Highland Circle of Stones

Florence Love Karsner

SeaDog Press, LLC

Ponte Vedra Beach, Florida

SeaDog Press, LLC
Ponte Vedra Beach, Florida 32082

This book is a work of fiction. Any references to historical events, real people, or real places are used fictitiously. Other names, characters, places, and events are products of the author's imagination, and any resemblance to actual events or places or persons, living or dead, is entirely coincidental.

Cover Design: Dar Albert, Wicked Smart Designs
Ship Logo: © Dn Br | Shutterstock
Ouroboros Design: Caroline Karsner Bowen
Copyright © 2015 Florence Love Karsner

Dedication

To my beloved mother-in-law and father-in-law, Ethel and Clinton Karsner, who brought joy to my life in so many ways. Though they are gone, they are still alive in our hearts and minds.

The serpent is an ancient symbol of healing and is seen in early drawings wrapped around the caduceus of the Greek god, Hermes. Many ancient cultures regarded the serpent as sacred and used it in healing rituals. A serpent devouring its tail is called an ouroboros. It is symbolic of immortality, the eternal unity of all things, and the cycle of birth and death. It unites opposites such as the conscious and unconscious mind. It has a meaning of infinity or wholeness, and is the Western world equivalent of Yin-Yang.

Acknowledgements

Thank you, readers, for making my experiences as an author so rewarding. Your support and encouragement keep me writing even on days when my muse keeps herself hidden.

Certainly a thank you to Elizabeth White, my editor, is in order. Her talents are too numerous to mention and she is an exceptional find for this author.

I offer a special thank you to Garry, my unpaid, untiring, husband who cheers me on even when I know what I just wrote needs to be trashed! Without his encouragement these novels would never get from the computer to my readers.

CHAPTER 1

*W*inter *had been slow coming to the Lowlands, but in the upper Highlands it had no trouble announcing its arrival. The dark, brooding mountains were peaked with snow, and on this frigid night a sharp, scissoring wind left frost-furred windows in the lodge, and a mournful howl followed in its wake.*

A fine mist hovered over the moor and a thick fog crept along the frozen ground, further reducing visibility. There was only one who could make his way in this eerie darkness. He had roamed these moors and mountains his entire life, and his great rack spoke of his longevity and intelligence. Tonight he stood on the crest of this moor as he had other nights, knowing he was safe in his surroundings. Those that dwelt in this place would never harm him. But on this night, even the great stag felt the stirrings of unforeseen events on the horizon. His great wisdom and guile had kept him safe over the years, and the same would be needed by the inhabitants of the lodge below if they were to survive the trials awaiting them.

"Oh, Holy Jesus, Caitlin. No lass, don't bring the lightning — ye'll kill us for sure. Alex, ye need yer arse kicked for bringing her here. She's as dangerous as a keg of powder I tell ye!"

Jack's loud voice carried throughout the lodge as he came flying out of his bedroom, running down the hallway wearing nothing but a long nightshirt that flapped about his hairy knees. He was the largest of the MacKinnon brothers, known for his short fuse and hot temper.

1

A cracking bolt of lightning lit up the sky, its brightness and powerful magnetism consuming the lodge. An ear-shattering cascade of thunder rumbled across the moor, echoing for what seemed like an eternity. Finally, a slight quivering of the earth brought another moment of uneasiness as nature's Kabuki dancers gracefully executed their carefully choreographed moves.

For a few seconds, the silence in the MacKinnon lodge was palpable. No one made a sound. No one moved. No one had the courage to speak up. But each of them had the same thought: was this the first indication of yet another harrowing event about to take place?

Jack had been fast asleep and was tired, as all the men were. But when the thunder rolled across the moor and the lightning illuminated the landscape, he had jumped out of bed and grabbed his pistol.

"Caitlin, control yer powers lass — don't let 'em get away from ye," he yelled as he continued down the hallway, moving quickly for a man his size.

A scream got his attention and he saw his brother, Alex, running from the other end of the hallway. The men shared a look that needed no words. Other than their large build and height, they looked nothing like brothers. Jack was auburn haired and blue eyed, whereas Alex and the other brothers had dark hair and eyes like Da. Alex also had a cleft chin — another trait he shared with Da. One other notable difference was that unlike Jack, Alex was always in control of his thoughts and emotions.

"Caitlin, is that man still alive? I just knew he wasn't dead. But don't bring the lightning again. Control ye powers, lass, lest they bring disaster to all of us," Jack yelled out.

He continued down the hall, pistol in hand, ready to take action. Alex grabbed his younger brother by his arms and stopped him before he got any farther.

"Jack, hold on now. There's no one here. It's just a storm, brother, just a storm."

Alex removed the pistol from Jack's hand and gave him a

2

moment to come to his senses. "I heard someone scream, Alex. That wasn't a dream." Jack's breath was coming in shallow gasps.

As if on cue, everyone decided to react at once. Caitlin came hurrying into the hallway that ran the length of the lodge. Her floor-length dressing gown was wrapped around her, and her long, curly, fiery hair streamed behind her as she rushed along. Her great protector, a large black wolf named Willie, was running beside her, his growl growing louder by the minute. Willie stayed as close to Caitlin as possible, but other than his growl, he wasn't showing any signs of alarm—no standing hackles or baring of canines. His sheer size was often enough to ward off any offender.

The scream that had awakened the men had come from Caitlin, and now she stood shivering in the hallway looking as if she might release another one.

"What is it, *mo chridhe*? (my heart) Another nightmare?" Alex asked.

Caitlin was a small woman, and in Alex's opinion very attractive. He took her by her shoulders and saw sheer terror on her face. Caitlin's anger usually flared when she was afraid, but at this moment she was uncharacteristically calm, and her look was beyond fear.

"No, no nightmare. Didn't you hear the thunder, and feel the quivering of the earth?" Her arms were wrapped around her, as if in defense of something as yet undefined and unseen.

"Yes, Caitlin, I heard it, too. 'Tis just a storm, lass, just a storm."

Another piercing cry filled the air, and a woman fled into the hallway carrying a small bairn close to her breast. This woman, Millie (Lady Millicent Sinclair), was the opposite of Caitlin. She stood six feet tall and was a striking beauty. Her long, ebony mane was swirling about her head and her face was flushed with the fear she felt inside.

3

Her normally well-modulated Lady's voice was louder now and could be heard throughout the lodge.

"Jack, where are you? What's going on? What's that shaking? Jack, what's happening?" She peered down the hallway and, seeing Jack, ran to him seeking comfort or explanation for what was transpiring. As tall as she was, Jack stood even taller.

Jack's memories of recent events were seared into his brain, and some of them had been seared into his hands at the time. Presently, his fears relating to Caitlin's powers had come front and center. So far he had managed to keep his qualms to himself regarding the healer's extraordinary gifts, but having been awakened from a deep sleep his worries had made themselves known. And his words had registered with Alex.

Far in the recesses of his mind, Jack wasn't convinced the soldier who had been chasing Caitlin, Commander Campbell, had been killed even though Alex assured him he had seen the soldier breathe his last breath.

Jack shook his head. "I didn't just dream that, Alex. I heard a scream I tell ye."

"Yes, Jack. Caitlin and Millie were awakened by the storm and ye heard them screaming. These ladies are not accustomed to the wretched weather we have up here, ye ken?"

Alex knew Jack was never at his best when awakened abruptly. In fact, it was a joke within the family. As a young lad, Jack would sleep walk and the brothers would tease him about being the "sleeping giant" as he was six feet tall even at that young age. Well, apparently he still had difficulty thinking straight when he was awakened in the middle of the night.

Is that man still alive . . . lass, don't bring the lightning again . . . control yer powers.

Alex had heard Jack's question about Commander Campbell, and his comments regarding Caitlin. Jack was unsure about Caitlin and her powers. To say he feared her to some extent might be more to the point. But Alex was sure his dirk, along with the streak of fire coming from Caitlin's fingertips, had taken Commander Campbell's life. The event was still fresh in everyone's mind, and it was fair to say the recent experiences had taken a toll on each person in the lodge.

What if Jack's right? What if she is dangerous? Should I reconsider my plan to marry her?

Alex had his own questions — fears, too, if he admitted it — regarding Caitlin's powers. But the lass was ever so important to him, and he'd not let anything come between them. Since Jack obviously had worries on this subject, maybe they should have a meeting of minds, but later, after they all had slept and could think rationally. Alex was aware he would have to lead the way, as Jack was prone to act first and think later.

"Now, lasses, it's just a storm passing through. These Highlands are known for producing some of the worst weather in Scotland. There's nothing to worry about. Come on, now. Let's all get to bed and tomorrow it'll all be over."

Then, almost as an afterthought, two more doors were flung open at the far end of the hallway. Two oldsters, Da and Uncle Andrew, stood there wearing their long nightshirts. Da looked about. Seeing the lads and the women, he shook his head slightly then turned to Andrew.

"'Tis just the youngsters, Andrew. Maybe having troubles with their women. We're too old to get involved with that."

He yawned and they both returned to their rooms.

Jack took the child from Millie. She'd been born just a short while ago, in the middle of a snowstorm. In fact, it was the event that had brought Millie and Caitlin together. The healer had come upon Millie, alone in the forest, pregnant and in distress. She had helped deliver her child and the two women had become friends instantly.

Jack felt the infant snuggle up to his neck, which pleased both of them. He was not her father, but anyone witnessing this scene would certainly have thought so. She had slept through the entire episode, as children seem to be able to do. Millie, a lady by anyone's standards, managed to get her emotions under control and walked with Jack to her quarters, located on the second floor at the west end of the lodge. These were formerly the master's rooms. When they had first arrived at the lodge, Jack had insisted Millie and the bairn needed more room, and there was no use arguing with him.

Alex put an arm around Caitlin and escorted her to Mam's sewing room, where she had slept since they arrived. She'd refused a larger room when it was offered later. This room suited her and Willie and she felt a connection with the person who had dwelled in it before.

Alex said goodnight to Caitlin at the door to Mam's room. When she had first gotten to the lodge, Caitlin was nursing a broken leg sustained in an accident at Cameron Castle, an estate belonging to Millie's grandmother and where they sought refuge from the snowstorm. Alex, being the oldest and leader of the MacKinnon clan of brothers, and the intellectual of the group, insisted Caitlin use this room as it was located on the lower level of the lodge and was the warmest room in the house. His mother, Mam, had used it as a sewing room, and also spent her last days there as she could view the moor outside the large, multi-paned windows. The cancer took away her strength and certainly all her abilities, but she could still enjoy watching nature through these windows. Even on her bleakest days, the view brought comfort to her.

Likewise, on this cold evening, Caitlin peered through those same windowpanes, tracing the icy edges with her finger. Sleep was difficult most nights, and after the event this evening she knew it would be impossible. She stood at the window, her *arisaid* (tartan wrap) held tightly about her shoulders. She was able to see clearly as the full moon flooded the moor with its brightness. She once again marveled at the beauty that lay out there, just waiting for her to immerse herself in it —the mountains in the distance, each one tipped with a blanket of pristine snow, the tall pines, the small rowans and elm trees that reached to the sky, and the rolling, unending moor that always called to her.

These Highlands were so different than the Western Isles, the part of Scotland she had come from. How strange, she thought, that she felt she belonged here, at this place.

She, too, had heard Jack's comments relating to her powers — the same concerns were running through her mind also.

My life has changed so much recently. If the MacKinnon brothers hadn't come along, I probably would not have survived my battle with Commander Campbell and Lord Warwick. But if I marry Alex, will I be able to continue my work as a healer? And what about these powers I've been given? Will I be able to use them for good and not harm my loved ones? Will Alex accept me with these powers? Will his brothers always be afraid of me? And there are so many MacKinnons. I've been a loner all my life — what if I can't adjust to being with a crowd? Will I ever belong?

Knowing it was useless to go to bed and hope for sleep to come, she stood at the window for the longest time, just thinking.

~ * ~

The latest in a long line of healers, Caitlin had spent her entire life on the Isle of Skye. When her mother died in childbirth, her father had fallen into an abyss of grief that left him unable to care for a child. His parents took over his responsibilities and he boarded a ship bound for the West Indies. No one had seen him since. That was twenty plus years ago. Upon the death of her grandparents, an eccentric old man Caitlin knew as Uncle Wabi took her in and acted as both her protector and mentor.

For years she did not know Uncle Wabi was not a blood relation, but merely a family friend. Only recently had she become aware he possessed unusual skills, or rather, powers. He was, in fact, what you might call a wizard. Children are much more accepting of differences in folk, and Caitlin never questioned any of his eccentric ways; she just accepted Uncle Wabi was different than others.

A few months ago, Caitlin had been forced to flee her home on Skye. She and Uncle Wabi, as well as other locals within the village, were part of the Jacobite Uprising that many of her countrymen were participating in, trying to return Bonnie Prince Charlie to his rightful place on the throne.

During an errand to buy a jug of wine for Uncle Wabi, Caitlin had overheard Thomas, the owner and barkeep of the Wild Boar Inn and Pub, and an Englishman, Lord Edward Warwick, planning to harm these Jacobites, steal their properties, and do away with their families. The barkeep had seen Caitlin and realized she'd overheard them. He and Lord Warwick knew she could make trouble for them, so they began to search for her before she could reveal their plans to the authorities.

Caitlin was certainly in a predicament, which was not exactly an unusual state for her — trouble seemed to follow in her wake wherever she went. But at that point she'd had a decision to make.

She knew the men were ruthless and had no doubt they would harm her, Uncle Wabi and her friends, too. She knew she must leave immediately and try to protect those she cared about.

She'd left the Isle in the middle of the night, her destination unknown. She ultimately found a cave south of Inverness, where she practiced her healing skills in a nearby village and cared for the soldiers returning from the bloody Battle of Culloden. As fate would have it, one of the soldiers in her care died despite her best efforts to save him. His father, Commander Campbell, was consumed with grief and accused her of being a witch who had taken his son's life. So he began to pursue her as well.

On one particular afternoon, she had been returning to her cave from the village when she was accosted by the MacKinnon brothers, who all but trampled her with their horses.

"Hey, ye there, are ye the healer? We need yer help, now!"

The large man who'd spoken dismounted, as did two others. Another was draped over his horse, apparently unconscious. The men were all huge, and their presence was most daunting as they encircled her, almost daring her to escape them.

The young man draped over the horse was their youngest brother, Ian. An enterprising lad of only fourteen or so, with a real penchant for not following his brothers' orders to stay at home, he had found his way to them at a battle site called Culloden. That battle turned out to be the worst battle of all, and the young lad was severely wounded when a British soldier slashed his leg with a Lockerber axe. Seeing the battle was lost, the MacKinnon brothers deserted the camp in search of someone who might help Ian. Finally they found the young healer, Caitlin, who was especially gifted. With her skills and knowledge she managed to save Ian's life, albeit at the expense of amputating the lower part of his leg. She cared for the boy until he was able to travel with his brothers.

The MacKinnons were anxious to return to their home in the Highlands and resume their lives. However, they were most uncomfortable leaving the young woman alone. She had only her protector, a very large black wolf who never left her side. Perhaps that would be sufficient in most circumstances, but they knew she was being pursued by Commander Campbell and the insane English Lord Warwick, who also wanted to see the end of her. The brothers, particularly Alex, did not like leaving the young woman with just a wolf for protection.

"Lass, are ye sure ye won't come with us? We've a large home and ye could practice yer healing in the Highlands. There are folks up there who could benefit from yer skills."

"Thanks, but I'll stay here in my cave. I'm safe here. If anyone should venture too close, Willie will take care of them. He's quite a good protector."

"Aye, but there's a soldier and an insane Lord looking for ye. Can't ye see they could make a lot of trouble?" *Damn silly woman.*

She stood quietly, arms akimbo, and looked the tall Highlander in the eye. Her temper was raging inside. "I said I appreciate your offer, but I'll be staying here."

That was Alex's first experience with the woman's stubborn streak and quick temper, and her answer did not sit well with him. But she refused to listen to any argument he made, so they left without her, headed to their home.

Shortly after their departure, Commander Campbell managed to find Caitlin in her cave and almost killed her. With the help of her wolf, Willie, she escaped and fled in the middle of the night, hoping to find her way to the MacKinnon homestead in the upper Highlands.

As she traveled, only at night, she came upon a young woman who was about to have a bairn in the middle of a snowstorm.

"Holy Rusephus, Willie, this woman is about to give birth!"

Caitlin assisted the woman, who gave her name as Millie, and after the birth they made their way to Cameron Castle, an estate that belonged to Millie's grandmother and aunt. The two had recently been murdered, but Millie was unaware of this situation. Millie, actually Lady Millie Sinclair Warwick, was trying to escape her tyrant of a husband, Lord Warwick—the same lord who was chasing Caitlin, which gave the two women a lot in common.

During their harrowing journey, Caitlin became aware of unusual powers she had never known she possessed — perhaps Uncle Wabi was blood kin after all?

The adventure had ended with the MacKinnon brothers— Alex and Jack— coming to the assistance of the women. Uncle Wabi had shown up at just the right moment too. Coincidence?

In the end, Caitlin's powers had brought about the death of Commander Campbell and Lord Warwick as well. She had literally melted Warwick with a bolt of lightning, reducing him to ashes and charred bone. Commander Campbell's fate had been to be on the receiving end of a streak of fire from Caitlin's fingertips that fried his hands. Alex MacKinnon had delivered the final blow with a dirk that hit its target —Campbell's heart.

Between the two of them, and with a little assist from Uncle Wabi and his powers, both assassins were dispatched and the two women and the new bairn went with the MacKinnon brothers to their Highland lodge. Caitlin had suffered a broken leg in the adventure, but Uncle Wabi had helped reset it and all was healing as it should. The MacKinnon brothers, however, were left with the memory of Caitlin's extraordinary powers.

~ * ~

Now here the MacKinnon brothers were, just a few months later, about to make these women part of their clan — one a *Sassenach* (a Lady from England at that), and the other with unusual abilities.

Still, Alex was convinced Caitlin should be with him, and was not bothered by her powers. He wanted her regardless of her unusual abilities and had addressed his brothers, making his feelings known to all of them.

"I tell ye, I don't care that she's got these powers. She's going to be mine."

Jack was just as enamored with Millie and wanted her to stay at the lodge also. But now, with both brothers' decisions to marry having been announced, Jack was wondering if Alex had thought this through.

The morning after the storm, Jack cornered Millie with his thoughts. "Millie, what if Caitlin *is* a witch? She could bring danger to all of us." Millie sighed and shook her head. She had no qualms about Caitlin. The healer had proved herself to Millie by helping her birth little Midge, so she'd accept her even with her unusual powers.

But Jack had witnessed Caitlin's lethal ability firsthand, and it was a sight not easily forgotten. He knew Alex was determined to wed the lass from the Skye, and he also knew Alex was by far the most intelligent and thoughtful of the entire clan — when he made a decision, it usually was a good one. He was also aware Alex usually held his tongue more than most, but he could be riled given enough reason, so Jack knew he may have a fight on his hands if he tried to convince Alex to wait a while on the marriage.

Still, she really did a number on that commander and that lord. I'm going to have to talk to him.

CHAPTER 2

The first few weeks Caitlin, Millie and little Midge spent at the MacKinnon farm were anything but boring. It seemed everyone on the farm had specific jobs and were good at them. Millie knew she could learn her way around a kitchen, and that thought appealed to her. Therefore, she had come into the MacKinnon kitchen — Hector's kitchen — and in her usual, efficient fashion had begun making changes. It was apparent to her these men were doing fairly well without a woman around, but Mam's touch was definitely missing in Millie's opinion.

When Mam had passed away, it only took a few weeks for the men to realize they needed some help around the house. Mam had always managed to keep the laundry caught up and the place was always filled with great smelling and tasting food. She had the Widow Murray come in one day a week to help her, and as her health gradually declined from the cancer the Widow came even more often. With no husband, the few extra coins she earned were helpful. The brothers agreed to ask her to come the same as she had when Mam was there, so even though the home was not as organized as when Mam was in charge, they had clean clothes and there was at least a semblance of order.

But even with that help, Millie and Caitlin had their hands full just keeping up with the daily chores that must be done. They put their heads together and decided there must be a better way of operating the lodge and when Millie had finally had enough, she made a firm decision.

"I might not know how to cook well but I have had experience running a large household, and this one could certainly use attention." Using her keen powers of persuasion, she enlisted the young hired hands to help her.

"Here, lads, do you think we could put a few hooks in the ceiling? Then we can hang the pots from them. That way we can reach them and not have to rummage through the cabinets when we need one. And over here, could you maybe add another shelf or two in the pantry so we've enough room for the flour, oats and other dry goods we use daily? I hate having to run out to the storage room when I need more flour."

The lads were getting use to this new lady and her gentle way of asking for their help. They hadn't seen anyone quite so beautiful, and she had them eating out of her hand.

"Do you think you could move the large table, the one out in the barn, inside? It would seat all of us and we wouldn't be so crowded at dinner."

The two young lads, Kenny and Hamish, would do her bidding just to have the pleasure of being near her. Getting the lads to help her was easy enough, and the new arrangements in the kitchen really did make it more workable. The only problem with making all these changes was she hadn't asked Hector's approval beforehand. That oversight resulted in a flaring of tempers from both he and Millie.

"Nae, lass. I don't mind ye helping, but I've been in charge of feeding this lot since our Mam left us. She taught us all to cook a bit, and I've been designated to take up where she left off. But I could use help in here, even though it doesn't look like ye've been in a kitchen very often," Hector yelled.

Despite his tirade, Hector, the second oldest brother, was actually the one with the best negotiating skills. At the moment, he seemed to have lost this ability. He did welcome her help, as feeding this crowd took a lot of effort, but this woman was trying his patience.

"Aye, Hector, you're right. I was never allowed to be in the kitchen as a child, and certainly not in Warwick's castle. That was considered beneath the dignity of a Lady."

Hector held his tongue, but jumped Jack the moment he entered the room.

"Jack, ye've gotta talk to Millie. She's just taking over me kitchen. I'm glad to have her help, but it'll work better if she asks my opinion before she makes any more changes."

Jack stood there, scratching his head. He hadn't found anything about Millie that wasn't to his liking, but could see his brother was not keen on anyone taking over his domain, and that person a woman to boot.

"Aye, brother. I'll talk to her. She's got a lot to learn about living with a bunch of sheep farmers. Give her time, if ye can."

Hector threw down a dishtowel and walked out the door, slamming it behind him.

Jack hadn't seen him this angry in a while. In fact, it took a lot to rile Hector, so Jack might need to ponder this a bit. *That's the most emotion I've seen from him in years.*

Having been the daughter of a Lord and then wife to one, Millie had been a Lady all her life. She'd never had to ask anyone's permission to do most anything, certainly not when it concerned running a household. Of course, she'd never had the experience of having a sibling, or any contact with children, either. So she had quite a bit to learn about living with a houseful of Highland men, and now she also had a child to contend with.

~ * ~

Caitlin's life had been one dedicated to healing, and even though she stayed busy, she was a loner. She'd always hoped to wed, but so far she'd not found a man who met her requirements. The few men she'd known had been intimidated by her intelligence and her commitment to her calling of being a healer. So none of those relationships had ever worked out, and Uncle Wabi was her only kin. She'd all but given up on her dreams of children, family gatherings and holiday rituals.

Hopefully this Highlander, Alex, would make those dreams come true. She'd agreed to wed him, and was excited about becoming a part of this clan. But Caitlin had fears about their relationship also. She was aware not everyone was as happy about that event as Alex.

The only other dream she still held on to was increasing her healing knowledge. There was much to be learned if she could only get to a place where that knowledge was available. The Isle of Skye had nothing more to offer, and she doubted these Highlands did either.

~ * ~

Alex had waited patiently for his perfect mate. He had thought he'd found her as a young man, at university, but that woman wouldn't follow him to the upper Highlands, the only place he was interested in spending his life. But this one, this healer, had such spirit and dedication to her ideals that Alex was drawn like a magnet.

"Jack, I tell ye she's a fine woman. She's committed to her

16

work as a healer and has her heart set on a home and bairns as well. She's exactly what I've been looking for."

Alex had tried to convince Jack this woman was *the* one, but had sensed Jack's concerns about Caitlin even before the incident on the night of the storm. He, himself, never had any second thoughts about joining with this woman. And truth be told, when she entered the room he followed her every movement and his pulse always quickened. There was something about her that he couldn't resist — and he had no plans to try.

Just as Hector and Millie, though, Alex and Caitlin had their disagreements also. Today Alex went through the lodge looking for Caitlin.

"Caitlin? Where are ye, lass?" he called out as he strode through the great room.

Not finding her inside, he went outside to look for her. When they first arrived at the home place Caitlin had made use of Ian's crutch, the one the lad used before Uncle Wabi, Da and old Jamie had created his new prosthesis. She'd used it to work her way outside to the birch tree next to the old hut.

There was a small stream that ran next to the hut, and it was a good place to sit and reflect. Caitlin had spotted the hut when they first arrived, and she could be found there most days, with Willie at her side. Alex had learned to look there first, but today she wasn't there either.

Going back inside, he wandered to the kitchen knowing Millie would be working on a new dish. She was really taking to her new responsibilities and she and Hector were working through their problems. A truce had been called for the moment.

"Millie, have ye seen Caitlin this morning? She's not out by the birch tree and I don't see her anywhere."

"She was here earlier, maybe an hour ago. But I haven't seen her since. You know Caitlin — she needs her quiet time. She's still adjusting to so many people around. But she's where she wants to be, Alex. She's probably just taking a short walk. Her leg is much better and walking is good for her. Willie's always with her, so I wouldn't be too alarmed."

"Aye. Well, I think I'll saddle up and go for a ride. She'll turn up I'm sure."

Alex mounted and made one more trip to the birch tree. Looking closely at the ground, he could see marks where the crutch had made indentations in the earth. She had been here apparently. Then she must have wandered farther out onto the moor.

Dang it all, woman, I specifically told ye not to go too far from the lodge. Ye've got to start listening to me.

Alex was accustomed to his orders being followed, and he definitely remembered cautioning both ladies not to leave the immediate area. There were any number of dangers always waiting in the Highlands. Where there were sheep, there were always wolves nearby. Wild boars roamed everywhere, as well as coyotes and fierce, wild dogs. Then, too, what often looked like grass might be an area of boggy peat moss that could give way if any weight was put on it.

Alex followed the tracks of the crutch and was surprised to see where they were headed. Caitlin had to have walked for quite a while to get so far up the moor. How long had that taken her with her leg? After riding for a few more minutes, he stood in the stirrups and looked higher, to the top of the moor. There was Caitlin, with Willie close at her side, both standing in the circle of stones next to the burial ground. Mam had taught Alex and his brothers that only the "called" were to enter the circle and that they should always approach the area with reverence. He'd never utter it to Caitlin, but in his mind the place held secrets and was a place he and his brothers all feared to a certain degree, though they were unsure just why. Seeing Caitlin inside was most disturbing.

Holy Jesus, she's inside the circle! What if Jack's right after all? What in heaven's name am I to think about this scene? Oh, Mam, if yer anywhere close, send me some of yer wisdom. At this moment I'm more frightened than I've ever been in my life. Maybe Jack's worries are justified. Maybe she is a witch and can harm all of us. Jesus, what am I going to do?

Sitting back in the saddle he rode up closer to the circle. He sat quietly for a moment, thinking, before dismounting. Then he did what he always did when faced with a difficult situation — he met it — in this case the woman who held his heart — head-on.

"Caitlin, *mo chridhe*. What are ye doing up here?" he called out.

She didn't move, as if she hadn't heard him.

Angry words were on the tip of his tongue and he almost gave in to an impulse to release them. As he got closer, however, he was mesmerized by the sight before him. Caitlin's tartan wrap was draped about her shoulders, her flaming hair blowing in the wind, whipping about her face, and her aqua eyes sent out flashes of light that almost blinded him.

Alex stood still, and for a quick instant thought he had interrupted a private moment of communication between Caitlin and an unknown entity. He had never seen this look on her face before. It was an expression of complete joy and contentment.

Then, as if she had awakened from a dream, Caitlin looked at him and smiled brightly. "Alex, did you know this circle was here? It's magnificent! Have you ever stood within it?"

"Nae, lass. Mam said only the called are to go inside."

Caitlin looked at the Highlander, this man who was more than she ever hoped for.

Is that fear I see on his face?

"Something has been calling to me since I got here, Alex.

19

Today I followed that calling and this is where it led me. This circle of stones feels so familiar to me. I don't understand it, but standing within it brought a peace to me that I haven't felt in ever so long."

Alex looked down at his little healer, so small she didn't even reach his shoulders.

"Then so be it. Mam told us it's called a henge, a circle of stones, and it's a special place for special folk. Let's just leave it at that, lass. If it soothes yer soul, then perhaps ye were meant to enter. But Caitlin, there are dangers here. Please don't come again without one of us coming with ye."

Caitlin nodded. "I didn't think about that, Alex. I just went without considering my actions first. I never meant to frighten you. It'll not happen again."

Alex wordlessly accepted her apology with a kind look and a gentle hand on her shoulder, then helped her into the saddle for their return to the lodge. Caitlin rode in front of him, ever so carefully, trying not to jostle her still-healing leg. Part of her didn't want to leave the stone circle, but she could feel Alex's anxiety and kept her thoughts to herself. She thought she would probably return — and he was certain she would.

CHAPTER 3

The lodge was a busy place and they were all trying to figure out how to make the arrival of the two ladies and the bairn work with their usual routine. The home had been without a woman around for a while, and it was going to take adjustments for all of them.

During the storm, Jack's anxieties about Caitlin's powers had come forth and though he didn't dare voice it, his real fear was that Caitlin herself might have brought about the thunder and lightning —another exhibition of her powers. He was still a bit afraid of those if he were honest with himself. But even more than that, he was afraid for Alex. His brother was so taken with that woman he would never listen to any qualms anyone had about her or her powers. The fact remained, however, that she was the reason they were all still alive. Her powers had made themselves known when they needed them, and she had not even been aware of them herself before then apparently.

A few days had passed since the night of the storm and the household was running as usual—not one word had been mentioned about the events of the stormy evening. It was as if nothing had happened. But Jack had made a decision before he returned to his bed that evening. He'd never feel right if he didn't caution Alex about what bringing Caitlin into the family could mean — to all of them.

He pulled his boots on, grabbed his morning cup of Hector's strong coffee, and started to the shearing shed, where he knew Alex would be giving instructions to the local men he had called on to help with the shearing. He'd make sure they were all clear about what they were to do.

"Alex? Ye in here?" Jack called, opening the large door to the shed.

"Yeah, brother, back here."

Alex was back in the rear of the building looking for a warmer pair of boots as his were a bit thin about the soles, and he was tired of having wet feet. The snow wasn't so heavy this year, but after all day walking about the farm the thin soles allowed the cold to seep in.

"Heavens but it's cold out here. What are ye doing? Let's get back to the lodge and have a bite of breakfast before we leave."

"Be right there. Just looking for warmer boots. Mam always had several pairs stored out here, some that had a little more wear if we needed a pair."

Alex sat on a bale of hay and removed his wet boots, replacing them with another pair, also worn, but with a better sole on them.

"What are ye doing out here so early? We don't have to get underway quite yet." Alex looked at Jack.

"Yeah, I know. But we got to have a talk. I can't put it off any longer, ye ken? It's about Caitlin."

"Caitlin? What about Caitlin? Haven't seen her yet this morning, so maybe she's sleeping in a bit."

"Aye. Alex, remember the storm the other night? The loud thunder and lightning that sizzled across the whole moor, and wind that threatened to tear the roof off? Quite a storm it was, I'd say."

"Yeah. Don't need any more of those. Gets the sheep and animals in an uproar; I'm sure we'll find strays that were spooked that night."

Jack sat across from Alex, sipped on his coffee, holding the mug with two hands, enjoying the warmth it provided. He looked directly at his older brother.

"Alex, in the middle of that storm did it ever occur to ye that maybe it was Caitlin causing it?"

Alex remained quiet, kept his head down and continued to lace his boots.

"When we went to bed there wasn't any indication we would have a storm —and we usually can tell. Then, just a few hours later, the whole house is awakened by Caitlin and Millie's screams, and a storm out of nowhere."

"What are ye trying to say?" Alex looked up, his piecing eyes never leaving his brother's face.

"I was just thinking, remembering what happened at the well at Cameron Castle, and what happened to Commander Campbell and Lord Warwick."

"So ye think Caitlin may have brought the storm? Is that what yer saying?"

"I'm not saying she did, I'm just asking if it crossed yer mind."

"Nae, it never did. Caitlin wouldn't bring a storm upon us. She saved our lives in case ye've forgotten that." He tied the boots and stood, still looking at his little brother, who was actually the taller one.

Jack stood then as well. "Nae, I remember that well enough. But how do we know she won't do something that could put us all in danger, what with these "powers" she seems to have been given. I mean —Jesus, that Lord Warwick never had a chance against her.

Did you see his body? It scared the daylights out of me I can tell ye."

"Jack, I think yer reading way too much into these powers. Caitlin would never harm any of us, or anyone else if she could help it. I hear what yer saying, but I'm willing to trust her and figure we'll never see any evidence of these powers again. Ye gotta remember, brother, Mam always thought there were folk who had been given special talents, and I believe Caitlin is one of those."

"But yer gonna marry her. What about any sons or daughters ye may have? How do ye know they won't be some sort of strange bairns, or witches?"

With a bit of effort, Alex called on one of his greatest assets — his ability to remain calm when he most wanted to yell. Then he spoke quietly to his brother.

"Listen to me. Caitlin is not a witch, and that's the end of this discussion. Yes, I'm going to wed her, just as ye are going to wed Millie. If my memory serves me, it's going to be real soon — next week. Now, stop yer whining and worrying about something ye need not worry about. Caitlin's a fine woman and I'm not going to let her go."

"Aye, but I had to tell ye my worries."

"And so ye have, so ye have." He put an arm around his "little" brother's shoulders. "And have ye forgotten another small fact? Yer about to marry a *Sassenach* yerself . . . and there are those who think that's even worse than a witch."

"But . . . well, Millie's different. She's no regular *Sassenach*, ye ken? She's only half *Sassenach.*"

"I don't think anyone here is too concerned about that fact. Millie's found a place with us. Just reminding ye Caitlin's not the only woman with a few special qualities. Come on now, we got work to do. With the ewes about to come into season, more hands will be needed to keep the rams in the right pastures. I've called on several of the local lads to help out for a few days."

"Aye. And I suppose the two of us should go down next week, after the ceremonies, and bring another flock to our place," Jack responded.

Until then, they both had their hands full doing chores and trying to help Caitlin and Millie get everything ready for the weddings that were to take place at the end of next week.

According to the ladies, much needed to be done around the lodge. They needed to decorate for the *ceilidh* (celebration with dancing) that would be held the evening of the ceremony, and Hector was planning enough vittles for the entire village. Most of the villagers would come as there were far too few celebrations anymore, and one at the MacKinnon lodge would certainly be one not to miss.

Caitlin and Millie had been here a few months now, and everyone was in agreement that a double ceremony was in order. The banns had been posted and the vicar had agreed to conduct the ceremony at the kirk in the village, not so far from the lodge. It was small, but there would only be a few folk from the MacKinnon side and only Uncle Wabi from Caitlin's side. Millie had no one to come, so Uncle Andrew had agreed to walk her down the aisle, as they called it. He was delighted with the idea, and Uncle Wabi would be there to escort Caitlin.

Uncle Andrew regaled them with his evening tales around the fire. His stories were ever so interesting to Caitlin, who knew absolutely nothing about her own family. Millie never mentioned hers, so no one knew what memories she might be keeping to herself.

Having never had family around, Caitlin delighted in learning about Alex's clan. Da and Uncle Andrew were the rocks of the group. And old Jamie? Well, there was just something about that old one's face, so richly lined with life experience, which Caitlin found so very interesting. There was a feeling of recognition.

This evening, thanks to Hector and Millie, they had filled their bellies with a dinner of lamb stew, followed by plum pudding. They were satiated and drifting off to sleep in their chairs. Finally, Da suggested they find their beds and get a bit of proper rest.

As had become a nightly ritual, Jack walked Millie and little Midge to their room in the far west end of the lodge, and Alex escorted Caitlin to Mam's sewing room.

After saying their goodnights, they all got to bed and were sleeping soundly. Living on a sheep farm insured that all would be ready for bed when night came, and this family was no different. Now, hours later, the new phenomenon that had started about a week ago played itself out again. It fact, it was becoming a nightly event.

"No. Not yet. Not yet. No… don't leave me!" Caitlin's voice could be heard throughout the lodge.

Alex came dashing into the bedroom, finding Caitlin drenched in perspiration and crying uncontrollably. "Caitlin, whatever is wrong?"

"Oh, Alex, it's you. It's you."

Alex pulled her close and stroked the curls hanging down her back. He still liked to feel the silkiness, and smiled when he pulled a curl and watched it creep up where it had been originally. Having never had sisters, this was a new experience for him. But he was becoming concerned about Caitlin. She was recovering well physically from the accident at the castle, but in the last week they had all been awakened every night by her screams, just like tonight. What was causing these nightmares?

"Ah, Caitlin. What must we do to stop this nightly visitor

who brings such anguish to ye, *mo chridhe?* Ye do well enough in the daylight hours, but at night something creeps into that beautiful head and causes ye much pain, I'm thinking."

"Aye. You're right. I've given it thought, but just when I think I'm about to discover this person or this unknown entity in my dreams, it slips away — just leaves in a fog or a mist. Then I look for it but I get lost and I can never find my way home. It's difficult to explain. I don't even understand it myself."

"Aye. I see that. Rest now and we'll talk more about it in the morning. Sleep now, lass."

He left her with just the softest, gentlest kiss he could manage. But that was getting more difficult every day. Alex was ready to get the courtship part of the relationship over and move on to the next — where they were wed and Caitlin slept in *his* bed. He understood her wanting to "walk down the aisle" with Uncle Wabi as her escort and the day would be coming shortly.

Alex wasn't the only MacKinnon man wanting to get on with this ceremony business. Jack, too, was tired of whispering his goodnights to Millie and baby Midge at her door. But he would bide his time as Alex was, knowing he would never find a woman he desired as much as he did this one. Mam had taught them all that most things happened when they were supposed to, and patience was definitely a virtue — but not necessarily one that was easily come by.

Caitlin lay in bed after Alex left and knew sleep would not come this night. Her mind dashed to the evening of the storm and she recalled how frightened she had been. Jack wasn't the only one who was afraid of her powers. She, herself, found them quite daunting too.

What if I find myself in another stressful situation? Will these powers come on their own, as they did the last time? Or will I discover the trigger that must be pulled before they become evident? And these nightmares? What are they about? Maybe I should just steal away in the night as I have before. Perhaps removing myself from the picture is what I should do if I really care about all these folk — and I do.

~ * ~

The next morning Alex found Caitlin where he usually did, sitting outside under the birch tree wrapped in her tartan. Caitlin and Willie liked the serenity the old hut and tree provided, and together they were both recovering well. The hut was behind the lodge and protected from the harsh winds, but it was still cold out there and she had brought a blanket for Willie. He, too, had been wounded at the castle. Today his wounds were almost totally healed and protecting her was still his first priority.

The hut was where Mam kept her keepsakes, as she had called them. As far as Alex knew, they were still there. No one would dare throw anything away until Mam had given permission. Of course since she died no one wanted to part with anything that was hers.

Caitlin and Willie spent hours sitting under the tree, she wrapped in her arisaid and he snuggled at her feet. During this season, the limbs of the birch tree were bare. Their silver trunks were etched with fine lines as if they were ancient, and their beauty and simplicity appealed to her. When spring came, she knew the tree would be draped with branches gracefully curving toward the small stream below it, like fingers dripping from each branch.

"Morning to ye, my lovely lass. Ye think it might be a mite too cold to be sitting out here?"

Alex had brought her a hot cup of tea, and sipping their brew together had become a morning ritual for the two of them.

28

"I just needed to be outside for a moment. I'm feeling much better and am so sorry to keep waking you every night. You can't keep getting up and coming to see about me."

She gratefully took the tea and sipped quietly as he sat next to her, placing an arm about her shoulders.

Alex looked at her and wondered how he had ever been so lucky as to win this woman's heart. She was beyond beautiful with her aqua eyes and that luscious hair, and her keen intelligence was even more appealing.

"Lass, ye are everything to me. Coming to see about ye is not a chore, ye ken?"

"Aye, I know. But they're confusing, these nightmares. In these dreams it's like I'm in a place I almost recognize, but then I get lost. I'm always looking for someone, but I never find them. And the scents are so familiar, but I can't place them. It's frustrating."

"Ye've been through quite an ordeal in the last few months. Maybe ye just need to try to quiet yer mind as Mam would say. 'Just be one with nature' would have been her suggestion." His eyes crinkled as he remembered Mam's words fondly.

"Huh. That sounds like something Uncle Wabi would say."

Caitlin smiled at this man sitting next to her. When in his presence, her heart overflowed with a warmth she didn't quite understand yet. But whatever it was, she knew she would stay with this Highlander. She looked up at him, and her physical response to him never ceased to amaze her. His dark eyes always seemed to pierce into her as if he could read her mind. He towered over her and yet she fit perfectly into his arms when he held her. Her body always responded to his touch, and her mind always followed suit.

Yes, he's exactly what I've been looking for. But he'll have to learn that I make my own decisions.

"Now, about yer nightmares. What do ye think could be

Florence Love Karsner

causing them?"

"It's beyond me. I've tried to think about everything that has happened, but as unpleasant as it all was, I don't believe any of that is responsible for these nightly demons that come calling."

"Ye don't recognize anything about the place where ye find yerself?"

"No, not really. When I have the dream, it feels like I travel to a place where I've been before, but that's not possible. I can only see shadows. And this place—it has that same soft, golden glow that was in my cave when I would light the candles, the one where I treated Ian."

"What do ye think we could do to help ye figure this out?"

"The only person who could possibly help me would be Uncle Wabi. But I don't want to bother him about my dreams."

"Don't think Wabi is bothered about much," laughed Alex. "He's quite a piece of work, and I'm thankful for him every day. He had a great influence on ye, and ye turned out mighty fine, lass."

"You're kind to say that, but I'm aware these new powers I have are unsettling to you. Well, rest assured the whole bit is strange to me, too. I'm thinking Uncle Wabi is just going to have to come up and work with me. What if I'm called on to use them again and don't know exactly how? What if I hurt someone I care about? What do I—?"

"Whoa. Hold on now, lass." He took her hands and pulled her closer. "Yer right. I'm a bit unsure about the happenings meself. But I want ye, no matter what comes with the package. Now, enough of that talk. I think maybe ye should ask Wabi to come a few days before the ceremonies. He might be able to set all our minds at ease if we just listen to him. So if ye like, I'll go down to Skye and bring him back to the lodge with me."

Caitlin glanced over at him. "Hmm. Actually, I think there's an easier way than that." The look on his face was one of non-comprehension. Caitlin smiled, just a small smile, unsure whether to proceed. The one bit of helpful knowledge that had come about as result of Caitlin using her powers was that Uncle Wabi had promised to come and explain more about them and aide in her understanding of her status as a called one. He had also informed her that his bird, Owl, was a special bird she could dispatch for him if ever she needed his assistance. Perhaps this was the time to see if that process worked. She had not missed the fact that, for some reason, the great-horned owl had stayed here in the upper Highlands after Uncle Wabi had returned to the Isle.

You're just keeping an eye on me, Uncle Wabi. I am quite sure of that. She laughed to herself.

"We'll ask Owl to get a message to Uncle Wabi. That bird loves flying at breakneck speed and making the trip for him is not difficult."

Alex stared at her. Images of lightning bolts and sounds of rumbling thunder ran through his mind. He wasn't overly concerned about her powers, but he also had not forgotten those events. He reached up and rubbed the back of his neck. That owl had played a part in helping them, too. He was a constant companion of Uncle Wabi — if one was around, the other would be close by also. Alex was quite sure he didn't understand the nature of the wizard and owl's relationship, but as with Caitlin, he just accepted that they were to be trusted. Mam had thought you should trust others until you knew that trust was misplaced. Mam left her mark on all of them and a good one it was, too.

"Ah, well then. If ye think that's the way, then get on about it, lass."

Alex certainly didn't understand Caitlin's newly discovered

31

powers, nor her wizard uncle and his owl, but wasn't ready to ask any questions — not yet. He stood and kissed her lightly on the cheek.

"Let's get in. It's really cold out here. I'll get on about my work, too. We're moving a large flock to MacDonald's place, so we could be gone for a few days. Jack will go with me, and Hector's going to Cameron Castle. Millie promised them she'd come back, but in the meantime she's asked him to check on the place for her. Da and Uncle Andrew will stay here with ye and Millie. Jamie and the lads will be about, too. They'll likely be corralling the ewes that are about to come into season, and a few of the local men are here to help them. Plus, we've hired Boder, a new hand. He's quiet, but that's all right. Don't need him to talk, just work. Da thinks we should do everything ourselves, but that's just not possible with such large flocks now. It'll take us the rest of today to get the sheep herded, so we won't leave until tomorrow, early if we can."

"Don't worry about me. I've never had so many menfolk looking out for me. Millie and little Midge can hold their own, as you've seen for yourself."

Caitlin had grown fond of this family, especially old Jamie, Da and Uncle Andrew, the old bard who entertained them with his tales of MacKinnon ancestors. She was sure he embellished some of the stories, but there was probably an element of truth in all of them. Old Jamie was her favorite. Her spirit recognized him and she so enjoyed listening to him when he spoke, which wasn't very often. His quiet presence always brought a peace that she relished. She knew nothing about her own family. Her grandparents, her father's parents, had cared for her early on, but as a child it never occurred to her to ask questions about her father or mother. Then, when her grandparents passed away, Uncle Wabi stepped in and her life was so full of adventure living with him that she never missed having kin around.

But recently, listening to Uncle Andrew at night, she found herself wishing she knew more about her ancestors. How would she ever find out anything about them? Wabi had known her mother and father, of course, but he had never made comments that she recalled.

Huh. That's strange now that I think about it. Why have I never wondered about my folks before now? Uncle Wabi is my only family.

She thought once again about just disappearing in the middle of the night. Willie would always be with her, so she would have his protection. Millie would understand why she left, and Jack would most probably be glad. She sensed his fear and it was always just on the edge, waiting to express itself. She'd miss Ian, Hector, Da and Uncle Andrew. Most of all, she'd miss old Jamie. He had a place in her heart unlike the others.

But just the thought of leaving Alex was unbearable. He had a place in her soul — a place she hadn't even been aware of. How would she ever forget his smile, the crinkles around his dark eyes, his quiet, thoughtful ways? Just hearing his deep voice could send shivers down her spine. And with his touch he had branded her as his. So while a part of her felt she should leave, another kept her here, surrounded by this clan of brothers and her friend.

I'm sure I was meant to be a healer, almost as if I had no choice. But will my life forever be one in which I am constantly being challenged to follow a destiny written for me? Or will I choose to write a new one for myself?

~ * ~

Alex saddled Zeus, mounted and started out to take his morning ride around the farm. This had been his routine for several years now, and today he found himself on the northeast side of the property, the same place where he had found Caitlin recently at the henge. Reining Zeus to a halt, he stopped and looked about. All was quiet, no sounds whatsoever.

Why have I come here? This is not where I usually go. There's nothing up here except the burial plot and that area where the circle of stones was placed, eons before we MacKinnons were here.

For a second Alex recalled seeing Caitlin standing within the circle, that look of contentment on her face. Mam always told him the stones were put here by folk called Druids, so the stones had been here for thousands of years. She believed the stone circle was only to be entered by folks that had been called to perform extraordinary feats, not for common folk. And she never wanted the stones to be moved. They still stood as they always had.

The graves of a number of MacKinnons were located here, some from long ago. Of course, the most recent gravestone was that of Mam—Alice M. MacKinnon. Alex climbed down from Zeus and let the reins loose, knowing the horse would stay there until he called for him.

Mam's grave looked almost as fresh as it had the day they buried her. Alex had an inkling it was kept in such fine shape by Da, but he felt he shouldn't ask about it. Today there was a fresh bouquet of holly, its bright red berries peeping through the snow that had fallen the night before. Certainly they all missed Mam, but surely Da felt her loss even more so.

He walked a bit closer to the gravesite then knelt, leaned back on his heels, and wondered again why he had come here. Well, no, that's not exactly right. He knew why he had come, but wasn't exactly sure what he thought to accomplish by coming. He reached and brushed the snow away from the holly.

Ah, Mam, ye wouldn't believe all that has happened to us — all of us: Da, Hector, Jack and Ian, and me, too. Maybe by telling ye about it I'll get a better understanding of it meself. But it's a bit complicated.

Ye would be so proud of young Ian, yer favorite. Aye, we all knew that, but then he's our favorite too, so not to worry. He suffered mightily from a wound he got at Culloden. Mam, Culloden was an awful battle. Men from every clan were there. Some of them survived, but many didn't. I won't go into detail, but just know that we had to find help for Ian.

As luck was with us, we found a young woman, a healer called Caitlin, just south of Inverness. She lived in a cave and we took our Ian to her. She saved his life, Mam, and we are ever so glad to have him still with us. But he lost a foot in the process, ye see, and was getting about on crutches, and doing fairly well at that. Then Da, Uncle Wabi, and old Jamie made him a new foot attached to a boot. Ye had to see it to believe it. He gets around now just like always.

Wabi? Oh, he's uncle to Caitlin. Now that's another story, and maybe I'll come again and tell ye more about that. But as it is, Caitlin and I are to wed soon, as are Jack and Millie. Millie is a fine Lady, Mam. And our Jack is so smitten with her and her little one, Midge. So now, in addition to all us menfolk, we have two fine ladies and a young bairn to keeps things a bit lively around here.

We all miss ye, ye ken, but yer still with us. Everywhere we look we still see yer touch, and yer name always brings a smile to our faces. Today, however, I'm not sure what to do, ye ken? Caitlin is having a real problem with a nightmare that won't let her be at peace. She's a most unusual woman, Mam, and I'm no real sure how to tell ye about her.

First of all, she's a very independent lass. She's got a mind of her own and sometimes I don't agree with her way of doing things, but I'm sure she'll come around to my way of thinking if I'm patient long enough. She's been given special powers, and I can't say I'm understanding them just yet. She saved my life, as well as Jack's and Millie's. She's special, Mam. Ye always told me, 'listen to yer heart, Alex. It'll no tell ye wrong.' And my heart tells me to hold this woman close and be thankful she belongs to me. Aye. I'll do just that.

He stood, brushed the snow from his knees and mounted again. He had come here a couple of times before, but thought now he might make it a regular habit. Sharing his thoughts with Mam eased his soul. He wondered for a second if Caitlin had spoken to someone special here, too.

CHAPTER 4

Wabi's life had gotten back to normal and he was busy with Maximo, the young beagle pup he'd been working with. Having completed his training, the dog was ready to go to his new owner. Wabi really didn't want to let this one go. The little fellow had taken to sleeping on Wabi's bed at night, right next to Groucho, his ancient feline, and the three guys made quite a full bed. This was the part of the job Wabi disliked —turning the dogs he had worked so closely with over to the new owners. But it had to be done. A dog trainer knows better than to get too attached to the animals he trains. Still, this particular small beagle had wound his way into Wabi's heart, and letting him go would definitely be difficult.

"Max. Come boy. We need to go."

The wooden floor resounded with the patter of beagle paws as Maximo hurried from the bedroom to the front door where Wabi was retrieving a leash — not that either of them needed it, but the new owner might.

Max's compact little body all but pranced as he stood next to Wabi, eagerly waiting for either a hand signal or a verbal command. Wabi had convinced him he was the best beagle ever, and the pup was determined to prove him right. The old wizard picked him up, snuggling him close.

"Ok, pal. We're off to the village. Told Laird Gordon I'd bring you to his place today, so we might as well get it done."

They walked out the door and started down the lane leading to the village. Wabi's ears perked as a humming noise came riding on the wind, a sound that always brought a smile to his face. A visitor, and one he especially enjoyed.

Owl came to a screeching halt in mid-air — he still liked to impress his Master with his abilities — and slowly fluttered his wings, gently landing on Wabi's shoulder.

"Owl, what a pleasant surprise."

Master Wabi. And Maximo, I see. And where are you two headed?

Wabi smiled. Owl's clipped British accent was in full bloom this morning. Wabi knew that in one of his lives Owl had resided with a proper Englishman and had adopted his manner of speaking, which Wabi found entertaining. And to think that today he was keeping company with Wabi, an old wizard who spoke with a gruff Scottish brogue, and certainly not proper English.

"As it happens, we're going to the village where I'll turn this little fellow over to Laird Gordon. His training is complete and he'll make the laird a fine hunting dog."

Ah. Then you've been successful as usual, Master.

"Well, he was a treat from day one. He's not any ordinary dog, Owl."

They never are, Master.

"Just so. Now, as glad as I am to see you, I guess that you didn't just drop by for a chat."

Right you are. I've been sent from the Highlands. Caitlin is doing well, the leg is almost totally healed, and she's getting about a bit. As of late, she's been plagued with disturbing nightmares — for more than a week now. They have her in a quandary, Master. She's unable to understand them and they get worse each night. Not only is she not getting any rest, neither is Alex.

"Oh? Wonder what's causing her to have nightmares? Hmm.

She's had a lot of changes in the last few months, Owl. Maybe that."

She's most concerned, Master. She would like you to come and help sort her out. Of course, the weddings are next week. She is wondering if maybe you could come a few days before and help her decipher these nightmares.

"I see. Of course I'll do whatever Caitlin wants, but you know, Owl, Alex may not especially welcome me coming to her side every time a problem comes up that she's not sure how to deal with. He's her mate now and I expect he's more than able to handle most situations. Nightmares don't usually happen without a good reason though. Just let me take care of getting Max to the laird, then I'll start out immediately."

As you wish, Master. I'll be on my way. It's a magnificent flight from the Highlands. You should see it from my vantage point.

Wabi and Maximo watched as Owl wheeled high and entertained them with a couple of spiraling aerial maneuvers, leaving the old wizard and Maximo standing in the lane.

Letting go of Caitlin is proving to be more difficult than I thought it would be. It's something I must get a grip on, though. My caring for her was necessary, but now Alex is the one she should call on. And I must remember that. I must let her go.

CHAPTER 5

C aitlin? Are you out here?" Millie walked out to the hut with a snoozing Midge resting on her shoulder — the child could sleep anywhere it seemed.

"Here. Over here, Millie."

"Thought you might be. I find myself wandering out to this spot also, just for a bit of peace and quiet, you see."

"Well, you know, it may take a while before we get used to a lot of folks around, and all of them men." Caitlin laughed as Millie sat on the bench next to her.

"Isn't it just so different? I do love being here, though. And I'd never want to be anywhere else. But you know, just an occasional reprieve from a lot of male voices and discussion about sheep and who's got to go where would be nice."

Caitlin was laughing aloud now.

"I believe we brought this on ourselves. You were running and so was I. Who knew we'd end up in the northern Highlands with a bunch of sheepherders with voracious appetites?"

Millie was also laughing, though both women knew how fortunate they were. They could have easily never seen the light of day again had these men not come to their assistance on that fateful morning.

"Aye. At that moment I don't think I even cared. I was just

past living with Edward another day, and anything was better than that."

Millie's life as the wife of Lord Edward Warwick had been a living hell from the first moment. She thanked her lucky stars for the changes that had come about through Caitlin, Jack, Alex, and her most beloved little child, Midge. Her life today couldn't be more satisfying.

"I wasn't running from a husband, but Warwick and that soldier certainly made my life miserable for a bit there. But you know, Uncle Wabi believes life has a way of bringing us experiences that lead us to greater understanding and, if we survive, then we become better persons as a result."

"Hmm, that's probably true. I don't ever wish to go through another experience like that one. Maybe because I had a babe it was different, but I'm certainly more thankful for everything now, and know I belong here in this place with these people.

"So now, what are we going to do about these nightmares you're having? Alex was talking about them with Jack and Da. They all want to 'fix' the situation you know — typical male response to anything we ladies might complain about."

This comment led them into another fit of laugher, which was good for their souls.

"The nightmares really are becoming a problem, Millie. The only person I think can help is Uncle Wabi. And even he may not know what to do."

"Then let's send one of the men to get him—today."

Caitlin smiled at her friend. "It's taken care of already. Owl has left and will take a message to Wabi."

Millie had already accepted that Caitlin and Wabi were unique, out of the ordinary. What they were exactly she didn't know, but she didn't care either. She and Midge were safe because of them. She'd let that be enough.

"Then let's hope he can get to the bottom of this. He's a wise man, no doubt. And I know you trust him."

Caitlin looked around, toward the old hut. "Have you ever looked inside the hut? Alex says Mam kept her special things there, but he doesn't know what they are. Do you think we could maybe look inside? I'm anxious to know more about this woman. All the brothers speak of her still. It's as if she left a large emptiness and they haven't been able to fill it yet. Sleeping in her sewing room, I often feel her presence. There's something about her that calls to me."

"Then maybe she's trying to know you, too. After all, you've stolen the heart of her firstborn, and I know a little about how special that first one can be. But my bet is they're all special, no matter what the birth order. To answer your question, no, I've never looked inside the hut. But I believe we may be called on to clean it out soon."

"Oh? Why would we need to do that?"

"Uncle Andrew has asked for one of the huts to be made available to him. It could be this one, I suppose, as it's the largest. Although there are several others farther away from the lodge."

"Why would he want to move to a hut? He's lived in the lodge for years now, ever since Florence passed away."

"It seems he found more than just family history on his trips to Edinburgh. According to Jack, Uncle Andrew is bringing a 'friend' to the farm to live — with him. She's one of the ladies who helped him go through the ledgers from the old kirks, and she's an expert on clan history. It seems they have an 'understanding,' as Jack put it."

"What does that mean, an understanding?"

"Jack says they've decided to make a home together, but are not going through any sort of official ceremony, as we are planning. It seems they've agreed to have a "hand fasting" as was done in the olden days. They think they're old enough to follow their own inclinations about such."

"What? Uncle Andrew and a woman? Holy Rusephus, what's going to happen next?" Both women dissolved into another of their female giggle fits as Jack called them.

"I've used all the herbs I found in Mam's storeroom and I've only got enough juniper berries and wild garlic to make a couple more batches of my tinctures. I need to gather herbs, but I'm not sure where to even start looking for them. As soon as I'm walking better, I'll go scouting. But until then, I need to find a person in the village who may have herbs they'll sell me. Last week I met a young lass from Spain—Lourdes—that sells her flowers down in the village — she had a few herbs too. Maybe I can buy from her until I can gather my own."

"Jack talks about an old woman who used to come by before Mam passed on. She'd trade her herbs for Mam's jams and jellies. Mam wasn't a healer as such, but she did know how to put together a few remedies for small problems, apparently. I'll ask him where we can find her."

"Good. Once I get enough remedies and ointments prepared, maybe I can talk Alex into letting me practice my healing again. He's overly protective in my opinion, and still thinks he can make my decisions."

"Yes, don't they all. Certainly they all mean well. Hector and I are struggling to work out our differences, and with so many mouths to feed, we do need to work together. Today he's at Cameron Castle working with the resident hands, Clint and Winston. Jack told me that Hector can 'talk a jackass into braying at the moon,' which I suppose means he's good at talking people into helping him. I know I must go myself at some point and get a feel for what is happening now that grandmother and Aunt Moira are gone."

The estate was hers now, what with her grandmother and aunt having been killed by a highwayman just a few days before she and Caitlin had sought refuge at the castle. During their couple of days at the castle, Millie had been surprised and pleased to have a visit from Dorothea, her childhood nursemaid and friend of a lifetime. They had been apart for several years now as shortly after he married Millie, Lord Warwick sent Dorothea back to Scotland and Millie had not heard from her since. When she had seen her recently at the estate, Millie had promised Dorothea she would return. And she would. Just as soon as things settled here at the home place.

Just before he left, she had handed Hector a letter to give to Dorothea. "Don't forget to give this letter to Dorothea, please."

"I'll make sure she gets it. Don't worry about that."

With all the men gone for a few days it was quiet around the lodge. Come nightfall, Caitlin hesitated to go to bed. Finally, she had to make herself retire for the evening.

A few hours later the dream came again, only now she could hear voices coming from a far distance and tinkling sounds — maybe bells — and soft singing far in the background. The scents were so familiar she could almost taste them. But again, the moment she could almost grasp something or someone, the dream floated away and she was left in the fog. When she awakened her heart was racing and there was a deep longing for something she couldn't even define.

Uncle Wabi, I hope you get here soon.

CHAPTER 6

Hector had agreed to go to Cameron Castle and try to get it working again. Millie was most concerned that the old ones — primarily Clint, Winston, Ethel and a few others who had worked at her grandmother's place — had means to keep on surviving. They'd worked at the castle all their lives and now, with the deaths of her grandmother and aunt, Millie felt a responsibility to them. Plus, they were part of her childhood memories.

When Millie was a child, Clint and Winston were young men. There was always plenty of work at hand, but they would still take time to hook up the pony cart for the youngsters, those being Millie and children of the staff. Millie would follow them around as they went about their chores. She liked visiting her grandmother, grandfather and aunt because she had such freedom there unlike at her father's castle in England, where she had to always be a Lady and never was allowed to associate with the local children.

Coming around behind the castle, Hector walked his horse to the stable. Normally he would have been met by a stable hand. But since the murders, most of the staff had fled in fear of becoming the next victim. He observed that there was water and fresh oats at each stall, so apparently Clint and Winston were still around.

A voice called out to him from the front of the stable. "Hello. And who might ye be?"

The old man had seen the horse and rider approaching and made it his business to find out why the rider was stopping here. Since the deaths of their mistresses, Clint and Winston were wary of everyone. They had told Lady Millie they'd watch out for the place, and they would.

Hector stepped forward and offered his hand to the old gentleman. "Good morning to ye, sir. I'm Hector MacKinnon, brother to the two MacKinnons ye already met. They bought sheep from Mistress Cameron a couple of years ago. And most recently, they were escorting Lady Millie and her bairn to our place in the Highlands. Remember? I believe ye must be Clint. Millie told me I'd find ye here."

The oldster studied the young man's face for a moment. "Yeah, ye do have that look about ye. Yer all different, but there's a familiar look ye all have. Yep, I remember fairly well, considering me age. Lady Millie told us she'd be coming back, but we ain't seen her yet. Is she all right then?"

"Yes sir. She's never been better. She and her new bairn are settled in at our lodge. And she and Jack, one of my brothers, are about to be married."

"Bless me, but weren't she already married to that there Lord feller, the one that conked me on the head and was trying to catch her?"

"It seems Lord Warwick met an untimely end, according to Alex, my older brother. But Millie was in danger, as were the others traveling with her, so it didn't seem there was much choice but to take care of him."

"Then that's the best news ye coulda brought me. That Lord fellow was a right dreadful man. Our Lady Millie's safe and that's a relief. Do ye think she's still planning to come back? We're at a loss as to what we should be doing, ye ken?"

"Aye, that's why I'm here. Millie asked me to get with you and another fellow, Winston was it? She wants to make sure you, Winston, and any others who have been with the family for years are taken care of. And she wants the place to be kept in good repair. She wanted to make sure you understood the place should be run the way her grandmother and Aunt Moira had run it."

"Then we'll be sure to do that. As it is, though, we done run out of funds. Me and Winston have managed to keep the horses fed and the chickens looked after but we've nothing to work with now. Hay needs to be cut for the horses, and the sheep, what few we still have, need to be readied for shearing, and the missus' gardens are done gone to weeds. She would be most upset about that, ye ken? She practically fed half the village with her vegetables and such."

"What do ye mean, fed half the village?"

"Ah, but then ye wouldn't know about that, of course. Well, ye see, the families have difficulty just feeding their wee ones, 'specially now that so many of the men died at Culloden. The women were left without a man to help, so Mistress Cameron had her gardeners, and the cook, my Ethel, always preparing food to be taken to the folk in the village. Me and Winston would load it on the cart and go to the main street. That food would be gone in a matter of minutes. It was a real help to them. Now, I don't know what's become of 'em."

"I see. Then I'd better put my thinking cap on and see what we need to do. I'll need yer help, and Winston's, too. Ye think we can count on him?"

"Aye. He's as much a part of this place as I am. He ain't going nowhere."

"Don't worry, we'll find funds for ye to operate with. Millie has some of her own and I've been instructed to use them where they can serve a good purpose. Looks to me like we got work to do."

"Aye, lad. I'll find Winston and we'll follow your lead. We might be a little long in the tooth, ye ken, but we still got our marbles and ain't much we can't do."

The old man walked away feeling lighter than his years should allow. Speaking aloud, perhaps to himself, he said, "Yes sir, our Lady Millie didn't forget us."

Hector thought to create an office of sorts in the castle, a place where he could begin to create a list of things that needed to be done. Just looking around, it didn't look as if anyone had entered the building since Millie, Caitlin, and his brothers had left here a few months ago. In fact, no one had ventured upstairs since the murders had taken place.

He walked about taking in his surroundings. Yes, Jack had told it right. This was quite an exquisite place. There was fine furniture in every room, hand-woven rugs, what Mam would have called "real china," and a number of original paintings hanging along the walls. Perhaps they were portraits of ancestors. Certainly, none of the women were as beautiful as Millie. He still wondered how his oaf of a brother had managed to charm that beautiful woman. As for himself, he hadn't found any woman he thought interesting enough to get involved with, nor had he found any he was inclined to spend time with either. Well, maybe Mam was right about things happening when they were supposed to.

Thinking to set up shop in a corner of the great room where the fireplace could provide warmth, he found a small table and chair, more like a lady's desk he thought. And it probably had been. There were letters strewn on the top so he stacked them neatly and brought out his own papers, which were just a few ledgers and empty pages for making notes. He had a mind that thrived on organization and a head for figures. He'd make a list of the stock, the household furnishings, figure out the acreage, etc., until he had a clear picture of what Millie had here. Perhaps he'd find papers in the castle that might help him.

Before tackling his new tasks, however, he started up the stairs to get an idea of how many rooms were on the second floor. Millie had told him there were a number of bedrooms, but she didn't remember how many. He stood at the top of the stairs scanning the upper level. It was amazing — the floor shone so brightly it looked as if it someone had cleaned it today. But there were no cleaning girls at the moment so he didn't think that could be right. The hallway at the top of the stairs was wide and a magnificent, colorful Persian rug ran the length of it. On either side of the hallway there were four doors. All of them were closed.

Just as he was about to continue on, he paused. What was that? A rattling noise? He was sure he had heard something. But standing there for another moment he heard nothing more. Still, he was sure he had not imagined that sound. Maybe just vermin.

Then, when he had convinced himself it was nothing more than rats, he heard another sound — something scraping — coming from the end of the hallway.

Now, I know I heard that.

The hair on the back of his neck stood to attention and he held his breath. Whoever had killed Millie's grandmother and aunt was still on the loose. Not one person had come forth with information that might help the constable find the killer or killers. These days the villagers kept close to home and the women never went anywhere without an escort.

He halted, listening closely. He pulled out his pistol and crept closer to the first door on the left. He pushed gently at the door and it slowly opened. He peeked in holding his pistol carefully. This would have been the mistress' bedroom. Or some woman's for certain. Hand-tatted lace bed linens covered the four-poster bed, and the room still smelled like a woman—something of heather or other flowers. Female. Empty.

He closed the door and slowly walked farther along the hallway, still listening. He heard a muffled noise, muted, and followed it to the last door on the right. He quietly pushed on the door, but it didn't open. He pushed a little harder but it still didn't budge. His heart was racing, but holding his pistol with both hands he lifted his booted foot and kicked the door with all his strength. The door quickly sprang open, causing him to practically fall into the room.

No matter what he had thought to find, he was not prepared for this sight. In the middle of the room gathered on a small woven rug sat three children. The oldest was perhaps seven and the other two even younger. Hector didn't have much experience with children, so guessing their ages was not easy.

"Holy Jesus, what are ye bairns doing in here?"

He wasn't sure who was the most surprised and frightened, him or the children. He was without words. What did you say to three small children sitting in a castle bedroom, munching on what looked like some kind of old oat cakes.

"We never meant to steal the cakes, mister, but we be awful hungry, ye ken?"

The oldest child, a young lad, stood and faced him, trying his best to stand in front of the younger ones — almost a gesture of protection. His eyes never left Hector's gun and his voice quivered when he spoke. Following the lad's eyes, Hector quickly stuck the pistol in the rear of his kilt. He figured he'd probably scared the living daylights out of the lad.

"No, no. That's all right. Ye eat all the cakes ye want."

He looked about, thinking surely there must be someone here to help him make sense of this situation. This was a most unexpected development. "What are ye doing here? Who are ye?"

The lad's face lost color. He was not sure how to answer the gentleman. If he told the truth, the man may take a limb to his hide. At this moment, the demands of his stomach were overtaking his ability to use his brain, so he came out with the truth.

"We got no home anymore. Our Da didn't come back from the fighting — the Culloden. And our landlord told our Mam we would have to leave. Said he had to have payin' tenants. But our Mam was sick — and then she went to sleep. And she wouldn't wake up, no matter how much we called to her. After a week our food was gone too, and we snuck in here. It was cold outside and we come up the stairs. There was some cakes in the kitchen so we took some. We didn't take all of them, though."

Hector's brain was finally functioning again. Millie had sent him to take care of business, but no one had ever dreamed about this state of affairs.

"Don't fret now, lad. No one's going to hurt any of ye. Just sit here until I can sort this out. It'll all work out, lad. Stay here until I come for ye. Don't leave. I'll help all of ye."

Hector found Clint and explained what he had discovered upstairs.

"By the rood! Ye mean they just camped out in our castle here? Where's they Mam and Da?"

Hector told the story as best he could and the old one just shook his head. He'd seen a lot in his day, but this took the cake.

"Bairns hiding in the castle right under me nose? Since Lady Millie left we hadn't seen any reason to go upstairs. Whatever cakes those wee ones found had to be several months old now. They must be like stone. But then, I guess anything is better than nothing. I'll see about getting them some vittles. I'll tell Ethel. She'll take care of that problem. Yep. I'll fetch Ethel. She'll know what to do with the wee ones. She'll feed them for sure."

"I thought she was at the inn, cooking?"

"Aye. But she'll be on home here shortly. She always has enough food around for an army. Don't even worry 'bout that." He removed his old tattered tam, scratched his sparsely sprigged head, and then looked again at Hector.

"Now that I think for a second, I know one who would know more what to do with them bairns than Ethel. Ethel never had a bairn, ye ken? But Dorothea, well she's spent her entire life looking out for bairns. She was nursemaid to our Lady Millie. She'd be the one we need to help us."

"Then you get on about finding her and I'll try to figure out what else we need to do."

Hector, Dorothea, Clint and Winston were quite a team and in short order they had sorted out what had to be done. Hector had to get home for the festivities, but he assured them he and Millie would return in just a matter of days. Just before he left, he remembered Millie's instruction.

"Oh, Dorothea. I've brought a letter from Millie. She wanted to make sure I didn't forget to give it to you." He handed the letter to the small woman, who gently took it from his hands.

"Thank you. I'll take it home and read it carefully."

Dorothea was more than excited to get a letter from Millie. The bond they shared would never be broken. She had cared for Millie from the day the child was born, her entire life, until Lord Warwick had sent her away just a few years ago. But when Millie had shown up at the estate fleeing her husband, Dorothea had come to her. Perhaps they could manage to see each other occasionally now. She tucked the letter in her coat pocket and looked forward to reading it, word for word, at home.

CHAPTER 7

W abi slowly began walking away from Laird Gordon's place. He had told himself he wouldn't look back. Maximo was the property of this gentleman now, and he would be well cared for here. But just as he closed the tall, ornately scrolled iron gates that surrounded the estate, he couldn't resist just one more glance at the young pup. Max apparently had the same thought as well. Their eyes met and Wabi smiled, then moved on. The little beagle watched as far as he could, then scampered after Laird Gordon, waiting for instruction.

A trek to the upper Highlands was quite an undertaking for anyone, but Wabi was definitely beginning to feel his arthritis these days. He walked with the aide of a crooked staff and, after a few hours, sat by the roadway to rest his bones a bit. He began a conversation with himself —an old habit.

All right, you old wizard. You know there's an easier route to the Highlands, but it'll take a toll on your body and mind. So be it. Caitlin must be needing you, or Owl wouldn't have come. And you know you must stop running each time she calls. Taking care of her is Alex's job now. But maybe just this last time you should see about her. So get yourself up there and quit making excuses. You can take the "long" way on the trip home, but right now you need to help her.

With this decision made, he laid his staff on the ground and got on bended knees. He slowly lifted his arms to the sky and began a quiet, slow-cadenced chant, using a language as old as time and known only to himself and a very few others. His chanting reverberated in the air above him and the sound was soothing. He then lay prone, with his head pointed to the North. This ritual demanded that his entire being be consumed within the elements of nature: earth, water, air and fire.

He began to chant once more, and raindrops slowly made their way to the earth. The rain built in intensity until it poured from the heavens in a deluge and rivulets ran in all directions. The old wizard was drenched totally and now raised his raspy voice and called out to an unseen god and goddess. The sky darkened, the wind swirled about him, howling as it did so. Great rolls of thunder pealed and it seemed the entire world vibrated with such force that it would surely split apart. He continued his chanting and an earth-shattering streak of lightning lit the sky and brought a trail of fire that started far above him and struck the ground just above his head. Still lying prone, he reached out and grabbed a handful of earth in each hand. Another quick, but scathing, lightning bolt scorched the earth next to where he was lying. He lifted both hands, as if in supplication to the gods of the sky. At that moment, one last, blistering blaze of fire struck him, and the ground beneath him crumbled. A great plume of smoke filled the space where the old wizard had lain before he disappeared.

Wabi was careful when he traveled in this manner. Those who opted to time weave had to take precautions. Not all who pass through the portals are clean in spirit and mind. If these unclean ones manage to squeeze through, they can bring much danger to those on the other side.

The old one now traveled at a speed that had stars melting, suns blazing, and the colors of the Aurora Borealis racing across the sky, blending in a manner that created symmetry in the universe. He smiled to himself. This trip would have even been pleasant to Owl, who so despised time weaving.

As often happens when using time weaving as a means of travel, his landing in a field of heather in the Highlands could have been smoother. He landed with a thud and rubbed his backside as he stood. Slowly regaining his equilibrium, he remembered to thank his Creator for this gift, this ability to move about quickly. It was not given to all the called, and Wabi was judicious in his use of it.

He immediately recognized the lodge at the top of the ridge. "Ah, good. Not too far to walk, now."

He retrieved his staff and began the short walk across the pasture. It was only a second later that Owl swooped from the sky and alighted on his shoulder.

Master, I didn't expect you so soon. I know how you must have gotten here in such a short period of time. Certainly glad I didn't have to travel with you today. That just ruffles my feathers!

"My friend, it was a most pleasant trip. I don't even feel exhausted as I usually do. Well, maybe a bit, but nothing I can't live with. Come, let's find Caitlin."

~ * ~

Caitlin was getting around using Ian's crutch, which he no longer needed these days thanks to Wabi, Da and Jamie. Walking with that was certainly better than sitting around being waited on, thought Caitlin. She'd had enough of resting and watching as others got about the farm and made themselves useful. She knew her day would come, and her healing skills would be in great demand. But she was ready to get on with her life.

Just then her scalp began to tingle and her nose registered the scent of leather, cinnamon and oranges — Uncle Wabi.

"Uncle Wabi's here, Millie."

Millie came to Caitlin's side, standing on the porch. "I don't see anyone."

Then, a few moments later, just a short way down the lane, she saw Uncle Wabi, stopping to lean on his staff a moment. Willie immediately jumped from the porch and ran out to meet the old one, his bushy tail frantically waving. The great wolf was rewarded with a quick ruff behind his ears and a moment of wizard-to-wolf meeting of the minds. Yes, they were of the same ilk.

Caitlin watched and, for a quick moment, saw how old Uncle Wabi had become. She still thought of him as the eccentric uncle that took care of her for most of her life. Just this instant, she saw an old man, tall and rather thin with a weathered face and a white beard. He wore a belted shirt over his trousers, and his smile could be seen even from this distance. Her dear old uncle wouldn't be here forever. She knew that, but until now had never given it much thought.

"Uncle Wabi, you're here." Caitlin called to him.

Millie walked out to greet him and Caitlin waited for the two to return to the porch.

"Millie, it's a pleasure to see you again, and you're looking well I might add."

Wabi gave the tall woman a gentle hug, and once again, as at their first meeting, Millie felt the warmth that emanated from him. Then he walked over to where his niece was standing.

"Caitlin, my dear girl. You look like the Highland air is certainly agreeing with you." He laughed and hugged her close, taking in the lavender and mint scent that was as much a part of her as her luxurious hair.

"Not sure it's the air, Wabi, but aye, everything here agrees with me. Well, almost everything, that is."

"Ah, yes, the reason for my early visit. Owl tells me you're having disturbing dreams. Having had a few of those myself, I remember what a drain they can be on one — and on others that are close to you also."

"That's exactly right."

Wabi watched as Caitlin moved about the room. "I see Ian's crutch is coming in handy for you. And how is that young lad doing with his new foot?"

"See for yourself. Here he comes now. He must have seen you coming," Caitlin responded.

Ian was trotting, not running, but close.

"Well, now that's what I call a fine piece of work if I say so myself."

Wabi was pleased that the efforts of Da, Jamie and himself had paid off. Young Ian could now go on with his life and not be hindered by a leg he had to drag behind.

"Uncle Wabi, I didn't know ye was coming." Ian beamed and grabbed Wabi for a hug. He had been drawn to the old wizard from the moment they met. He had plenty of brothers and a couple of uncles, but there was a quality about the old man that drew Ian to him and made him feel as if he had known him for eons. When Wabi had been here the first time, he had included the young lad in discussions that Ian found exciting and interesting.

Ian remembered every conversation with the old man. They had discussed the unique qualities that animals have that allow them to survive, and Wabi had gone on to suggest that perhaps they even had abilities greater than those of humans. He was also of the opinion they could communicate with other species. Ian was mesmerized by this kind of conversation and was thrilled to find someone who found other species as interesting as he did. It was his first experience with discussions with someone outside his family, and Wabi knew much more about the world than anyone he had ever known. One particular conversation was embedded in the lad's mind and he thirsted for more. He recalled every word of it.

"Ian, there are more worlds out there than the one we know about. The Creator has created so many magnificent species, peoples and countries that we can't even count them. He has a plan for each of us and it is within our power to discover the path that is ours."

What that really possible? What did that really mean? He had no concept of any other worlds or peoples, but Wabi had now planted a seed that Ian needed to nourish, and he was ready to do so.

The old man actually treated him as if he were as important as his older brothers. Plus, Wabi was the one who had come up with the idea of creating a prosthesis for him. Working on that project had put the two of them together and a bond of sorts had already been made. So now Ian was even more anxious to be with this most interesting man. He was unlike anyone the lad had ever come across. He hoped Wabi could explain more about the early Vikings and woads that lived in Scotland and the Isles in the past. The wizard had told Ian stories about these folk and the boy was intrigued.

Millie went inside and brought out a pot of tea and the small cakes she had made earlier. "Come, let's have a bit of a celebration. It's not every day we have such an esteemed visitor."

They sat around the old pine breakfast table, its worn surface gleaming with the lemon oil Millie had rubbed into it, and creating scrumptious goodies was almost second nature to Millie these days.

"I see you've accomplished much since I was here, Millie. These cakes are as delicious as those Mrs. Favré brings to me. Think you may have found your own calling, my girl."

"Oh, I don't know about that, Wabi. But the air here agrees with me as well. And Midge is content to be passed from one shoulder to another, so no complaints from her."

They all laughed, and Wabi felt satisfied that Caitlin was at the right place.

After clearing the table, Ian and Millie gave the two a little privacy. Wabi sensed Caitlin wasn't sure where to start, so he allayed her thoughts with one statement.

"Caitlin, my girl, I believe this move to the Highlands was a good one for you. Or maybe it's just that Alex is here. Whatever the reason, you look well. But now tell me. Now that you're not being pursued by a soldier and a mad lord, are you satisfied with your life? You were always so busy back home that I had difficulty just keeping up with your daily schedule. Do you think this is the place for you?"

"Wabi, it's such a relief to not be running, struggling to stay alive, and wondering what tomorrow will bring. Alex is ever so patient with me, but he seems to think he is the only one who can make a good decision. Sitting around doing nothing doesn't work well for me— there are days I think I'll go mad. Yes, it's been necessary for my healing, but it won't work for the future. I must use my healing skills, and from what I've seen so far they are greatly needed here. The stories I've heard are unbelievable. Folks dying from nothing more than an infection that was not treated properly. If the Creator has a plan for me as you believe, then it's for me to help these folk, and I must find a way to do that. Of course, the first thing I have to do is convince Alex that anything else won't work. He wants a family, as do I. But I'm a healer and that's what I'll always be, even if we do have children. Once in a while, I'd like to just whack him over the head when he hovers over me and treats me like an invalid. So far I've managed to keep my tantrums in bounds, but you know what a chore that can be for me."

63

The old uncle smiled at his niece, nodding his head. "It appears to me you know what you are called to do. And if so, then you and Alex will sort this out. Now tell me what you can remember about these dreams."

"Oh, it's difficult to put into words. When the dream comes I feel I'm searching for someone, or maybe some place, and I think I'm there. But then the place is lost in a fine mist, a fog. There are voices, but the voices fade away and I'm left in limbo. There are even scents that call to me and they are so familiar, but I can't remember what they are. And there's a golden glow, always — it reminds me of my cave, where I lived before I ran from the soldier. Oh, Wabi. I realize it sounds ridiculous, but that's about all I can tell you."

"No, my girl, none of it sounds ridiculous. Dreams most often are based on memories that have been tucked away for safekeeping, or even sent to us from the past — maybe not even our own memories, but ones that are necessary for us to learn a lesson from. Dreams are images that tell a story in a way words never can. They can bring forth longings or desires we may not be aware of. But primarily they are a way of bringing us to a greater understanding of our place, our purpose, our destiny perhaps. These dreams have a definite purpose and you must work through them in order to be at peace again."

"They're frightening to me. Why are they coming now? I never had them before."

"Why now? I can't answer that. Maybe being here in this new home is prodding you to consider a new way of thinking about your life and where you're to go from here. Only you will be able to discern the meaning of these dreams. Tell me. What's so different here than you've experienced in life before now? Anything particularly enticing or interesting to you?"

"Hmm. The first thing that comes to mind, and a ritual I find most interesting, is our evening story time, as I call it. Uncle Andrew tells us a new story every evening as he knows the MacKinnon family history for generations. He remembers a lot of it, but what he didn't know he recently documented from records in the kirks and the official documents in Edinburgh and Inverness, and now wants to make a trip to Skye to add even more.

"He's amazing, Uncle Wabi. Listening to him each evening, I've become more and more aware that I know nothing about my own family. Why have I never asked questions about my own people before now? Was I just so self-absorbed I never gave thought to those before me? I don't even know where my people came from for goodness sake."

"There's no shame in not knowing about family. Some clans have stayed in the same region or country for generations, so knowing family history is not difficult. Take the MacKinnons for example. There are quite a few of them in Skye and several other villages nearby. And, of course, a branch of them has been in this region for many years, so finding their histories is not so difficult. However, not all families are that easy to locate or find records for. I'm wondering if hearing these stories has gotten your inquisitive mind into high gear, and it's telling you it's time you discovered your own history, your own people. I'm not surprised. Once you started accepting your powers there was bound to be questions about other aspects of your life. Just know that you, too, will come to understand more than you know now, but none of us ever know all that's in store for us. Why, that would be so much less fun." He tried a little levity to lighten the situation, but understood she was troubled.

"Wabi, you're the only person I know who may have any information about my family. Do you think you can remember anything that might help me?" Caitlin's face revealed she was ready to find answers, and the sooner the better.

Wabi had been expecting this question for a while now.

"Yes, my girl. I can tell you a bit, but not all. What I can do is let you find out for yourself. As you have no doubt begun to realize, this life is not the only one I have lived. There have been many, some of which I remember in detail, but some I remember little about — especially if they were in the distant past. The more recent the events, the better my memory. Memories of your grandmother, Ci-Cero, and your mother, Flinn, are still fairly fresh. It's a family you can be proud to have come from — a fine lineage, my girl.

"What? You knew my grandmother, too? How can that be?"

"It's difficult to explain, but we'll spend time together and I'll tell you what I know. As it was, your grandmother could read and write, almost unheard of skills in her time — skills that I taught her. Being that she was skilled, she kept a journal, actually a book, in which she tells the story of her life and how she and her parents came from Scotland to the shores of North America. She called it The Wolf, The Wizard and the Woad.

"Her life and mine were intertwined for such a long time and we worked on this journal, this book, together. She asked that I pass it on to those who would come after her. For the longest time, I hoped that Flinn might read it; but she never embraced her calling, thus she never read the story. She only knew bits and pieces that I told her. But I have preserved the journal as Ci-Cero asked and planned to give it to you if and when you were ready. Apparently, the time has finally come for me to put it in your hands.

"The Wolf, the Wizard and the Woad. What a strange title," Caitlin murmured.

"Perhaps, but once you read it you will understand why she

called it that." Wabi smiled within remembering Ci-Cero's insistence on the title.

"And North America? You mean America? But, then how did my mother get here to Scotland?"

"Ah, there's much for you to learn, my girl. Your great-grandfather, Ci-Cero's father, was a Viking and your great-grandmother was a woad."

"A Viking and a woad? But, isn't a woad one of those small people that painted their bodies with blue paint from the woad plant? I know about that plant. It can be fatal if not used properly."

"Yes, precisely. But, like you, your female ancestors were all healers. They knew how to use the dye properly. But, knowing where you came from, who your people were, may help you understand your place in the Creator's universe."

"Oh, Wabi. There's so much I don't know. More than anything I would like to know about my family."

"Then I'll bring the book on my next trip. It belongs to you now. I can fill in many details that may need further explanation. It is quite a story about a most exceptional young lass. And you are so like her." Caitlin nodded without commenting any further.

"Where is everybody anyway?"

"Alex and Jack are moving sheep, Uncle Andrew's at the library in Edinburgh, again, and Da and old Jamie are working out in the shed. Don't worry. As soon as it gets close to evening, they'll all come looking for Millie's vittles, as Uncle Andrew calls them."

"And Hector?"

"He's due any day now. He made a trip to Cameron Castle a few weeks ago and returned with information that Millie was surprised to learn. It seems the estate needs some care, and he now has made his second trip to take care of some business there. Millie has given him leave to make decisions for her. He's quite a whiz with numbers, so the estate will be in working order shortly. Millie wants to take care of the old hands who have spent their lives on the estate. They need to establish order again."

"Then perhaps he can be of assistance to them."

Caitlin stood and took her crutch. She would make her way to the birch tree, where she would mull over her thoughts of her ancestors. A Viking and a woad?

"And what's young Ian doing with himself these days?"

"Good question. He's out front on the porch. He's a bit of an enigma, I'm afraid. At his age, I'd think that's not unusual."

Wabi particularly wanted to see more of this young man. He, too, felt a connection, and knew exactly what it was. He'd talk with the lad and feel him out about various thoughts that were running through his mind. The boy was more than ready for a mentor, but Wabi didn't want to make any hasty decisions. He'd find a way to decipher where the boy stood in his own mind regarding his, as yet unspoken, yearnings. Patience. Patience.

Wabi went to his room for a few minutes, then walked outside to the front steps where Ian was sitting. The young lad was trying to read a book, but twilight was upon them and he was having difficulty as darkness was closing in.

"What's that you're reading, my lad?"

Ian held the book a bit higher so the old wizard could take a good look at it. As Wabi reached for the book, he put his hand on Ian's shoulder as he started to sit down. The jolt of electricity that shot up his arm shook him to his core.

Oh, good glory! I knew he was one of the called, but the vibrations coming from him are stronger than what I ever would have expected. No doubt the lad is experiencing his "awakening" of powers and is undoubtedly in great psychic, perhaps even physical pain. He has told no one, of course — he wouldn't dare to do so. Who could he tell? No one would even have an inkling of understanding. His Mam would have, but she's not here. Whatever I had planned for this trip, helping him understand his situation must take precedence over all other plans, perhaps even Caitlin's issues. She needs some help too, but she's more mature and better able to manage her powers. He's vulnerable and frightened. And this amount of power can be dangerous.

He sat down slowly, still pondering how to approach the lad about his plan.

"It's a book Alex brought home from his university days. It's called *Notebooks of Leonardo da Vinci*. He was a genius, Uncle Wabi. He was a sculptor, an architect, a musician, a mathematician, an engineer, a writer. And a botanist. And he was an artist, too. How could one man be so talented? I mean, how could he have learned to do all that?"

"Leonardo de Vinci, huh? Well, I agree he was a genius if ever there was one. And certainly most of us are not as gifted as da Vinci, although some of us have talents we aren't aware of until they are ready to be found. They just sorta stay hidden, waiting for the right time and circumstance to show themselves."

"Yeah? Then maybe one day I'll discover a few talents I don't know about yet. Right now all I can do well is make a good pot of tea. That's all right, as Mam taught me that. But Da, Alex and Jack, and Hector too, they all can do just about anything they set their minds to."

"Yes, I've seen them in action, and you're right. They're capable men. But as capable as your Da and brothers are, Ian, I can assure you that your own abilities and gifts are even greater. When we first met, it was apparent to me that you have been given special talents. And now, as I sit here next to you, I am even more certain. Just as Caitlin and I, you have been chosen by the Creator. You are to be one of his ambassadors, also.

69

"I am quite sure your mind is beginning to experience some situations that are unsettling to you. As with all of us called ones, when we first become aware of our abilities it is most frightening and we try to ignore them. This period is called the awakening, and is a most difficult time for those going through it. Your thoughts may seem to be running wild and you may sometimes be so restless you can't remain still. You may even experience episodes of moving items about, just through using your mind, or you may have vivid dreams that seem very real to you. Your powers are beginning to manifest themselves and that may frighten you.

"Each of us has our own personal situations, but rest assured what you are going through is familiar to all of us. What you must not do is let your powers rule you. Rather, you must become aware of when and where they should be used. Of course, powers are only to be used for making the world a better place, lad. When one is as young as you, it will be tempting to use them for personal gain or as a weapon to be used just because we have this ability. I'll teach you how to control them and guide you in learning how to use them properly. So, tomorrow we'll begin with the basic lessons and talk at length about how to proceed from there. Don't be afraid of these gifts, Ian. They have been kept in secret until now, but they were given specifically to you by the Creator, and he rarely makes a mistake about whom he gives them to."

Once again he laid his hand on the young lad's shoulder and again felt the sizzling vibration of the amazing power that rested within this special boy. The old man rose and started to walk away.

Ian wasn't sure whether he was relieved or even more afraid. The fact that Wabi had sensed he was experiencing unusual thoughts and moments of surprising happenings was comforting. He hadn't said a word to anyone, but apparently Wabi already knew what he was going through. Perhaps that explained the connection he felt to him early on. Could he really be a called one like Wabi? That thought had never occurred to him, but the old one was right about his mind reeling. Yesterday he had found himself opening the barn door with just a thought. He had not even been aware he was making the effort, so it was very disconcerting. Yes, he was certainly glad Wabi was here. There was no one else to turn to.

Wabi had his hand on the doorknob, and as he opened it Ian called to him.

"Speaking of secrets, I think there are some about our place that no one is talking about."

"Secrets you say?"

"Yes sir. Not only that, but I can tell ye there are some dark powers about this place. If ye understand me."

"Aye. Then we'd better talk about this dark power. But let it wait until tomorrow when I feel a bit more refreshed." He walked away, but his mind was already churning with questions regarding this dark power Ian had referred to. Tomorrow.

He closed the door behind himself and continued to his quarters. He had much to think about now, but he needed to retire and let his body and mind rest, even if only for a short time. The power that lay within the lad could be destructive if not guided carefully, and Wabi's concern for Ian weighed heavily on his mind.

Just for a second, Ian watched as Owl quietly sailed by, executing one of his delicate maneuvers as he did so, then settled himself in the birch tree. The owl had become part of the scenery at the MacKinnon homestead and no one questioned his presence.

CHAPTER 8

When Hector returned from this first trip to the estate, Millie couldn't believe what he told her. Her eyes had grown large and her mouth had dropped open, in a very unladylike fashion.

"What? What do you mean bairns in the castle? Where's their mother? And what are they doing in the estate castle?" Millie had known she needed to get back there, but certainly she hadn't anticipated anything like this.

"Uh, well, that's a bit complicated, Millie. But suffice it to say they had been camped out for several days. The oldest lad told me his Da never returned from the fighting at Culloden, and with no man to help with expenses the landlord told his mam she would have to leave. He needed paying tenants in his place. Then their mam had a sickness and died and they had no one and no place to go."

"But how were they surviving?"

"When I came across them they were eating old cakes they found in the castle kitchen. Probably from the last batch Ethel cooked there."

"Oh, no. We can't have that. You didn't just leave them, did you?"

Millie was pacing from one end of the kitchen to the other, her mind zipping about in a hundred directions.

"Of course I didn't just leave them. Clint suggested I call on a woman I believe you know well — Dorothea. She's there with them at the moment. She didn't have enough room in her cottage for all the children, so she and her boy, Garry, came to the castle so she could take care of the wee ones."

"Dorothea, yes, what a fine solution. They'll have better care than anyone could wish for. Other than their own mother, of course. Dorothea will know just how to handle them. What a most unexpected situation for you to deal with, but apparently you were up to the task."

"Clint enlisted Ethel's help and they've got tasty vittles. Had a little of them myself. Clint and Winston are taking care of the animals and keeping buildings in repair. But, Millie, there's more to the story."

"More? What do you mean?"

Hector began to reel off the numerous projects that needed to be taken in hand. "Clint and Winston have taken good care of the horses, chickens, and the small flock of sheep. But there's no one to tend the vegetable garden, or rather gardens. There are about half a dozen."

"Why would Grandmother need half a dozen vegetable gardens? There was only her and Aunt Moira. And of course she fed the estate hands."

"Your grandmother and Aunt Moira have been feeding half the village for quite a while now. They had gardeners pick the vegetables and take them to the village where they were handed out to anyone who needed them. There was never any left at the end of the day. Apparently the villagers depended on your grandmother's generosity and are presently having difficulty feeding their families. It's pretty rough for a great number of them. And like the three bairns I discovered, there are women that have no menfolk about to help with anything."

Millie sat down slowly. "I've never even considered the full ramifications of Grandmother's death. I've thought of the old ones like Clint and Winston, but I had no idea the village itself was so needy. Here I am sitting in a fine lodge with more food than I can ever eat and a family that cares for me and my bairn. The situation at the estate is untenable. I have some thinking and planning to do. Hector, you've done me such a great service. I don't know how to thank you. The way you handled this tells me I need you to stay close. We'll talk again."

She planted a kiss on his cheek and walked away. Briefly he thought of Mam. She always pecked him on the cheek before she retired.

~ * ~

Another couple of months had passed and Millie couldn't wait for Hector to return and give her his latest report from his second visit. He had proved to be quite a capable businessman. Perhaps she could talk him into staying at the estate a while — just until the place was sorted, of course.

CHAPTER 9

*E*vening came and Wabi sensed Caitlin's hesitance to retire for the evening, and he certainly knew why.

"Caitlin, go to bed, child. If the dream comes again, I'll be here. It's only a dream, dear girl."

"I know, Wabi. But it's real at the moment."

Finally she went to Mam's sewing room. Mam's spirit still rested there and that was comforting to her. Wabi walked to his own sleeping quarters. He felt sure Caitlin's dream visitor would make an appearance again tonight. So be it. He waited for a short while, then decided he would sit by Caitlin's bedside and try to gain some understanding of what she was experiencing. His rest would just have to wait.

Hours later, the tall old clock in the hallway began to chime, the sound deep and reverberating. The clarity of its tone was soothing, and Wabi listened as it began its beckoning call.

Bong, bong, bong. Three o'clock.

Then, just a few seconds later, Caitlin's screams rattled the rafters throughout the lodge.

"No! Not again. I'm still here. Don't leave me!"

Wabi sat in the chair next to Caitlin's bed. Seeing she was still asleep, he took her hands, feeling a low-key, rapidly pulsing vibration when his hand touched hers. He was surprised. Vibrations like these were usually an indication that communication with another entity, or spirit, was transpiring.

This is more than a nightmare, then. But who is she communicating with at this moment? It's not me, so who else would it be?

Wabi then did something he never thought he would. Touching his fingers to her temples, he took a moment to peer inside Caitlin's mind, a liberty he had never taken before even though he always could have done so.

He almost wished he hadn't. Aside from the fact he felt he was stepping beyond his boundaries, he felt an immediate stirring of his own. This entity was indeed powerful and Wabi knew he must allow Caitlin and this visitor to continue their encounter, wherever it might lead Caitlin. He could not interfere with this, of that he was certain. There was more at work here than just a disturbing nightmare. Someone was calling to her, certainly, but it was not clear to him who it was. She must make the decision to answer this call, or not — it was not a task he could do for her.

What I can do is stay close to her and help her discover the nature of this calling.

He removed his fingers from her temples then whispered in her ear. The words were unintelligible to anyone except her and they allowed her to drift to a place where she could rest and sleep, finally.

The next morning Wabi eventually surfaced and left his room, making his way to the kitchen simply by following his nose. Apparently Millie had made herself at home here, and her baked goods were just what he needed.

"Millie, my girl. I believe you've mastered the art of cooking. I believe that talent's been fermenting inside you. You just needed a chance to let it express itself."

Millie smiled at the old wizard. He brought such a spirit of happiness with him and Millie liked having him around. Having never had the pleasure of any uncles herself, she adopted him as her uncle, too.

"Wabi, I think you might be right. Nothing makes me any happier than getting my hands into flour and seeing what I can create. It wasn't anything I was ever allowed to do in the past, so now that I can I find it surprisingly enjoyable."

"So you are content here, then?"

"More than content, Wabi, I'm happy and more. Of course, we have had moments with all these men and only two women. But we're figuring it out."

"And Caitlin? Is she as enamored with this place as you? She's certainly having issues at the moment, but from past experience with her that's not surprising." He smiled.

"Aye. She's found a place, too, I believe. But you're right, she is a bit more complicated than other folk. I keep thinking it's just that she's never been around so many people and now we're both surrounded all day. I, myself, seek refuge and find myself wandering about the moor just to hear nothing but nature's sounds. Of course, that's nothing new for me — a holdover from childhood, I suppose. Then I was seeking the company of the animals, whereas now I seek the solace that I find there."

"You'll get no argument from me, my dear. I, too, find solace in nature."

"We're almost ready for the ceremonies, Wabi. You haven't forgotten that have you?"

"Oh, no, I haven't forgotten you two refined ladies are about to wed two Highland ruffians. Hope you both know what you're getting into." He laughed and went out, carrying his cup of tea and one of Millie's warm apple tarts with him.

The sheep farm was a flurry of activity in any direction you looked. Alex and Jack had not returned yet, but Da, Jamie and the farmhands were in constant motion keeping the sheep tended and in the proper pastures. Wabi found himself in awe of these men who had created a home and life in these Highlands. He could see the appeal this place might have for Caitlin, but he had unsettled feelings about her this morning. As soon as she came out, he would talk with her and try to help her get her mind settled once again.

But first he needed to take a short walk and test a theory that had been niggling at his brain following his visit with Caitlin last evening. Walking across the moor slowly, watching the working dogs as they herded the sheep and brought them into the fold, Wabi liked the feeling that permeated this place. There was a feeling of permanence, a wholesomeness, almost an innocence, as if time had stopped and nothing would ever change here. Of course, Wabi understood that was not the case. Life is nothing if not constant change. But he did admit he often wished it weren't so. If he knew but one thing, he was confident his Caitlin would flourish here in this wild, wonderful, Highland home. But as Ian had alluded to, he sensed there were secrets here that were not known to all, and it was only a matter of time before Caitlin would become aware of them. Would she be able to meet the challenges he knew were coming her way?

~ * ~

"Millie? Are ye here?"

The back door flew open and young Ian came dashing through. He had been so excited about his new prosthesis that he hadn't stopped running since he found out he could. Not stopping to wipe his feet, he continued yelling throughout the lodge.

"Caitlin? Millie? Where is everybody?"

He had been excited when he saw Wabi coming down the path yesterday. The old wizard brought a sense of expectation that Ian found exciting, and their short discussion last evening had his mind flitting about even more than usual. Wabi had stimulated his mind during his last trip and Ian was hoping to stay close to him this time also.

Finding no one in the house he went out the front door and started to make his way across the top of the moor toward Mam's gravesite where he seemed to spend a lot of time lately. He didn't understand that need either, but then maybe he didn't need to understand it.

It was deep December, just a few days before Christmas, and a blanket of snow still lay on the ground as far as the eye could see. Ian spent a few minutes collecting red berries from the holly trees, and evergreen boughs as well. He never went to Mam's grave without taking a bouquet he knew she would enjoy. Usually, he just sat and talked to her. It wasn't a one-sided conversation either. He felt she heard every word and he sensed her presence.

Coming to the top of the moor and looking ahead, he saw someone standing at Mam's gravesite. Who was that? No one ever came here except him. Closer inspection revealed the visitor to be the person he most wanted to talk to, Uncle Wabi.

"Wabi, what are ye doing here? I've been looking for ye."

"Ian, my lad. Just the person I was hoping to see as well. What brings you up here?"

"Oh, nothing in particular. I just come up here to talk to me mam. Somehow she seems to be closer up here." He laid the evergreen boughs on the grave and arranged the colorful berries around the edges.

Wabi watched as the young man gingerly worked with the berries and the greenery, carefully arranging each piece on his mother's resting place — such tenderness in his every movement. He felt the young lad's pain.

"As long as she remains in your heart, Ian, she's never gone."

Wabi put an arm around the boy and allowed a measure of warmth to flow between the two. Today he wasn't shocked by the depth of the throbbing vibrations coming from Ian, as he had been yesterday.

"She's almost closer now than when she was here, Wabi. Is that possible?"

"It's not only possible, but probable in your case. It's obvious to me you worship your da and your brothers as well, and they are worthy of your adoration, no doubt. But Ian, you have a special place in this universe. Trust me when I tell you that you bring a quality to this world that cannot be duplicated. It belongs only to you, was designed with you in mind. And this quality that is unique to you will come to your awareness slowly, but with deliberation and purpose from the Creator. Your only requirement is that you listen, and learn to hear the message. It is within your reach now already. You must accept and acknowledge the reality of it. As I told you last evening, Caitlin, too, has been called to a special service to the Creator, as have I. This doesn't mean we are more precious to him than any others, but he has chosen us to assist in his plan for this world, this universe. If we are to feel anything, it is to be humbled that he has chosen us to be his ambassadors."

"I don't know how to think about all this, Uncle Wabi. Why did the Creator choose me? I'm just a lad and no one listens to me. But there are some things I don't understand and yer right, some of them are scary. Just yesterday I thought I felt something in the air. I can't explain it, but I know it was dark . . . something dreadful. And it was all about our place. It scared me, Uncle Wabi."

"Ah, yes, the dark power you mentioned last evening. Perhaps we should meet in the library where we can be undisturbed and discuss this power you sensed. Dark power is strong, lad. But I've met it before, so we'll recognize each other. There's no way it can defeat you, Caitlin, and myself. Don't fret about it. It'll show itself if it is intent on staying about. Now, young man, the first thing we will do in your beginning session is take a look at your book by da Vinci. I believe we may find worthwhile reading there."

The two walked side by side toward the lodge. Wabi, and perhaps Ian also, knew this was the first of many walks they would take together.

CHAPTER 10

Following dinner, Ian and Wabi made their way to the library. Wabi had been astounded to find the lodge had one. There was quite a large collection of not only books, periodicals, and medical tracts, but also a number of highly regarded, leather-bound editions of classics. He could see why Ian was drawn to this particular room. There on a large writing table was the book about de Vinci the lad had talked about. For the next two hours, Wabi and Ian devoured the book with Wabi explaining theories Ian had never heard of but was thrilled to learn about. His mind was already making room for this new knowledge and he was anxious to continue even longer. However, Wabi was experienced enough to know they must proceed slowly and methodically.

"That's where we'll stop this evening. Some knowledge has to be absorbed slowly and this book is one of those." He stood and stretched his legs after sitting so long. The two of them then joined the others in the great room where they had gathered for their usual evening discussion time.

"I must say that's quite an impressive library you have, Daniel. Why, I never expected to find such on a sheep farm. You have a treasure there, sir."

Da, having never received any formal education, was proud of his library even though he did admit it wasn't his idea.

"When Alice came to the Highlands with me, we brought all her trunks, loaded on the wagon until it could hold no more and I thought we'd never make it. I wondered where in the world she was going to wear all those clothes. I tried to explain to her that she wouldn't need a whole lot here in these Highlands, but she insisted on all the trunks so I didn't argue with her. I was learning quickly how determined the woman could be. When we finally arrived at the crofter's hut, which was what I had to offer her at the time, she began to unpack her trunks. She had a number of fine dresses and some lace petticoats as well. But after she finished unpacking the first trunk and opened the next one, I couldn't believe it. It was full of books, as were the rest of her trunks.

'Woman, whatever are ye going to do with these books?' I asked.

'Books are for reading, Daniel MacKinnon,' she said. 'And I'll select a couple for you to start with.'

"I suppose she thought I needed a little educating, which was true enough. So she selected one for me to start, that evening, ye ken, and she was smart about her selection. She knew I was interested in history. She put a large book into my hands. It was titled *The Iliad*, by a writer named Homer.

"As it was, I couldn't even pronounce the title, but Alice convinced me that if I would just give it a try I might find out it was an exciting book. 'Course, she forgot to tell me how difficult the reading might be. But right she was. As I learned over the years, the woman was right about many things. Reading became a passion for me and we spent our evenings discussing the various books we might be reading. I always had a taste for history, though, no matter what other subjects I tried. And Alice, well, she always favored stories about early Scottish heroes, such as William Wallace or Robert the

Bruce. But together, we must have read Shakespeare's works a dozen or more times over the years. She particularly loved *A Midsummer Night's Dream*, and the character Tatiana, Queen of the Fairies."

Da loved to tell the story of how he had captured Alice's heart and had to bring her to the Highlands because she wouldn't let him out of her sight.

"Lads, ye shoulda seen that woman. She was the loveliest thing I ever did see. And the MacDonald's *ceilidh* was always a place where a lad could count on meeting a beautiful girl. Maybe not one to keep, but certainly one for the evening. Well, this young lass, with that auburn hair hanging in curls down her back, took a liking to me immediately. She kept sashaying around me and finally I decided to put her out of her misery and asked her to dance. Of course, she told me I'd have to wait my turn, but that was only to make me think she wasn't too keen on me, ye ken? But after just one dance about the room, she stuck to me side like molasses."

The lads laughed when they heard the story. They had indeed heard it a thousand times, but still liked to hear Da repeat it. They were all aware it brought back fond memories, so they were eager to indulge him. However, they all knew the real story also, or as much as Mam and Da had told them. Their mam was attracted to Da that evening, but he was not exactly what her parents had in mind for her. But according to her, she simply followed her heart and, after a few weeks of seeing each other daily, she left against her parents wishes, went with Daniel and they made a life in the Highlands.

"And never once did I regret that decision," she'd said.

CHAPTER 11

"Jack MacKinnon! When I need ye to fight my battles for me, I'll let ye know. 'Til then I'll thank ye to keep yer arse out of me business!" Millie abruptly handed little Midge to him, turned on her heels and stomped out the door, slamming it so hard it rattled on its hinges.

Jack, accustomed to having the bairn on his shoulder, held her with one hand and, dumbfounded, scratched his head, shaking it from side to side.

"Women. What in heaven's name brought that on?" He looked over at Caitlin, who was doubled over in laugher, as were Alex and Hector.

"Now, what was it ye said to me, Jack?" Alex asked. "She's easygoing, not one to cause any problems, will go along with what I suggest." Alex grinned at his brother, enjoying the moment.

"And did you hear her, the Lady Sinclair? She sounded like a woman raised in the Highlands. Ye and yer —why her tutors would turn over in their graves!" laughed Caitlin. She hadn't laughed so much since they came to the northern Highlands. But this was indeed a situation that caused her to appreciate how different her life, as well as Millie's, had become.

"Ah, just wedding nerves, Jack. Don't give it too much thought," Alex said.

"But she said she wasn't pleased with the dressmaker's progress and all I did was to tell her I'd go to the woman and tell her she needed to hurry up with the work. What's wrong with that?"

"Who's making your dresses?" Alex asked, turning his attention to Caitlin.

Caitlin thought for a moment. "Um, I can't exactly recall her name, but it's maybe Dora, or maybe it was Deirdre? Yes, Deirdre. Da took me to the village to buy herbs from the old woman, Nezzie, the one who lives down in the forest. She had quite a selection, so I bought a bit of dried agrimony and milk thistle to make ointments I'm totally out of. I made arrangements for her to keep me supplied with herbs until I'm more familiar with the countryside here and know where to find what I need. Between her and Lourdes I should have plenty.

"Nezzie was selling potions to a young woman she introduced to me as Deirdre. The young woman apparently knows you all well as she grew up here in the Highlands. The old woman was a bit on the strange side, but Deirdre seemed to know her. Anyway, when I told her we were to wed, she insisted on making gowns for both Millie and me. I don't have the skills for that, and I rather doubt Millie does either. So we agreed she would make them."

Alex sent a look to Jack, who just rolled his eyes in response.

Oh, Jesus. Not Deirdre.

"Yeah, well, yes we do know her. She's a bit of a hothead her own self, if I remember correctly," Alex replied.

And she still remembers my refusal of her favors.

He had known Deirdre his entire life as she had grown up just a few miles from the MacKinnons. She had taken quite a fancy to Alex a couple of years ago, but he was not attracted to her for a number of reasons. First of all, he didn't find her attractive, physically or otherwise. She was given to complaining about much and was not a kind person. Alex had witnessed her cruel manner in her treatment of her elderly mother, who needed constant care these days. Her mother was a widow and bedridden with arthritis so severe she couldn't get about. Deirdre resented having to provide this care, so she only did the minimum. In Alex's opinion, the old woman should be cared for much better than what he had observed.

Deirdre began to come to the farm, making all sorts of excuses for coming, and making it clear that she was "available" to Alex, on any terms.

She had arrived one afternoon, ostensibly to ask Alex's help with finding someone to do some fencing, and she sauntered up next to Alex. "Ye gotta be needing a woman, Alex MacKinnon. Yer a man and that's just a known fact—a man needs a woman." She came closer to him, too close in Alex's opinion, and took his hand.

Taking her by the shoulders and moving her a few steps back, Alex looked her in the eyes and responded quietly, but firmly. "I believe it best that ye go on home, lass. I've plenty of work to keep me occupied, and when I'm ready for a woman, I'll take care of the situation."

He turned away from her and started to the stable to finish his chores. Chasing after him and jerking him by his arm, Deirdre addressed him. "Ye going to turn me down, just like that, Alex? Ye think to find a woman that suits ye better? Well, in case ye haven't noticed, there aren't a lot of women here in these Highlands. And ye'll not find one who can please ye like I can!"

In a calm, clear, voice, Alex responded. "Go now before I say more than ye want to hear." And he walked away with his back to her.

"Ye'll be sorry you refused me offer, Alex MacKinnon. And I'll not forget this day. Ye'll pay for your humiliation of me." She picked up her skirts and stomped off.

She had left, seething to the bone. That had been more than a year ago now, but she still wanted Alex. Finally, she went to visit Nezzie, the old woman who lived in the forest over behind the cave and was said to have powers —dark ones. Deirdre couldn't care less about how dark they may be. If they could bring Alex MacKinnon to her, then that was fine.

As she came into the forest it was twilight, just before the sun totally gave way to the moon. Deirdre was afraid after seeing a number of bats, with their funneled, furry ears, making their way even deeper into the glen, but she followed them. She'd seen them before. Sure enough, they alit on the edge of the thatched roof of a dilapidated hut, hanging upside down in their strange manner. She went in, not quite as sure about this decision as she had been earlier. The place was creepy and smelled strange. But she was determined to get Alex MacKinnon at all costs.

Nezzie had been in these deep woods for as long as anyone could remember. She kept to her hut during the day, as the light hurt her eyes. Any moving about she did at night, and no one had ever seen her face, or not all of it as she wore a cloak with a hood that partially covered her features.

She had a reputation for being a healer, and there were folk who swore by her potions. Deirdre herself had seen her own mother perk up after using one of them. She had also witnessed the old one caring for her old dog after he had been caught in a trap that had been set for wolves. Her soft words and gentle hands spoke of one who had an understanding of suffering, and the young woman was surprised to see such care coming from her. Her old hut was filled with dried skins and it smelled to high heaven. Deirdre had been in it a couple of times, but it had been early in the day, not late like now.

There were animal skeletons, foul smelling tins of medicines, and several feral looking cats roaming about the hut.

There were rumors of strange events over the years, and some believed Nezzie could conjure up the devil himself if she so desired. Well, Deirdre knew those stories were just folktales and she'd turned to Nezzie for help — a little dark power might be just the thing. Then, once she had Alex in her bed, she'd keep him there.

"Nezzie, I've brought ye a currant pie. I need yer help with a small problem. Would ye be able to do that?"

~ * ~

Alex looked at Caitlin and was glad she had come into his life. Maybe the fact Deirdre was making the dresses meant she was over her disappointment about Alex. He hoped so.

"Jack, both Millie and I are in a tizzy trying to get our dresses ready, the food for the celebration in order, and our heads are full of more details than either of us can handle. But don't worry, we'll all get through the ceremony and I'm sure we'll all be glad when that's done. I never realized getting married would be such an ordeal."

Willie was sitting next to Caitlin, though often these days he would wander over and rest next to Alex as well. He, too, thought this was a good thing — these two being together. As far as the sheep issue, he had made it clear he wasn't a sheepherder and that relieved all of them.

"So tomorrow is the day then, lass?" Wabi asked as he entered the room.

"Aye, Wabi. I suppose it is. And it can't be soon enough. Millie and I are exhausted with making food, keeping the seamstress busy and listening to Hector complain about the amount of food the *ceilidh* will require."

"Nah, he's happy as a lark, lass. Right down his alley, getting food ready for a crowd. He'll have enough to feed everyone who shows their face. Don't worry so," Jack said.

He, too, was ready for all this fuss to come to a halt and the farm to return to its normal routine. Making changes was difficult for him but he had begun to realize there would be some, like it or not.

Wabi and Caitlin took a walk out to the hut where she and Willie found their quiet moments. She would eventually get used to a lot of people around, but this place was a respite she needed. The three of them ambled on, watching the bright shards of light bouncing off the snow.

"Wabi, I remember you coming into my room last night, but I must have fallen asleep, as I can't remember much about the dream. But it did come, I know it did."

"Yes, I was there. You need not worry about these dreams, my girl. I agree with you that someone is trying to communicate with you, but my brief encounter with the entity led me to know there is nothing dangerous about this spirit. It will find a way to make a connection with you and will eventually disappear. If it were a harmful spirit, it would have made its intentions known by now. I can tell you the answer to understanding these dreams lies in the circle of stones — the one at the top of the moor where the burial plot is located. I'm sure you've been there."

"Yes, that place calls to me. Alex doesn't like me to wander that far without an escort, but when I feel compelled to go, I really don't want anyone with me. It's as if the place wants to share something and at the same time it feels as if it needs something from me. But what? I can't figure it out, but I must. The pull gets stronger each day, and Alex needs to learn that he can't dictate everything I can and cannot do."

"With all the activities planned for the next days, I'd try to put all thoughts of this matter aside and concentrate on it when your mind is not so burdened as it is now."

"Aye, it certainly is full at the moment. But tomorrow the sun will rise and we'll get this joining underway. Everyone is ready, and certainly Millie and I are."

CHAPTER 12

W here are ye, Jack? Hurry up man, we're gonna be late, I tell ye. And where's Hector and Ian? They're all supposed to be here now. And where's Wabi? And Andrew and Jamie? They're supposed to be here, too."

Da smiled as he watched his firstborn, Alexander, pacing the room, taking long quick strides that spoke of his anxiety, an emotion he never had much experience with.

Ah, yes, my oldest lad. The intellectual one, always logical. Decisive.

"Ah, stop yer yelling, brother. We'll all get there. Now hush before ye get everyone else as worked up as yerself. I'll get ye to the kirk on time and I won't let Caitlin box yer ears."

Hmm, my number three lad, Jack, the protector — and a good one he is.

"Alex, this outfit is getting so tight I can hardly breathe. Are ye sure I have to wear it? I mean, I think ye and Jack getting married and all is fine, but is it really necessary for us to get so fussed up?"

Daniel's smile got even wider. *My youngest lad, Ian. So much wants to be like his brothers. But this young lad is, um, well he's special. Yes, special, Alice, just like ye always said.*

"Will the lot of ye try to get along for just a few minutes without a referee? I don't know how ye get through the day without someone to keep the peace."

97

And that would be my number two lad, Hector, ever the peacemaker, negotiator. Has a little of ye in him to be sure, mo chridhe.

Da looked at this small group of men, the sons he and Alice had raised. It wasn't always an easy task, but he was ever so glad they were his lads. Each man had qualities any father would have been proud of, and certainly any mother.

Alice, they're fine lads— and fine-looking, too.

Now here they all were, outfitted in the finest clothing they had. Mam had made sure each one had a complete outfit for a celebration of any kind—perhaps it would be a funeral, a christening, or maybe one of them may marry one day. Daniel recalled it had cost him most of a year's profits from the sheep farm to manage to pay for it all. But just now, he so wished his Alice could see them.

Each man was wearing a fitted wool jacket, a white shirt with turndown collar and French cuffs, a five-button black waistcoat, kilt from the MacKinnon plaid, a tie, and black ghillie brogues. Of course, they sported hose with flashers to match their kilt, and a black, leather sporran with their clan symbol emblazoned on it. Each man had a *sgian-dubh* (small knife) tucked into the top of his hose. Mam had been careful to attach Alex's to his left leg, as he was left-handed. And lastly, their Highland bonnets were in place.

"Well, now that's quite a display of MacKinnons, I do say," Da said, smiling broadly.

Wabi and Uncle Andrew walked in together and finally old Jamie showed up. Andrew had returned last evening from Edinburgh and he and Jamie were attired in their finest Highland wear also. As for Wabi, everyone stared for just a moment. They had all grown accustomed to his peculiar ways and understood he was an unusual man, so his choice of apparel went unquestioned, with only slight nods from everyone.

Wabi's lineage had never been explained to Caitlin, but she knew it was most unusual. So here he was at this gathering, wearing his chosen garb. He had donned a floor-length silk robe, a most resplendent one — a deep forest green with unusual symbols around the hem. Maybe a language they thought, but again, didn't question it. His one bit of attire they did recognize was a cummerbund made from the MacKinnon plaid. It was a gesture on his part to indicate his belonging to the clan as well, and they all approved of that gesture.

Before Wabi had come out, he had asked Owl to inspect his garment. "Let's make sure there aren't any loose threads or rips that I've missed." Wabi slowly turned around, making sure Owl could see all sides.

Master, I do believe this garment is from another time. It even has a unique scent that I remember from a previous life. And our Caitlin will detect that, no doubt. But yes, I believe it is exactly what you should wear on this special occasion. Most elegant. I wholeheartedly approve. Of course, each word had been clipped in his most officious English manner.

Now that everyone was here, Da walked forward and turned, facing them.

"If one of ye'll fill the cups, I would like to make a toast."

Hector hurried to complete this task and stood in line with his brothers.

"A toast is traditional, I'm told. As ye all know, I'm not good with words, but today is a fine day for we MacKinnons. We have two lovely ladies joining us, and fortunate we are to be so blessed. Yer mam would be happy to know ye've chosen such fine ladies and that they've been so taken with ye they agreed to wed ye. She'd be just as proud of ye as I am. Ye are the finest men I've ever known and I'm proud to be yer da."

Everyone tossed the liquid back, even Ian, who tried his

hardest not to cough. He did turn bright red in the face, however, but not a brother commented on it.

"Speaking of ladies, where are they?" Alex asked, wondering why he hadn't thought of that already.

"They've already gone to the kirk. The dressmaker will do the last of her stitching there. According to Millie, it's traditional to never try the dress on before the actual day. Whatever last minute alterations are necessary will be made then. So now that everyone's accounted for, Alex, relax," Jack smiled at his older brother.

~ * ~

"Millie, if ye don't be still I'll never get this neckline finished. It's almost time now."

Deirdre had to stand on a small stool in order to reach Millie's collar to complete the final stitching. Yes, this was a rather tall woman and very beautiful. Even Deirdre knew Millie was a real Lady. That fact was evident to anyone who spent any time in her presence.

"There. That's done. Now, Caitlin, come over here and stand on the stool."

Unlike Millie, Caitlin was so short she needed to stand on the stool instead of Deirdre. The dressmaker was quite a bit taller than Caitlin, and had to bend to work on her dress—hence the need for the stool.

"The waistline is a tad too big. I'll try to tighten it if I can. Not much meat on yer bones, ye ken? Certainly not much to keep a Highlander warm on a cold December night."

Caitlin glanced at Deirdre, not sure why she would make such a remark. But she didn't make an issue of it.

"Almost done, just one more stitch," and she proceeded to

make her alteration.

"Ouch! That smarts." Caitlin flinched as the seamstress stuck the needle into her side. Accident certainly.

"Oops. Sorry. Never meant to stick ye."

Deirdre was boiling inside just thinking about this small, red-haired lass from the Isle claiming *her* Highlander, Alex MacKinnon. He'd be sorry he had chosen this woman. She'd make sure of that.

"Ok, ladies, yer as ready as I can make ye. Stand here and I'll weave a little white heather and moth orchids in yer hair — for good luck, ye ken?" She proceeded to take ribbon and wrap it around the heather, then attached it to their locks, carefully tucking in a few small orchids as well. All the while she was wishing the lasses were weaving ribbons and heather in her own hair. Somehow, though, she knew that would never be.

"Wherever did you get moth orchids this time of year?" Caitlin asked.

"Oh— that young lass — the one from Spain or was it Greece? I forget. She's a wee lass if I ever saw one — she's even smaller than you, Caitlin. And she's verra easy on the eyes. I noted several lads looking her way when she dropped these off. That long, shining, dark hair and those eyes that twinkle when she speaks. And that accent — it's strange, but I could understand her well enough. She insisted that I put these in your hair. Seems they're considered good luck in her country also."

"Oh, you mean Lourdes, and you're right, she's from Spain. She just arrived here a few months ago. I think she's married to that older man . . . uhm, McGowan, or McGuire? Not sure. But I met her in the village recently where she was selling the most beautiful flowers. She told me she grows them in a small room that she keeps very warm with a small peat fire. According to her, the flowers will grow in there year round. She obviously has a very green thumb as she also had some herbs that looked very healthy. I'll be sure to stop by and thank her for the orchids." Caitlin smiled as she watched Deirdre arrange the delicate flowers in her hair.

"Hold on. Let me see if the signal for ye to come out has been given."

Cracking the door ever so slightly, Deirdre could hear the pipes as they began their whine.

"Aye, 'tis time for ye to join yer escorts. Millie, yer to go first."

And Millie, looking so perfect in her dress, a full-length, cream-colored lace with a train, calmly stepped through the door and began to walk across the cobblestone path where Uncle Andrew stood, smiling as he watched her approach.

"Ah, lass. Yer even lovelier today than ye were yesterday," he beamed.

The old man was honored to have been asked to escort this fine woman who was to marry his nephew. Millie walked as she always did, as elegantly as any queen. She took Uncle Andrew's arm and smiled at him.

"Thank you, kind sir. I think we should go inside now."

They proceeded along the curving, cobblestone walkway and entered the kirk.

Millie smiled when she saw the transformation the kirk had undergone. The villagers had been so excited about the MacKinnon lads finally finding women. The young lasses, though wishing it had been them, had spent hours adorning the kirk with flowers from their own gardens. They had hung ribbons and heather on the lampposts and doorways, and flowers were placed in vases at the front of the altar.

As they approached the first pew, the pipes were playing a haunting, flowing piece with a fiddle echoing in the background. The pipes were calling to the fiddle and it was responding in a yin-yang song that seemed to have been written precisely for the two. Millie didn't think she had ever heard anything so moving. She had only heard the pipes making off-key sounds 'til now, but this was music, beautiful music.

Uncle Andrew delivered Millie to the right side of the altar, where Jack grinned from one ear to the other. His auburn hair had been brushed till it shone in the morning sunlight coming through the stained glass window. He held out an arm and Millie took it, desperate for anything to keep her feet on the ground.

"All right, now ye, Caitlin. It's time."

Deirdre could hardly get the words out of her mouth. They tasted like bitter bile and she had to work exceptionally hard to keep her emotions under control and her feelings to herself.

Not yet . . . but soon . . . soon.

Caitlin lifted the front of her dress, a soft, pale blue satin that, too, had a lengthy train. She took a deep breath, stepped forward and made her way to the edge of the cobblestone path. She saw Uncle Wabi coming her way and he looked splendid in his eloquent clothing.

"Uncle Wabi, how dashing you look. Where did you ever find such a robe?" She looked at the garment carefully and observed the symbols stitched along the hem.

"Is that a language, Wabi?"

Then she slowly turned her head from one side to the other, lifting her nose and sniffing, much like Willie would have done.

"Do you smell the aroma that drifts from the robe? That's an interesting scent that I'm not familiar with. What is it?"

"It's a very old garment, Caitlin, and I particularly enjoy wearing it on special occasions. And today is a special one, my girl. I'm so pleased to be a part of this ceremony. And the aroma...from the Orient, I would think." He kissed her cheek lightly. "Now, we should be going in."

Caitlin just nodded her head.

Yes, we should be going in.

The pipes and fiddle were still performing their yin-yang dance and Caitlin found it most alluring. Never had she thought pipes could produce such stirring music.

As they walked down the aisle, however, Caitlin could see little, due to her small stature. What she could see was that the young lasses had strewn flower petals about the floor and bouquets were tied to the pews and adorned the doorways. They couldn't have made it any more beautiful.

However, as Millie and Uncle Andrew walked to the right side of the altar, Caitlin could see everything and everyone. Apparently the whole village had come. She stopped abruptly. She could now see the entire group that was assembled at the front of the kirk, on the altar, waiting for her to join them. The sight took her breath away.

Never had she seen such an array of so many striking men . . . and all of them MacKinnons. They always appeared handsome to her, but now, in their finest clothing, the bonnets, MacKinnon kilt, hose, and sporrans, they were stunning. Uncle Andrew, Jamie and Da had even trimmed their beards, a chore they never enjoyed. Oh what a sight! And that tall, most handsome one on the far left was her man, her Highlander, her Alex. And she couldn't take her eyes off him.

Uncle Wabi felt her vibration and sensed her emotions. "It is quite a magnificent gathering of MacKinnons, is it not?"

He smiled and nodded at her and began to lead her forward again. She was having difficulty getting her feet to move and even greater trouble keeping her emotions under control — but knew she must.

However, she needn't have worried so. She looked up at that moment and was ever so relieved. Alex had stepped from the altar and was striding down the aisle, coming to meet her. It seemed he couldn't wait another moment. Her heart was full, and as she reached out for his arm, Uncle Wabi stepped aside, understanding that his niece was in very capable hands now. His heart was full also, but a great measure of relief flooded him as well. Now she had a protector even better than the wolf. Then, as if he had read Wabi's thoughts, Willie came running through the kirk entry and joined Alex and Caitlin as they made their way to the altar. Alex may be her new protector, but Willie would always be at her side.

~ * ~

The bells in the tower pealed out as Millie and Caitlin walked out of the kirk, escorted by their fine-looking gentlemen, and they were both smiling as they approached the carriage waiting for them at the end of the walkway. Apparently the young lasses had gotten to the horses, too. They had woven heather and ribbons into their manes and tails and bouquets were tied to the sides of the carriage. No doubt those young lasses wished it was their special day. And no men could be finer looking than the MacKinnon lads.

Jack climbed up and held the reins as Alex helped the ladies to their seats. Their cumbersome dresses were a challenge for him but he managed, then took his seat next to Caitlin.

"Jack, my man. I do believe we have just joined the league of old married men."

"Aye, brother. What were we thinking?" Jack laughed.

Alex lifted Caitlin's hand and kissed the back of it lightly— a gesture she would remember one day years from now — sending shivers up her arm.

The brides and grooms had stayed for a short time at the kirk talking with the vicar who had insisted they share a wee dram with him before leaving, but finally they were on their way. Jack clucked to the horses and they picked up their pace.

"Well, the celebration can't very well get underway until the brides and grooms arrive," Jack laughed. However, a short while later, as they pulled the carriage close to the lodge it was obvious no one had thought of waiting for them to begin the celebration. Many of the villagers had already arrived and from the sounds coming from within, they were all having a great time.

"Well, I suppose that tells us how necessary we are to the party," Millie laughed.

"They may have started without us, but I'll bet there's not a one of 'em who can do a proper reel." Alex grinned and handed Caitlin down from the carriage.

Opening the door, they were surprised to see several of the young lads and lasses already moving about the floor, even Ian, who was having no trouble with his new prosthesis. He and Hector had left the wedding and hurried home to help get the celebration underway. The brothers nodded to each other when they saw the lad twirling a pretty fair-haired lass. There were several fiddles, a base, a banjo, and a young woman whom neither of the brothers recognized sat at Mam's harpsichord. The place was filled with toe-tapping music and Hector had the cider flowing generously. Caitlin looked around, stunned at the number of people crowded into the lodge.

"I thought it would be just family and a few friends, but it looks like the whole village has come," Caitlin said. Alex took note of how many folk had made the effort to celebrate this occasion with them. He wished Mam could have been here.

"Ah, about time ye got here. We waited for a few seconds, but then decided to commence with the festivities," Hector said, handing them a cup of his tasty cider.

Alex took a thirst-quenching swallow and turned to Caitlin. "My lady, let's show 'em how the Gay Gordons should be done!"

"What? You dance? Alex MacKinnon you are full of surprises."

With that she found herself being pulled onto the dance floor, trying desperately to keep pace with her Highland fool. She would never have thought this quiet, reserved, man would engage in such an undertaking. Something told her this might be the first of more surprises to come.

Millie and Jack were more content to watch from the sidelines, but both were glad the day had finally come and happy to have so many well-wishers at the celebration.

Alex, aware that Caitlin was tiring a bit, took her over to her uncle.

"Wabi, she's just unable to keep up with me, ye ken? So I'll leave her here with ye for a few minutes. I'll see if Millie will give it a try."

Alex was thoroughly enjoying the evening. He had planned to marry only once, and he wanted it to be right. So far, it was the best day ever.

Jack wasn't much on dancing, even though Mam had spent an enormous amount of time teaching each of them the proper steps to many reels. But Alex took care of that. Millie was thrilled to find herself twirling about the floor, and it only took a few reels for her to be exhausted.

"Alex, that's more than enough for now."

Millie had drunk a cup of cider and found her dress just too confining and, at the moment, rather warm. She excused herself to go change.

"Where ye going lass?" Jack stood as if to follow her.

"Oh, just going to find Deirdre and see if she'll help me get out of this dress. It's lovely, but I think something more comfortable would be in order."

Millie waved at Deirdre across the room and the seamstress knew what she wanted. She had counted on it, in fact. *Good. Now my plan can be put into action.*

"Aye, Millie, let's go to the rear storage room. There's a closet in there to hang yer dress and ye can come later and put it away. It's a bit cold there, but we'll only be a minute."

"The cold would be welcome just now. This dress is awfully warm. Of course, the cider might be a factor too."

The two women laughed and went on to the storage room and entered, closing the door behind them.

"Hold on just another second. OK, now. Step out of yer dress and slip this one on. I made it just for you, Millie. The color is perfect for your hair and skin."

"I can't thank you enough, Deirdre. I had nothing to wear when I came here, and this is such a treat. I just hope Jack likes it. I don't usually wear red, but with Christmas just a few days away, this is just perfect."

"Oh, he'll like it, lass. He'll like anything that ye wear."

Deirdre had managed so far to keep her intentions to herself, but her patience was running thin. These two women coming here and taking not just one man but two was too exasperating for words. Highland men were a breed unto themselves, and these MacKinnon men could have had any lass they wanted. But in Deirdre's case, none of them seemed to desire her. Be that as it may, they would all be sorry they had rejected her, especially Alex.

"All right then. Back to the party. Send Caitlin and I'll help her too. She's bound to be getting a mite warm herself," Deirdre said.

Uncle Wabi had stood at Caitlin's side when Alex left her with him. "My girl, that was the finest ceremony I've ever seen. And I couldn't be more pleased with your Highlander. He's exactly what I would have chosen for you — as if I ever had the opportunity."

"Aye, Uncle Wabi. He's special to me. And he's just what I want, too. I think this entire day has been a success."

"Then ye'll not mind if I make myself scarce? I believe I'll start my trip to Skye. There's something niggling at the edges of my mind. Or maybe someone. Can't really tell, but I feel I should be getting home. I need to check on a few things."

"Of course I don't mind. But wouldn't it be better if you waited until morning? Traveling in the dark and through this snow could be dangerous."

"Well, I'll be there in just a few moments, Caitlin. And Owl will go with me, though he'll complain about it all the way."

Caitlin just stared at her uncle for a brief moment. Then she remembered.

"Aye. I see. You'll use that time-weaving, place-weaving thing… whatever it is you do. Maybe one day you'll explain it to me. But do be careful. You're not as young as you used to be."

"And don't I know it. But all will be well and I'll be back soon. I've spent some time with Ian and promised to come back soon and continue our sessions. He's special, Caitlin, as I have told you. We have an understanding, you see. And, my girl, remember — about your nightmares — visit the circle of stones."

"Um, yes, I'll remember. As for Ian, well, he's his own person, true. And a bit different from the other brothers. But he's still young and could use guidance. He misses his mam a lot, I do know that."

109

Uncle Wabi had spent as much time as he could with Ian this trip, doing his best to continue his mentoring of the lad. There was so much the young boy needed to know, and he was like a sponge soaking up everything Wabi taught him. In their most recent session, Wabi had stressed to Ian the necessity of being thoughtful before acting. The lad had such a great amount of power that Wabi was most concerned he could get into trouble before he even knew it.

"Ian, when you are one of the called, you will often find that having powers can be quite a burden and responsibility. Even I still have situations that require me to think long and hard before I act. For a young person such as yourself, it will be even more taxing. Remember that I am always within your reach and I have taught you how to call me. I must warn you there might come a time when the powers make themselves known rapidly and strongly. You must strive to keep them under control and think though the situation before acting." The lad was making great progress, but Wabi knew he needed extensive mentoring in order to fully become the wizard he was to be.

Now, as he was about to take his leave from the wedding celebration, Wabi took a few minutes to say good-bye to Ian, who was still paying court to the lass with the golden hair. Wabi kept his good-bye short, but wanted to be sure the lad knew he was planning to return. The old wizard figured his sessions with the lad had gotten his brain into overdrive, and his mind was churning with thoughts he'd never experienced before. He put an arm around the young man's shoulder briefly, then handed him a folded piece of paper.

"Here lad, take this. It's something I would like to ask you to keep for me. And I'll ask you not to read it — just yet. But a situation may arise that will have you wondering what I've written on the page. If that time comes, then you should read it carefully and follow it to the letter. It will be of utmost importance that you do. Can you do that for me?"

"Aye, Uncle Wabi. I'll take care of it for ye. And I won't read it. Ye don't have to worry about that. I keep secrets better than anybody." He put the folded paper in his jacket pocket for safekeeping.

Wabi quietly walked out the front door and immediately Owl flew in and alighted on his shoulder.

Are we leaving so soon, Master?

"Yes, Owl, I think I should go home, now. Something brewing there, maybe. Are you ready?"

I suppose you mean time weaving, Master?

"Well, yes. It's the fastest way and the weather isn't the best for walking."

If we must. But don't take any detours —just get us there quickly.

Wabi started laughing and stroked his friend's head.

"You know, Owl, on second thought, I wonder if perhaps you might stay just for a short while. Just to see that Caitlin is all right. I know, I know. I've got to let her go and let her find her own way. And I will, but if you could watch just for a short while, then I'll release her into Alex's hands for good."

As you wish, Master. Alex is very capable and I know you'll keep your promise of letting her go. Eventually.

The great bird headed to the night sky and found his way to the birch tree, relieved to skip this time weaving event.

And in the twinkling of a star that was moving overhead, the old wizard disappeared into the darkness. And the star twinkled even brighter than before.

~ * ~

Millie needn't have worried about Jack liking her red dress. Jack thought she was beautiful in anything, but his eyes did sparkle when he saw her coming across the room, trying to make her way through the throng of dancers.

"I was getting worried about ye, lass. What were ye doing?"

"Jack, unbuttoning a thousand buttons is tedious. Remind me to never have a dress made with that number of buttons again. But Deirdre did a fine job with this one. What do you think?"

"Lass, red is my favorite color, and ye are my favorite lass. So that about sums it up for me." Millie stood next to him, and it was such a joy to be able to stand next to him and have him be taller than she. She liked that.

Shortly, Alex wound his way through the crowd and caught Millie by the sleeve.

"Have ye seen Caitlin? I seem to have misplaced her."

"Aye, Alex. She's in the rear storage room changing her dress. Deirdre's helping her. She's got a thousand buttons on her dress, just like mine, and that takes a bit of work to get those undone. She'll be here shortly. Go now. Find another unsuspecting lass and wear her out on the floor."

Alex smiled and walked over to speak to Hector.

"Brother, looks like ye outdid yerself with this *ceilidh*. Verra fine vittles in my opinion. I thank ye for yer efforts."

"Nah. Wasn't so much work. Millie helped quite a bit and we managed to pull it off. Now that we've done it, we might just do it more often."

He smiled and sipped his cider. Looking around the room, he failed to see any lass he thought might suit him. But now that Alex and Jack had wed, there would be pressure for him to do the same.

Well. When I'm ready, he thought.

Caitlin found her way to the storage room where the dressmaker was waiting for her.

"Ach. Ye must be ready to take that dress off, Caitlin. It's bound to be warm by now."

"I really would like to keep it on, but it is pretty warm and heavy. But it's even more beautiful than I had pictured, and you did such a fine job making it. Your work is excellent. I'll have to get with you to have more made."

"Right ye are. Now here, step forward and I'll start to work on those buttons. Here, have some cider while I get this job done."

Caitlin drank deeply from the cup and it felt so cool, relieving the dryness in her throat. It really was warm with all these people in the lodge.

"Now, step back once more and we'll get rid of that petticoat."

Caitlin did as instructed and Deirdre brought out a dress created for Caitlin also. But not red. Hers was green. Another color of the season.

"Oh, it's a beauty, and my favorite color. Did you know that?"

"It suits ye. What with that flaming hair. Alex will like it for sure."

Caitlin was glad to hear that comment. There was something about Deirdre that made her scalp tingle, but she couldn't define it yet.

"Here, this one needs a stitch at the waistline too. Ye've got to start eating more, lass, or ye'll blow away."

"Ouch! Not again, Deirdre! Ye've got to be more careful with your needl….need. . .ne . . "

Abruptly, she sank to the floor in a puddle of silk.

O h glory. I didn't think the concoction would work so fast. Devil berries she called them. They were supposed to make her sleep, not die! Oh, what have I done? Alex will kill me for sure! But I don't care. This woman is not going to have what's supposed to be mine. I'll fix her so he won't even want to look at her face!

It seemed when Deirdre made a decision lately, it was one that brought her deeper and deeper into a place that had little light and her soul was becoming blacker and blacker.

She had visited Nezzie and asked her for a potion or medicine that would make one sleep, but not really harm them. She told the old woman it was for her ailing mother.

"She never gets any sleep. Says her arthritis keeps her awake."

The old potion mixer dug through her basket containing an assortment of herbs, and came out with a handful. "Here, give her these. They're called devil berries. Crush them and add some water. They'll relieve the pain, and help her sleep. But be careful, ye hear. Don't give her too much or she might not wake. Don't think ye want that do ye?"

Well, that had worked on her mother, so it would work on the red-haired lass, too. Now that Caitlin had succumbed to the cider laced with "devil berries," Deirdre had to get her into her cart, which she had driven to the rear door when she arrived. She knew every room in this lodge, having been here before when Mistress MacKinnon was alive. She knew this would be the best place to have the ladies undress.

Now, however, she was struggling to get Caitlin into the cart. She was certainly a tiny thing, but a limp body was hard to manage. She pulled and shoved until she got her in the cart, then covered her with a blanket. She lashed the whip at the pony pulling her cart, and they were down the lane headed to a place only Deirdre knew about.

The evening was wearing on and there was one more surprise in store for Caitlin — for everyone. Until Mam passed away a couple of years ago, most evenings she would have the lads standing next to the harpsichord. She had begun teaching them to sing when they were but wee ones at her knee. With the four of them, she had a bass (Alex), a baritone (Jack), a tenor (Hector), and Ian . . . well, his voice couldn't be counted on to stay in any range just yet, but he was willing to sing with them. Mam knew he would eventually figure out where he wanted to land. So the finale of the evening would be the lads serenading the group *a cappella.* Mam always played the harpsichord for them, but they did well with no accompaniment, too.

Alex was off to find Caitlin so she didn't miss out on this treat. Walking to the rear of the lodge, Alex wondered why the ladies would have come here, so far away from the front where it was warm. He knocked on the door and waited a moment. No one came.

"Hello. Caitlin? We need ye out here. Come on now, lass, hurry."

Still no answer. He knocked again and opened the door, calling out as he entered.

"Caitlin? Deirdre? Where are ye?"

He still didn't see nor hear anyone, so he walked the length of the room and went around the corner to the closet. The ladies were not there. As he started to leave the room, however, an odd sight caught his attention.

"What does this mean?"

He bent over and lightly touched the satin, blue dress laying on the floor. That was Caitlin's wedding dress, and it was laying in a heap here in the storage room. Caitlin was meticulous about the few items of clothing she had acquired since arriving in the Highlands. He was sure she would never leave her dress in a puddle on the floor.

Something was not right.

It only took his agile brain a second to make a few connections.

"Deirdre. No. Surely ye aren't that deranged."

But no sooner had the thought entered his mind than he knew he was right. Deirdre had taken Caitlin. He recalled her saying "ye'll be sorry ye humiliated me, Alex. Ye'll pay for that." He had thought she was just angry. But now, he had no doubt she was keeping her promise.

He hurried to the great room. As tall as he was, he could see over all the heads in the room. He quickly caught Jack's eye and no words were necessary. Jack nodded and struggled to get through the dancers as they continued their reels. Finally, he was at Alex's side.

"What's wrong, brother? I know that look."

"Caitlin's gone, Jack. She's not here at the lodge."

"What? Whadda ye mean she's gone?"

"She's with Deirdre. But I don't know where."

"Why in the world would she leave with Deirdre?"

"I don't think it was by choice. I believe Deirdre has taken her someplace. Apparently she never got over my refusal of her attentions and this is her way of repaying me."

"Jesus, do ye think she's that vengeful?"

"Aye. She has a mean streak, and I've witnessed it on more than one occasion. She's cruel to her own mother, so that tells me she'd not hesitate to hurt Caitlin. We've got to find her. And now."

"Aye. We will, Alex. We will. I'll have Hector get the folks to leave now and I'll talk to Millie, tell her what's happening. We'll be out of here in just a few minutes. Let's get out of these clothes first. I'll meet you in the stables."

"Aye. And Jack, I'm asking Ian to go with us. He's a better

tracker than any of the three of us . . . something about that keen nose of his. And he's old enough now to take part in family affairs."

Jack was glad Alex was including the lad. He had earned the right to be part of this band of brothers, for sure. He'd learned a lot from his Culloden experience and Alex was showing a new willingness to let someone other than himself make decisions. Jack knew that was difficult for his older brother.

"Aye. Ye get him and tell Da what's going on. He'll want to ride too, but he and Andrew need to stay here. Millie won't like being here by herself with little Midge."

"Be with ye in a few minutes."

Alex scanned the crowd looking for Ian. The lad was getting tall himself, just like his brothers, so finding him wasn't difficult.

Alex spotted the lad grinning at that same lass he'd seen him talking with earlier. Pretty little thing, no doubt. He hated to interrupt, but he needed the boy's help.

"Ian, could I have a word, just for a moment, lad?"

"Alex, can't it wait? I'm just a bit busy at the moment." He had cornered this little lass and didn't especially appreciate Alex interrupting.

"Sorry, lad. It's important."

Ian made his excuses and came over to where Alex was pacing the floor. "What's got ye so riled? I could sense it across the room."

"Caitlin's been taken. We've got to find her, and we need yer help. Ye could always track better than the rest of us, and with the night and the snow yer nose will come in handy."

"What? Who's taken Caitlin? Why?" He was having trouble following the conversation. It made no sense to him.

"I'll answer yer questions later. Right now, I need ye to be changing and getting saddled. I'll see ye in the stable." Alex's worry

117

was overwhelming, but nothing compared to the anger that was building inside him. He had enough maturity and experience to know, however, that anger needed to stay on the back burner until the proper time. A cool head worked better than a hot one.

He left quickly, and as he went through the room he could hear Hector addressing the crowd.

"Ok, we should all say goodnight. The brides and grooms tell me they need a little rest, so ye need to be getting on about finding yer own beds."

This brought laughter from the men and giggles from the ladies. The men were already in their cups and the women were more than ready to call it a night. A *ceilidh* at the MacKinnon lodge had been a grand evening, certainly one they would all remember.

Alex was stopped by Da as he hurried through the kitchen, headed to the stables.

"What's going on, lad?"

"Da, Caitlin's been taken. By Deirdre. We're going to search for them. Hector's disbursing the well-wishers, so if ye could go help him that would be good."

Da never blinked an eye. He had no difficulty understanding that Deirdre would do such a thing. He had never liked her from day one, and remembered her Da in the same way.

"Aye. But I'll come with ye, and Andrew, too. We both still know how to track, lad."

"We were hoping ye and Andrew would stay here in case they might come back to the lodge. Millie would need help if Deirdre did show up. I think it would be comforting for her to know the two of ye are here with her and the bairn."

"I see what ye mean. All right then. But ye lads need to be careful. It's slushy out there and yer mounts aren't going to thank ye

118

for taking them out in this weather."

Da immediately went to the front door and shook hands with the men and gave hugs to the ladies as they left.

"Ah, Daniel, 'tis fine ladies yer lads have there. I was beginning to think they'd never find anyone. And now just look. Two lads wed on the same day."

This particular neighbor had a daughter that he had hoped might snag one of the MacKinnons lads. But, looked like she'd have to look elsewhere now. He laughed heartily and slapped Daniel on the back.

Da closed the door on the last guest and leaned against it. He had seen his lads in action and knew they would find Caitlin. He wasn't sure what they might do to Deirdre, however. She could have done a lot better than to make an enemy of the MacKinnon men.

CHAPTER 13

A lex led Zeus out of his stall, talking to him the whole time — a habit of long standing. The two had been together a number of years and Alex knew the horse wouldn't complain about the weather as Da had mentioned.

"Where's Ian? Is he coming?" Jack called out. He had arrived with Hector close on his heels.

"Do ye think he can mange this? I know his leg's doing well, but what if this is too much?" Hector was not as sure of this plan as Alex.

"He'll be fine. He's got a nose like Mam's — and Caitlin's too, now that I think about it. He's always been able to track better than the three of us. More than that, he needs to feel he's a part of this family. Let's give him a chance to make his mark."

Alex had taken the reins as leader a few years ago, just as Da had planned. And now he was allowing Ian to pull his weight. Hector nodded.

Well, then. Maybe Alex is finding his way to including others in his decision making and allowing them to bring ideas as well.

Ian came running into the stable, a bit frustrated as it took him longer to get his boots on than it did the others. But no comments were coming from them, so he brought his young gelding out and threw a saddle over him quickly. This beauty was a gift from

121

Da a couple of years ago. He was totally black, except for one white blaze down his face. Ian had named him Merlin, a character from his favorite book, Le Morte d'Arthur by Sir Thomas Malory. He had found it in the library and read it often.

Alex was back to giving orders, as usual, and no one was going to challenge his plans this night.

"Jack, you go over on the west side of the property. It's rugged over there, so I wouldn't expect they would have gone that way, but we gotta check everywhere. Hector, you go to the south end as far as that old crofter's hut. Maybe Deirdre would try to hide in there for the evening. She's not in her right mind, so we don't know what she might be thinking. Ian, I want you to come with me. We'll go to the top of the moor, at the crest, and see if you can smell anything. The wind there will carry scents a far distance. Now, if anyone sees anything or hears anything, fire one shot as a signal to the rest of us and we'll all come in that direction. We'll meet back here at daybreak. Let's hope we find them before then, but if not, we'll get more help. Now off with ye."

Jack took off headed west, and Hector made tracks to the hut. Alex and Ian started at a fast pace. The moon was lighting their way fairly well as it was only a day til it would reach its fullness. As they got to the top of the moor, Ian suddenly stopped, pulling quickly on the reins. Merlin stomped and snorted, annoyed at such an abrupt command.

"What's wrong? Do you smell something?"

Ian shook his head. "Nae, but we forgot something. We gotta go back."

"We can't go back. We've gotta find Caitlin quickly, lad."

"Alex, my nose is good — but Willie's is even better. We gotta get him."

"Damnation! What was I thinking? Getting married and losing yer bride in the same day turns yer brain to mush. Yer right. Let's get Willie."

They flew down the moor and rushed to the stable where they had put Willie so the women at the celebration wouldn't be afraid. Alex was quite sure Willie would not have harmed anyone, but it was better that the wolf be put away for the evening.

When Alex and Ian opened the stall door, Willie was standing at attention as if waiting for them, right next to his new friend who had appeared at the barn a few days ago. It was the strangest looking cat any of them had ever seen. In fact, no one had ever seen such a cat. It was larger than most, and its body was a soft pale yellow, and its ears were tipped in black as was his tail. Then, most unusual, it had blue eyes. The farm lads had all commented on it, but Willie seemed to think the cat was acceptable, and allowed the animal to curl next to him for a quick "cat nap."

"Willie, come boy. We've got to find Caitlin."

The words were hardly out of Alex's mouth before the wolf ran out of the stable and headed to the moor. Alex wondered if the animal hadn't understood every word. The cat looked at both men, then settled into the hay, licking at his front paws.

Willie was at the crest of the moor several minutes before Alex and Ian. But he had sat down, almost as if he had already tired of this chase.

"Willie, do you smell something, fella?"

Alex looked about, but didn't see nor hear anything. Turning to Ian, Alex look puzzled.

"What do you think Ian? He's acting as if he wants to stay here."

"I don't know, Alex. But I do know he's a special wolf. Wabi told me enough to know we should trust Willie's instincts over our own."

Alex looked at Ian. The expression on the lad's face stopped him in his tracks.

"What's wrong? Did ye hear a noise — or smell something?"

"Nae, but I gotta go to the lodge. It's important. Ye just gotta trust me now. Go on and I'll catch up with ye. I can't explain it just now. But go. I'll be back in a few minutes."

"Ian, I can't wait, lad. Caitlin's out there. I've got to find her and soon. Hurry yerself. I'm going on without ye." Alex couldn't for the life of him understand why the lad was insistent on going to the lodge. He knew he and Willie must keep on the trail, if they could find one.

Ian tore through the place, frantically looking in jacket pockets to find an important piece of paper. Finally, finding the right jacket hanging on one of the pegs, he reached inside and his fingers felt the folded piece of parchment he had placed there. It was the paper Wabi had given to him with the instruction, "Don't read it, not just yet anyway. But if a time should come when you wonder what I've written on the page, then that is when you must read it. And it's most important that you follow the instructions, exactly as they are written."

There was no doubt in Ian's mind that this was the moment. Every nerve in his body screamed for him to do this now. Slowly unfolding the paper, he read the words carefully and felt a rush of anxiety he was not sure what to do with. He was becoming more and more aware lately that there was something he must do, but what it was exactly he did not yet know. Just now, however, he also remembered other words of Wabi's in one of their discussions.

"Ian, lad, when the time comes you must open your mind, your heart, your spirit, and embrace the experience. Don't be afraid.

Just follow your intuition. It will not lead you astray."

Holy sheep shite! Should I really follow his directions?

~ * ~

Alex waited for only a few minutes, then he had to move. Had to do something.

"Come fella. We gotta find her. She's in trouble."

Willie understood completely, but when Alex called him, he continued to sit, just outside the circle of stones.

"Come on, boy. Let's move on."

Finally, Willie obeyed Alex's command, but kept turning his head toward the stones, as if he could see something that perhaps Alex couldn't. But Alex was in command. Willie would follow.

Ian left the lodge and was at the crest of the moor. Alex was gone apparently, as was Willie. He stopped and dismounted, then following the instructions on Wabi's paper, walked a few steps forward and reached the circle of stones. *Only the called ones are to enter...*he remembered Mam's words.

Ian knew he was to enter the sacred circle, and even though he was afraid, he continued until he reached the middle of the space. He stood atop a small flat stone that was only about two feet by two feet. There was such a feeling of peace in this place.

He had not known what to expect, but peace was not something he thought to find. Then he felt the wind rise and he could hear voices, far away, singing a song . . . almost like a lullaby . . . and it seemed familiar.

Following the instructions on Wabi's paper, he raised his arms skyward. As he did so, he began to chant in a language he had not known he could speak, but one that had been used for millennia by others of his ilk. His words were echoed back to him by other chanters, and he understood their meaning. Then, in a hushed whisper that he almost missed, one voice stood out from all the others, and he fell to his knees in reverence. He knew that voice. Mam. Her spirit was ever so real and he was so wrapped in her presence he could hardly breathe.

"Yes, dear boy. I'm always here for you. Always in this place."

Then she drifted away and he felt such a loss. But as she left, his mind was suddenly filled with images, one after the other — and they meant nothing to him.

"Embrace the experience, Ian. Follow your intuition." Wabi's words rang in his head.

He stood again and this time when he raised his arms he opened his center and let his mind fly as far as it wished. The images began to become clearer and clearer. A dark place. Cold. Water dripping. Lavender and mint. Voices, female. And another image — no, not image — a sense — evil. This place was filled with darkness. Something powerful and evil was in this place. And so was Caitlin.

His fear resurfaced and he was so tempted to leave this place of images. Where was this? Caitlin was here. He must look again . . . and listen . . . and smell. Another scent, or more accurately, an odor . . . sulphur . . . and a sound he couldn't place. Wind whistling? Perhaps. As the images began to waver and disintegrate, the last one caught his attention—a fleeting image of the letter X, just for the briefest of moments, then the images were gone and the singing stopped. All that remained was the delicate scent of roses, which Mam always left in her wake.

Alex still had found no tracks, nothing to give even a clue as to where Deirdre may have taken Caitlin. The more time passed, the more agitated the Highlander became. With no sense of where to go next, he stopped, dismounted and tried to think, if that were possible.

Kneeling on one knee, he stroked Willie's muzzle, wishing he had never put the wolf in the stable during the celebration. He would have kept Caitlin safe from Deirdre, of that Alex was certain. But then, that was his job now, wasn't it?

Well, Alex, my man, ye've not done so well as a protector so far. Maybe ye better let Willie keep that position 'til ye get better at it.

Exasperation was not an emotion that Alex cared for. Neither was fear.

Willie had stood still for the Highlander's attentions, but when Alex rose, Willie did something Alex had never seen him do. The wolf threw his great head back and called to his ancestral past. "HOOOOWWWWWWW!" That howl would have awakened the dead. It even had the hair on Alex's neck standing at attention. The next second the wolf tore off across the path to the moor. Alex had enough sense to realize this animal knew something he didn't, so he jumped on Zeus and he, too, made a short trip of getting back. However, when he arrived he was unsure of the scene before him.

There, in the center of the circle of stones, stood Ian, hands raised in the air and a golden glow shone on his body.

Just like the light that wavered over Caitlin's body when I found her in the circle.

What that meant he didn't know, but he'd take whatever help he could get now and ask questions later. Or maybe not even then.

Willie entered the circle and lay at Ian's feet, almost in supplication. Another four-footed beast was there also, the great cat with the black tipped ears and black tail. He, too, lay prone, as if waiting for an event to occur.

Not knowing what to do or say, Alex dismounted and stood quietly. Only a second was necessary as Ian lowered his hands, bowed his head for a short moment, then left the circle with Willie and the cat following.

"Have ye something to tell me, lad?" Alex spoke quietly, and waited for a response.

"I have information that may help. But it'll take all of us to figure out what it means. Just images. But I know they're important to finding Caitlin."

"Aye, then we'll call Jack and Hector and sort this out."

He fired one shot from his pistol and the echo from that single shot resonated from one end of the moor to the other. Alex knew his brothers would follow that echo and be here as soon as their mounts could find their way.

"I'll ask ye no questions, just as I asked Caitlin none. But are ye sure your images come from a place, or person, we can trust?"

"I don't know much more than ye do. But Wabi told me to trust my intuition, so I will. Don't think we got much else to go on anyway."

"Aye, ye got that right. But damnation, this waiting around and getting nowhere is not to my liking. We've got to find her!"

The night grew colder and colder. The wind was whipping around, first in one direction then another, as if it couldn't decide where it wanted to go. But the clouds had cleared and the moon provided even better light for the bewildered band of brothers.

In what seemed like ages to Alex, but was only a few minutes, Willie jumped up and began to pace the ground. Alex and Ian heard nothing at first, but shortly their ears, too, picked up the sound — horses coming at a fast pace.

"Thanks be to the Creator," Alex mumbled.

Now they could make a plan or develop a strategy. He'd never felt so inept. The two, Jack and Hector, listened as Ian told them what he had seen in his vision. They, too, asked no questions. It had never been Hector's nature to question much, but Jack usually wanted every detail. Since meeting Wabi and Caitlin, however, he'd learned to accept there was much in this world he knew nothing about. Right now he'd listen to anything that might help them in their search for Caitlin. He'd never seen Alex in a state of inertia. It was as if he couldn't get that fine brain of his to function. But now, with information recently received through Ian, perhaps they could make some headway.

"All right, lad, tell us once again what ye saw."

"Jack, it was just images. Some very clear, others not so much so. And scents . . . and sounds."

Alex came to stand in front of the lad. "Think hard on these images. Caitlin's life depends on them."

"Aye. Aye. There was darkness. The place was cold, but not freezing. And I heard a sound, like the wind whistling as it does just before a storm. And there were a number of scents — a few that I recognized, but others that I didn't."

"What scents? What did you recognize?" Alex was desperate for any information.

"Alex, I don't wish to upset ye, but I could smell lavender and mint. I don't know if ye are aware of it, but that's Caitlin's scent. It's just part of her, like roses were a part of Mam."

"Keep going, lad." Alex was indeed aware of Caitlin's scent.

"Any other scents ye could get a whiff of?"

"Yeah. A strong odor of sulphur. It was not pleasant, but I know that's what it was."

"Sulphur. Where would we find that smell?" Jack started pacing to and fro. "Sulphur, sulphur."

"What about any other images?" Alex was still prodding, hoping to find a clue that would give them direction.

"Oh, there was the sound of running water. A constant running."

"That's it?" Jack was frustrated with not being able to

connect all these smells, sounds, and images.

"Well, no. There were a couple more things. But I don't think yer gonna like it."

"Come out with it, Ian!" Alex, not one to lose control easily, had shouted at the boy.

"There was evil there, all around the place. I can't tell ye any more than that, but it was frightening, I tell ye."

"What frightens me is not knowing what state of mind Deirdre's in. Let's hope she's regained her senses and realizes this scheme of hers was not such a good idea." Alex had his doubts about that happening.

"Oh, and one more thing. The letter X appeared, just for a second, then it was lost in the fog, but it kept flashing for another moment."

"X? What the hell does that mean?" Jack was not one for figuring out puzzles. He preferred to take action. Any kind of action was better than this.

Ian just shook his head. He had no idea what it meant.

"Then let Willie lead the way. He's been prancing now for ten minutes like he's ready to go," Jack said. He needed to get moving.

Alex got on his haunches and took Willie by the jowls, looking deeply into the wolf's eyes, as he had seen Caitlin do when she wanted his full attention. "Willie. We need ye to find Caitlin. Come on, now. We need yer help."

Willie ran to the circle of stones, sniffed around for a few seconds, then was halfway across the moor before they could even get mounted.

"Let's hope he knows where we're headed. God knows I don't," Alex muttered.

He spurred Zeus and the horse responded immediately. The thunderous sound made by this group of men on horseback could be heard across the moor. Certainly the two men standing on the front porch of the lodge heard it.

"Come on in now, Daniel. Those lads will find her. Never known any of 'em to not complete any task. Come on. Let's have a wee dram and find our beds."

Andrew opened the door and let Daniel walk through. These two had seen much in their years, but this latest event had them worried. Daniel would like nothing better than to talk with Alice about now. She always had a way of pulling information together more quickly than others. If ye asked her about it, she'd just tell you it was woman's intuition. Maybe, thought Daniel, maybe.

CHAPTER 14

W ake up, ye hear? Wake up now!" Deirdre lightly slapped Caitlin's cheek but there was no response. She had thought the woman would surely have come to by now. Whatever had she done? She never intended to kill her—not just yet. She just wanted to scare Alex a bit and make him take notice of her. She had her own abilities and he just needed to become aware of them. The latest ones, she knew, had come from the old woman, and in her sane moments she knew these powers came from an unholy place. Her mother had warned her about that old woman, but she'd use whatever means she could to trap her man.

"He's mine, ye hear? Mine!"

Deirdre stood and walked to the opening of her hiding place. She had chosen this place carefully and knew she could come and go without anyone seeing her. This place was known to only one other person, Nezzie.

"Here, take these berries," she'd said. "It'll make the woman sleep. Then, when ye get the chance to be with the man, have him drink a bit of this potion. It'll bring him to ye bedside, that I promise ye. But ye may have to disguise it in his whiskey, or cider. It's right vile tasting. But it'll work. If ye need more, come here at night. And be sure to let me know when ye have the flame-haired woman. I can help ye with her."

Deirdre's plan was to hurry home with her horse and cart and go about her daily routine as if nothing had occurred. Her mother would never even know she had been gone most of the night. In fact, she probably expected Deirdre to be late coming from the ceremony and the celebration afterward.

Of course, Deirdre knew Alex would eventually come and ply her with questions. She would deny she knew anything about Caitlin's whereabouts. No one had seen her leave with the woman, so there was no way he could prove she had anything to do with her disappearance. She would keep the woman addled for a few days, then eventually she'd have to permanently do away with her. That was the part she hadn't quite figured out just yet.

She had committed a number of fairly cruel deeds, even to her own mother, but she had never killed anyone. But her hatred for this healer grew more every day, and the idea was getting more and more attractive. Then, while Alex was deep in grief, she would work her way into his good graces. She would show him that he needed her, just as she needed him.

Aye, I like that plan.

She covered Caitlin with a blanket and made sure her hands were tied. It didn't look like the girl would awaken any time soon, and tomorrow she'd come back and make her drink just a little more of the devil berry concoction. She wouldn't be much of a problem, not as small as she was. Why, lifting her was like lifting a child.

"That'll keep ye tonight. This cave isn't warm, but ye'll not freeze to death. Tomorrow I'll decide what to do with ye, ye wretched girl. Did you think I'd just let ye take my Alex? Not in this lifetime. Nae."

She grabbed her wrap and left the cave, pulling the thick brush over the opening. She'd be home shortly in her own warm bed, while that tiny lass would shiver in this cold cave.

~ * ~

Millie and Midge were in their quarters, neither of them sleeping. Millie's memory of her past life flooded her brain. Life with Lord Warwick was an unbearable existence but with the help of the MacKinnons and Caitlin she had escaped it. She had to believe Caitlin, too, would escape her captor, whoever it was. Millie was beside herself. Caitlin had come to her aid on a cold, dark, night and here she was, cozy, warm and safe as could be. But she knew she could do nothing more than continue her prayers. Why would Deirdre, do such a thing? Some wedding night this had turned out to be.

There must be more to the story than I know. I had thought once we got here to the Highlands all those problems would be behind us. Looks like I was wrong about that. Still, Caitlin has more help here than she would have had anywhere. And you and I are safe, little one.

She was wearing the rug out with her pacing. Unable to stay still, she put on a warm robe, wrapped Midge in a snuggly blanket and went to the kitchen. This had become a place of refuge for her. She'd never been needed for anything in her life, but here, on this farm, she was needed and had already proved her worth. Hector had taught her how to cook a myriad of dishes, and she had learned to make others on her own. Cooking suited her.

Early on, the only thing she thought she might have wanted to do was to teach. The one pleasant thing about her childhood had been the special tutoring that had been provided. She was good at math, science and history, and spoke English, French, and Gaelic as well. She had approached her father about going to the local village and teaching the children as most of them never had the first bit of education. But he had refused to even entertain the idea. She was a

Lady, and Ladies did *not* mingle with the lower classes, and certainly didn't teach them. So that was the end of that. Now, however, as she rumbled about putting on a pot of tea, the thought of teaching returned to her mind.

Maybe I couldn't do it then, but I could now. Maybe I'll see what Jack thinks of the idea. Realizing she no longer had to fear her father, or her husband, was still new to her. She had lived a lifetime with one or the other, and being free to live her life as she chose was a new experience. One that she liked a lot.

Then, Midge, we should give more thought to that idea.

She placed the child in the small crib Jack had brought inside. All the MacKinnon bairns had used it, and it could work for one more. That way Millie could cook and keep an eye on her, too. Of course, Midge never stayed in a crib very long. Someone always came by and picked her up and she had napped on several shoulders. Everyone was taken with a bairn in residence and Midge never complained about any attention they wanted to give her.

Da and Andrew were headed to get a dram when they heard noise coming from the kitchen.

"Ah, lass, did we wake ye?" Da asked.

"No, Daniel. We were both wide-awake so I thought to make a pot of tea. Don't think any of us are going to get any sleep until the men get home — with Caitlin."

"Right ye be, lass. Sleep has a way of escaping us when our minds are so full of worry we can't let it rest. Yep, a spot of tea would be the thing."

Da was so pleased for his sons, Jack and Alex, finding such fine women. He wasn't so sure about Hector, however, as the lad had never had a serious relationship. Not one that Da knew about anyway. Of all the brothers, Hector kept things more to himself.

Daniel and Andrew pulled up a chair, poured a cup and began to tell Millie stories of the lads in their younger years. Both the old ones had memories like an elephant—well, about the old days, that is—what happened yesterday often escaped them.

~ * ~

Riding hard and fast with Willie out front, the brothers were past exhaustion but Willie looked as if he could run forever. Pulling his reins, Alex called for a short break as even Zeus was beginning to show fatigue.

"Let's stop here for just a few minutes. Let the horses have a breather. And let's compare our thoughts. I've been thinking and I know ye have too."

The four of them squatted, but Ian shortly had to stretch his leg out full. There were just a few things he found uncomfortable with his new foot, and squatting was one of them.

"If memory serves me correctly, I believe there's a sulphur spring over on the McLeod property. Old McLeod was always complaining about the smell of the waterfall, that one deep in the forest. Remember where we would go on a hot day and plunge off the waterfall into the pool at the bottom? Course we never told Mam about it, as she'd have hanged us by our toes if she ever knew it. I think Da knew, but he kept it to himself."

That brought a smile to Jack's face, as he did remember going down that waterfall. He'd been so scared he could hardly stand it. But if Alex could do it, then so could he. And of course Hector was game. By the time Ian arrived, though, they were too old for such games and Alex didn't think they ever took him there.

"Waterfall? Where? I don't know anything about a waterfall in this area." Ian wished he had been born sooner. Listening to his brothers, it seemed he may have missed out on a lot of fun.

137

"It's pretty far back in the glen, " Hector said, then looked at Jack, who nodded.

"Yeah, he's right about that. I'm not sure we can find it in the dark, Alex."

"What? Of course we'll find it. There's got to be a path. We'll find it lads." Alex stood and began stomping about, trying his best to relieve his raging fear and anxiety.

"I just thought maybe we should come in the daylight, when we can make better progress. It's so black out here we could get lost ourselves if we're not careful." Hector tried to negotiate a plan that made sense to him.

"Then go on if ye must. But I'll not stop until I find her, ye hear?" Alex mounted and Willie leapt in front, leading the way once again.

The other three brothers exchanged looks of contriteness, and then were right behind him. They'd not let Alex down. Tired or not, they'd stay with him.

It couldn't be too far from daylight, surely, thought Alex. He was tired too, but Caitlin was more than life to him. She was everything. He'd find her or die trying.

Willie came to a screeching halt, lifted his great head, sniffed the air and made a sharp turn to the left, going down a steep bank. The men followed and the horses snorted and blew loudly as they struggled to maintain their balance on the terrain.

"Easy, Willie, slowly fella. We're trying to keep up."

Alex leaned back in the saddle, trying to keep his own balance. It was a rough path certainly.

Abruptly, Willie stood still, then raised his hackles and made another hair-raising call to his ancestors. His howl was so loud and mournful the brothers felt it shiver through their bones. They were all off their horses leading them, and now found themselves trudging through thick brush as Willie crawled underneath, moving more quickly than they could.

"He's onto something," Jack said.

He would follow the wolf wherever he led him. He'd seen this one in action before and he knew he was one fierce protector. If Willie got there before they did, whoever had taken Caitlin was in more trouble than they had ever bargained for. The only worse thing would be for Alex to get there first. He just might be even more dangerous than the wolf.

"Listen. Ye hear that? That's got to be the waterfall."

"Jesus, do ye smell that awful stench?" Hector never had cared much for the smell of sulphur, even though he knew it had practical uses for military purposes. Soldiers would soak cloths in various substances, including sulphur, which could be toxic. They would bombard the enemy with these airborne weapons and smoke would fill the air, usually destroying everything in its path.

"I don't remember it smelling so bad when we were here in our younger years." Jack didn't much like the odor either. But Willie kept going, and they followed the best they could.

As the sun began to peek over the mountain, with just a sliver of pink light on the horizon, Willie crawled out of the thick brambles and began to bark incessantly, running back and forth before some tall brush until Alex got there.

"Hold on, fella. We're right here. Let's see what ye found."

Alex didn't see anything, but now with the day just dawning he looked about, and listened. "That's water. Hear it? And it's real close."

Jack walked a few feet around to the right side of the brush they had struggled so hard to get through. "Alex, here's the waterfall. Right here. Man, it looks taller than I remember. This thing is really high."

Alex rushed over and took a look for himself. There was the waterfall, and Jack was right—it really did seem larger than what he remembered.

"Jack, I don't think that's the same waterfall. Ye know, I believe there must be a smaller one somewhere close by. We were daring, sure, but even we wouldn't have been so stupid as to leap from that."

He went to the place Willie had refused to leave. The wolf's hackles were standing tall and, he began a deep-voiced growl that Alex knew meant trouble for someone.

"Easy, Willie. Easy now."

Alex carefully looked about. The light had gradually crept over the mountain — dawn had broken. Alex thought for a moment, then nodded to Jack. "There. Those tall bushes. Ye think they look a bit taller than the others? And look at the edges. Those brown ones, they're dead, like they've been cut a while ago."

"Aye, I think yer right. Let's see."

Jack and Hector began to pull at the tall brush limbs. With a bit of tugging by four strong arms, the limbs tumbled forward and they had to step back quickly before they toppled on them.

"Come on, this is an opening. I think it's a cave." Alex rushed forward ready to get in as quickly as he could. "Hold on, Alex. It'll be darker than hades in there. We won't be able to see anything." Jack really disliked this creepy place.

Ian stepped forward and with a nod of his head and a flick of his wrist, he handed Alex a lighted torch. It smelled of tar and black smoke rose from it. "Here, this will help ye see where yer going."

Alex stared at his young brother and one look from him told

Jack and Hector to let it pass. They didn't need to understand right now. They just needed to find Caitlin.

Before Alex could squeeze through the opening, however, Willie shot through the hole and they could hear his bark as it trailed off.

"Jesus, that's a tight squeeze." Jack wasn't sure he was going to be able to maneuver his large frame through the opening. Hector watched as his big brother turned sideways in order to make himself a bit smaller. Finally, grunting and muttering a few choice words, he followed Alex who was much thinner than he.

"Hurry. Alex's leaving us. No telling what he might find." Hector grumbled under his breath and with greater ease than Jack, managed to squeeze through.

Ian stayed behind with the horses and was glad to do so. He sensed the evil that was close by. "I'll wait here and stay on guard." He needed Wabi's instruction to know how to deal with this kind of evil.

The other three continued slowly. "Jesus, what is this place? I didn't know we had any caves in this area. What do you think?" Jack asked.

Hector shook his head — he had no idea. He wasn't especially fond of caves, or any other close spaces as far as that went. He recalled being really glad when they left Caitlin's cave when Ian was in her care. It was clean and she had made it comfortable, but still, it was just too confining for his taste. Just now he thought he caught a glimpse of something slithering across the floor, but it disappeared quickly. He decided it might be better to keep that knowledge to himself as Jack was mortally afraid of snakes.

Alex continued to move and still had not caught up with Willie, but could tell he was gaining on him. Then, Willie stopped barking. Alex could still hear him, but now it was not a bark — it had now become a whimper. That got Alex's own hackles on end and he dashed forward, taking another left turn, holding the torch as high as he could.

Rounding the corner, he all but fell over Willie who was stretched out, his paws resting on a body lying on the floor. The body was as still as any Alex had ever seen, and he waited a second before daring to touch it.

"Oh, Holy Jesus. Don't let her be dead. Don't let her be dead," Alex whispered.

Putting the torch aside, he brought his hands together just beneath his chin — as close to a prayer as he had come in a while — then reached over and lifted the blanket that covered her face. And there she was, as lovely as he remembered. She looked so peaceful, as if she were just taking a nap.

"No. No. Not my Caitlin."

Alex lifted her and held her close. Her limp body draped over his arm like a ragdoll. She never moved a muscle — and he knew she was gone.

"Ah, Caitlin. Oh, *mo chridhe*, ye can't be gone!"

The word agony was insufficient for his feelings. He'd never experienced emotions such as these, ones that took control of his very being. His mind was vacant — his heart shattered. Holding her close was all he was able to manage. And he'd never let her go.

"Is it Caitlin? Alex?" Jack called out as he finally caught up with him.

One look at his brother's face told Jack the worst had happened. Caitlin was no longer with them. If that was the case, then neither was Alex.

"Alex, we gotta get her home now, brother. Let's get her home." Jack stepped closer and tried to pry her body away from

Alex. "Ye need to let her go, Alex. I'll take her."

Alex stared up at his brother with hollow, sorrow-filled eyes that said more than any words could have.

"No. I'll carry her. She's mine. All mine."

The Highlander stood, easily lifting her small, lifeless body. Jack stepped closer and saw Caitlin's face. He, too, thought how peaceful she looked. And how young to have left this earth. Too young.

How will he ever get through this?

Hector said nothing but watched as Alex held Caitlin close. There was no point in saying any words; Alex wouldn't hear them. So he kept silent and led the way out of the cave, carrying the torch aloft to light the way, hoping nothing slithered by his feet.

"Let's put ye on the horse and I'll hand her to ye. Or if ye want, I'll hold her. She's not heavy and I can manage her if ye need me to."

"No. I'll hold her. Let's take her home now."

Alex handed her over to Jack, mounted Zeus, and leaned to take her. Willie had never left her side and whimpered so loudly Alex could hardly bear it. The wolf, too, felt the same loss. Alex was certain of that.

"Alex, are ye sure ye want to hold her?"

"Yes. I'm verra sure, Jack. Hand her to me."

Such a stoic response was not uncharacteristic, but it spoke volumes to Jack. Alex was already crawling inside a shell that he'd never come out of. They had not only lost Caitlin today, Alex was gone too.

"Aye. Here she is."

Jack gingerly lifted her and Alex pulled her close, feeling how warm she still was, and how right she felt next to him. How could this be? This was just so wrong. They belonged together. Of that he was certain.

Willie began prancing, as if walking on hot coals, when Jack handed her to Alex.

"It's all right, Willie. We're taking her home. Come on boy." Jack touched the wolf on his head and was surprised when the beast showed his fangs and let out a growl that Jack had not been on the receiving end of before. "Willie, boy, it's ok. We'll take her home now."

Alex repositioned himself in the saddle and reached for the reins. Suddenly, he felt Caitlin's body begin to slip from his arms. "Help me, Jack. I'm losing her!" He couldn't believe he was having trouble holding her tiny body, but he was.

Then, one loud, quick groan — OOHHH! —and a voice splintered the silence.

"Oh, Holy Rusephus! Alex? What are you doing? This is not very comfortable. I'd rather have my own horse. And why have you tied my hands together?"

Caitlin turned in his arms and looked about. "What are you all doing? It's cold out here!" She could not imagine what they all doing out in the cold, holding a torch. And whose idea had it been to tie her hands?

Alex was laughing and crying at the same time. "Oh, lass, ye didn't die! Thanks be to the Creator! Yer still alive!" He held her so tightly she could hardly get her breath.

Jack and Hector stared at the two of them — one laughing and crying, the other complaining about her accommodations.

"Alex? You haven't answered my question. What are we all doing out here in the cold? Can't we go home? And for heavens sake, untie me!" Willie reached his paws up and began to lick her hands. His mistress still lived.

Ian had stood by watching, scanning the entire area. Where was the X? He saw nothing that resembled the image he had seen. But one element that had been revealed in the vision was definitely here, even now — the evil he had sensed. It was still close by and he could feel it in his bones. He'd never felt this before and for a moment was tempted to strike out at it. But not just yet. He wasn't ready yet.

He was ever so glad to see Caitlin giving orders like always and Alex's face come back to life. From death to life . . . all within a few seconds. Was that the way when one died he wondered? From life to death . . . then back to life? Was that what happened to Mam? There was much he needed to discuss with Uncle Wabi.

CHAPTER 15

Millie was the first to hear the commotion out front. Da and Daniel had gone to the great room to wait, and Millie had made her first attempt at baking scones, knowing it was better to keep her hands and mind occupied. Caitlin was so important to all of them and Millie couldn't think how they would all get along without her. She wouldn't let her mind think of anything other than seeing her walk through the door.

Hearing the noise, however, she was almost afraid to go out. What if they hadn't found her? No. They would. She just knew they would. She breathed a sigh of relief as she watched Alex come striding through the door, carrying a very agitated Caitlin.

"Why do you insist on carrying me? I can walk very well on my own," Caitlin complained as she struggled against his arms. Alex laughed as he set her down.

"It's our wedding day or what's left of it. If ye recall, lass, it's tradition for the groom to carry the bride over the threshold."

The men were all laughing and clapping each other on the back. Da and Daniel had come running when they heard the horses and relief flooded their old bones too.

"Lass, 'tis good to hear ye giving me lads a piece of yer mind. Their mam was good at that, and she'd be right proud to know another lass still keeps 'em in line."

This new daughter-in-law will do. Yes sir, she'll do,

Millie embraced Caitlin and the two ladies shared a moment in which no words were needed. Millie had never felt such relief. This woman was more than a friend; she was more like the sister Millie never had.

"I knew these scones would come in handy. Come on. Let's have a spot of tea and see what you think of them."

Millie was close to tears, but she had discovered Jack absolutely couldn't deal with crying women. He seemed to think he had to make everything right for everyone. And for her, he always did.

Sitting at the table, Caitlin took a bite of Millie's latest creation. Licking her fingers, she nodded to Millie, then turned her attention to Alex, who had just made the most ridiculous statement.

"What? You think Deirdre kidnapped me? What kind of nonsense is that? Why would she do that? She couldn't have been any kinder to me. And the dresses she made? Why, she took extra care to make sure they fit properly. No, you're wrong. She didn't do that."

Alex kept his thoughts to himself, at least for the moment. As it was, Caitlin couldn't remember anything after she went to the rear storage room to have Deirdre help her with her dress.

"No, I tell you. She helped me change my dress, and she gave me a cup of cider. That's the last I remember. But I just don't think she's capable of such a devious act."

"Well, there's history with her that ye don't know about, *mo chridhe*. It's a verra boring story, but she was hoping I'd show her some attention a while back. But she's not my cup of tea, ye ken? I made it clear to her that I wasn't interested. And she promised to make me pay for humiliating her. I believe those were her words."

"But how do we really know she did kidnap Caitlin?" Hector asked. "I mean, we have no proof, even if we do think so."

"Aye. I realize that, but my instincts haven't been wrong often, and I trust them in this instance too." Alex would keep his plans to himself but he was definitely going to find a way to know what had happened here. Until then, he'd make sure Caitlin was never in the presence of Deirdre without one of the brothers being with her. The fury banked up inside him would not stop until he had found her and dealt with her. Presently, he knew he would kill her if he had the chance.

"Then what? We just assume someone else took her then?" Jack didn't like this at all. If it wasn't Deirdre, then who? Was there another person who wanted to hurt Caitlin? Or maybe they wanted to hurt Alex? Or another family member? Jack was at the boiling point with no place to vent his anger. He agreed with Alex. Deirdre was responsible for this. And he'd make sure she got her due.

"Ian, ye got any thoughts lad?" Alex had not missed the fact the boy had been responsible for them finding Caitlin. How had he done that? Alex didn't especially care how, he was just glad he had.

"As I told ye at the cave, I felt a darkness there — and at the waterfall, too. I can't explain what I felt, but it was wicked, frightening. That much I do know."

There were nods around the table but no one questioned him. The only one who understood what he was saying was Caitlin. She'd been too drugged to feel much, but there was a vague memory of a dark entity, and it had left a mark in her mind. She decided to keep this knowledge to herself as well. Alex didn't need to know everything.

"So we just go about our usual business and we'll all keep our ears and eyes open. But Caitlin, yer not to go anywhere without an escort."

Caitlin's temper was aroused immediately. She stood and came to stand next to Alex at the table. "What? An escort? No. Alex, I won't be told what to do and where I can go. Do you hear me? Besides, I have a constant escort and he's protected me his entire life."

Pulling her close, Alex reiterated his statement. "Just the same, I'd feel better if ye would let one of us go with ye if yer going verra far." He bit back more words, trying to keep himself from saying too much. She liked her independence and he knew she'd resent his taking over. He'd just pay close attention to her until he got this sorted out. He had no doubt it was Deirdre's doing, but he'd have to prove it. He would, too.

CHAPTER 16

Early the next morning, Deirdre found her way to the cave, fully expecting to find her captive more alert — and angry. She couldn't care less how that woman felt. Actually, she was past caring what anyone else felt and this situation was no different.

When she got to the cave, however, her heart skipped a beat. The brush limbs had been pulled away and were lying to the side of the entrance. The brothers had just pulled on them and they had toppled over. They didn't move them far.

No. Has that skinny little wench found her way out? But she couldn't have. She was far too drugged and it was too dark. Plus, I tied her hands.

Hurrying down the tunnel to the left, she stopped and looked about. That woman was gone. The blanket was gone.

Someone had to have helped ye. Ye got away this time, so I'll just have to create a new plan. I'll never stop until I've sent ye to hell! Next time I won't hesitate to complete the job. I'll make it quick. Ye may have escaped me for now, but I'll not make the mistake of keeping ye next time. I'll find a way to finish ye off . . . and in a hurry. Alex MacKinnon, ye belong to me... me!

Anger rose inside her and she felt the darkness growing. She had felt it when she visited the old woman, and it was becoming more familiar to her now as it grew. She loved the feeling of power it generated in her soul. She couldn't remember when it had started, but knew the old woman was the connection. And now, she had begun to understand the dark power was guiding her thoughts and actions. It was power, dark though it was, and she would use the power when the day came.

~ * ~

Alex stood, stretching his stiff legs. He was ready for this whole episode to pass. "Let this day be over. Getting married has turned out to be even more exciting than I expected but now, I'll bid ye all goodnight."

He took Caitlin's hand and led her from the room. At Alex's instruction, the lads had moved her belongings from Mam's sewing room to the upstairs quarters in the east wing, where Alex had always slept. He had two rooms adjoining each other. The rooms were large and he liked sleeping there. It was quiet and both rooms had windows that overlooked the moor. He often stood at them, looking over the farm—his home.

He waited patiently as Caitlin insisted a bath was in order. This had been an unbelievable day and she finally climbed out of the large tub and wrapped herself in her long robe and sat down at the dressing table. Alex helped her unpin her hair and brush it out. It had become quite a mess during her ordeal and he was enjoying the process of helping her remove the tangles and seeing it return to its usual style streaming down her back.

"It's been a verra long day I know, mo chridhe, but if ye'll indulge me one more moment I have something for ye — a wedding gift Mam would have called it."

He reached inside a box in the corner of the room and brought out a small package wrapped in a rough piece of burlap with a small sprig of heather attached to it.

"What? A wedding gift? I didn't realize brides and grooms gave each other gifts, Alex. I have nothing for you."

"Ah, well then. Maybe they don't, but I know this one is meant for ye, lass."

She looked up at him as he placed the package in her hands.

152

She wondered if Millie had had a hand in the wrapping process — she knew how much Caitlin liked heather. No matter. She couldn't imagine what he thought was meant for her.

As she unfolded the burlap, however, she understood immediately and her face revealed her pleasure. She was holding the very small clay teapot that she had traded her healing services for with the old woman in the village near Inverness when she lived in her cave. She had been so taken with the carvings on the side as they reminded her of a similar teapot that Uncle Wabi had. There was the etching of a young girl, with long curly hair falling down her back. Next to her was a wolf, and a large raven was seen soaring overhead, his wings ever so enormous.

"I can't believe it! How did you find this? I had completely forgotten about it."

"When I went searching for ye I discovered it in yer cave. Actually, finding it told me that ye had left in a hurry as I know ye would never have left it otherwise. I know it means a lot to ye and it seemed I should make sure ye got it back."

"It's very special to me and I will cherish it always. Just as I will always cherish you." She stood up and pulled his head down to hers and felt his body tremble as she touched her lips to his.

Jack walked Millie back to her rooms. These quarters also allowed a view of the peaks that were snow-covered this time of year. This part of the lodge was quiet also, and Millie was thankful for a place where she could go with the bairn and not be disturbed.

Da had claimed the small room next to the kitchen, and Uncle Andrew had quarters on the first floor as well, at the end of the hall. Those two agreed that climbing stairs was for the younger set. Old Jamie, however, had decided to stay upstairs in a room just at the top of the stairs. He'd been there so many years that he didn't wish to leave it, and he had a large bed that was very comfortable.

When he'd been about ten years old, Ian had laid claim to a room even more removed than all the others—an attic space Mam had asked Daniel to install at the top of the central section of the lodge. He had his own small collection of books there. Had you been strolling the moor, most nights you'd see candlelight from that window as the lad would often read far into the night. As it was, each person had a place to call their own and there were several other rooms unoccupied. For the moment, anyway.

~ * ~

Sheep farming didn't leave much room for idle time. Caitlin and Millie realized shortly that if they were going to make any changes then they would need to be adamant about their wishes. Otherwise, the men would just continue on with everything the same as it had always been. And in the women's opinions, there were definitely a few areas where improvement would be in order.

Caitlin's temper easily jumped out front and center still. When she resided with Uncle Wabi he had been able to keep it under wraps, usually. However, this morning's conversation had her at wit's end and she stood, arms akimbo, looking up at her Highlander. Her usually soft voice had a definite edge to it and she spoke quickly with conviction.

"Alex, I don't think you understand what I'm trying to say to you. Yes, I do like being here on the farm. And yes, I can always find plenty to do. But there aren't a lot of folk here close to the lodge who need treatment by a healer. I want to take a cart, my medicines, and of course Willie, and make a trip to the village a couple of days a week. That way the old ones can get attention. It's difficult for them to come all the way out here. And it's not a chore for me. It's what I want to do. The best part of my day is when I see you coming in at night, but the days can get pretty tedious. So I'm asking you to understand this is something I must do — something I am going to do."

She lowered her arms, and her voice. She had made her case. But her tongue hurt from biting back more words she could have uttered.

Alex thought for a moment before answering her. He smiled inwardly as he realized Caitlin and Jack shared a common trait — a temper that had to be contained on occasion. But he'd spent a lifetime with Jack and knew how to handle him. With Caitlin, he was learning she would only back down when you convinced her your way was better. And yes, his penchant for ordering others about had been brought to his attention.

"*Mo chridhe*, I wish more than anything for ye to be happy here. This place has come alive again, with ye and Millie bringing back the sunshine that Mam always brought. Da, Jack, Hector, Ian —all of us —we've never been so content. As for not wanting ye to practice yer healing, lass, that's how I met ye. And I'll not stand in yer way. But wait just a short while. I'm still not ready to let ye go by yerself. We still don't know who captured ye, ye ken? But we will know. I promise ye that."

"That was a while ago and nothing has happened since. I'm of the opinion it was a prank by local lads. They never meant to hurt me." She stood looking up at him, determination written on her face.

"Well, that could be I suppose. But I'll think on yer plan as ye asked. Just give me a couple of days."

"I'm going to the village next week and that's the end of that. I don't need your approval." The fire in her eyes left no room for debate.

Alex gave her a long look, but said nothing more. He finished his cup of tea, placed the mug on the table and walked to the door, deciding to let the matter go for the moment. The rigid line of his back and his taut face said more than any words would have anyway. Always able to read body language better than most, Caitlin longed to go to him and put her arms around his waist and lean against him, but couldn't get her feet to follow her thoughts. This was the first time she had felt Alex pull away from her emotionally, and she immediately experienced a painful emptiness. He walked out and she watched him as he calmly mounted Zeus without ever looking back.

He was headed to his sheep and to his thoughts about who had kidnapped Caitlin. He was almost ready to approach the one responsible for that adventure. He'd let her think the ordeal was over, but that would never happen when you crossed Alex MacKinnon, especially if you'd tried to harm one he cared for. Deirdre's days were numbered as far as he was concerned. Even he was surprised at the depth of his anger at the woman.

His feelings toward Caitlin following their disagreement were not those of anger, but rather, fear. Presently, he spurred Zeus on and made haste to get to the sheep. Before long, however, he reined him in and sat staring out into space.

Why can't she see that I'm trying to protect her, not control her? She refuses to see that Deirdre could be responsible, but I've never been more sure of anything. I must settle this problem once and for all before she becomes victim to her again.

After Alex left Caitlin tried to get regain her composure, then walked out to the hut by the stream. She had seen Millie leave the house as she and Alex began their confrontation.

"Millie? Are you here?"

"I'm here, inside the hut," Millie called out. She'd left when it became clear Alex and Caitlin were going to cross swords again. However, she still overheard enough to know it was quite a row.

Caitlin pulled at the heavy door and stepped over the threshold. The hut was quite old but Da had made it pretty airtight as Mam wanted to put her special items in here.

Just some things I don't want to part with, Daniel. They'll not take much room. So if ye please, just humor me in this. Ye'll not have to move them again. Just help me store them here.

Daniel went about filling all cracks and making sure the roof would hold. He even put stronger timbers inside to support the thatching. And now, all these years later, Alice's treasures still looked almost like they did the day she placed them here.

"That sounded like a bit of clashing of tempers from here." Millie smiled at her friend.

"Yes, it was that and more. That Highlander can get me fired up quicker than anyone I've ever known. He's even more stubborn than I am, and that says a lot." She shook her head, as if clearing away unwanted thoughts.

Millie continued to smile, then turned back to the items in

front of her. "You won't believe what I found. Come over here. Look at this."

Even from the doorway Caitlin could see several large rectangular items. A couple were laying on the floor, and others leaning against the wall. "What are they? Can you uncover one?"

"Aye. I did already. This is a surprise for sure." She pulled the covering off the first item. "It's an oil painting, and a very good one at that."

"What? Mam collected art? Alex never told me that. I've seen a few charcoal drawings in the lodge, but no paintings."

"This work is better than good. It's very fine. But I don't think Mam collected art. Look closely, in the lower right hand corner. It's signed." Millie was smiling and Caitlin came closer.

A.M. was clearly seen even in the poorly lit hut.

"Millie, do you think what I think?"

"Yes, that's her initials. Alice MacKinnon. Mam was an artist. Why didn't anyone tell us that? Why are the paintings out here in this hut? They should be inside where we can all enjoy them. They're beautiful and would bring color to the walls of the lodge. Do you think we should move them inside?"

"I don't know why not. It would be a treat for my eyes. I'll bet the men would appreciate the change, too. They never give much thought to such. They're more interested in what your next vittles will be than such as this. They could all use a little taste of refinement, but you and I will have to provide that I'm afraid."

The two ladies carefully unwrapped several paintings, brought them into the lodge, and spent the entire afternoon deciding where they should hang them.

"Over the fireplace. That scene of the sun just barely peeking over the mountain is perfect there. Look at the colors. Green from the forest, the white on the mountaintop, and the two hinds walking through the stream, with a stag in the distance. Even the men will like that." Millie was excited about finding such treasures.

"Aye. Then we'll put the floral ones in the bedrooms, where we can enjoy them. They'll be so surprised. I can't wait to see their faces."

Millie had lived in a castle filled with original art and even Caitlin had some pieces Uncle Wabi had collected in his travels. But they were in Skye. Both women were thrilled to bring a touch of color to the all-male, drab lodge. Certainly when Mam was alive there were more feminine touches, but these paintings would add so much to the place.

~ * ~

Food on the table was always the first order of business at the end of the day. The men washed first, then they would have a wee dram or maybe a cup of cider. The table conversation most often revolved around happenings on the farm and who needed to do what, when.

The men had come through the door, headed to their baths, then hurried to the great room for a cup of cider which would be followed by a tasty dinner Millie would have prepared for them. She was more in charge of the cooking than she ever thought she would be, but that was to her liking. She had plans for Hector, which naturally meant she would be busy in the kitchen.

Alex had greeted Caitlin at the door as usual, with a quick kiss on the forehead, and didn't mention the scene that had taken place that morning. She was relieved, but knew the matter was far from over. When the men assembled in the great room, seeking a bit of warmth from the fireplace, they could hardly miss seeing the large painting the lads had hung at Caitlin and Millie's direction. Alex was the first to notice the piece and the smile on his face spoke of his pleasure.

"Caitlin? Where did this come from? It's quite a piece of art. I studied a bit of art history at university, and this reminds me of some of the paintings in the textbooks."

Jack wondered if perhaps Hector had brought it with him this last trip. "Millie, is that one ye had sent up from yer grandmother's place?"

Millie was sure they must have seen these before. "None of

you have ever seen this before? Maybe in your early years?"

"Nae, lass. I'd remember this. It's so lifelike. Look at that stag's antlers. Looks like that old one that shows his face occasionally out on the moor. I've seen him from my upstairs window. He knows he's safe from us. Mam never would let us shoot one of those," Alex said.

They began discussing the colors and how the painting brightened the room. The ladies had not yet gotten around to pointing out the initials in the right hand corner. Of course, dinner was never served until all the men had washed and gathered together in the great room. All were here except for Da. So they sipped their cider another moment. Finally, Daniel came in, wondering what all the commotion was about.

"Did I miss the party? Yer all making quite a racket."

Then his eyes rested on the painting over the fireplace. He dropped his cup of cider, the contents spilling across the wood-planked floor.

Millie rushed to get a mop.

Da stood there, taking in every inch of the painting, not speaking a word. His voice cracked when he finally did find it. "I see ye've been in the old hut."

Millie returned with a mop and she and Caitlin looked at each other. It had not occurred to them that perhaps they should have asked permission. They were so delighted about the find they assumed everyone else would be, too. But perhaps not.

"Yes, Daniel. I see now that we should have spoken with you beforehand. We weren't thinking very clearly, it appears. Please accept our apologies for making ourselves at home here," Caitlin said. She had learned early from Uncle Wabi to always admit your mistakes.

Daniel turned to his new daughter-in-law. "Nae, lass. Ye've done nothing to apologize for. It's just that it's been a while since I've looked on that work. Yes, a verra long time."

Alex, Jack, Hector and Ian looked at Da. No one could understand the look on his face. He was close to tears.

Alex finally approached him and laid a hand on the old man's arms. "Da, ye've seen this painting before? Where did it come from?"

"Well, my lad. That's a story ye wouldn't know about. But I suppose it's way past time it should have been told. Let's have our supper first, then I'll tell ye a new tale, one that might surprise ye."

Supper was as usual — men asking for seconds, Hector getting more cider for everyone, and Jack feeding himself and little Midge from the same plate. The two were practically inseparable these days and Millie never failed to be surprised by the man's abilities. How this brash, short-tempered man could have this other side, this caring, patient side that always showed itself where Midge was concerned, was touching — a surprise certainly to Millie, but also the brothers, who had watched this change with interest.

After clearing away the table, which they all helped with as Mam had taught them, they retired to the great room and everyone found a seat. Da sat in his usual place, close to the fire where he enjoyed poking at it with his fire iron. Caitlin pulled her chair over next to Alex. Hector sat across from them and Ian lay on the floor with his head on a pillow. His leg would most likely always prefer a stretched out position over all others. But he was young, so lying on the floor didn't bother him. Millie and Jack claimed the old sofa and Midge had gone to sleep in her crib.

"Yer mam is probably watching us here, so I hope I get it right."

That brought quiet laughter from the lads.

"First of all, Millie and Caitlin, ye've done us all a favor by bringing the paintings inside. Should have done it years ago. It's good that they're here, and the paintings are the first of several other subjects that should have been brought to light. If ye look closely at the painting, me lads, you'll see the artist signed it, way in the lower right corner.

"Yeah. I can see it from here. It looks like A.M. But it might be A.N. Not sure." Hector squinted and decided it was A.M.

"A.M. That's right. Alice McCormick, not MacKinnon. Yer mam painted that, and a number of others before I met her."

160

"Mam was an artist? But Da, why would she keep her paintings out in the hut? She could have had them here, in the lodge."

"Aye. She could have. But she choose not to, lad. It's a bit complicated, but she decided her paintings belonged to another life, the one she led before we found each other and she came to the Highlands with me. I never liked that she put that part of her life away, but it was not my decision to make. It was obvious to me she was a talented artist, but I learned early on she'd make her own decisions. And most of the time she was kind enough to discuss them with me." He chuckled under his breath.

"But why would she wish to keep such a beautiful painting hidden away?" Caitlin was in awe of anyone who could produce such art. Not a talent that she possessed, certainly.

"I think it was just as she said. It represented her life before she came here. When she made that decision, to come with me, it was not exactly with the blessing of her family, ye ken? Now, ye know ye have a few distant cousins in the lowlands, right at the border, but that's about it. Yer Mam's parents were much older when I met her. She, like Ian, had been a late-life baby for them. There had been two other children, both boys, one of whom died in infancy, so Alice was their only daughter. Her father, Laird McCormick, was a verra wealthy man, ye ken. She had been sent to school in Edinburgh when she was just a young girl, and had begun her studies at university about a year before we met. Naturally, she was expected to marry into the same social class to which she belonged. So as was common then, her father made arrangements for her to be introduced to the finest young men in the country at the annual McDonald *ceilidh*.

"And she did meet a number of the sons of landowners. Lovely as she was, she could have had her pick. But for a reason I'll never understand, she chose me, a poor Highlander who just happened to be helping MacDonald herd his sheep to the border. MacDonald insisted I, and the other two young lads with me, Andrew and Jamie, come to the party and that's where the story started. There I was, with nothing but a few acres of land, a small flock of sheep, and a couple of crofter's huts to boot. In fact, I tried my best to tell her she wouldn't like it here.

"It's a bit of a struggle, living in the Highlands, Alice. Ye'll be wishing to be with yer servants and wearing yer fine clothing soon. And yer kin will be there if ye need them.

'I don't want to marry any one of these lads. I've known most of them all my life, and there's not one I'd think of spending a minute with. Most of them are only interested in me because I'll inherit my father's lands. And that's not enough for me. I'll choose the man I marry. And that's you, Alex MacKinnon.'"

"She must have been quite a lady, then, I would guess," Caitlin said.

"Well, aye. She was Lady Alicia McCormick. And I thought she was the finest Lady I'd ever seen. There wasn't any question on my part, certainly. So after informing her parents of our plans, Alice packed her trunks and we left. Her father threatened to disown her and to leave all his properties to her brother if she went through with this arrangement. Obviously, she made her decision and she always reminded me that she never regretted it.

'My life with you, our lads, and these Highlands, has been more than I ever hoped for.'

"Those were the words she left me with on her last day. I'll let them be enough. But now, I think we can hang her paintings and let that part of her be shared with us also. She'd be pleased with this. I know she would."

Daniel slowly stood and made his way to the front door, preferring to walk on the moor, winding his way to the top. Alice would be waiting for him there.

CHAPTER 17

school? Ye want to start a school? Now why would ye wish to do that, lass?"

Jack, as well as the other men, had been schooled pretty much by Mam. She had instilled a love for reading in all of them, and Jack understood how important that was. But create a school here at the lodge?

"There are quite a few children up here and most of them have never seen the inside of a classroom. We could make such a difference in their lives. Everyone needs to know how to read and they could learn a little about history, how things grow, and how to add a line of figures. I could teach all of that. Plus, those who wanted to learn French could do so. I might as well make use of the fine education that Father so insisted on."

Millie's mind was made up, but in this endeavor she would definitely need Jack's approval, as well as that of the other family members.

"But Millie, ye've got Midge to take care of, and the kitchen keeps ye busy already. How are ye gonna find time to teach? That's a lot of change, if ye ask me. And by now ye know how I feel about changes."

"I'm just asking you to consider the idea. It would benefit the entire village and those who have no chance of any education otherwise."

"I don't know. But I'll think on it, lass. A lot of change." He started to walk away, then turned back to Millie "Have ye discussed it with Caitlin?"

"She's all for creating a school. But she's got plans of her own

163

that will take a lot of her time. She just needs to talk with Alex and get his thoughts."

"What kind of plans?" Jack was still a bit unsure about Caitlin. So far, she hadn't brought any lightning on them. But what could she be making plans for?

"That's not for me to be telling, Jack MacKinnon. She'll let you know when she's settled her mind about it." And she returned to her baking.

~ * ~

Wabi's antennae had come to attention. Mrs. Love, owner of a large hunting estate in Skye, had turned over the care and training of her dogs to him. He couldn't think of anything he'd rather do, and presently he'd been making a bed in the barn for her old bitch, who was about to have a litter any day now. But what was it that had his scalp tingling? He stopped a moment, closed his eyes and opened his center, listening closely. Whoever it was that was calling was certainly persistent. His scalp was practically burning by this point.

Ah, Ian, yes. I hear you, lad, I hear you. Slow down, now. Slow down. Yes. Are you sure? Then I'll make my way to you. If there's another incident and I'm not there yet, trust me when I say you can handle it. The power is there for your taking, but take care to think the situation through before acting. Make sure it's necessary to use your power before you do so. Careful, lad, careful.

~ * ~

Several months had passed since the wedding ceremonies. Wabi had left the celebration before it was over, as he'd felt a need to go home. But when he arrived, all seemed to be in order.

Now Ian was trying his hand at communicating with Wabi. As Wabi expected, he got through immediately. Wabi's sense of this young lad was right. He would be a powerful tool for the Creator. He knew the time had come for him to put everything else aside and mentor the boy.

I wonder . . . if he would come here I could give him even more attention. Maybe I should talk to Daniel about the lad's special qualities. Pretty sure he won't be surprised.

Owl had recently returned from the Highlands as Wabi had decided Caitlin was in good hands now and had called for his friend to return to him.

"I'm headed to the Highlands again, Owl, are you coming?"

The great owl turned his head, almost all the way around, and focused his all-seeing eyes on Wabi.

If you need me, Master, of course I shall come.

"Well, I know how you dislike time weaving, so if you like, stay here and look after the place. If you get bored with the scenery here then join me in the Highlands as that scenery will certainly renew one's spirits. I'm headed there at Ian's request. He believes there's dark power about and he's afraid of it. Not that he would admit it, but I sensed it in his voice. And I'm glad he fears it. It can be difficult for a novice to conquer — even difficult for me occasionally. So I'll get myself there and see what's what."

~ * ~

Hector, Millie, and Jack were headed to the Cameron estate. Millie had to see for herself that all was well with the old ones. And though she knew Dorothea would take excellent care of the three children who had been hiding in the castle, she needed to satisfy herself that this solution was working for everyone.

"Lady Millie, I knew ye'd keep yer word, I did." Clint helped her off the cart and quickly removed his tattered tam. His Mam had taught him it was the proper thing to do in the presence of a Lady. And even though she was married to this Highlander now, Clint still thought of her as Lady Millie.

Millie took his old weathered hand in hers. "Of course I did. You are all important to me, as you have been to my grandmother and aunt for all these years. Without you this place would have fallen apart long ago."

She had such a way with words that old Clint just liked to listen to her.

"Is Dorothea here? I would like to see her, please."

As the words were spoken, several children raced out the door, laughing as they went dashing through the bailey.

"Are those the children Hector discovered?"

A voice called to her. "Yes, m'lady. Those are the ones. Give me a minute and I'll have them come in for an introduction. They're a handful, but with a little work they'll be just fine."

Dorothea never doubted Lady Millie would return, but she was pleased to see her. Once everyone was inside and had been given a cup of tea, Dorothea gave her report.

"I don't know exactly how long they were hiding here, Lady Millie, but it must have been several days — maybe more. They had head lice, infected sores and hadn't had a bath for a bit. I'm not sure, but they likely had some of that before they came. I've taken care of those issues and they're now well-fed and clean. And I'm doing my best to teach them a few basic manners. 'Tis a challenge, though."

Hector, Jack and Clint talked business for a while, and Millie and Dorothea relived old times. Finally, Hector could put it off not another minute. "Millie, we've got to come to a conclusion about what to do with these children. Ethel's been feeding them, Dorothea's been caring for them, and Clint tries to keep the place warm enough for them. But this can't be a permanent arrangement. What did ye have in mind? I know ye've been thinking a while on this. But we need to know where to go from here."

Jack waited for Millie to speak, but when she hesitated, he stepped in.

"Millie's got her mind set on starting a school up at our lodge. And I've bought into that idea. We all need to talk about it, so we'll discuss it at home, with Alex and Da. And Ian, too. Here at the estate, she hopes ye might help her put together a staff for the place, with Clint, Winston and Ethel still in charge, of course. But this staff would be a bit different than what's been here before. Millie wants to provide food for the village again, just as her grandmother had done. Also, perhaps this could be a temporary home for the children and wives who lost their das and their husbands during the fighting."

Millie was glad Jack had started the conversation. He had

been surprised when she first mentioned the idea of a home for the children. But as she knew, he had a fondness for children that others may not understand. And with a suggestion coming from him, Hector might be more inclined to agree.

"I want us to continue with the gardens as Grandmother had. And this is a perfect place for us to establish a place to help the wives and children of the men lost in the fighting — a temporary refuge until they can sort out their situations. My place is in the Highlands with Jack and Midge. I have no plans to live on this estate, but it could serve a great purpose. With Clint, Ethel and Winston's help, we could make this a sanctuary of sorts. That would mean a safe, secure place for the children and it would mean employment for a few."

"A home for children and widows. A sanctuary." Hector stared at Millie as though just seeing her for the first time. "The place would need to be arranged differently. We'd need to turn bedrooms into sleeping quarters for several people. And there would have to be a dining hall. And food. Ethel could take care of that."

Millie smiled at Jack as they watched Hector already making his plans aloud. The idea obviously appealed to him.

"And it would be work — at first. Take a lot of my time. Just to get things organized and sorted properly. What do ye think Alex will say about that? He usually needs all hands working with the sheep."

"He's already on board, brother. He's given his blessing and Caitlin thinks it's a great plan for the estate. If we need to, we'll take on a new helper or two while ye get this taken care of."

At the end of the day, Hector decided to stay at the estate, get his thoughts together and start making a plan. This would need to be carefully done, with a mind for how the place would pay for itself. There were still a few sheep, but if they could get the farm going again, the flock might need to be increased. They could sell the wool and that would bring in funds that could be used for the other necessities. Hector's mind was rushing like wildfire.

CHAPTER 18

Caitlin listened for a moment. Silence. Heaven. She walked outside and Willie trailed behind her, sniffing the path. Winter still had them in its grasp, but Caitlin's nose detected a scent that spoke of spring. Maybe just in her memory. She would be glad when the weather did change to something not quite so fierce.

This silence was golden. Millie, Jack, Midge and Hector had gone back to the Cameron Estate and would be gone for several days. Alex and Daniel were in the south pasture with the lads trying to retrieve several sheep that had been trapped in the bog. And according to Alex, this was a dangerous undertaking. And Ian? She had no idea where that lad was off to. He'd just rushed in and rattled off some words about needing to make a quick trip down the mountain.

She was alone for the first time since she'd arrived in the Highlands. It was a nice reprieve from a regular day filled with people coming and going. Most of the time there was much talk and laughter, and once in a while a few angry words would be tossed about, but not often. It was so different from her life with Uncle Wabi. But she knew she was meant to be here. And she intended to follow through next week with her plan to start her healing in the village. She and Alex still had not discussed the matter since the day of their heated argument. It was a subject that was still the elephant in the room and she planned to discuss it with him this very evening. Might as well hash it out until they could come to some understanding. She doubted he'd ever agree with her, but she'd waited long enough now. Healing was her calling, and their difference of opinion was certainly putting a strain on their relationship. Alex still wanted to make all decisions, and she still wanted to resort to a temper fit.

Today she again felt a pull to return to the circle of stones. Her nightmares still came, though less often, and she recalled Uncle Wabi's belief the solution to her dreams would be found in the circle. She knew full well Alex would be steaming mad if she went back there, but Willie would be with her and he'd take care of anything that might try to harm her.

Pulling her a*risaid* around her shoulders, she started the climb up the moor. It was eerily quiet. No sounds anywhere. No wind. Most unusual. The closer she got, the more insistent the compulsion to enter the circle became. It was like being pulled by an unseen hand. As she reached the top of the moor, the wind immediately began to whip in every direction and began to howl.

"Willie, the wind is making that same sound you make when you call to your ancestors. Listen to that. I've never heard that before."

If Willie thought it was unusual, he didn't indicate it. His nose was lifted, as always, and he stayed close to Caitlin. Walking closer to the circle of stones, the urge to enter was so great she never even considered not doing so.

Willie entered with her and lay prone, next to her feet. She once again saw the golden light that had surrounded her before. And that peaceful feeling, it was still here. Now, however, something else was here as well. Was that a voice whispering in her ear? No, that was just the wind. Then again. Whispering? Was it a voice? Maybe. But it was so far away. Not a voice. More a feeling of being called, needed. By whom?

The feeling grew stronger and Caitlin knelt. Her hands went to the small stone in the center, and she felt a small, pulsing vibration that warmed her throughout. The stone was smooth, the edges even. As her hands moved over it, she saw a very faint image, just as Ian had. But this image made no sense. It was a small child. No, not a child. An infant in a christening gown. And it called to Caitlin. Not a voice, but an emotional urging — a feeling that this child was crying, calling to her. In just a short moment, however, the crying drifted away, farther and farther . . . and finally the image faded and Caitlin knew it was gone and would not return this day. She bathed herself for another moment in the golden light and the calm spirit of the circle, then stepped out again into the harsh, real world.

As she walked back down the path, the wind shifted and came full blast from the opposite direction. The force of it frightened Caitlin and she stood still for a moment, now detecting something else.

"What's that odor? It's like something dead. No, worse than that."

The smell was so odious as to have her stomach in turmoil and a wave of nausea swept through her. Quickly her mind turned to the warnings that Alex had given her about going to the circle of stones alone. Did he know more than he had voiced to her? Perhaps he felt the same darkness that she did now. With her next step, she felt the darkness coming closer, pulling at her. She found herself off balance and fell to her knees. The darkness had tentacles that wrapped around her even as she tried to pull away from them. Her only hope was that her protector could help her. She finally managed to stand again and with trembling body she called out.

"Willie! I need you!"

She really didn't need to call him. He had already caught the scent himself and was responding with his teeth bared and hackles standing tall.

Her voice quivered, "There's evil here, Willie. I feel it."

Willie roughly nudged her behind her knee. She had learned long ago that this was his way of telling her to run quickly. She began to flee and he stayed close to her. Finally they reached the lodge, leaving the darkness behind.

Caitlin wished Uncle Wabi were here. He would know how to handle this situation. With that last incident, she knew she would take Alex's warnings to heart. But that image of the child. What did that mean? Again, she knew she would return.

~ * ~

It was still early when Caitlin got home. She went with Willie to the stable to check on Henson, his new friend. Caitlin was taken with the unusual cat, as they all were. He was more the size of a small bobcat than a house cat. She had noticed he often followed Ian up the stairs to bed at night. Sometimes, though, he would camp out here in the stable with the horses and Willie had found the stable to be a cozy place as well.

She returned to the lodge and her two companions tagged at her heels. Then, still looking for a task to occupy herself, she made another decision she knew wouldn't sit well with Alex. As it was, she and Alex gave each other a lot of room. She needed quiet on occasion and he gave it to her. If she had a problem, she always wanted to talk it out, whereas he wanted to brood over the issue for a while. Their lives were so full and both of them realized what a treasure the other was. Her skin still tingled at his touch and she hoped that would never change. He went to sleep every night with a strand of her hair wrapped around his finger.

"That way I'll know if ye try to sneak away."

His greatest fear was that she would tire of the Highlands and leave him. An unthinkable event.

Today, however, she just needed a change of pace and Alex needn't know about it.

"Willie, we're going to take a ride. We won't go far, but I need to see something besides this lodge. I can't sit here another minute twiddling my thumbs. Come."

She gathered her wrap and her medicine bag, an item she never went anywhere without, as she knew she might come upon one who needed her help. Then she returned to the stable and saddled her horse, the same horse she had stolen from Commander Campbell. She'd decided to call him Soldier — that seemed appropriate.

Caitlin had become quite at ease on a horse after having

172

ridden one all the way from Inverness to the Cameron estate. And now as she began to canter, Willie stayed right with her. She had no idea where she would go but just a change of scenery would do her good. She let Soldier have his head for a ways and she loved feeling the wind blowing through her hair. Willie kept pace with them easily.

A short while later she came to a fork in the road and wasn't sure which way to go. Willie took off running to the right, so she decided that was as good a way as any, but she had trouble staying with him. Then he stopped rather abruptly right in front of Soldier, causing him to prance sideways and snort loudly.

"Willie? What's wrong?"

His growl was deep. Caitlin dismounted and tried to follow the beast as he fled into the woods.

"Hold on, Willie. I can't go so fast," she called out.

Then, from some distance away, she heard a cry.

"Help me. Please help me!" A woman's voice came crying through the trees. Caitlin listened again and followed the sound. Willie was headed down an incline and she was trying her darndest to stay with him.

"Willie, wait. It's steep."

She could hear water flowing nearby. A lot of water. And the smell that emanated from the entire area was not especially a pleasant one — sulphur. At home in Skye there were a number of sulphur springs and the locals often immersed themselves in them for therapeutic purposes. Caitlin knew sulphur was a good remedy for skin irritations and it also relieved arthritis.

For a moment a blurred memory drifted across her mind. A memory of the night she was kidnapped. This odor? But that night was fuzzy in her mind, so she put aside the thought and focused on finding the voice.

"Willie, that's a waterfall. See it? It's a ways from the top to the bottom."

"Help me. Can ye hear me? Please help me!" The voice was hysterical at this point.

Caitlin could tell the voice was female and that it was coming from behind the water, close to the bottom of the waterfall. Getting to her would take a few minutes.

"Yes, I hear you. Hold on. I'm coming. Be still and don't move. I'll help you."

The climb was not an easy one. As she slowly made her way, Caitlin was wondering how she would get this woman back to the top.

"Patience, dear girl. Patience." Uncle Wabi's voice whispered in her ears.

Willie had already scampered far ahead of her and she could hear him barking. Then the barking ceased, and the sound she heard now got her attention — a deep-throated growl.

It was a sound she knew meant someone was in danger from one angry wolf. But why in the world would Willie be growling at a woman who was obviously in pain and needed help?

"Willie. Stay now. Stay."

Caitlin reached the bottom of the incline and called out. "Where are you? I can't see you."

"I'm here, underneath the waterfall. I'm hurt and I can't move my leg. Help me!"

Caitlin looked carefully over the waterfall then quickly moved back again, retreating from the edge.

Holy Rusephus, that's a long way down there.

She kept her spine flat against the rock wall and followed the path that led behind the flowing water. There she found the woman splayed out on a rocky ledge about halfway down the waterfall. She hadn't fallen all the way, but far enough to have caused injury for sure. She was lucky to have landed on the ledge where she had.

How am I ever going to get the two of us to the top?

Caitlin's mind was spinning, trying to think what to do in this situation.

"Hold on, I'm almost there."

She made her way onto the ledge, knelt down and lifted the woman's head gently. The woman looked at Caitlin and it was

174

difficult to tell who was the more surprised, Caitlin or the injured woman.

"Deirdre? What happened? What are you doing out here?"

"Oh, Caitlin. I was taking a bath in the sulphur water. It's warm and I thought to ease my aching back and soothe the blisters on my hands. I burned them trying to make stew for me mam. She's not eating much these days, but she'll eat a bite of lamb stew if I prepare it. I spilled it on my hands and there were blisters in just a few minutes."

"Let me take a look at you. Where do you hurt? Can you move?"

"Aye. I can move, but I landed on my hip. It hurts like the very devil. But my foot is the worst. I don't know if I can stand on it. Now my back hurts even more than before I got in the water. I don't know if I can walk, Caitlin. What am I going to do?"

Caitlin took a few moments to make her assessment. She couldn't tell if there were any broken bones, but Deirdre definitely had suffered a hard fall. Her hip may indeed be fractured, and she had either sprained or broken her ankle in the fall. In any event, they had to get to the top and make their way home.

The struggle to get to the top was more than Caitlin had bargained for. She pulled and lifted Deirdre, stopping every few feet. Every muscle in her body was screaming out in pain, all but refusing to lift anything another second.

"I'm about done for, myself, Deirdre. But we're almost there now and we'll have Willie bring Soldier closer. That'll save us a few steps. Here, rest a moment."

Caitlin had not failed to notice Willie continued a low-level growl the entire time they were climbing, but she'd not think about that now. They needed to get Deirdre home so she could see what she could do to help her.

The healer took the wolf by his jowls and looked directly into his dark eyes. "Willie, get Soldier. Bring him here. Quickly. Go now."

Deirdre watched as the great beast flew through the forest.

"Do ye think he understood ye?"

175

Caitlin smiled, as she'd been asked this before. "Oh, aye. He understands more than you would believe. Not sure but what he can even read my mind."

Soldier was standing at the top of the incline shortly and Caitlin forced herself to make a final effort. "Come on, now. We've got to do this. Just keep your arm around my shoulders and we'll make it."

"Caitlin, I don't think I can get on that horse. My foot is broken. I know it is."

"Come on now. I'll help you. We'll manage."

Caitlin dragged Deirdre the last few steps and, finally, with the woman screaming and crying, coerced her to try and get into the saddle.

"Put your foot in my hand, I'll give you a boost. You can make it. Now, come on. I'll lift you."

Deirdre tried to get on the horse several times before she succeeded.

"Caitlin, it hurts. Aieeeeee!"

Deirdre understood she was in trouble and needed help, but Caitlin was the last person she would have ever expected to help her. Now she wondered if maybe Alex had not figured out she was responsible for Caitlin's disappearance. However, she knew Alex MacKinnon was an intelligent man, and she'd do well to remember that.

"Good. Now I'll get behind you. It's not too terribly far to the lodge from here. Come, Willie, let's get home."

She eased the reins and Soldier started for home. He knew the way even better than she did. She shook her head as her next worry came to her. *Whatever am I going to tell Alex?*

CHAPTER 19

Da and Alex were exhausted. Getting two of the larger ewes free from the bog had been an ordeal. The old gals were heavy and not smart enough to stop fighting you when you tried to help them. Finally, Alex put a rope around their necks and had Zeus do the pulling. Not much of an effort for him, but now he was covered with muck as well as the men. So the first order would be to clean the horse and then himself.

Da went to the lodge after cleaning most of the mire off outside in the shower Jack had rigged for them. They used it in the summer months, but in the winter a bath in one of the rectangular baths that Da had installed inside was much better. He'd put one in for Mam originally, then as the lads came he'd added two more, one in each wing. He headed to one of those to wash. He'd never speak of it, but he was beginning to feel his age. The cold seemed to have seeped into his bones. A warm bath and a wee dram would take care of that, though. He got his bath and went to sit by the fire, where Andrew and Jamie were discussing their ailments.

Uncle Andrew was just a couple of years younger than Daniel, and the only sibling still living. There had been several others, but all died in infancy. Thus it was that these two brothers were exceptionally close. For most of his life, Andrew had lived on the sheep farm. His Florence had passed away a number of years ago now, and he moved into the lodge. His own place was just too lonely without her. So now the two were both widowers and took pains to be as useful as possible.

Old Jamie, a distant cousin, rounded out the trio of oldsters. He had lived in the lodge for years too, and was about most of the time. He was rather quiet, and kept his thoughts to himself. But he still contributed to the running of the place and was very much a part of the family.

"A little arthritis now and then. And the heartburn, fer sure," Da reported.

"Aye, and as it should be," Andrew said when Daniel made mention of his ailments.

"Jamie, ye got any complaints that need airing?" Da smiled at his old friend and cousin.

"Nae, none that would be any worse than what ye two talk about." He laughed and sipped at his cider. The three of them could tell stories till the sheep came home.

"Not one of us is what ye'd call spring chickens, Daniel, but we ain't done fer just yet. In fact, I'm feeling younger than I have in years." Andrew grinned.

"Ye think maybe it might be those trips to Edinburgh? Checking out those records?"

"Yep. Could be. Could be."

Daniel nodded to his brother, and winked at old Jamie. "So when are ye going to bring her here? She'll have to pass our inspection, ye ken?"

"What? How did ye know about her? Why, a fellow can't keep a secret to himself around this place." But he smiled and the three of them shared a dram and reminisced about the good old days.

~ * ~

Alex worked to clean the mire off Zeus and then quickly got the worst off himself. The sticky muck clung to his shoulders. But Jesus, that was cold! He was finishing as Da came out the door.

"Alex, do ye know where Caitlin's got off to? I told her I'd help get the vittles on the table, but she's not in the lodge. Was she headed to the village maybe?"

Alex stepped out of the cold shower, wrapped a large towel around his body and stared at Da.

"She's not inside? She knows not to leave without one of us

178

going with her. Maybe she's upstairs. What about Willie? Is he inside?"

"Nae, lad. They're not in the lodge. I checked everywhere."

Alex hurried inside, washed quickly, put on a clean kilt and shirt and tried to find a pair of boots that were dry enough to put on. Walking in this snow all winter didn't allow much time for drying out.

"Da, I've got to go look for her. What if Deirdre's found her again? I tell ye it was her. I haven't been able to prove it yet, but my gut knows it was her."

"Hold on a minute. I'll go with ye."

"Nae, Da. Stay here. It's getting even colder out there now."

"Lad, I know how cold it is and I'll thank ye to let me make my own decisions as long as I can. Now let's stop talking and get to the stable." Da could make a point when he needed to.

Alex was only halfway across the yard, however, when he heard a voice calling.

"Alex, we're coming. Over here!"

Caitlin had seen Alex when he came out the back door of the lodge. She'd never been so glad to see anyone. She had no doubt he would be angry, but also knew he would come to her side now and help her with Deirdre. The anger would hold for a while.

"Jesus, Caitlin, what's happened?"

He helped Caitlin off first, then, looking at the other woman who was slumped over, he saw red. Deirdre! Even in his angry state, however, it was apparent to him that she needed help.

"Have ye lost yer mind? I told ye she's the one who kidnapped ye. Didn't ye even think about that before ye brought her here? She's the enemy, lass. Listen to me, ye ken?"

"I found her out under the waterfall, lying on a ledge. I couldn't just leave her there. She's in a bad way whether we like it or not. Now help me with her."

Alex's first inclination was to take the woman and tie her up so she couldn't harm anyone. When he got closer to her, however, he saw she was in no position to harm anyone. So against his better

179

judgment, he looked at Caitlin, who nodded at him, then turned to Deirdre.

"Here. Lean over here. I'll take ye, now."

Alex felt the woman lean slightly in his direction and he cradled her in his arms and headed for the lodge.

"Let's put her in Mam's sewing room. I spent weeks recovering in there and I can tell you it's a most comforting room. Trust me on this."

Alex would rather not have this woman anywhere near Caitlin, or any of them as far as that went, but there didn't seem to be anything to do but follow Caitlin's suggestion.

"Caitlin, I don't want that woman in our home for one minute. Do ye not understand what a danger she is to ye, to all of us? Ye have to hear me on this lass. Listen to me, I tell ye." Containing his anger was very challenging.

"Perhaps what you say is true. But we can't just turn her out to fend for herself under the circumstances. Now, put her here on the bed and I'll give her a good going over. Then we'll talk."

Alex stood next to Caitlin, unwilling to leave her side. Willie stood so close to her she could hardly move. Alex had not missed the underlying, reverberating growl coming from the beast. He was certain the wolf felt the same way he did, and neither of them was going to leave Caitlin alone with Deirdre.

Caitlin lifted the woman's head and poured some liquid down her throat, causing her to cough. "I've given her a dose of laudanum. She'll sleep now and tomorrow she'll be able to tell us what she was doing out there. You can go now, Alex. She's unable to harm anyone at this moment. Willie can stay here with me. I'll watch her a few moments, then I'll join you."

Alex stood there for another minute, then walked out, confident Willie would stand guard.

"That wolf has better sense than his master. Damnation! She's got to realize this woman might have killed her." Alex vented his frustration, and Da just nodded and poured both of them a dram to settle their nerves.

"Lad, Caitlin's no fool. But her first calling is to heal. Ye'll never get her to let go of that. I have to tell ye, lad, she and yer mam have a number of similar traits. My advice to ye is to hold yer tongue and accommodate whenever possible. It's a lot easier that way." He laughed as he watched Alex's expression.

The effects of the laudanum only lasted a couple of hours, which was most unusual. Caitlin heard Deirdre calling, so she and Willie, followed by Alex, went to see about her. She was complaining about her foot and her hip.

"You've got a sprained ankle and a nasty bruise on your hip. Those will heal and you'll be good as new. For now, just rest here and we'll see how you feel tomorrow."

"There's another problem."

"What? You're hurting? Where?"

"No. Not that. It's me mam. She's all alone. I'm the only one to take care of her and she's bedridden, ye ken? She'll wonder what happened to me. And she can't get her own food. I have to go to her."

Caitlin glanced at Alex, who stood by the bedside, still unwilling to leave Caitlin alone in the same room with Deirdre. He didn't trust her for a second.

"We'll get over to yer mam's place. Don't worry about her. Do what Caitlin tells ye now. We'll take care of yer mam."

"Alex, I'm afraid of that wolf. He growls at me constantly. Don't leave him in here with me, please."

Caitlin ran her hand along Willie's back then scratched him briefly behind his ears. "I'll put him away. He's got a place in the stable. He'll not mind staying there a night or so. He's got a friend that likes to sleep out there so he'll not be alone."

Alex looked at Caitlin as they left the room and she closed the door behind her. "Caitlin, ye can't be alone with that woman. I tell ye she's not to be trusted. Ye must hear me on this, lass."

"She's not well, Alex. Just look at her skin. She'll be better tomorrow. Then we'll decide what to do."

"Better or not, she leaves tomorrow. I'll drag her out myself

181

if I must, but she will leave here tomorrow. Now I'll get over to the Taggart place and check on her mam. The old woman's not in good shape, either, but maybe I can take food and see how she's faring. If she needs more than that, I'll go to the village and find one of the young lasses to stay with her. But you stay with Da and don't go into that room without him being with ye. She's dangerous and she'll still try to hurt ye."

Deirdre could feel the medicine working again. Sleep would be good. She hadn't gotten much of it lately. No matter how hard she tried, she didn't sleep much and certainly not well. When she did sleep her dreams were filled with disturbing images. It was like being pulled into a dark tunnel, hands pulling at you as you walked past. What did they want? Who were they? She always awoke in a sweat and the only relief she got was from drinking just a taste of Nezzie's potion, the one she had prepared for Deirdre to give to Alex. She'd tried it once and learned that it helped soothe her nerves and allowed sleep for short periods. But she needed to save the rest of it to put in Alex's whiskey.

At the moment, just before sleep did finally rescue her, she remembered the feel of Alex's arms when he lifted her from the horse and carried her to this room.

Warm, caring. Safe. He's supposed to be mine. Mine.

Taking Daniel aside, Alex explained his plan. "Da, I'm off to see about Mrs. Taggart. I'll check on her and if she needs someone to stay with her I'll go to the village and find a lass. But while I'm gone, I'm counting on ye to not let Caitlin be alone in the room with Deirdre. Trust me, she's not in her right mind. I can't get Caitlin to understand that, but I know that woman. She cares only for herself."

"I'm here and so is Jamie. We'll take care of Caitlin, lad. Go now."

Alex left and Caitlin took Willie to the barn as promised. He continued growling when they left Deirdre's room. Caitlin put him in the stable even as he made it plain this was not what he wanted. He actually barked at her and refused her command at first.

"Willie, come here. It's just for the night. I know you don't care for the woman, but I'll be fine. She's too tired and sick to cause any trouble. Stay here with Henson."

She closed the door and Willie whimpered again, not liking this arrangement.

CHAPTER 20

Caitlin hadn't known where Ian was going when he left the lodge, but then, neither had he. He only knew the evil he had felt at the top of the moor near the circle of stones was real. The fact he had awakened in the night aware of its presence again had him wondering what he was meant to do. Was it creeping about in the lodge where everyone was sleeping, unaware of the danger it might present?

Wabi, where are ye? Ye need to get here soon. Every day that darkness seems to grow and grow. I don't know how to keep it away from us. Hurry, Wabi.

Why did he find himself here, following a path he knew only led deep into the woods, just a few miles from the lodge? When he was younger, he had often packed a lunch and hiked over here, always with a book tucked in his saddlebag. It wasn't often he was given free time, as he learned early that sheep farmers worked all day, every day. But occasionally, being the youngest, Mam had let him have a few free moments. She seemed to understand he had a need for time alone. And this destination was a place he knew he would not be bothered.

At some time, far in the past, it had apparently been a place of worship. There were the remains of an ancient kirk, perhaps centuries old. The building was all but totally gone now, but one small section of the original structure still stood. It had the remnants of a roof, and Ian would sit inside it, liking the solace he found there. He often thought he heard singing, but perhaps that was just his imagination. As a child he didn't even question why he came, he just

185

did.

Now here he was again. It had been a while since he had made a trip to the old kirk. Again, it soothed him as he sat in his usual place next to some old stones that had been piled in the corner. He smiled when he saw the wooden, toy soldiers laying on the ground. He must have left them here. He always liked playing soldier, though after Culloden he wasn't so keen on that anymore.

In the last few months his life had taken off in a new direction, one in which he wasn't at all sure he knew how to maneuver. He could only wait and hope Uncle Wabi had understood how important it was to get here. After a short while he closed his book, packed it in his bag and headed to the lodge. Of all his places of safety, he was aware home was safer than any other. Home with Da and his brothers. And he knew Wabi would be there soon.

~ * ~

Leaving Hector behind was easy for Jack and Millie. They could tell he was excited about making plans for the estate to be turned into a sanctuary and a place that would continue to employ the old ones that Millie cared so much about. And to her delight, Millie saw that Dorothea was excited about her part in their scheme. Once everything was settled, Dorothea would come to the Highlands and care for little Midge. Dorothea had only her son, Garry, so she was more than excited about being with Lady Millie and her child. They would become her family now. Millie had loved this woman her entire life. It was only fitting that they bring her to their new home. And little Midge couldn't be in better hands. Even Jack realized that another person to help with Midge would be a good idea.

"She was just as I remember her being when I was small — ever so patient with those children, though I could tell them they'd be smart to not be fooled by her soft voice. She put me in a corner more than once when I got out of hand. She's as happy as I've ever seen her, and I can rest now that everyone has a purpose, a way to contribute their own special skills to making this project work. I know how it feels to be virtually useless, unwanted, and unneeded."

"Aye. Hector will get that place in shape. He's at his best when he's working with numbers and making plans. Just relax. He'll make it work."

Jack felt better now that Millie was settled about the future of the estate. Their life on the farm was exactly what he wanted and he felt Millie was content as well. He was finding that some changes weren't so bad after all.

"What about Caitlin? Did she ever talk to Alex? You never did tell me what that was about." Jack looked over at Millie and saw her smiling to herself.

"I told you, Jack. That's for her to tell. She'll let you know when she's ready."

Women. Trying to understand their logic is just not possible.

"I just hope she doesn't bring the lightning again."

They both laughed. It looked like Caitlin had either lost her powers or decided they were not needed. Either way, Jack was relieved she hadn't exercised them. Once was enough for him.

~ * ~

When Millie was away, Da made himself at home in the kitchen. Caitlin helped, but that area was not her best place. She was a healer, and she had to convince Alex that having her clinic in the village, just a couple of days a week, was a good idea. Perhaps she'd gone about it the wrong way.

Daniel and Jamie had stayed close by Caitlin, and after she was assured Deirdre was settled for the night, they headed to prepare dinner. Jamie served the stew Millie had left for them and brought out her freshly made bread. No sooner had they sat than Ian came in, hungry as always.

"Come on, lad. There's barley bread. I know ye like that well enough. And just like yer brothers at your age, that stomach of yers always seems to be empty."

Da was only slightly sad to see his youngest becoming a man. The lad would walk a different path, Daniel was certain of that.

But where that path would take him was a mystery.

Ian, Da, Jamie and Caitlin decided to eat and not wait for Alex. It could be late before he returned and there would be plenty left for him.

"Daniel, I want to ask your opinion about a situation, if I may." Caitlin and Daniel were on the best of terms. He loved his son and so did she. That's all that Daniel needed to know. And she was so like his Alice that he smiled.

"What's that lass? If it's about sheep, then I can probably help ye. Other than that, I'm usually not much to listen to."

"Nope, not about sheep. About healing. Providing care for the oldsters in the village. And others too, perhaps, but mostly for those who can't care for themselves. I've been wondering about the possibility of going to the village, two days a week maybe, and having a clinic. You know, where the folks can come to me and I'll provide whatever relief I can. From what I've observed so far, these Highlands are a place where it's difficult to find a healer. Millie's got her hands full planning meals and taking care of Midge. And all you menfolk are about before daylight taking care of your sheep. And what am I doing? Mostly, I'm pulling at my hair, twiddling my thumbs, and hoping one of ye gets hurt — just slightly mind you — so I have a patient to take care of."

Daniel and old Jamie laughed, and Ian shook his head. Caitlin laughed, too, as she tried to get the message across without sounding too desperate.

"It's true. There's not a thing that I contribute to this place. And that isn't my idea of what my life should be about. I believe I was put here for a purpose, taking care of sick folk, and there has to be a way I can do that."

"Then, lass, let's have a family conference and see what we can do. Alice was always a good one to help us see our way to doing most anything she wanted. Ye probably have that same ability. Though ye have to have figured out by now, Alex is always the last to agree to something that wasn't his idea to begin with," laughed Da.

~ * ~

Alex rode quickly to the Taggart place. At one point, Taggart had helped on the farm during lambing season. But in his last years he'd not been able to do much due to an ailment — having to do with his lungs, Mam thought. And finally he had passed away a number of years ago. That left Mrs. Taggart and Deirdre to look out for themselves. With help from their neighbors, such as the MacKinnons, the two ladies always had food and shelter. But in the last few years, Mrs. Taggart's arthritis kept her in bed and Deirdre was left to take care of everything. Maybe that's why she'd become so bitter and neglectful of her mother. But that didn't sit well with Alex.

He knocked and waited for a minute.

"Hello. Mrs. Taggart? It's Alex MacKinnon. I know ye can't get out of bed, so I'll just come on in. I've come to see how ye fare. Do you hear me?"

Still no answer.

He stood at the doorway, calling out to her. "I've come about Deirdre. She sent me to check on ye." Still no one answered. The home was a typical hut, to which Taggart had added a couple of rooms. There was only the one child, so they hadn't needed much.

When he opened the door to come inside, the stench of the place took his breath. As he stood looking about, Alex was appalled at the state of the room. The floor was littered with leaves and scraps of food. And clothing was draped about, laying on the floor as well. Dirty dishes were stacked on the small counter and the odor in the room was unbearable. What had happened here?

Jesus. I knew she was angry about having to care for her mother, but there's something wrong here.

Alex called out once again. "Mrs. Taggart?" And once again had no response. He entered the next room and immediately knew why the place smelled to high heaven.

Good Lord, lass. Have ye truly become unhinged?

Mrs. Taggart was lying in her bed. Alex didn't have to check

189

her pulse to know she'd been dead a while now. His nose told him that.

Oh glory. What do I do now?

He left the hut, closing the door behind himself, and was gone as quickly as possible. His mind was reeling, trying to make sense out of this development. Why would Deirdre have sent him over to check on her mother? Obviously she knew he would find her body.

The best thing I can do is get back to the lodge. Anyone who would leave her mother's body to rot in her own bed is capable of doing anything.

He called for Zeus to get them home in a hurry.

~ * ~

Jack, Millie and Midge arrived at the hut on the edge of MacKinnon property. It was the same one where they spent the night on their first trip to the MacKinnon lodge. It was here that her husband, Lord Warwick, had come upon them, and was the place where Caitlin's powers were first exhibited.

"I'm not sure I want to go in there, Jack. The memories of that day are still pretty fresh. But if you stay close by me, then I'll get over those and replace them with good ones."

"This hut has been a lifesaver for us over the years. And we could say for ye, too. Yer life changed on that day. The hut's still standing after more years than I can number. Da says it was here when he and Mam came up the mountain and it'll be here after we're all gone. There's a lifetime of good memories here. Don't let one bad one drive ye away."

"Aye. I'll just remember it as the place where my life began its new course, with you and Midge."

Jack pulled the wagon close to the hut, helped Millie and the bairn off, then got on about building a fire. They had a night of quiet and much discussion about the plans for the estate.

~ * ~

Everyone was in bed when Alex got home. He came through the kitchen and never stopped. Eating was the last thing on his mind. That scene at Taggart's hut would have turned anyone's stomach. At this moment his only thought was to find Caitlin and make sure she was safe.

The door to Mam's sewing room was closed and Da was sitting in the hallway as planned, making sure Deirdre stayed put. Alex spoke briefly to him and told him about Mrs. Taggart, then climbed the stairs and quietly opened the door to the rooms where he and Caitlin slept. He sat down and sighed, glad for this day to come to an end.

Caitlin was asleep, her hair spread out on her pillow and her knees pulled to her chest. Apparently she would get cold in the night, but never could wake enough to find the covers. He undressed, slipped in beside her, pulled the blanket up and brought her closer to him.

Lass, if I have to stay by ye every minute until Deirdre's out of our home, then I'll do it.

And he meant it. Tomorrow they'd have to decide how to handle the situation at Taggart's and, even more importantly, how to handle Deirdre.

A bit later, Ian climbed his own stairs all the way to the attic. He really liked this room, high above the rest of the house. He could hear stairs creak when anyone went down, he could smell Da's coffee early in the morning, and at night he could see all across the moor, especially when the moon was at its fullest.

But tonight, he lay in his bed and just listened . . . with all his senses. The evil he had felt at the circle of stones and again at the cave left an imprint in his mind. He felt a tingle in his gut, his center, of something malignant and dark. Was it just his imagination, which he admitted could be overly active, or was it the same evil he had felt before? No. Surely not. Not in their lodge. Wabi had warned him he may experience unusual feelings as he acknowledged his abilities, but he wasn't sure what this was.

Hurry, Wabi. We need ye.

Finally, he closed off his extraordinary senses and drifted off to sleep.

Next morning Da and Jamie were about before everyone else. They had the coffee brewing and the rich aroma crept up the stairs tempting Alex to leave his warm bed where Caitlin was snuggled close, her hair all but covering his face. He gently left the bed, careful to tuck the blanket around Caitlin, and headed downstairs. He needed to talk to Da.

"It's hard to believe Mrs. Taggart's dead. How come we didn't know about it? Ye'd think that girl would have told us," Jamie said. Alex had informed Da last evening, but as Jamie had been sleeping, he had not awakened him. Naturally, he was shocked at Alex's news.

Just a few moments later, Caitlin came down following that same delicious aroma of coffee that had lured Alex from their bed. She reached for the cup as Daniel handed to her. He'd already learned she liked it heavy with cream and just a small dollop of honey. As for Caitlin, it warmed her heart that the old man paid that much attention to her likes, but he had.

"Did you say Mrs. Taggart's dead? What caused her death? Arthritis can be crippling, certainly, but doesn't cause death as a rule."

"The hut reeks of death — it's as bad as a dead animal. We need to send the lads over to take care of her remains."

"Wait, Alex. I need to see her body. Deirdre's obviously not well either. Last night I observed that her skin is sallow and that blue tinge around her mouth tells me she's ingested an herb, or another concoction, that's affecting her body. And maybe her mind. Give me a minute and we'll go over there together."

"But . . . Caitlin. . ."

Alex didn't especially want to return to that hut. He couldn't put his finger on what it was, but he didn't like the sense of foreboding he'd felt there. And most of all, he didn't want Caitlin anywhere near that place.

However, listening to her footsteps just now, bounding the stairs with more energy and purpose than he'd heard in some time, it was obvious she was in her element. If she wasn't busy practicing her healing, then she was pouring over the medical journals she had found in the library. Mam had a collection of them, some of them ancient. Several of them were histories of the old Greek physicians, such as Galen and Hippocrates, and Caitlin spent hours reading and rereading them.

She was back shortly and she and Alex, along with two of the farmhands, made their way to Taggart's place. Alex wanted to get this task over with and quickly. They walked up the pathway and approached the door. Alex went in first with Caitlin right behind him.

"Holy Rusephus, what an odor! And what's all this? This place looks more like a pig's sty than a home. Whatever has happened? Surely Deirdre wouldn't let her mother live in this mess. There's something not right here, Alex."

"Aye. Couldn't agree with ye more, lass. Let's get this done. Are ye sure ye want to see that body? It's pretty foul smelling."

"Yes. I've smelled dead bodies before, so let's go on in."

However, when she reached the bedside, even she wasn't prepared for the overpowering stench. Taking a handkerchief from her medical bag, she held it to her nose and choked back a strong impulse to vomit. Even a healer could only stomach so much, apparently.

Alex walked to the other side of the bed. "Look, here, Caitlin. That same blue tinge is around her lips, too. Just like Deirdre's."

193

"Yes, but this blue tinge is always present in a body after death. This is not the same as the color around Deirdre's. I need to look in her mouth, Alex."

"Jesus, Caitlin! Do ye really need to do that?"

With a nod from her, he took his hands and carefully pried the woman's mouth open, and shuddered as he did so.

"Look here. The tongue completely fills the mouth cavity. This woman has been dead for about three days. See how flexible her limbs are? Rigor mortis has already passed and she's gone from being stiff back to being limp. All of that's normal. You know, the oldsters call a body like this a "limber corpse.""

"Never heard of that. What does it mean?" Alex hesitated to even ask the question. He wanted to get out of this place and quickly.

"The old ones believe that the corpse has supernatural powers when in this condition. Just folklore, Alex. Just folklore. But, in this case, there's nothing here that points to anything other than a natural death."

"Well, that's good news. But I don't like the feeling I get in this place. Let's ask the lads to wrap her body and we'll get the vicar to say his words. Old man Taggart is buried on the east side of their property. We'll put her next to him."

"Aye. Oh, one more thing, Alex. Turn her towards you and let me take a look at her back."

Alex grimaced but gently pulled the woman's body and rolled it toward him, allowing Caitlin to view her from the rear.

Mrs. Taggart was wearing a long-sleeved, high-necked gown in order to keep warm in the cold Highland nights. Caitlin carefully unbuttoned the first four buttons and opened the neck of the nightgown and inspected her lower back.

"Yes, this pooling of blood confirms the same, about three

days ago." She started to button the gown when she saw something else that told her even more.

"Oh, but Alex — look at this. Apparently I spoke too, soon. This woman didn't die a natural death. She was strangled."

Alex peeked over the body and there, just at the base of her neck, were bruises in the shape of fingers. She'd been strangled and her murderer had left incriminating evidence.

"Jesus. Deirdre's killed her own mother. What has happened to her? She was always a rather unpleasant person, but I never would have thought she could do this. Good God."

Alex's thoughts were coming so fast he hardly knew how to act on them. The most important thing they needed to do now was get to the lodge.

If she's crazy enough to kill her own mother, she'd not think a moment about killing anyone else — like Da or Jamie or Andrew.

"Let's get home, Caitlin. I'll tell the lads to prepare her body and get the vicar to come."

He disappeared for a moment and the two lads came inside. The odor was so putrid they wanted to finish this job and get to the farm. They'd never complain about smelly sheep again. Then they got busy wrapping the body and Alex and Caitlin hurried back to the lodge.

~ * ~

Jack and Millie arrived shortly after Alex and Caitlin. They were relieved to have gotten the plans for the estate laid out, and were glad Hector was willing to put them into action.

"It's good to be home," Jack said as he climbed from the wagon. He was about to take little Midge from Millie, but another pair of hands beat him to it.

"And it's about time ye brought our favorite bairn back to

us, lad." Da reached and took the baby from Millie and held her close, letting her rest her sleepy head on his shoulder. The little lass had worked her way into more hearts than one.

Caitlin and Alex were discussing the events of last evening and this morning when Jack and Millie walked in.

"Who are ye talking about? Who died?"

Jack looked from Alex to Caitlin.

"Mrs. Taggart. She's dead and the lads are over there now, taking care of her body."

Jack nodded. "So she just couldn't hold out, I guess? Deirdre will be alone now, then."

"Deirdre's here at the moment, Jack." Caitlin knew this would not be information Jack would like to hear.

"What? What's she doing here? I'm telling ye she's the one that took ye, Caitlin, I know it and one day we'll be able to prove it. Why is she here?" He looked at Alex as if he had lost his mind.

"That's an interesting story, brother. But she's got a sprained ankle and she's got to rest another day. For the moment, Caitlin's taking care of her."

No sooner had that statement been made than Deirdre herself came hobbling into the room, using the same crutch Ian and Caitlin had used earlier.

"What are ye saying? Are ye talking about me mam?"

Alex looked at Caitlin and nodded. She helped Deirdre to the nearest chair and then, taking a seat next to her, began to explain the situation.

"There's no easy way to tell you, but your mam has passed away. Apparently she died in her sleep."

"What? Me mam?" Deirdre looked from Caitlin over to Alex, as if she needed him to confirm the statement.

"Aye, she's telling ye the truth. I went to see her last evening and found her in her bed. She's gone to her rest, now. We took the lads over and they'll take care of her and lay her next to yer da. When yer able, can get about, ye can go visit her. The vicar will say the proper words, and that's the best we can do at the moment."

Caitlin watched the woman closely to see how she would respond to this information. Had she known her mother was dead? If so, then why did she send Alex to check on her? She was certain Deirdre was under the influence of an herbal concoction and was unable to think clearly.

"Your ankle will not thank you for trying to use it so early after a sprain. I think you'd better get to bed and we'll see if tomorrow's not better. You had quite a fall and your body needs to recover."

"That room, where I'm resting. There's something in there I don't like. It's haunted I tell ye. Haunted."

Alex looked over to Caitlin. Maybe she should give Deirdre a drink to make her sleep. Obviously the woman was unable to deal with her problems at the moment.

"Come. I'll help you to bed. Millie will soon have a good meal for us. I can guarantee that. Let's get you back on your feet so you can get home. That's always the best place to recuperate." Caitlin led her to Mam's sewing room and the cot, with Alex following closely behind. As Caitlin closed the door, she made an interesting observation, one that Alex, too, had noticed.

"She never asked how her mother died and there was not a sign of a tear."

"Now do you believe me when I say she's a danger to ye? She leaves today, Caitlin." He turned away, unwilling to entertain any comments to the contrary.

Coming back to the kitchen they found Jack still fuming. "So

197

we're just gonna let her stay here in our house even though we both know she's the one that took Caitlin? That's crazy, Alex. Why, she could hurt any of us. Millie, Midge, Da . . . any of us," Jack ranted.

"Jack, we didn't have much choice. Caitlin found her clinging to a ledge beneath the waterfall. Apparently she fell and landed on that ledge, which probably saved her life. Caitlin thinks she's under the influence of some kind of herbal concoction. Some of those herbal medicines can be potent, according to Caitlin. But usually if the person stops drinking it, they'll come to their senses."

"She's never appeared to have much sense to me. And ye say it was that waterfall near the cave where we found Caitlin? That same one?" Jack's memory of that evening was pretty vivid still.

"Aye. I don't know what she was doing there, but I plan to ask her when she's able to answer questions."

Da put in his two shillings worth. "Lads, don't worry so. Jamie and me are watching her every minute. And if we need him, Andrew will give us a hand. He's headed to Edinburgh tomorrow, so let him rest today. The girl is obviously not right in her head. But yer mam would have done just what Caitlin is doing — she'd have seen to her, then as soon as possible she'd have sent her on her way. I think we have to keep her one more night, then tomorrow I'll help ye get her to town to the constable. Tonight me and Jamie will take turns just like we did last night. We don't sleep well anyway, so sitting is not a chore for us old men. So let it rest now lads, let it rest. I don't think she can hurt any of us in her condition."

Alex and Jack never crossed Da unless there was no other way. In this instance, with Caitlin and Da in agreement, the two brothers exchanged a look that spoke of their displeasure at the situation, but also of their understanding that they would have to let it go — at least for the moment.

Da and old Jamie were delighted to be of assistance. Sure, they still worked about with the sheep, but both were aware that their contributions were not what they once were. Sitting outside Deirdre's door through the night again was an easy task, but a vital one, and they were proud to do it.

What had already been a tiring day became an even more tiring evening. Millie and Jack headed to the west wing and Alex and Caitlin to the east wing. If the lodge could talk, its stories would fill a few volumes in Daniel's library. But secrets were safe here and they would remain so.

As the evening wore on and bedtime came about, Da rose and started back to Mam's sewing room. "Jamie, I'll take the first watch, till about 2:00 am, then I'll let ye take over. She'll leave tomorrow and we'll all be glad of that."

"Aye, Daniel. And none too soon to suit me. Never did care for that lass. She's got her own problems, now, but I'll be glad to see her from the rear walking out."

Daniel brought his book and settled in the old stuffed chair in the hallway. He lighted a candle and read. He didn't like to admit it, but reading was becoming quite difficult for him. Maybe he would think about going to Edinburgh with Andrew and seeing that doctor he'd heard about. Andrew had a pair of spectacles that doctor had made for him and he could read everything. A short while later, the book fell sideways, resting on Daniel's knees. It was dog-eared, having been read many times before. He let his eyes rest . . . just for a moment.

Deirdre listened at the door for what seemed like an eternity. She'd not stay in this room another night. There was something in here that frightened her and the sooner she could get away from it, the better. She'd decided to not drink the mixture Caitlin had left by her bed. She figured it was meant to make her sleep — maybe permanently.

Most likely ye'd try to poison me, just like I did ye.

As she put her ear to the door now, a few hours later, she could hear the old man snoring. She quietly peeked out the door and saw he was dead to the world. If she was going to leave, then she needed to do it now. She wrapped herself in a blanket she found in the closet. It would provide a bit of warmth as she worked her way to her hiding place, where she'd be able to have another taste of Nezzie's potion. It would soothe her, and she'd figure out how she was going to finish the job she'd started with that red-haired healer. A sprained ankle would not stop her.

CHAPTER 21

Wabi was glad Owl had decided to stay behind as he knew the great owl would keep watch over his place. Before he left, Wabi had taken great pains to fill his leather pouch with a couple of items that he might need, primarily his rowan twig and some jam Mrs. Favré was sending to Caitlin. Of course he donned his cloak and grabbed his crooked staff. At the very last minute, he remembered to pack the book for Caitlin, the one that told the life of her ancestors that her grandmother, Ci-Cero, had written.

Flying along at the speed of starlight was absolutely the only way to travel. He'd zipped past several universes in just a matter of minutes and the sights and sounds he experienced were exhilarating. Now, he'd brought himself back to this earthly plane and had appeared on the top of the moor near the MacKinnon lodge.

The old wizard pulled his cloak tightly to his body. He'd forgotten how cold it could get in the Highlands. His nose detected pine burning, most probably at the lodge. But for now, he had decided to keep his presence known only to the forest creatures. He'd thought about Ian's comments about sensing darkness, an evil presence about. He did not doubt the lad was correct, but the boy was new at this.

Perhaps it's not as dire a situation as Ian thinks. Either way, I'll look around the area before I go to the lodge.

Following a small path on the far side of the moor, he walked slowly into the forest and was seen only by his feathered and furred friends.

~ * ~

Alex had awakened early, as usual. But something was different. Something missing. What? He lay close to Caitlin, who had turned over for another few moments of warmth before arising. Alex thought for a second and then realized what was wrong.

Coffee. No smell of coffee.

He stood, quickly wrapped himself in his kilt, grabbed a shirt and hurried down the stairs. Da always had the coffee brewing before now. Had Deirdre harmed him? His heart raced and he took a deep breath as he reached the bottom stair and turned toward the hallway where Deirdre slept in Mam's room.

There was Da, slumped in the old chair, his book still in his lap, snoring to high heaven. Relief rushed through Alex and he let out the breath he'd been holding.

He walked over to Da and touched him gently on the shoulder. "Da? Are ye all right then? Da?"

The old man slowly opened his eyes and looked at his son, confusion written on his face. What was Alex doing waking him? He was expecting Jamie. Surely Jamie should have relieved him by now.

"Alex? What are ye doing, lad? Is it time to relieve me? Where's Jamie?"

"No, Da. It's morning already. I guess Jamie slept through the night. Are ye all right?"

"Aye. Aye. But sure am stiff from sleeping in this chair all night. Could do with a little coffee meself. Let's get up and about."

"You go get the coffee brewing. I'll get Jamie. He'll be upset he slept through his shift. Better get coffee ready for him, too, I expect."

Alex found his way to Jamie's room. He knocked lightly and let himself in. Jamie was a bit older than Da and a cousin, but Alex never had understood the proper connection. He'd lived here most of his life, having lost his wife, Margaret, early on. After her death he moved into the lodge and they treated him the same as they did Uncle Andrew.

"Jamie. It's morning. Time to rise. Da's got coffee going."

Alex walked a little closer. The old gentleman was lying across the bed, still dressed, with his boots on.

Why in the world would he sleep in his clothes and boots?

Alex squatted next to the bed and put a hand on the old man's arm. Cold. He was cold. Then, knowing it was unnecessary, he felt for a pulse. The old fella was gone.

Oh, Jesus.

Alex thought for a second before he stood again. Had Deirdre caused this, too? Did she come in here and strangle him as she had her mother? If Jamie had any ailments, he'd kept them to himself. But then, that was the MacKinnon way, wasn't it?

Think Alex. Think. That's what yer good at.

Before he even went to tell Da, he hurried to get Caitlin. She'd know more what she was looking at than he would. Passing Ian in the hallway, he called out to his youngest brother.

"Go on down, Ian. I'll be there shortly."

He found Caitlin still under the covers, but awake. "Caitlin, hurry lass. Jamie's died during the night. I need ye to take a look at him."

"What? Jamie? No, he can't be dead! He was fine last night."

203

She pulled her dressing gown on and followed Alex to Jamie's room. Her first thought was the same as Alex's. Had Deirdre done this?

Why Jamie? He was such a gentle soul. My spirit recognized him even when I didn't. But this is no time for tears and reflections. I need to try to figure this out.

"Alex, we need to look at his neck. See if it has marks like Mrs. Taggart."

Alex carefully turned Jamie's body over and they both looked. No prints anywhere. Caitlin made a head-to-toe assessment and could find nothing to indicate any violence. There were no bruises anywhere, no scratches and certainly no finger marks on his neck.

"I think he may have truly just died in his sleep. He mentioned to me recently he had a little heartburn now and then, but I didn't give that too much thought. He never complained of any other physical problem that I was aware of."

"Nae, lass. But if he even told ye he had a 'little heartburn,' then ye can bet it was more than that."

"Then the only thing I think makes sense is that he had heart problems. But we'll never know for sure. Oh, Alex. He was just the kindest old man. This place will not be the same without his quiet presence. For one who spoke so little, he always seemed to say so much."

"Come. We need to tell Da and the others."

She nodded, determined to hold her tears.

They went to the kitchen, which by now had become the gathering place for everyone. Jack and Millie were there, Midge was asleep in the crib, and Da was pouring coffee. Ian sat quietly just listening, sipping his coffee.

"Here ye go, lass." Da handed Caitlin her coffee, prepared just the way she liked it.

"Is Jamie on the way? I'll pour his cup, too."

"Nae, Da. Jamie's not coming this morning. Ye need to sit now. It's bad news we bring I'm afraid." Alex said. He so wished he didn't have to tell Da about Jamie.

"Sit? Why do I need to sit, lad?"

"We don't know what has happened, but Jamie's dead, Da. He's lying on his bed fully dressed. He apparently passed away during the night."

"What? Jamie? Whatever do ye mean? He's never had a sick day in his life."

"Aye, I know Da. But it must have been his time, as Mam would have told ye."

Da slowly sat down in his chair and shook his head. "Jamie, dead? He's been like a brother — just like Andrew. I know we only have a certain number of days on this earth, but I wasn't ready to see him go jest yet, ye ken? Caitlin, what do ye think, lass? What happened to him?"

Caitlin came over and put her arms around Da's shoulder. "Probably his heart, Daniel. But we'll never really know."

There were no words that could ease his pain, but she knew just the touch of another could be comforting. And this role was one she was well suited for.

Da stood slowly and addressed Alex. "When Andrew comes, tell him I'm out for a walk. He'll know where to find me."

Jack had held his patience about as long as he could stand it. When Da took his coffee and walked outside, he finally vented his thoughts. "Alex, are ye sure Deirdre didn't cause Jamie's death? How do we know she didn't? She killed her own mam for God's sake!" His face was about as red as his hair when he got this riled.

"I believe he must have had heart problems, Jack. Deirdre's still asleep, but when she wakes, we'll question her at length." Even as she said them, Caitlin wasn't sure she believed her own words.

"Then I'll take her home myself — today. I don't want her here another second." Jack stormed out the door before he exploded with what he really wanted to say.

They waited another half hour, but when Deirdre still hadn't come out, Millie fixed a breakfast plate and handed it to Caitlin. "Take her a tray, Caitlin. A bit of breakfast and hot cocoa might help."

"Aye, Millie. That'll give her a little energy that she'll surely need today."

She carried the tray gingerly, knocked softly and opened the door. "Good morning, Deirdre." Then she hurriedly put the tray down before she dropped it. The lass was gone. Was she in another room perhaps? She'd complained about Mam's room, but Caitlin had put her in there because it was the warmest room in the house. But now, she was not here.

Hurrying to the kitchen Caitlin caught Alex just as he was about to go out. "She's gone, Alex. Deirdre's gone."

Alex stared at her. "Gone? Where could she be? Her foot would keep her from going far."

Alex thought the morning couldn't get any worse, but he was wrong. Jamie had died, and now a mentally disturbed woman was on the loose. What else could go wrong?

"Ian, lad, do ye think ye can go and get the vicar? Maybe he can help settle Da and Andrew. Talk to them or whatever it is he does. And we'll need the lads to get a coffin ready. We'll need to bury Jamie soon, lad."

"Aye, I'll take care of everything. Ye go on and try to find

Deirdre. But be careful, Alex. There's evil in her. I feel it whenever I'm in the room with her."

Caitlin could think of nothing to ease their worries. "She's not well, Alex. I believe she's drinking a potion that has her mind confused. That doesn't mean she's a killer, though. We just need to find her and keep her confined until we can figure out what's going on with her."

Caitlin always had difficulty believing anyone could be evil through and through, but in this instance, it just might be the case.

Alex was determined to find Deirdre and take her to the local authorities. He wasn't particularly interested in figuring out her "confusion" problems. He just wanted her out of their home and nowhere near Caitlin.

"She needs help, Alex. Maybe you don't think it's a good thing for her to be in our home, but she's not well. Is there no kin left at all? No one to look after her?"

"Nae. Not to my knowledge. She and her mam have been alone for several years now. I know she's a vile person, but even I have trouble thinking she'd kill her own mam. Do ye think this herbal potion could cause her to act that way? To kill another? Why would she drink such a thing?"

"There are herbal drinks that bring a kind of elated feeling, makes one feel as if they can conquer the world . . . or makes them forget their problems. There are folk that like these feelings and will do whatever they can to keep their minds in that place."

"Ye mean like the ones I've read about in the opium dens in the Orient? Herbal remedies can do that too?"

"Herbs are useful in preparing medicines, ointments and potions for drinking. But these same herbs can be mixed with others and may be lethal. Deirdre either knows how to make this potion, or knows someone who does. From her behavior I'd say she's been using it for a while now. It has left her unable to make good decisions, or even rational ones, apparently."

"Then all the more reason to not bring her here. Jack's fears are the same as mine. If I find her, I'm not going to bring her here. I'll take her to the village to the constable's office and let him figure out what to do with her. But no matter the situation or her condition, she's not coming back here."

He strode out of the room, his long legs making short work of the distance to the stable. He'd finish this business with Deirdre and keep his loved ones safe. If that meant destroying the woman, then so be it. He'd do so and not have a moment's regret.

~ * ~

Caitlin paced the bedroom, trying to find a connection between the morning's events. So far, she'd been unable to connect any dots. Had Jamie just died in his sleep? Or did Deirdre play a part in his death? At this minute, the call to visit the circle of stones was screaming louder than ever. Was there an answer in that place that would help her get to the bottom of these questions?

Last evening the nightmare had come again. Why now after not coming for several weeks?

Someone is calling me, or their spirit is. It's such a soft voice. What is it saying? Why can't I understand the words? It's the same sound over and over.

She was positive the circle held answers, even though she didn't know what the questions were. There was definitely something in the circle she was to connect with. Or maybe someone. But if she went there, Alex would be even angrier with her than he already was. He hadn't made any comment yet, but she knew he hadn't liked her taking a ride and coming upon Deirdre at the falls.

She'd not been called on to use her newly found powers since dispensing with Lord Warwick and Commander Campbell, but she felt the time may be soon when she may have to use them again. Uncle Wabi had talked with her at length about her powers when he was here and he had suggested that Ian, too, may possess unusual abilities as well. What would the brothers think about that? Or did they already know? There was much she still didn't know about the MacKinnons.

Do I dare go to the circle again?

Her emotions were in turmoil. She'd always thought it better to follow your head when making decisions. It was her experience that listening to the heart tended to get one into compromising situations.

All right, I'll not go to the circle this morning. I'll tell Alex how strong the urge is. He'll just have to understand that I must act on these feelings sooner or later. And he has to understand that I must make my decisions about the circle — not him.

CHAPTER 22

Wabi wandered far into the woods listening and observing with every sense and learning more about this region. There was such a variety of creatures here that he found himself engrossed in naming each one. In Skye, they had sea creatures such as harbor seals and otters, and his pine trees were full of red squirrels. But here in the Highlands there were other critters that Wabi found interesting, particularly the fowl.

He watched as a golden eagle glided high above him, and out of the corner of his eye he spied two peregrine falcons dipping and diving in an apparent mating ritual. He wasn't exactly sure why he was continuing to go deeper into the woods, but his intuition had yet to fail him, so he'd go until such time as it felt like he should stop. So far, nothing had his scalp tingling or his skin itching.

~ * ~

Mid-morning found Uncle Andrew and Da outside, even though it was chilly still. Da had felt a need to walk about, anything to ease the pain in his heart. Andrew would not leave for Edinburgh as planned. Not today. He and Daniel would see that Jamie was properly buried with family about and the vicar speeding him to his next place. Daniel, Jamie, and Andrew had spent hours discussing the hereafter and still hadn't come to any conclusions that brought them to any greater understanding.

Andrew's Florence had died years ago from an illness they were calling influenza in Edinburgh. He'd done his reading on the subject on one of his trips. Edinburgh was the place to find information on about any subject one could think of.

Then Da had lost his Alice. Of course, her ailment wasn't one that was discussed in public. She had died of a type of cancer — that dreaded word — which had all but eaten away her body. She was as thin as a rail when she finally passed on. Daniel had more than one doctor and several healers look at her, but none of them had any magickal potion to stop the spread of that hideous disease.

She'd been buried on the moor in the burial plot, close to the circle of stones as she'd asked. She'd given him specific instructions to follow regarding her burial as well as his. And he had followed them to the letter. Something he needed to discuss with Alex, too, soon. No one had expected Jamie to be gone so quickly, and Daniel was only a couple of years younger than Jamie.

"Daniel, it grieves me so to know he's gone. But if anyone was ready, it was Jamie. He was at peace in most any situation he found himself. I believe maybe we can count on him to find us a place and have it waiting for us. Not that we need to rush to it just yet, however." Andrew smiled at his brother. They'd both buried wives, and now a cousin who was also a dear friend. But Daniel had been blessed with enough sons for the two of them, and just recently Andrew had found another person who would bring joy to him in his final years. The Creator was merciful.

Alex had started the day headed to the Taggart place thinking the lass would most likely have gone home. Surely she'd want to say farewell to her mam. Maybe that was the best after all, going home that is. Caitlin didn't seem to think the woman was a killer, but Alex would not let his guard down again.

He brought Zeus to a halt, walked along the cobblestone path and knocked on the front door. No answer. So he went around to the rear where he thought he might find Deirdre at the gravesite. But the only thing standing by the newly dug grave was a small white cross. The vicar would have brought that. There was also a small bouquet of wildflowers at the head of the grave — Millie would have sent that. There was no gravestone yet as those were usually put in place later. Perhaps he would send a lad to help Deirdre with that. But he'd never allow her to be in Caitlin's presence.

Where else would he look? There were no relatives and the nearest neighbor was a family with half a dozen children. She might have gone there. In spite of her numerous despicable traits, she always liked children and had hoped to have one herself. Alex remembered that bit of information. That might be the next place to look. Now, however, he'd get back to the lodge and help the others get on with getting Jamie taken care of.

Maybe he and Jack would cover more ground tomorrow after the burial was over. They'd find her all right. Right now he was more concerned about Da and Uncle Andrew and how they were faring. Those three old men had been inseparable. This death would be hard for the two remaining ones.

He took one slow walk about the place but saw nothing to make him think Deirdre had been here. Well, she had to be near, and he would find her. As long as she was out there he feared they may all be in danger.

He mounted and started home. He liked this time of year especially. Winter was losing its grip and spring was just around the corner. Despite the furor of the weddings and kidnapping, Christmas had been a rather quiet affair compared to past celebrations. He had missed everyone gathering around Mam's harpsichord and singing

Christmas carols. Next year. They'd get to that next year. By then perhaps Ian's voice will have found a range that could be counted on.

Alex smiled, thinking about the last time they all sang together. There was such richness with all the voices blending, but Ian's would occasionally squeak and bring all of them to their knees in laughter — because they had all been through the same thing when they were his age.

"That's all right, me lad. Give it time. Ye'll have a voice that will call to the heavens." Mam was in her element when playing that harpsichord and listening to her personal, all-male choir. Da was content to listen and keep the cider poured. He was proud his lads could sing, but he, himself, had a tin ear.

The lads were busy out in the shed putting together a coffin for old Jamie. He would not have wanted anyone to go to a lot of trouble and certainly he would have only wanted his family to gather around. He was a very quiet, unassuming old gentleman, and he would be greatly missed.

Alex found Caitlin in Mam's sewing room, clearing away leftovers from Deirdre. "Millie's made a flower arrangement for the gravesite and I took care of wrapping Jamie in a clean soft shroud. I've done that for others in the past, but as we have discussed before, only now that he's gone do I realize how important he was to all of us. His gentle ways and quiet manner were his trademarks."

She turned away and walked out of the room, not wishing her tears to add to Alex's grief. She'd never had any kin before joining the MacKinnons. Now, feeling this pain, she thought perhaps it was easier when you didn't have anyone to care about. She'd been very young when her grandparents died, and she'd only had Uncle Wabi until now. She found herself wishing he were here. She still missed

214

seeing him every day and discussing her thoughts with him. Of course, she and Alex always discussed their daily events. But with Wabi, she didn't have to leave out the parts about sensing something, or being aware of something unseen. She often left out those thoughts when she talked with Alex for fear he wouldn't be comfortable with that part of her.

CHAPTER 23

Nezzie hadn't been this excited in years — decades, actually. She'd been around for eons and through use of her dark powers would be able to continue existing even longer. This time around though she would finally settle an account from another lifetime. In fact, she'd been trying to bring this issue to a close for ever so long.

Deirdre was exactly what she had been looking for — a young woman with a reason to come to her for help. She'd tried to use several other women in the past, but invariably they were never able to bring her plots together. It would take years for her to lay her plans only to have them disappear in a second when the women would no longer participate and play their role.

But this one, this girl, she had been wounded by the Highlander, Alex.

And a wounded animal is a dangerous one. One that can be manipulated easily.

This time Nezzie had no doubt she had worked out every detail and she'd succeed at last. Not only was Deirdre wounded, but whatever life had dished out to her had left her bitter, resentful and vengeful. She would relish playing a part in Nezzie's spiteful scheme. Of course, she'd not know the extent of her participation until it was too late to turn back.

217

Yes, you're just perfect for this adventure. I've waited for the right person and the right moment. Just thinking about the pleasure I'll get, just watching his face, is more than enough to continue to be patient with you, my dear. And together we'll make my little plan work.

True, Deirdre had not quite been able to bring the woman to her yet, but with a little more help from Nezzie the fiery-haired one would be in her hands and Deirdre would have her Highland prize. And Nezzie would return all the gifts *he* had bestowed on her so many years ago. Gifts that had lasted several lifetimes now. Gifts that even her dark powers could not rid her of. Only *he* could do that.

Nezzie had instructed Deirdre to bring Caitlin to the cave and she would take over from there. But the healer had managed to get away with the help of the Highlander and his brothers.

I only want her. But if I must take care of the brothers, too, then so be it. I'll call in reinforcements if I have to. But this time I will prevail.

The old woman refused to let this plan go awry. She'd waited, and now she would get her revenge on *him*.

~ * ~

Deirdre had found her way to the cave near the waterfall. *What was I doing out on that ledge?*

She had no memory of why she had gone to the falls, and even less of how she landed on the ledge. And what had Caitlin been doing out there? Did she remember this was the place Deirdre had brought her to?

No. She doesn't remember anything. If she did, she wouldn't go to the trouble to help me. No. She doesn't remember.

But just a day of rest in the MacKinnon lodge had allowed Deirdre's confused mind to begin to make a little sense of events. She had gone to Nezzie's hut for more of the potion. Had she drunk all of it herself? It made her feel better and she loved that feeling of being on top of the world and knowing she would be able to make Alex MacKinnon desire her. Just a small sip of the potion and he would be hers. But something else was on her mind.

Mam? Did he say Mam was dead? She was alive when I left her. Was that yesterday? No. That can't be right. I'll get my potion from Nezzie then go home and see about her. Alex is just telling me that to get back at me. He knows. He's smarter than the others. He would like me to think that just to get even.

She continued into the cave where she would wait until twilight when the vengeful old woman would come by.

~ * ~

Nezzie had waited until dusk to start her trek to the cave. It's wasn't so far, but she waited until the darkness would hide her. She expected Deirdre to keep her end of the bargain. She was to bring Caitlin to the cave and Nezzie would have her potion ready and, if need be, she'd help her get the Highlander to drink it. But it was evening already and the girl wasn't here. Why hadn't Deirdre brought Caitlin to her?

Then, just as she thought the girl was not coming, she heard movement at the front of the cave. She herself had entered from a rear opening and walked the crumbling path to the front.

"Ah, Deirdre. I was about to give up on you. Is she coming? The flame-haired one?"

"Nezzie, there's been a little difficulty, just a minor problem. I'm truly in need of the potion, ye ken? I'm afraid it's almost gone already. But I know Alex will be coming for me, any moment now. He's looking for me, ye ken? Then, once I get him, Caitlin's bound to come looking for him too. Then ye can have her for yerself."

"Oh, I see. You think a little more potion is what you need? Are you sure he's looking for you?"

"Oh, yes. He'll come for me. Just now, though, if I could have just a wee taste of your potion I'd feel ever so much better."

Handing over a small vial, Nezzie smiled as she watched Deirdre toss the liquid down, shivering as it ran down her throat.

Yes, you're in my power now and soon my mission will be accomplished.

CHAPTER 24

The day started out with a dreary drizzle that finally stopped midmorning, leaving a layer of fog over the moor and farm. Jamie was laid to rest next to his Margaret, who had been buried here when she had passed away years ago. The four brothers carried his coffin from the pony cart and gently placed it in the recently dug grave. Then they joined Da, Uncle Andrew, Caitlin and Millie to stand next to the site. All the farmhands were there as well.

Willie and Henson had found their way inside the circle of stones and lay atop the small one in the center. Caitlin was the only one to see that both were bathed in a ray of golden light — just for a second — and then it was gone. Even they understood the family had lost a loved one. Caitlin felt the familiar tug once again, but she knew this was not the time to enter the circle. She would come again, later.

The vicar read a short scripture and sprinkled holy water on Jamie's coffin, then offered a final prayer for his soul. The lads had agreed to complete the burial process and Millie handed them the floral arrangement to lay on the grave once they finished. The small group slowly walked to the lodge together — a family with a dear one missing now.

Entering the lodge and making their way to the kitchen, Daniel and Andrew had coffee laced with a wee dram. They had lived long enough to know time would offer a small reprieve from grief, but only when it was ready. Daniel went to his room and Andrew decided to ready himself for his trip to Edinburgh. Millie put Midge in her crib and began to prepare supper for the lot. She would prepare a dish that would stick to their bones in the damp chill that still hung around the lodge.

Jack and Alex gathered by the fireplace, ostensibly planning strategy for finding Deirdre. They didn't have to compare notes and thoughts; they were in agreement that she was the culprit. Early tomorrow they would get underway and take steps to insure she would not be around to hurt anyone else.

This day was set aside for observing Jamie's contributions to their lives, a tradition that Mam had instituted. Rather than going around brooding and grieving over the death of a loved one or neighbor, Mam thought it much better to recall fond memories of them and share them with each other.

"As long as they are alive in your memory, they're never gone from you."

Mam had said that so often they all believed it was gospel.

~ * ~

Early next morning, everyone tried to begin the day with purpose. Millie worked on her plans for the school, Uncle Andrew started out for Edinburgh again, and Caitlin decided she'd start an inventory of herbs she would need for making tinctures and ointments for her clinic. She would not abandon this idea. She just needed to work harder on Alex to get his agreement. Alex and Jack left in search of Deirdre again.

"You go to the Taggart place, Jack. Deirdre may well have gone to pay her respects to her mam. Caitlin still thinks the lass is under the influence of an herb or potion. But I personally think she's capable of just about anything. I've witnessed firsthand how she treated her mam over the years."

"Aye, I feel the same way. The girl never was very bright, but still, that's no excuse for treating her mam with disrespect. Our own mam would have pinned her ears, I can tell ye that much."

"Aye, and then some. I'll go to the cave and see if I can find anything there that might help us locate her. We'll meet at the lodge at nightfall. See where we go from there. If either of us finds her, let's agree to take her to the constable in the village. Let him figure out what to do with the idiot woman."

"Agreed. Then I'll see ye this evening at home. And Alex, be careful, brother. She still carries a torch for ye, and that's a fact. Ye know, a 'woman scorned' and all that stuff."

"Well, this is the last time I plan on having to deal with her again. If I have to take care of her myself, take her to an asylum or whatever, I'll do it. She's not going to come within an inch of Caitlin again . . . ever."

They departed, each going his own way. Alex had thought long about where to find Deirdre and decided she would either be at home or in that cave, so he was not surprised when he saw a soft light coming from the cave entrance. He entered quietly, listening and watching before heading on back. He could smell her, and even though it was a floral smell, he associated it with disgust.

"Alex? Is that you? I knew you would come for me. I knew you would." Deirdre sat on the floor smiling at him as he came closer.

Alex stopped, all the while fighting a great urge to strike this woman. Or even something more drastic. He actually wanted to kill her. Unable to control his anger any longer, he reached out and jerked her to her feet, causing her to spill her tea and to gasp at his rough handling.

"Alex, what's wrong?"

Coming to grips with his anger, he knew he must try to deal with her and get her to the constable. He released her and she sat back down on the floor, then proceeded to pour another cup of tea for herself and one for him. It was as if she failed to see the desperate situation she was in.

"Yes, Deirdre. I'm here. We need to get ye home. Let's go now, lass."

"Come, Alex. Let's have a cup of tea together first. Then I'll go with ye. I need ye to take me to check on me mam. She's poorly, ye ken?"

Alex stood looking at the woman. How had the lass become so unhinged, become so hideous?

"Here, just a quick sip of tea. Then we'll go." She patted the blanket beside her, indicating he was to sit there, close to her.

Taking the cup, he sat down next to her and sipped the warm tea. It felt good. It had become darn cold outside and this warmed his insides. Then he took a long swallow of the tasty liquid and turned to her. "Why did you leave? Caitlin was trying to take care of ye. She's quite a skilled healer and… she…sh…"

He slumped over, his tea spilling across the blanket.

Deirdre smiled and called out. "Nezzie! Nezzie, he's sleeping now. Help me."

Nezzie came hobbling into the room as quickly as her old legs would allow. "Good. That's good. Now that woman, that healer, will come looking for him. We've caught them now, my lass. Ye stay here now and wait for her. There are a few things I need to do before she gets here. Just stay here with the Highlander."

~ * ~

On the morning following Jamie's burial, Ian disappeared without a word to anyone as to where he was headed. He had hoped Uncle Wabi would have made an appearance by now, but so far he hadn't. After saddling Merlin, he threw a double-sided saddlebag on his back. He often packed the bags with his books and a few snacks when he went out riding. Now he started off, surprised to see Henson trotting behind him.

"Whoa, now, Merlin. If that cat wants to come that badly, then we'll take him with us."

He dismounted and plucked his new friend from the ground, cradling him under his arm.

"Come on. Ye'll tire yourself out trying to follow Merlin. He likes nothing better than to fly like the wind, and if I'm no careful, he'll tear off like a *bean nighe's* (banshee) after him. Here, settle yerself in this saddlebag. Ye'll like it once ye get used to it. Traveling *with* Merlin is a lot better than running beside him."

He gently placed the big cat in one side of the bag and remounted, not really sure where he was going. But he had to get away for just a short while. Seeing old Jamie being lowered into the ground brought memories of watching them lay Mam to rest. Ian thought he would rather they put him in with her, so great was his feeling of loss. But he had already learned she was still with him, every day, and some days he thought he could smell her rose scent riding the wind.

Henson settled quickly and off they went. In a short while they arrived at the old kirk where he always went when he was trying to figure out a problem. He dismounted, handed his friend down and walked around the old grounds, seeing bits and pieces of stones that must have been statues or urns.

Walking farther into the old ruins, he came again to the area

225

where he had played in his youth. Once again, he saw the little collection of wooden, toy soldiers that Da had carved, still lying there just as he had left them.

His feline friend was clawing at a small dug-out indentation next to the wall of the kirk. Ian reached out and untangling Henson's claws from a piece of fabric, saw it was a small burlap bag tied at the top. He sat cross-legged and opened the bag, emptying the contents into his hand. There were a dozen or more shards of colored rocks and several smooth stones. He had totally forgotten about those items, but now remembered he had collected them long ago. One stone in particular caught his attention. It was a small stone, about the size of a robin's egg. It was a deep amber color, almost totally translucent. Deep inside it he could see small flecks of green. If you held it to the light, the green specks sent out sparks of light as if the sun had been trapped inside. There was something about that amber colored crystal. What was it? A memory so old . . . he couldn't bring it to mind, but he knew it was an important memory. Not dwelling on it, he tucked it into his pocket, replaced the burlap bag, and lined the soldiers along the wall as he had always done.

Then he listened for a moment. A noise? But what? From where? There was no one else here, and these barely standing walls were all that was left of the old kirk. He walked behind the wall and listened again. Then, realizing he had never ventured farther back where the rear wall was covered with brush, Ian made his way through the thick tangle of vines and dead trees that were piled high. As he was becoming another one of those tall MacKinnon lads, he had to bend over just to get close to the wall. His nose caught a whiff of an odor that he recognized immediately — sulphur.

But there was no sulphur water here at the kirk. The only sulphur he knew about was located at the cave near where his brothers had played when they were children—at the waterfall where Caitlin had found Deirdre. Carefully inching his body, using the wall as a reference point, he continued to move deep within the brush, until he couldn't see. The brush had been growing here for years and it totally eclipsed any light from above.

Ian touched the wall, feeling the roughness of the stone of the old kirk. Then, just as he decided he would go back, his fingers felt a smoothness, a change in the texture of the stone. This area was not rough like the rest of the wall. The smooth area was about the size of a small book and Ian ran his fingers along all the edges, which were rounded on the corners. In a moment of insight, he pushed gently on the stone. At first nothing happened, but when he pushed again the smooth stone fell inward, dropping away from his hand. Before Ian could think what to do next, his companion cat made a flying leap and dashed through the opening in the wall.

"Wait, Henson. Wait."

The agile critter moved on as if he hadn't heard a word.

Ian reached inside and, stroking with his fingertips, felt a small handle on the inside of the opening. Not knowing what might happen, he pulled at the handle and the lower portion of the stone wall slowly opened. It was a doorway of sorts.

But it must have been built for midgets.

He'd read about those small people in one of Mam's books. Even at only fourteen years old, he was almost six feet tall and had to crawl on his knees to get inside.

Holy sheep shite! What is this place?

He hoped Mam wasn't listening, but he sure wished someone else was here with him. It was darker than Hades and he sat quietly and tried to figure out what to do next. Henson rubbed against him, letting him know he wasn't totally alone. Then the large feline started to walk away as if he knew exactly where he was headed.

"No, don't go farther in Henson. We don't know where this leads."

But the cat, in a usual independent feline way, dismissed him and walked on, meowing quietly as if to tell him which way he was going.

Ian crawled a few feet into the area, still not sure if he could stand. It was pitch-black.

If only I could see.

He had produced a lighted torch when they were looking for Caitlin, but he was still hesitant to use his powers unless absolutely necessary. And, actually, he was not sure he could do it again. Then as he looked at his kilt, he saw a dim light coming from his sporran. He reached inside and pulled out the amber stone, which was giving off a very faint glow, enough for him to see a bit. What kind of stone did that? He couldn't recall ever reading anything about a stone that glowed in the dark. But this one did, faint though it was. Once again the remnants of a memory niggled around the edges of his brain — but he still couldn't bring it to the surface.

Even in the dim glow he could see there was a tunnel leading off to the right and Henson had headed that way. He had no idea where this might lead, but he decided to follow his cat. He'd heard they had nine lives, but he wasn't so sure about himself.

~ * ~

Millie's supper was well underway and she was pouring over her papers, the plans she was making for opening a school at the lodge.

"Caitlin? Is that you? Come look at these plans and tell me what you think. Jack's behind me, but he won't discuss much of the details with me."

Caitlin took a seat at the old pine table and nursed her cocoa. It really had been just the thing to take away the chill of another dismal day. The dreary weather had begun yesterday with Jamie's burial.

"At least he's in agreement with you. I can't even get Alex to talk about me starting a clinic yet. And Millie, I'm not feeling like myself. I've got to have purpose to my life again. These Highlands are so full of folk in need of care. There could be twenty of me and that wouldn't be enough. But I could help a few of them. If only Alex would listen to me. I know what I'm doing."

"Aye. He's just so afraid for you. Jack says he's never seen Alex so agitated as now. Perhaps when all this confusion with Deirdre is finally over he'll come around. Don't despair, we'll work on him together. There's no doubt in my mind he wants you to continue your healing practice. And if I know these MacKinnons, they will draw this chapter to a close today."

"But you know, we both need to concentrate on getting the lads to help us with the hut, the larger one over on the east side of the property. That's the one Uncle Andrew has decided to make home for himself and his lady friend."

"Really? Have you ever seen an old gentleman so excited? You'd think he's a young lad again. You've got to respect that he's living life to the fullest. Maybe we should all try to do the same."

Caitlin was looking forward to seeing the old bard again and they all were anxious to lay their eyes on his new woman. That would be three women now at this sheep farm. For just a second, she wondered what Jack was thinking about another change at the lodge. He did so dislike change.

"I wonder what Mam would say if she could see us all now?" Caitlin looked around the room.

The two women dissolved into laughter and looked at the

229

plans once again.

Just before the sun had totally left the sky, Caitlin draped her wrap around her shoulders and walked to the top of the moor. The circle of stones had called yesterday at Jamie's funeral, but that was an inappropriate time. But now, when everyone else was occupied with their own tasks, she decided to answer this beckoning call.

She looked around the burial plot and after a small prayer, entered the henge. The warm feeling descended upon her immediately and she relished it. Sanctuary . . . safety . . . peace. The golden glow enveloped her and then, just as she was about to leave the place, she heard the sound again, the same sound. A child. Yes, now she was sure . . . a child crying. And then there was total silence, and the glow was gone.

She walked away with a new determination. There was something she would do before she came here again. She understood it was important, but didn't understand why. She returned to the lodge still hearing that small little voice, crying out to her.

~ * ~

As it got later and later, Caitlin's nerves were getting shorter and shorter. Why hadn't Alex come home yet? Jack had returned an hour ago, just as the sun was setting.

"Why isn't he back yet, Jack? Were you not together?"

"Nae, we went in different directions and agreed to meet here this evening. We had thought to turn Deirdre over to the constable if we found her. Then we were to come here. Don't worry so, give him a little more time. If he's not here shortly Ian and I will go looking for him. Where is Ian, anyway?"

"I thought he went with you two." Millie had watched the lad leave shortly after Jack and Alex. She just assumed he would be catching up with them.

"Nae. He didn't go with us. Maybe he's upstairs in his lair. He spends more time there or in the library than anywhere else. I'll go check."

A minute later Jack returned, shaking his head.

"He's not here. That lad just tears off anymore without telling anyone where he's going. At his age I wouldn't even dream of not telling Mam where I was going. She would have strung me up by my ears if I had."

"Aye, Jack. I just know you were an absolute angel at that age." Millie smiled at him and went on about her cooking.

"I'll wait one more hour. If Alex and Ian aren't here by then, Da and I will go out and look for them."

Caitlin paced the room. This life in the Highlands certainly was proving to be more exciting than her previous one. But no matter what happened, she'd take this life any day over that one. Alex MacKinnon made her heart sing and she'd stay with him.

When the hour passed with still no sign of Alex or Ian, Jack and Da left to search for them. Shortly after the two men left, Caitlin felt her scalp burning — sizzling, in fact.

Alex is in trouble! She knew it.

Without thinking, she took flight out the door and was on Soldier's back before she thought about any consequences. But this time she remembered to take Willie with her. She didn't know which way Jack and Daniel had gone, but she knew Willie would have a better idea of which path to take than anyone else.

"Willie, come boy. Let's find Alex."

The wolf was halfway down the path before her steed could even head in the right direction. With her skirt catching in the wind, she wished she had thought to put Ian's short trousers and shirt on. Riding in that outfit was a lot more logical than fighting these skirts that kept billowing about every second. When she reached the edge of the woods, she pulled on the reins and came to a stop. She closed her eyes, cleared her mind, found her center, and sent out a call to Uncle Wabi.

"Hear me, Wabi. I need you. Hear me."

She wasn't sure her newly found powers would assert themselves and the wizard would hear her, but she had to try to reach him. Then she dashed off again, hoping Willie knew where he was headed.

Willie traveled so fast he outran Soldier. The great wolf kept returning to horse and rider making sure they were following him. As they got closer, Caitlin knew where they were headed. The cave. She dismounted and looked around, then walked to the entrance, still hidden behind the tall bushes. Just before she entered, she felt a quivery vibration in the air — a feeling she couldn't quite understand — a presence.

What? What is it?

She closed her eyes as she had learned early on that she could often "see" better with her eyes closed. Then a warmth that could only come from one place enveloped her.

Wabi. You're here. Thanks be to the Creator.

She opened her eyes and there stood her dear old uncle, smiling as always. She embraced him and he stared at her strangely.

Oh! A vibration I've never felt from her before . . . but of course!

"Yes, dear girl. I do believe I'm just in time. Now, tell me what's going on. We need to proceed with caution. I don't know what's here, but according to Ian, it is evil indeed."

"Ian? You've seen Ian?"

"No, I haven't seen him. But he's been in touch. He's advancing in his powers so quickly, Caitlin. I need to guide him before he gets into trouble. He has powers he's not even aware of yet. But that's for another day."

While walking through the woods, Wabi had determined for himself that Ian was right. There was some dark power somewhere close by.

"We've got to find Alex, Wabi. He's missing."

"Right. We will, my girl, we will."

As she stood at the entrance to the cave, Caitlin knew Alex was there — his fresh, evergreen scent lingered and her heart skipped a beat. She wanted to rush in, but Wabi held her.

"Wait, Caitlin. Let's use all our senses before we charge in."

Walking slowly, listening, smelling and employing all their senses, the two called ones moved forward. Even before they got through the entrance, Wabi and Caitlin felt the darkness, and Willie stood erect, his great head lifting to the air. His deep growl sent out a resonating sound and vibration that could be heard and felt throughout the cave. Wabi had not expected to sense such malevolence. Who had this much power? The old wizard would be called on to use every ounce of his power and, most likely, Caitlin would have to use hers, too.

This foe is very powerful and will require my focused attention.

"Caitlin, wait here and keep close to Willie. I must place a layer of protection just outside this entrance. We need to put a strong barrier between the opening and the exterior. Hopefully we can keep the evil contained within the cave. I'll place the barrier and then we'll proceed."

The great wolf was agitated, trying to follow Caitlin's command to stay. Finally he had no choice but to follow his native instincts. He rushed to the rear of the cave where he found Deirdre. He snarled at the woman, revealing large, sharp teeth itching to make their mark. His growl got louder and louder as he backed the woman into a corner, waiting for a signal from Caitlin to attack.

At the cave entrance Wabi laid down a barrier, but while doing so his keen senses received information that was alarming, and he stood still, allowing himself to process what his senses were telling him.

No. It's not possible. Not possible. The old wizard needed to re-evaluate this situation.

He returned to Caitlin and they hurried farther into the cave, where they came upon Deirdre stumbling around the room crying, uttering unintelligible words and making no sense. She seemed unaware that Willie was in attack mode and she was his intended victim. Alex was lying on the floor, draped with a blanket.

Caitlin cried out and fell to her knees next to the Highlander.

"I'm keeping him warm. He's tired, ye ken?" Deirdre said. The woman was so addled she still paid no attention to the wolf who so wanted to be released on her.

~ * ~

Before Caitlin and Wabi arrived, Nezzie had disappeared out the front of the cave, completed her preparations and had now returned. Her plan was working perfectly and she'd finally give that old wizard his due. Now that it was dark, she could move about more quickly. But the instant she got close to the cave, she gasped.

No. It can't be. I sense a great amount of power, which means he's near already. I feel him. But even he doesn't have that much power. But who does? Who else has that kind of power?

Nezzie hadn't counted on battling more than Wabi. She knew her dark power was very strong, but now she realized the old wizard was not alone. She darted into the forest and made her way far into the woods, knowing she must enter the cave from the other

234

end, from the door she usually used — the small one at the old kirk.

~ * ~

Time seemed to stand still and it took Nezzie a while to get to the small opening. Finally, she entered the cave from the kirk and made her way through the winding tunnel. Even though Caitlin and Willie were far at the other end of the cave, Willie was aware of Nezzie's presence before she even got close to them.

Should he stay locked on Deirdre? Should he attack the latest threat whose presence he sensed? Deirdre was easy to deal with.

But this latest enemy, this one needed his attention, now. She positively reeked of evil. He ran farther into the cave and when Nezzie appeared Willie was ready for her. He leapt into the air, his fangs exposed, reaching for her throat.

Nezerra was ready for him too, however, and as she flicked her hands a handful of black dust filled the air around him. He fell to the floor, unable to move. He was aware, but paralyzed. He could only watch as Nezzie crept up behind his master, who was trying to lift Alex's head. The great protector saw Caitlin was about to be prey for the old witch, but was helpless to change the situation.

Nezerra slithered up behind Caitlin. *This is the moment I can get her. She's distracted. I can get her before the wizard gets here.* She placed her hands on Caitlin's temples, squeezing tightly.

Caitlin immediately recognized the woman by her scent. "Nezzie?" She felt the blackness as it flowed through Nezzie's hands. "No. I'll not let you … no . . ." Caitlin slowly slid to the floor, reaching for Alex.

Nezzie smiled, pleased to see her long ago laid scheme was working. "I need you, my girl. You're the key to my plan. You belong to me now, and you'll only awaken when I want you to."

Suddenly Nezzie's skin began to crawl.

235

He's here in the cave. I feel him.

She hadn't expected him to be here so quickly. She thought briefly about pulling Caitlin's body, trying to hide it before the old shaman saw it. But she frowned at this idea, realizing he would feel her presence anyway.

She closed her eyes and for the briefest of moments, she remembered with clarity the time they had shared. He was so attentive to her needs and she adored him. He was handsome and talented, and she young and beautiful. She doted on him, caring for him in a most loving way. During this time she also used her healing skills and cared for others in their area. But somewhere along the way she began to resent his spending time with others, primarily two young girls to whom he was passing on the art of making pottery. Ultimately, she caused such a scene and became so possessive of him that he banned her from his cave and she was left alone.

Finally, later on, she had tried to destroy another one of his young trainees, a young lass named Ci-Cero. This young girl was even more special to him than all his other trainees had been. She had been Caitlin's grandmother, which was why Nezerra found such pleasure in her current plan—to harm Ci-Cero's granddaughter would be such sweet revenge.

When Wabi discovered Nezerra was responsible for Ci-Cero's close call with death, he had stopped short of killing her and instead placed a curse on her that left her disfigured and hideous. He knew that would be more painful to Nezerra than death. She had so enjoyed being a beautiful woman, and now no one could bear to look upon her.

Nezerra had questioned why things had gone so wrong and regretted her actions more times than she could remember. She'd tried so many times to apologize to him, but he refused to even talk with her. The pain of that rejection and humiliation had grown over the years. As often occurs, rejection, pain and humiliation lead some to seek vengeance, as was the case with Nezerra. There had been many failed attempts, and even her use of dark magick had never brought about her desire to make Wabi pay for the curse he had bestowed on her.

That was eons ago now. She had not forgotten that he was a great wizard, but she had grown in her powers and felt sure she would complete her carefully laid out scenario. But things were not going exactly as she had planned. As her mind swirled about trying to come up with a solution to this latest hitch — him being here already — she could feel doubt beginning to enter her mind. Before that thought could even be completed, she sensed his presence and turned to face him.

"Hello Wabi . . . dearest."

"Nezerra. Still as hideous as I remember you, maybe even more so."

Wabi was stunned to see his old enemy. He knew she should have died a century ago. Still alive due to dark power, no doubt.

She's more desperate than she ever was, and even more dangerous.

Forgiveness for her treatment of Ci-Cero was not a thought he had ever entertained — nor ever would.

He saw Caitlin on the floor and could tell Alex was unconscious. Willie was lying immobile, his eyes riveted on the wizard but unable to move. Deirdre was stumbling around mumbling to herself, uttering incoherently. There was a lot going on, and Wabi wondered if he could take care of it by himself.

"You're responsible for my hideous looks, if you recall, and you can make me beautiful again, also. We both know that. That's all I want, Wabi. I just want you to remove the curse you bestowed on me in the former life we shared. If you will do that — and I know it's an easy task for such a powerful wizard as yourself — then I'll not let your precious niece die. Just as with your curse on me, only I can remove this one from her. And her dear husband? Well, let's just say he may expire any moment now if I don't administer an antidote for his potion — or perhaps I should say— poison. It's your choice, Wabi."

"Your power has grown considerably Nezerra, that's obvious. But it's still dark power and that will never be enough to overcome power bestowed by the Creator — His power. Surely even you know that."

"That's up for debate, Wabi. You're still around, but then so am I. And I have friends, just waiting in the hallway. In fact, I believe I hear them even as we speak."

The hum grew louder and louder and the cave was filled with a deafening screech as thousands of bats winged their way into the tunnel with the never-ending flapping of their wings. Then, as if obeying an unseen or unheard signal, they flocked to Wabi's body and attached themselves at every place where they could plant their tiny feet. The old wizard found himself unable to move for a few seconds.

In that few seconds, however, he heard a scream from Nezerra that had the hair on his neck standing tall.

"NOOOOOOOO! AIEEEEEEEEEEEE! Stop the pain! AIEEEEEEEEEE!"

Nezerra was consumed by more pain than she had ever imagined.

Wabi got his bearings once again and mentally dispatched the bats. They scattered in every direction, anxious to get away from the unbearable fire that came from contact with the old wizard. Their feet were burned to a crisp and, blind though they were, they found their way through the tunnel that led them outside.

Then the old wizard became aware of a seismic shockwave of power flooding the cave. It was unlike any he had ever experienced. It had him staggering to keep his balance. He looked about and there, standing just in the far corner of the cave, he saw Ian, his arms lifted high above his head, his hands crossed at his wrists with palms facing outward. He threw his head back and a hair-raising keening filled the cavern.

The call of the wild and the sign of the cross — the oldest and most powerful tools of all time.

Wabi had heard keening and seen the sign of the cross before, but this was the first time he had ever witnessed a deep, amber light shining from the palm of a wizard. Ian apparently had his own personal talisman. Wabi watched as the amber light glowed and bright green shards of light streamed from the young lad's palms. He should have prepared the lad more, but even he was not expecting this exhibition of power so soon. The boy was not ready yet. But ready or not, he was here and they were in a situation that required intervention from someone who had great power.

Oh, dear heavens. That lad has not had enough training to control his power yet. He could well kill us all in the blink of an eye. May the Creator be with us.

He bowed his head briefly and hoped his prayer was received. It was far too late to prevent the event that was transpiring in front of him. As for Nezerra, her soul had long ago been destroyed by evil and now, after Ian released the amber and green shards, his flood of power entering her body, what was left of her lay in shreds on the cave floor.

Relieved that only Nezerra had been destroyed, Wabi sent up a quick prayer of thanks. *The lad is new to this life, but what a powerful shaman he is already. The Creator has chosen well again.*

Wabi nodded quickly to Ian and they both headed to Caitlin, still lying unresponsive on the floor. Wabi realized he would have to go to extraordinary measures to bring her from the abyss where she resided at the moment. Nezerra was correct. It was almost impossible to remove a curse another wizard had placed on one.

"Ian, my lad. We'll have to do this together. Come place your hands on Caitlin's temples. I'll call on all the spirits I can, and if you have access to any, please call on them as well."

Ian carefully placed his fingers on Caitlin's temples, next to Wabi's. He could feel her pulse, faint but present. He'd not known Caitlin was here. Nor had he known that Wabi and Nezerra were here. He'd just found the entrance leading from the old kirk, followed his feline friend and traveled the path into the cave. He knew studying with Wabi would strengthen his abilities and he wouldn't always be working in the dark, with some things coming through and others not. But he had certainly played his part in keeping Nezerra's plans from working. He may have come through without Wabi's help, but he was glad his mentor had been here.

Wabi put all his effort into bringing his powers to Caitlin's aide. He summoned all help he could possibly tap into and those spirits that hovered nearby. But in her last moments of consciousness his niece had apparently used her own powers. He could not reach her no matter how hard he tried. She was certainly in trouble, and even with Ian's help she still slept the sleep of the dead.

It was obvious to Wabi he needed even more help, but where would he find it? The wizard knew that in her present state they would have to be extraordinarily careful with her.

"Ian, we need more help. Caitlin has blocked herself off from receiving us. She must have sensed Nezzie's presence before the old hag got to her, or immediately after. She took a wise precaution — blocking. When a called one blocks, it means no other power can enter their mind. It's used as a defensive measure when nothing else can be done. But it also means I can't get through to her either. We must have more help. This deep sleep is a natural reaction following exposure to a spell such as this one. She'll not die, but unless we can reach her, she'll stay in this state of limbo for an eternity. We must hurry now."

Ian looked at the old man. If this old wizard couldn't perform this miracle, what in the world were they going to do? His own powers were growing, but he was fearful now.

Think, Ian. Alex would tell ye to think.

"Wabi, we've got to get them, Caitlin and Alex, to the circle of stones. There's more power there than any place I know of. I've been in the circle and there were so many spirits at work I didn't want to leave it. They'll come to our aide. I know they will."

"My boy, you've got more than just power. You've got a mighty fine brain, too. Yes. The circle of stones."

"And Wabi, we've got to bring Willie, too. He'll die if we don't."

Ian had no doubt Caitlin would never forgive them if they didn't bring Willie within the circle also. He himself was just learning about the importance of a personal animal friend, and in Caitlin's case, a protector as well.

"Hold on, Ian. We may be able to help him here, now."

The wizard got on his knees and carefully took Willie's head into his hands. The wolf looked at him, recognition evident in his face. But he was still paralyzed and couldn't move a muscle.

"Look, Ian. See these black dust particles on his muzzle? That's the remains of a paralytic powder Nezerra used on him. It most often is short-lived. And Willie's a strong wolf. He has special abilities, also. If we call to him, he'll hear us. Come, let's work on him together a second."

They used the same procedure for Willie that they had tried on Caitlin. Ian put his hands on the great protector's head and Wabi lifted his, calling on assistance and chanting in his language. A quick dash of color raced into the cave. Ian was surprised to see it was Henson. The large feline came quickly over to them and proceeded to lay his own paws on Willie's body, next to Ian's.

"Ah, just so. Of course you would feel him. We welcome your touch too, Henson."

Wabi was not surprised to find the feline had his own special touch. He wondered if Ian yet realized this animal had chosen him to be his master. Wabi lowered his forehead and touched it to Willie's. The wolf could only stare — he couldn't even close his eyes. But these two had known each other in another time and place and Wabi resurrected those memories from this four-legged called one.

Within seconds there was a meeting of minds and the protector groaned from a place deep within. The great head was the first body part to respond as he lifted it higher, then shook it back and forth as if awakening from a nap.

"Ah, yes, my friend. It takes more than a little witch's dust to do you in. Come now, we need your help."

The great wolf licked Wabi's hand and was on all fours. Once he got his feet planted and could stand, he threw his great head back and released a howl that set Wabi's ears on edge.

"HOOOOOOWWWWWWWW!"

"I'd say he's back with us, wouldn't you?"

Ian smiled and felt a tremendous amount of relief. He most definitely didn't want Caitlin's wrath turned on him. He'd never witnessed it, but Jack had told him the story of how she "literally melted" Lord Warwick and then "struck down with lightning" the soldier that was after her. Jack probably embellished certainly, thought Ian, but even so, he'd prefer to stay in her good graces.

The wolf's first action was to run over to Deirdre, who was sitting in a stupor in the corner staring out into space. He only stood there a quick moment, then turned away. He sensed she was no longer a threat and he quickly went to Caitlin's side. Then, in a most uncharacteristic manner, he began whimpering.

"Yes, Willie. We know. She's only sleeping, fella. Only sleeping," Wabi whispered.

"Wabi, we only have one horse. We can't get there without help."

Wabi looked at the young shaman, then finally spoke. "I could get us there quickly, but Caitlin is in a very fragile state. For reasons known only to her, she's blocked off all communication. She's protecting herself from more evil I believe. It's the only thing that comes to mind. I'm afraid if I were to take her through a time-weaving trip she might not make it. We've got to get the pony cart for them."

Willie rubbed his nose on the back of Ian's knee.

"Jesus, Wabi. The wolf's got more sense than we have. Yes, Willie. I'll go and get Jack and the cart." Ian ruffed the wolf's neck.

Wabi looked at the young lad again. "That may take a while, for you to ride home. Time is of the essence, lad."

"No, Uncle Wabi. I don't have to ride. I can get there quickly, trust me." And with that he leaned his head to the right, released a low-pitched guttural sound and the air sizzled as he disappeared.

Powerful. Yes. Powerful.

Wabi smiled, as he knew there were days of excitement ahead for him working with this young lad.

Willie took his place next to Caitlin where he would stay until such time as he felt she was safe again. Henson had disappeared with Ian.

~ * ~

Ian and his feline friend appeared on the front porch of the lodge and the boy called out loudly. "Jack, I need you!"

The door opened and Jack stood there staring at the young lad. He and Daniel had returned after several hours searching and had not been able to find Alex and Ian. Their plan now was to get the farm lads, Kenny and Hamish, as well as the MacDonald men, to go out with them. One look at his little brother and he knew there was trouble.

"Holy Mother, where have ye been lad? We've been looking for ye. Where's Alex? What's going on?

"Caitlin and Alex need your help. We've got to get them to the circle of stones, quickly."

"The circle of stones? Why?"

"It's a place where we can get help from others. The spirits that live there can offer assistance we need to bring Caitlin back. As for Alex, I'm hopeful Deirdre's potion was one that wasn't too powerful and maybe its effects will wear off. Then he'll recover on his own. But we should take him too. There may be help for him there also."

"What? Where's Alex? And Caitlin? I thought Caitlin was upstairs sleeping. She never told us she was leaving. Jesus, but that woman can try my nerves." He stomped about the room.

"Aye, but right now we need you to bring the pony cart so we can get the two of them to the circle. Hurry now."

Jack yelled to Ian on his way out the door. "Get Da, Ian. He'll skin us alive if we don't take him with us."

Ian flew up the stairs and told his tale to Da. A short version, certainly. "We've got to get there quickly, Da. They're in real trouble."

"Then I think we need to stop jawing and get moving."

Daniel had taught these lads, these men, how to track, shoot, trap, and take care of each other. He was still useful and could ride better than all of them. He was in the saddle before Jack had the pony cart hooked to the horse. He strapped his pistol to his belt and had his dirk as well. When time was important, his age took a backseat in his mind.

"We'll be back, Millie. You and Caitlin aren't about to be widows this soon. I give ye my word on that. We'll find them . . . both of them."

Millie had gasped when Ian told her their predicament. "Oh, Ian. Be careful. Deirdre is so unbalanced. She's dangerous."

The trip to the cave took more time than they wanted it to, but a cart and horse can only move so fast. Ian was glad Jack hadn't asked him any questions about how he had gotten to the lodge. Obviously a family meeting would need to be held soon, and maybe Uncle Wabi could explain a few situations better than Ian could. Right now, however, they needed to take care of Alex and Caitlin.

CHAPTER 25

After Ian left, Wabi walked over to Deirdre. She had a far away, vacant stare and didn't appear to see him. He lay his hands on her head and sensed the evil residing there.

Such a sad affair. You're so young to be so filled with such hatred and evil.

His heart would not allow him to do away with her. He only permanently disposed of evil that had no chance of redemption. He wasn't sure about this woman yet.

I'll let you sleep for a while until we sort this out. Perhaps there is hope for you yet.

With that, he touched her forehead and whispered a chant that had her eyes closing in sleep.

We'll come for you. You're safe in this cave.

Wabi felt the men coming before he heard them. The tension that was present in their bodies traveled on the wind. Wabi had wrapped Caitlin in his cloak, hoping to keep a little warmth in her body. Her breathing was shallow and her body was cool to his touch. He placed his hands on her shoulders and sent a wave of warmth throughout her body, but it would last only a short while. He did the same for Alex. About this one he wasn't sure what was going on. He appeared to be in a deep sleep, but when he had tried to reach his mind Wabi found a wall there also. He wondered for a second if Caitlin had put a barrier on him as well. She would have only had a moment before Nezzie had taken control.

Da reached the cave before Jack and Ian. His life had changed completely in the last few months. He wished Alice were still with them. She would have loved all the talk around the kitchen table, the women laughing about something the lads had done, and the bairn, little Midge, would have thrilled her.

He was lost in his thoughts for just a moment before he heard the pony cart wheeling its way across the path. He refused to give much thought to Ian and what was going on with him. Some things would just have to wait. First things first. And at this moment, getting Caitlin and Alex to the circle of stones was paramount in his mind.

Bringing the cart to a halt and climbing off, Jack hurried down the path into the cave and memories of his last visit reeled through his mind. Caitlin had almost been killed then, too. And now again?

"Wabi? When did you get here?"

The fact that Wabi was here let Jack know this event was one of importance. The old wizard could come and go, Jack realized that, but he wasn't expecting to see him here in the cave. But he did admit he felt a bit more hopeful that Alex and Caitlin may survive if this old one was here.

"Let's get them into the cart, Jack. We must hurry."

Jack picked Caitlin up effortlessly and placed her on the cart. Next he lifted Alex, which was quite a chore even for Jack. It wasn't that he was so heavy, but he was quite a tall fellow. Jack grunted and was on the cart snapping the reins before Ian and Wabi had even completed their conversation.

"We'll meet you there, Jack."

Wabi called to Willie and Ian reached out and grabbed

Henson. A streak of blinding light illuminated the forest for the briefest second and they were all gone.

Jack never questioned that those two would be there before he would. That was just fine with him. Alex and Caitlin were obviously in a state way beyond his understanding, and he had that horse moving faster than the old boy had ever gone in his life.

~ * ~

"How could she have gotten both of them? Did she trick them?"

Millie found herself speaking aloud. For the first time since coming to the MacKinnon lodge she was alone. The quiet was unnerving. There had been a few days when she had wished for solitude. But now the silence was deafening and she understood how much she needed the noise of everyone coming and going, laughing, yelling about one thing or another. Her early life had been just that — solitude and emptiness. No, she didn't ever want that again. This was home. This rambunctious, loud, loving family was hers now. She lifted Midge and held her close.

"I hate standing here stirring stew while Caitlin and Alex are struggling for their lives."

She could hear the anxiety in her own voice. Millie was only too familiar with the fear that accompanied being in someone else's control. She'd lived with it all her life until the past few months.

She thought about a conversation she and Jack had just yesterday, when she was trying to figure out problems that could arise when she started her school.

"When Mam was worried about a problem she couldn't seem to work out, she'd go to the circle of stones and kneel. She felt there were others who had gone on before and they would hear prayers," Jack had told her.

I don't know much about that, Midge, but if that's where Jack and Ian are taking them it might be good for the two of us to be there and offer our own prayers as well. Don't believe it would hurt, and who knows, maybe it'll help. Beats sitting here literally stewing about the situation.

Little Midge gurgled her consent and after wrapping the bairn in a warm tartan, Millie started out for the circle.

~ * ~

Wabi and Ian appeared on the top of the moor and watched as the sheep stopped their movement and refrained from making their incessant noise. Perhaps they could feel the sizzle in the air that always accompanied these two wizards — the old one and the young one.

Jack lashed out again at the horse and it snorted it's feelings about that. Its coat was gleaming in the moonlight and certainly the animal would be glad to have this trip over with. He wasn't often on the receiving end of a lash. The MacKinnon men only resorted to such behavior when it was absolutely necessary. They had learned as children that most animals respond to kindness rather than the whip.

"Here, Jack. Bring them inside the circle. Lay them side by side."

Jack looked at Wabi, then at Ian. "Are ye sure? According to Mam, only the called ones are to enter the circle. I know ye and Caitlin belong to that ilk. And I'm getting that Ian may also. But Alex? He's not a member of that group that I'm aware of."

"All that you say is true, Jack. But within the circle there will be others who will protect Alex, even though he isn't one of us. Don't be alarmed. The power within this circle would amaze you. In fact, it may amaze us all. At this moment, we need all the help we can get."

Jack worked quickly to bring Caitlin inside the circle and walked toward the stone that lay in the center, with its smooth edges that stood out from all the others. He gently placed Caitlin there and brought Alex next, laying him close to her. Then, not sure what he was to do next, he slowly inched his way back out of the circle. He was fairly certain *he* didn't belong in there. And if he would admit it, he was a little afraid of the place. Mam had always thought it a special place, but he'd just as soon stay out of it.

He stepped farther back and looked around. The moon was ever so bright, and the wind almost non-existent. That was strange. There was always a brisk breeze at the circle. He looked around the area. The gravestones of his ancestors were visible, and over on the right side he saw where they had laid Mam. Just a little farther, Jamie's grave was visible, its floral wreath gleaming white in the moonlight. As far as he could see out on the moor, all was quiet and the silence of the lambs was deafening. Then he uttered the first prayer of the evening.

Ah, Mam, wish ye were here. We're in another bad place. Some of yer woman's intuition would be good right now.

Mam had always managed to remain calm when everyone else might be bustling about trying to make something happen.

Jack continued to stand well outside the circle and watched, feeling totally helpless. Alex and Caitlin might well be dead. Both of them lay perfectly still. Wabi and Ian entered the circle, followed by Willie and Henson. The two wizards joined hands and began to chant. Immediately the wind began to howl, whipping the trees in every direction, and clouds raced across the sky in a kaleidoscope of colors. Jack was surprised to feel his hair rising from his head. He wasn't sure if it was the wind, or if he was just that scared.

He felt a great sense of relief as he looked around and saw Millie and Midge walking up behind him. He took a few steps to meet them, taking Midge from Millie, holding her close. Millie walked over and stood next to Da, who seemed so forlorn standing by himself.

"Daniel, can you tell me anything?"

"Nae, lass. I think all we can do is stand here and watch quietly."

"And send a few prayers of our own," Millie said.

They watched and wondered and worried greatly.

The two wizards now lifted their arms skyward and the chanting grew louder. The sound was certainly more than two people could make. There were so many voices lifted to the wind and, like a giant chorus, there was a musical quality to the sound. The wind began to send small whirlwinds of leaves into the air, and Millie had to tug at her skirt to keep it from flying about.

"Do you understand any of the chanting, Daniel?"

Millie looked at the old man and he shook his head. "Millie, I've never heard such before, lass. But Alice always said this place was sacred, so I'll let that thought stay in me mind at this point."

Alice, mo chridhe, be with us all.

He might be afraid just a bit himself. Those two bodies, so still, just lying on the stones — his son and a new daughter-in-law whom he had come to love already.

The scene was one none of them would ever forget — Wabi and Ian, with arms lifted to the heavens, and hundreds of voices chanting with them. The two now knelt in reverence and lowered their arms and it was quiet—the chanting had stopped. Then, in a hair-raising act of beseechment, Willie's call to his ancestors flooded the sky, echoing from one side of the moor to the other and Henson's primal yowl tore through the path Willie had created.

Movement just above them got everyone's attention. A great

horned owl made a spectacular downward spiraling circle and quietly alighted on Wabi's shoulder.

"Now we're all here. Let us complete this task."

Wabi had spoken. He and Ian joined hands once again and the air began to shimmer, bathing the circle of stones in a golden light. So many spirits had joined in this ritual that Ian was overwhelmed. But, even in this state of total immersion in the moment, he felt *her* spirit as it slowly floated over her firstborn . . . and then over his chosen woman.

Mam. I knew ye would find us. We need ye — Alex and Caitlin need ye.

Ian waited quietly and felt her as she drifted away. He began to rise, but as he did so, he became aware of another spirit hovering over Caitlin's head . . . it wasn't Mam's spirit, but he knew it was filled with a mother's love. He remained kneeling and watched as Wabi acknowledged the spirit.

Ah, Flinn. Your spirit is as healing as Alice's. A mother's love is the greatest power of all.

She too drifted away and the old wizard and the young one both felt the moment when the blackness was lifted and the golden light brought the return of the two beloved family members. It was as though a tremendous weight dissipated into thin air.

"Thanks be to the Creator. He has found us worthy."

Wabi and Ian stood and watched as Alex first raised his head, then slowly got to his knees, looking around. He leaned over to Caitlin and brushed her hair from her face, then carefully lifted her head. She opened her eyes and looked into his face, reaching for him with outstretched arms.

"Alex? Where have you been? I've been looking for you."

The look on the Highlander's face was one she'd always remember.

"*Mo chridhe*, we've got to have a talk

CHAPTER 26

Hector selected a few items from the estate that he knew Millie would wish to keep. She had asked him to bring the small desk from her grandmother's bedroom. She could remember watching her write notes at the desk. She'd move the pen slowly, making sure each letter was perfectly written in her beautiful handwriting. Writing well was a point of pride for her.

He had loaded that piece onto the cart and selected several other items, including a small table that had been made by an old man in the village. This piece had carvings of animals in each corner. Hector thought it was particularly unique and knew Ian would like the carvings of the critters on it. There were several medium-sized paintings, original oils he thought he should bring also. They all were enjoying seeing Mam's paintings in the lodge, and these would fit right in.

Taking a large piece of canvas he draped it over the cart, covering everything well and he set out extremely early, with the crescent moon shining brightly. He planned to go all the way without stopping. If he kept on at a steady pace, he'd be there by nightfall, or maybe a little after, but not much. So off he went, the sky still littered with hundreds of stars blinking above him.

It was a difficult day, indeed, and Hector didn't arrive until well past nightfall. He was hoping Millie would have her usual array of delicious food ready. He'd enjoyed Ethel's cooking, but Millie's artistic ability was showing itself in her cooking. She seasoned her dishes in a way that he personally enjoyed. He supposed she had always had cooks from France, or wherever her father had wanted, and she'd learned now how to replicate those magnificent tastes in her everyday meals. Arriving at the lodge, he knew something was off.

"Hello? Where is everybody?" He called out again as he walked across the yard. "Alex? Jack?"

Normally, one or more of the brothers would have come out to greet him. He could see candlelight in the lodge, but no one came out. He walked inside and without going any farther, he was sure the place was empty.

So then, where is everyone?

He walked out onto the front porch and listened. Nothing at first, then a sound that had his skin crawling and his hair lifting from his scalp.

"HOOOOOOOOOOOOWWWW!"

That sound could only come from one animal — a wolf. But since Willie had come to the lodge they never saw wolves around anymore. And he'd never heard Willie make such a call, certainly not one so filled with anguish.

He left the porch and started to walk in the direction of the howl. The moon was bright and lit the entire area, and it was only a few moments before he saw the small gathering at the top of the moor. His people. He saw Jack, Da and Millie standing together.

Then he saw a scene that halted his movements. The circle of stones was bathed in a golden light that shone across the top of the moor. Inside the circle he saw Wabi and, to his great surprise, Ian, standing with their arms raised high. Then his eyes traveled lower, apparently of their own volition. On the ground, atop the small flat stone in the center, were Alex and Caitlin, lying as still as could be.

"Good God, what is happening?"

He didn't know whether to run to the circle or to stand still and watch. Before he could make the decision, the light faded slowly and he watched in amazement as Alex slowly rose and leaned over to Caitlin, who reached up and put her arms around his neck.

Oh, Mam. What am I supposed to think about this?

Mam often went to the burial plot and the circle and had instructed them to maintain a reverence when there. The circle was a place they all knew wasn't to be desecrated. Hector had never given a lot of thought to the place, but obviously something had just transpired that had his mind reeling.

I believe I'll just go inside and see what kind of explanations are coming forth when they get here.

He made a hasty retreat to the lodge, entering through the back door. Still not sure what he had just witnessed, he poured himself a cup of cider and waited patiently for the others to return.

~ * ~

Before the ensemble from the circle made their way to the lodge, Wabi asked for a moment. His first action following any incident that required him to use his special talents was to give thanks to his Creator.

"Let us be thankful the Creator has found us worthy of his intervention. We are all put here for a special purpose and our duty is to find it. And may we all be thankful for those who came to our side and helped us return these loved ones to our midst."

Wabi was aware Mam had been called on by Jack, Ian, Da and Hector. Was there more to her than they had known? Ah, perhaps he would ponder this thought.

"Uncle Wabi, we need to go to the cave and see about Deirdre. And what about Nezerra? Do we know she's finished?"

Ian had been surprised at how devastating his treatment of Wabi's old enemy had been. He had no idea that the power he sent out would be so deadly. It frightened him as it was happening, and perhaps even more so now. Yes, he needed time with Wabi for sure.

"Deirdre will sleep. She's not in any danger from anyone, certainly not Nezerra. She was just a pawn for that old crone. My connection with Nezerra is a really long story, and I am aware I need to explain it to you all. But let it wait until tomorrow, my lad. Everyone needs to rest tonight. We'll go early, you and I, to take care of Deirdre and clean the mess we left — Nezerra. Rest now, my lad. We've had a very draining evening."

The usual aftermath of exercising powers was already creeping up on the old wizard. Tomorrow he would feel it even more so.

~ * ~

The next morning they all got to the kitchen one by one. Da was first, then Hector, Jack and Millie. Alex came walking in with an arm around Caitlin, who looked a bit under the weather. Probably just the events of the previous day and evening. Da handed her a cup, which he had doctored as usual. Wabi and Ian were the last and they all found a chair at the large table.

Who would ever have thought there would be so many of us?

Da kept his thoughts to himself, but it still struck him as amusing to see these women around, an old man with eccentric abilities, and a small babe in arms.

Wabi was fully expecting the exhaustion that always

accompanied an event that called on him to use his powers. And this event, this saving of Alex and Caitlin, had been the most trying one he could recall. To his amazement, the effect the event had on Ian was just the opposite. The lad was so filled with energy this morning that Wabi shook his head in disbelief. He, himself, had barely found his way to Millie's kitchen where Da was passing out coffee.

"Ian, my boy. This is most unusual you understand — this energy spurt you seem to have. Why, even when I was your age this was tiring. Not as much as today, but still it did take a toll on my energy. We need to look at this carefully. I believe there's something at work here that we don't quite understand, but that will have to wait a day or two. My energies take a few days to replenish themselves. But before I rest, we'll go over to the cave and finish our work."

Ian took a swallow of his coffee — cream but no sugar — and looked at the old wizard, his mentor. *He does look tired. Maybe I should do the cleaning by myself.*

Wabi took a look around the room, reading the same questions in every face. What had happened? What had become of Deirdre? Why had Nezerra wished to harm Caitlin? And where did she fit into the picture?

The old wizard thought for a few moments about how best to explain these events to the group. They all readily accepted that he was different, as was Caitlin. And now they had to know that Ian was special in his own way. So far, no one had questioned Wabi about the happenings of yesterday, but that didn't mean they understood. So, as he usually did, he decided to just tell the truth and let it speak for itself.

"Daniel, you've raised some very fine men here, you and Alice, and I'm so glad Caitlin has found a place where she can use her talents and skills and lead her life in a manner that suits her. She is at home here. The events of the past few days have been trying for all of you, or I should say for all of us. I've faced challenges before, but this one was particularly difficult. Without Ian's help and assistance from others, I'm not sure what might have happened.

"Caitlin, I'll try to explain as best I can. You see, Nezerra, Nezzie, was not truly after you for any offense you may have committed. No, she was using you as a means to get to me. Using others for her wicked deeds has been a trademark of hers for centuries. Nezerra and I knew each other in a time that is long past now. Without trying to explain that, I just ask that you accept my words as true. They are.

"Nezerra was a beautiful, loving woman when we first met. And let's just say we were enthralled with each other and our lives were connected for a period. But as often happens, events occurred that caused us to go our separate ways. Then, shortly after our parting, a young woman came to me for mentoring, a woman even younger than you, Caitlin, but one who was alone with no family. My days were filled teaching her, increasing her knowledge, honing skills and helping her prepare for a destiny written for her in a distant place and time. It was an honor for me, you see, and sanctioned by the Creator.

"After learning of my young apprentice and my close connection to her, Nezerra believed if the girl were gone then I'd wish her to return to my life. Of course, that was not true. The young girl was like a daughter to me, and she has never left my mind or my heart. In fact, we still have a connection this day, through you, Caitlin—she was your grandmother, Ci-Cero.

"My grandmother — the one you said was a woad?"

"Yes, the Woad."

"There are several books in Daniel's library that tells stories about them. They were actually a people called Picts and the Romans called them woads. According to the legends, the Romans built Hadrian's Wall as a place to never go beyond as these very fierce peoples, the Picts, lived beyond that place. The Romans had dubbed them "woads" as before they went into battle, the Picts covered their bodies with paint made from blue dye that comes from the woad plant."

Caitlin watched Alex's face, but saw no reaction. It may be that he was not familiar with the term.

"Yes, but that's another story for another day. Nezerra brought about an event that caused the young girl, Ci-Cero, great physical and emotional damage. It became apparent to me that I had to take care of Nezerra in a way that would prevent her from harming anyone else. So I took great pains to punish her, but did not permanently do away with her. Killing is not a solution usually, and I try to avoid it if possible. It is only a deed that comes when there are no other possibilities and no other way to conquer the evil. I dealt with her, arranged for her to depart from the area, from my presence, and find her own kind elsewhere. Since then I have never come across her. In fact, my thoughts were that she had disappeared from this plane, this period, and had met her final end.

"But when I received the call from Ian —not from you — I knew things were not right. If you had sensed you were in trouble, then you would have called. But Ian was right to call me. The power that Nezerra had been able to gain was some of the darkest I have ever come across. Without Ian's help and the others at the circle of stones, I don't think I would have been successful. But we are all here, now, and we have seen the last of Nezerra.

"As for Deirdre, Ian and I will go over to the cave this morning and decide what must be done with her. Nezerra was most certainly using her. Whether Deirdre would have acted so on her

261

own, I can't know. But we will make sure she can't harm anyone else."

Caitlin sat a bit straighter, next to Alex. "So Nezerra had no grudge against me, only used me to cause you pain?" Caitlin was trying to understand this situation. It seemed so strange to her.

"And you knew my grandmother, Ci-Cero." Caitlin found this fact most interesting. She couldn't wait now to read the journal.

"Yes, dear girl, I did."

Alex had sat still and had not asked any questions. But now he spoke.

"Wabi, I appreciate what you did for us, both of us. But if ye don't mind, I'll go to the cave and see about Deirdre. She needs to hear from me that this ridiculous obsession she has with me is over. She has a home, she has a place in the community, and others will come to her aide. But we MacKinnons will not have any relationship with her. I'll never trust her, no matter what she does or says. And I'll not let Caitlin near her, ever again."

The Highlander had been pushed past his limit. If Deirdre would see reason, so much the better. If not, then he, himself, would take care of her. He had no compunction about doing away with her permanently if that was what was called for. And this was one decision he'd make without considering anyone's thoughts but his own.

Wabi and Ian nodded to each other. "Then come with us, Alex. Deirdre will still be in the cave sleeping. You can take her home or wherever you think she needs to go. Ian and I have a bit of a cleanup to do."

"Let me get my boots on. I'll meet ye in the stable."

He and Caitlin hurried up the stairs. Caitlin didn't think she wanted any breakfast this morning. Too much excitement, no doubt, so she'd just get herself put together and come down in a while. Alex, Ian, and Wabi rode out and made haste to get this cave business over with.

~ * ~

Daniel was helping Millie dish out pancakes and oatmeal for the crowd when there was a knock on the back door.

"Who's here this early? Not expecting the lads to come till later. It's Sunday morning. They usually sleep in on this day."

Jack rose and opened the door.

"Mister, can we see the Lady? And we're hungry. Do ye think we could have a piece of bread?"

Jack stared at the one asking the questions. It was a small lad, very thin and wearing only a pair of trousers — too short — and in his shirtsleeves. And it was darn cold out.

"Millie, come out here."

Jack was usually quick on his feet, but just now they seemed to be rooted to the floor, unable to move. His brain likewise.

"What is it?" Millie opened the door wider and looked out. There was a young lad standing in front of Jack, and just a few steps behind him stood two more children, another lad even smaller than the first and a wee lass, all shivering in the cold in only their shirtsleeves.

"Why, I know you. You're the children from the estate. However did you get here?"

Before they could answer, however, Millie had ushered them inside.

"Jack, find a blanket for each of them. They're freezing. Here, you three, inside with you. Hurry. It's cold out here. Come stand by the fire."

Coming inside, the children all huddled together, fear written on their little faces. They knew an explanation would be required, but weren't real sure what to say.

"Hector, get in here," Jack called out the front door.

Hector had stepped out on the front porch, checking to see what kind of weather the day might bring. Shortly, he heard his name being called. *What now?* He was still trying to sort out what he had learned from Wabi and now Jack was calling, and the tone of his voice told him it wasn't good.

"I believe ye had stowaways. Three of 'em, in fact."

Hector's mouth dropped open. He stared at the small trio. It was the same three children he had discovered on his first trip to the estate, the ones hiding in the castle. He thought Dorothea had been taking care of them.

"What are ye bairns doing here?"

"We just want to be with the Lady, sir. She's ever so nice, like our mam. And she kinda looks like her too, ye ken?"

The two brothers exchanged a look that spoke volumes, and Daniel sat down in his chair.

What will happen next? Three children? Who do they belong to?

He missed old Jamie more than ever. If he were still here, the two old ones would have slipped out the back door and stood by watching to see how the young men and women would handle this. They'd already done their share of "herding kittens" in their day. But today, with Jamie having passed on and Andrew in Edinburgh, Daniel felt alone.

Ye think they might could use a guiding hand, Daniel?

Aye, Alice, mo chridhe, aye.

Daniel walked over to the smallest lad, got on his knees, then wrapped a blanket about the young lad's shoulders. "Well now, let's see if a bit of oatmeal and pancakes wouldn't warm yer insides a bit."

Millie took the oldest boy by his hand, and Jack lifted the wee girl, holding her close.

"Come on, all of ye. Let's find a bowl of oats and pancakes for ye. Then we'll talk a bit."

~ * ~

Wabi, Ian and Alex were at the cave in just a short while. When Alex and his brothers had played there at the waterfall when they were youngsters, it had seemed like a great distance, far in the woods. But today it really wasn't so far, especially when you had made the trip a few times in such a short period, as they all had.

Alex wanted nothing more than to string Deirdre up by her feet and let her hang there until she expired. He'd never felt so much hatred for one as he did her. To think she would go after Caitlin expecting he would eventually come to her infuriated him. She was disgusting. Everything about her.

Wabi led the way through the winding tunnel. Deirdre was still sleeping, as he had left her. A vile-smelling area next to the wall got everyone's attention. The two wizards studied the floor where a black, jagged scar ran from one side of the cave to the other. It looked like where an old sore had festered and oozed onto the floor, and the liquid appeared to be blood mixed with oil. But even today, both Wabi and Ian could still feel dark energy emanating from the black, slimy puddles — remnants of Nezerra.

It still amazed Wabi that young Ian possessed such a great amount of power. Power is wonderful if used properly and at the right time, but if it's not controlled it can be used against you.

"It seems you did a fine job of decimating Nezerra. But as you see and can feel, there's a trace of dark power still looking for a vulnerable one to attach itself to. Makes me glad I put a protective barrier around Deirdre before I left her. Remember that lad. Never leave any person unprotected. Evil is always lurking about, just waiting for a vulnerable one to enter. And especially one such as Deirdre, where it has resided before."

"So how do we get rid of this leftover evil?" Ian was anxious to complete this task. There was a part of him that was excited about his newly found powers, but there was still a frightened young lad inside trying to make sense of his troubling emotions and feelings.

Reaching deep inside his coat, Wabi pulled out what appeared to be an ordinary small twig to Ian. It was only about six inches in length and fit perfectly inside Wabi's pocket.

"What's that?"

"It's only a twig from a rowan tree, Ian. But a very special twig that goes with me everywhere. It has properties that can erase the remaining evil."

With that statement, he shook the twig at the blackness on the floor. The twig began to drip small, silver-colored droplets that caused the remains of Nezerra to begin to bubble and hiss. They grew smaller and smaller until the floor was clear with no bits or pieces left. The black, ragged scar was gone. The puddles disappeared. The place was clean and Ian immediately felt the absence of the dark energy.

"I've got a lot to learn, Uncle Wabi. Yesterday, when I felt the evil in that woman, Nezerra, my body responded without me directing it. And the letter X that I saw earlier in my vision when I was in the circle of stones — I think that's what I was making with my wrists. And the keening? Well, Mam always said I would have a voice that 'called to the heavens,' so I suppose that was true.

"That wasn't the letter X, lad. That was the ancient sign of the Cross, which was always used in the olden times. But, I do agree with you about the voice — the keening was indeed a call to the heavens."

"I can tell ye it was a moment I'll never forget. But the power was controlling me, Wabi, not me controlling it. That scares me, ye ken?"

"Aye. I think we'll talk to Daniel about you going to Skye with me. Your instruction needs to begin immediately. Now let's see if Alex has come to any decision about what to do with Deirdre."

Walking over to where Alex stood looking at the woman, Wabi could feel the man's anger.

He's beyond angry. He's in a state of mind not too different from hers. He so wants to destroy her. Better awaken her and let him do what he must.

"Alex, let's wake her and see where to go from there." Touching Deirdre gently on her shoulder, Wabi called to her. "Deirdre. Wake now. Wake up. Open your eyes."

Wabi knelt and placed his hands on her head once again. The darkness he had felt there yesterday was gone. There was only a small humming sensation, perhaps vibration left from carrying such evil in her soul. He stood and addressed the Highlander.

"I don't sense the evil anymore. But Nezerra has controlled her for some time and it may take her a while to come to herself. Perhaps you can find a companion to stay with her." Then he stood back as Alex stepped forward.

Deirdre opened her eyes. Looking up, the face before her was the one she had yearned to see. *Alex. He's mine now. Nezzie's potion worked.*

Alex was standing over her, staring downward. It was almost more than he could do to not strike her. He loathed this woman.

"Come on, Deirdre. Ye've got to go home now." The tone of Alex's voice got her attention. *He's angry. Why is he angry? He's supposed to be happy. She promised he would be happy with me.*

"Yes, Alex. I'm ready now. Let's go home."

267

As she rose, a little unsteady on her feet, she reached for Alex's hand. He waited a moment then finally reached out to her and helped her regain her balance.

"I need to check on me mam, now. She's probably needing food and water. Come with me. Let's see to her."

Alex looked to Wabi, but even the old wizard had no answers for the questions that were running through Alex's mind.

"Take her to the village. Let the constable figure out what to do with her. She's living in her own world right now. Perhaps in a few days she'll regain her senses. Give her a chance."

Alex kept quiet, but nodded. He led Deirdre out of the cave and placed her on Zeus holding the reins tightly as the horse shied to one side; even he didn't trust this woman.

"Easy, fella. It'll only be a short ride." Alex would make sure of that.

Wabi brought Ian over to the area where Nezerra had finally met her end. "Ian, you've made this world a better place. Reducing Nezerra to ashes was the only solution."

"I have to tell you, Uncle Wabi, I didn't really know what I was doing. I just sorta reacted and that's what happened," Ian replied.

"The evil that abided in that woman could have lived on and on. But by using the power that you possess, it has ended once and for all. The Creator has given you abilities far greater than most any I've witnessed. But remember lad, to whom much is given, much is required. You will be challenged on more than one occasion. And we must get you ready. Now, let's complete this cleaning. The rowan twig removed the remnants of Nezerra, but the very earth underneath that vile heap needs to be cleansed as well."

They held their hands out in front of their bodies and a streak of fire from each fingertip ate its way through the first layers of earth.

Smoke rose in the cave and, with a nod from Wabi, an opening appeared in the ceiling of the cave and the smoke began to rise. Within a few seconds, the smoke had cleared and the ceiling came together again.

Ashes to ashes, dust to dust.

Wabi had delivered a final prayer over his old nemesis.

CHAPTER 27

H oly Rusephus, what is all that noise about?" Caitlin had dressed, tied a ribbon around her unruly hair, and decided to come downstairs. Her stomach felt better now so maybe she would have a bite of breakfast. As she started down the stairs she heard the voices of Jack, Millie, Hector, and Daniel, all talking at once. Whatever was going on?

"Millie, we need more oatmeal. This bowl's already gone and they're asking for more."

"What? Well, give them some toast and jam. It'll take a few minutes to make more oatmeal."

"Can we have some milk, Lady? Our mam always made us drink it every morning. And Miss Dorothea told us we had to drink it, too."

Hector stood in the doorway trying his darndest to figure out how the children had managed to hide themselves in his cart without him seeing them. And to think they had spent the night outside in the cold. Everyone in the lodge was running about trying to sort out what to do with them. Millie was dishing out oatmeal, Da was helping the wee girl drink her milk, and Jack was holding little Midge and spreading jam on toast.

"What's going on?" Caitlin walked over and stood next to Hector. She watched as Da, Jack and Millie scurried about. "Who are these children? Where did they come from?"

Hector shook his head. "Stowaways was the word Jack used. It appears I brought them with me and they spent the night outside in the cold."

"But where did they come from? Where are their folks?"

"They're the children I found hiding in a bedroom at Cameron Castle. Millie met them on her trip there and arranged for Dorothea to take care of them. Their Da died at Culloden, and just shortly after that their Mam passed away from an illness. They were homeless and found their way into the castle."

"But why did they leave Dorothea? She seemed like a perfect nanny to care for them."

"Seems they took a fancy to Millie so here they are."

"So I see. Well then, I believe you and I had better turn to and give the others a little break. So now we have four children to care for. That will take as many hands as we can get."

Caitlin looked at the scene. Total chaos. Everyone talking at once, the children squealing when Tess, the MacKinnon's old Border collie, came waltzing through and Jack calling for more oatmeal. But she knew this lodge could handle those children just as well as it had handled the MacKinnon lads. For a moment, she wondered if Da hadn't had second sight when he started adding more rooms way back then. She smiled and walked through the doorway, tying an apron around her waist as she did. For a loner, it was surprising how much she was enjoying this.

Well, isn't this what you've wanted? A large family? Looks like you've got it, so how are you going to deal with that fact?

~ * ~

The trip into the village was a short one. Deirdre had not spoken, which was fine with Alex. He had nothing to say to her. Or nothing she would have wanted to hear. He helped her dismount and she looked about as if just realizing he had not taken her to her home.

"I thought you were taking me home. What about me mam?"

"The constable will help you now, Deirdre. He'll know the best place to take you. Come on now. Let's get inside."

He put his hand at her back, directing her to the office door. Just touching her was enough to make him cringe with anger. He pulled his hand away for fear that he may give in to his craving to bury his dirk in her back — and then twist it.

Constable Stewart rose from his desk as they entered. "Alex, come in. Weren't expecting any callers today. 'Bout to go home. Been a hectic week. Old Cromartie's been here already, complaining about somebody stealing his cattle . . . again."

"Well, I hadn't planned on making a call, as ye say. But Deirdre here is having a bit of a problem, ye ken? She's not able to take care of herself just now. And Constable, her mam passed away a few days ago and the lass can't seem to get that into her head. Well, she didn't exactly pass away — someone strangled her, so ye might need to check that out. Deirdre's unable to make much sense just now, but she's the one responsible for kidnapping Caitlin. Ye do remember that incident don't ye? And just yesterday she tried to kill both Caitlin and me. It's yer place to find her a home — away from here. I don't even want to know where ye take her, but ye need to do it now. If she comes anywhere near my home, or close to Caitlin, my soul will be damned for I'll kill her for sure."

With that, Alex walked out, leaving the door standing open and a cold wind blowing through.

~ * ~

"All right, all of you. March yourselves upstairs. Follow me now. A bath would make you all a bit more loveable."

Caitlin had never been around children, but she was convincing these bairns that she knew what she was doing. She sounded like a commanding officer ordering his troops. Millie smiled and was glad to have Caitlin take charge of the three children for a while. She'd gotten them warmed and fed them, but three was a lot to handle. Midge was still just a babe that had to stay put when you placed her in a crib. But these three were running about the lodge, the oldest lad trying to ride old Tess, and the wee girl seemed to be leading the smaller lad around by his hand. They were close in age, but the lad was just slightly taller, and apparently very shy.

Caitlin had both tubs filled with water, waiting to receive the dirty little bodies. How they had gotten so filthy was still unclear to her. Dorothea would have insisted on a daily bath for sure. But who knows what they had gotten into before sneaking into Hector's cart.

Caitlin had insisted on giving each of them a bath herself. If these children were going to be here for any amount of time, she would check them out from head to toe. Did they have any open wounds or sores? Any lice? Any bites that needed treating? She found herself smiling — maybe they were her first patients. She had heard from Hector that there were more like these children, homeless, and without any family at all.

The older lad talked constantly and asked more questions than Caitlin could possibly answer. The smaller lad smiled, but didn't follow instructions very well. Or maybe he just chose to ignore them. She'd have to talk with him about that.

"Now, tell me your names again."

"He's Charlie and I'm Dugald," the oldest lad said.

"And what's your sister's name?"

"She's Bridget, Miss."

"I see. And my name's Caitlin and you may call me that."

"Why are ye looking in me ears? I know they be clean. Miss Dorothea made sure we washed every night."

"I'm sure she did. So why did you hide away in the cart? Didn't Dorothea take good care of you?"

"Yes, mum, she did. But the Lady is like our mam. She has that long, black hair just like our mam. And she smells like her too."

"Yes, well, let's get you two bathed and then I'll see about Bridget."

Caitlin called out loudly. "Daniel, can you find something for the lads to sleep in?"

"Aye. There's bound to be sleeping shirts in some of the old trunks upstairs. Give me a minute. Ye go now and see about the wee lass. I've not had any experience with the lasses, ye ken. She's got an imagination, that much I can tell ye. She's been talking me ears off and wanting me to read another story."

Da had found a new burst of energy the moment the children had appeared at the back door. Caitlin had noticed, and now, thinking a little more on it, was sure he was as at home with these children as he had been with his own four boys. He hadn't even questioned why they were here, but turned to making sure they were being cared for.

Caitlin bathed the young girl and a quick look told her the lass was thin, too thin. She'd have to watch her closely and see if she just didn't eat properly or was there more going on. She was, as Da had indicated, very talkative and obviously liking being pampered by Caitlin. The child was very different from her brothers, who were both dark eyed and dark haired. The lass was fair, with hair that was almost white and the bluest eyes ever. She was so small she could lie down completely in the tub and did so. She squealed with delight and Caitlin was totally drenched herself before the bath was finished.

She found a soft sleepshirt of Alex's and held it out to the lass.

"Here, Bridget. Slip this over your head. It'll keep you warm for sure."

The shirt came to the floor and the lass squealed with delight. "It's a beautiful gown that I can wear to the dance." She spun around, giggling as she did.

Yes, a very vivid imagination.

Finally, having gotten all three of them bathed and ready for bed, she decided to put them all in the same room. In the same bed, actually. They would certainly feel more secure than if she separated them. But where? Which room?

"Daniel, which room do you think I should put them in?"

The old man scratched his head then nodded. "Oh, I believe Jamie would be kind enough to share his room, don't ye?"

The bed in this room was one of the larger ones and it would work well for three small bairns. Caitlin smiled at the old man. "Aye, Daniel, I rather think he'd be pleased to share that room. And Da, do you think you could read them just 'one more story?' Maybe then they'll go to sleep. I'm done for."

"Would be my pleasure. Can't tell ye the number of stories I've read over the years. Alice always thought that was a special time for me to visit with me lads. I believe I can still manage to do that."

H gathered a couple of books under his arm and climbed the stairs, just as he had so many times before.

~ * ~

Ian and Wabi arrived just after sunset, with Alex close on their heels.

He came in the door and let out a very loud sigh. "Oh, what a relief. Just to come into this place of peace and quiet. This has been one heck of a day."

The laughter that followed that statement had Alex looking at the others as if they had all lost their good sense.

"Ah, just so, then. Peace and quiet. This is the place for that," Hector smiled.

Then he, Millie, Caitlin and Da were bursting with even more laughter. Ian and Wabi were just as dumbfounded as Alex.

"What's got into all of ye? Ye been having a few wee drams?" Alex wanted nothing more than a bath and a wee dram himself.

Da finally came to his rescue. "Nae, lad. We're just a bit tuckered out our own selves, ye ken? No doubt you, Ian, and Wabi had a trying day. But things were a bit hectic here at the lodge, too. So if we seem just a tad too giddy, it's just that we're all tired and not sure what to make of the happenings around here today."

"What happenings? What are ye talking about?"

Alex poured himself a small mug of Hector's cider and sat on the old sofa, next to Caitlin. He kissed her quickly on the forehead and she leaned into him, relieved to see him home and safe.

Jack took center stage and started pacing, trying his best to relay to Alex the events of the day. But when he had finished, Alex was more confused than ever.

"Three? Three children? Who are their folks? And where are they now?" Alex looked from one to the other and no one answered him.

Eventually, Hector, the negotiator, took the floor and began to connect a few details for Alex.

"But whatever are we going to do with three children?" Alex noticed that no one really jumped at answering that question either.

Da sat his cider down, stood, and looked directly at Alex. "I expect we'll find room for them somewhere, don't ye think? These rooms have had children in them for many years, what's a few more, huh?"

Da had spoken, and there would be no more discussion.

~ * ~

Hector brought out his papers from the estate. He'd gone over them several times to make sure his figures were correct before he'd discuss them with Millie. She was very sharp herself when it came to numbers. But that was not surprising thought Hector, she'd had tutors from her earliest years.

"Millie, I've gone over these figures and I think you can trust they're correct. Clint and Dorothea and I have drawn up several sets of drawings — for your approval, of course — that lay out how we think the place should be arranged. Ethel has agreed to run the kitchen, and she'll find the girls that used to work at the estate, your grandmother's lasses, to help with cleaning and keeping the place in order. Clint and Winston will take care of making sure the buildings are in shape and the animals are cared for. And Dorothea would like nothing better than to help these children with no homes, and the mothers without husbands. The estate can accommodate quite a few if we lay it out right. The only thing left is to find a couple of women to help manage the children with no mams, as there are a few of them, too, such as the three we know about. Surely we can find ladies in the village to help with that. It also occurs to me that we need at least one experienced woman who can run the place once I'm finished with my part. As yet, no one has come to mind. On the next trip I'll work on that problem."

Hector was just now realizing how he had enjoyed working on this project. It was even better than cooking. His life was most definitely taking off in a new direction.

"There will be a great deal of expense involved in order to make some of these changes. We'll have to pay the cleaning girls, and those who help with the children. And if we are able to find a manager, then she'll expect a salary also."

"Don't worry about the expenses. When I left Warwick's castle I took only two things — one of his prize horses and the jewels that Father had given to my mother and me over the years. Those jewels that my father draped my mother and me in will provide funds that will help make this school here, and the sanctuary at the estate, a reality. I'll never wear them and this is a good way for them to bring happiness to others. They never brought my mother or me any."

"Then we can make this a fine sanctuary. Yer grandmother would be pleased with yer plans and ye'd be following in her footsteps, caring for those needy ones, the locals in the village."

Then Millie spoke up. "Oh, just one bit of clarification, Hector. Eventually, after you have had a chance to get things in proper order, Dorothea will be coming here to live. She's agreed to help us with Midge, just as she cared for me. What with the other three children here now, her skills will be most welcome."

"Aye, she's quite good with the children."

No one voiced the words, but it was apparent the three homeless bairns would be staying at the lodge. The Lady never even considered sending them back. Jack wouldn't have let her if she had. Change was becoming a little easier for him, apparently.

~ * ~

Daniel knew where he would find them, Ian and Wabi—in the library, of course. The two of them were inseparable. He didn't even have to guess what they were doing, he already understood. He walked the empty hallway and entered the library, breathing in that unique scent that only comes from very old books. In Daniel's case, an intoxicating scent.

"That's the smell of knowledge," Alice would say.

"Thought I'd find you two huddled in here, combing through these old tomes. I always thought I would get around to reading all of them, but I'm still a ways from that." He laughed and pulled up a stool next to Ian. "Ian, my lad. If you grow any more ye'll be taller than Jack, and he may not take kindly to that idea. He's always been the big brother, even though Alex is the oldest. But ye may just do that. Ye've still a few years growth coming, so we'll see."

"Da, I don't think I'll ever be as big as Jack, and never as smart as Alex."

"Ye underestimate yerself, lad. I also know it's time for ye to find yer own way in this life, yer place, just as we all must. With ye and yer brothers I've been able to teach ye all about sheep farming and living in the Highlands. Being a MacKinnon ye've learned those lessons well and would make a fine sheep farmer. And that nose of yours can find things none of us ever can. But it's clear ye need special training for ye to find yer true place. Alice always knew ye would walk a different path. Now I understand what she could see early on. And if we can talk Wabi into it, perhaps he might take ye on as an apprentice. Do ye think that would work?"

Ian was speechless. He'd been dreading this discussion with Da. He'd just figured Da would expect him to stay on the farm and work with the sheep. He wasn't opposed to that particularly, but lately, especially after the last few days, he knew there was more he was called to do.

"Holy sheep shite, Da! Ye mean it? I could go with Uncle Wabi and learn from him?"

"Watch yer tongue, lad. Yer mam wouldn't tolerate that language and neither will I. But if going with Wabi is what the two of ye think is the right thing, then so be it. I don't pretend to understand this calling, but Alice would never have stopped ye and so I'll not either. The older I get the more I realize there's still much for us all to learn."

Wabi nodded to Daniel. "Being a called one doesn't mean he doesn't have a choice, Daniel. He does. It will always be his decision to answer the calling or not. But I can instruct him in ways that will help him come to his own decisions and know what will be expected of him. We are all responsible for our choices, the called as well as all others. But he has been given extraordinary gifts, Daniel. The Creator doesn't usually make mistakes about whom he bestows them on."

~ * ~

The three bairns belonged to everyone apparently. Millie had no trouble finding a place in her life for them, and neither did anyone else. And life on the sheep farm had been kicked up a notch for sure. Dugald, the oldest lad who was about seven or eight, had attached himself to Jack's back pocket. The big man now had a small shadow and learned to be careful before stepping backward.

"If yer going to follow me, ye gotta be careful. I'm not used to having anyone so close behind me, ye ken?"

But it was evident this boy and Jack would do well together. Recently Jack had put the lad on one of the older, gentler horses. The lad had gone to sleep that night still talking about "my" horse.

But Millie and Caitlin were struggling with Charlie, the younger lad. He didn't listen to either of them and they were both getting tired of repeating themselves all day. He was very shy, they all agreed on that. Bridget stayed pretty close to him and, being more verbal, answered a lot of questions for him.

"So far, he's only grunted more or less, but he'll never talk more if she continues to do his talking for him," Millie said.

"Charlie, you've got to start talking to us now. Bridget can't always answer for you. Speak now, lad." But the boy remained close-mouthed as he smiled at her. Millie could see this little one would need more attention than the others.

Today, however, even Caitlin had lost patience with the lad. She'd spent the morning gathering berries and herbs for making medicines and had told the bairns they were not to eat these. But, now, coming back into the room just a few minutes later, she found Charlie with his cheeks bulging out, having stuffed himself with a handful of her berries.

Standing right in front of him, she began repeating the same thing she'd just told him moments ago.

"Charlie, those berries are not for eating. I told you that. They're to be used for making medicines. Now, you need to pay attention when I'm talking." The lad nodded and she walked away, went out to the porch, and then came in a few minutes later only to find him eating the berries again.

"What? I just told you not to eat those, Charlie." She was becoming exasperated with this situation. He nodded again and continued to eat as if she had not spoken to him.

Suddenly, as if struck by a bolt of lightning, she had a thought. She walked around behind the boy and called his name — loudly. "Charlie! Charlie!"

He never moved. Never turned around. She clapped her hands loudly. Nothing.

Of course. Why didn't I think of that before?

Millie came through carrying an armload of laundry. Laundry was a chore that had to be done everyday

"Move, Charlie, I don't want to step on you."

The lad stood right in her way, never moving an inch.

"Charlie!"

"Millie, don't. He can't hear you. He's deaf."

"What? Charlie? He's deaf? Are you sure?"

"Yes. I'm sure. That's why he never does what we ask him. He never hears us. And that's also why Bridget stays close to him. She knows he's deaf whether anyone else does or not. There's only a year or so between their ages. I'm sure of it. She's been his ears since he was a baby, and when she's not around, he's lost."

"Oh, Caitlin. What do we do?"

"Well, nothing that I know about can restore his hearing. But Uncle Wabi may have knowledge I don't. He's seen a lot. But for now, let's help the lad by trying to show him what we want rather than just saying it to him.

Surely there must be a way to make his life easier. I'll give this problem careful thought.

Later that same evening, the wee lass, Bridget, found her way into Alex's lap and as usual, fell asleep there. Alex, certainly quieter than the other brothers, was more surprised at this than anyone. He hoped he and Caitlin would have bairns of their own, but this little lass was worming her way into his heart already.

CHAPTER 28

Wabi and Caitlin had a few quiet minutes together and she told him about Charlie's deafness. He made some suggestions which could be helpful. She finally got around to asking the question that had been in her mind, the one she wasn't sure she wanted to know the answer to.

"Uncle Wabi, in the cave, when Nezerra came upon Alex and me, I knew she was there. I caught her scent a few seconds before she arrived. When I saw her, however, none of my powers came to the surface. All I could think of was protecting us . . . Alex and myself. Do you think my powers have been taken away? I've not used them since reducing the soldier to dust. Perhaps they were only given for a short time."

"No, dear girl. Your powers are still with you. You did exactly what you should have done in your situation. You protected yourself and Alex. That was the most important action at the moment. And those actions were definitely your powers at work. There are situations that cause us to employ our powers in ways that are difficult to understand."

"But Wabi, she could have killed us both. Why would I resort to just putting us into a protective state where she couldn't reach us instead of just outright killing her?"

"That's a question you must ponder. But when you do think

on it, ask yourself one question — who is the most protective creature on this earth?"

Caitlin stared at her Uncle, but make no response. He knew more than he was telling her, but she didn't pursue the issue any further.

Yes, I'll think more on this.

Although she wasn't sure she would ever need them again, she was relieved to know she hadn't lost her powers. They had been most helpful with Lord Warwick and Commander Campbell. She had to believe they were given for a purpose.

Certainly Highlanders were a superstitious lot, no doubt. They believed there were those with special abilities, such as second sight, or curing disease. So it was not so strange that they accepted that Wabi, Caitlin and Ian were unusual and no questions asked.

~ * ~

The old wizard and the young one said their goodbyes to everyone. Again, no one asked any questions, which was a great relief to Ian, who was still asking questions in his own mind. He didn't know how many days or months he would be gone from the Highlands, but whatever the period, this place would always be home.

They walked to the top of the moor, and the wind began to rise and the trees began to sway.

"It's time we get home, my boy. Everybody ready?"

Wabi, with Owl perched on his shoulder, and Ian, with Henson tucked under his arm, took the short route to Skye. Owl could be heard squawking his complaints when Wabi caught the tail of a whirlwind as it passed over them.

Master. You promised this would be an easy trip!

At the other extreme, Ian's laughter could be heard ringing across the Highlands. His life with Wabi would be an interesting adventure for sure. Henson just closed his eyes tightly, burying his head under Ian's arm, his long, black tail jerking back and forth rapidly, a sign Ian would learn meant the critter was anxious. He was trusting that his new master knew what he was doing. He needed to have a feline-to-wizard talk with him.

~ * ~

Alex had made his way over to the Taggart place. There was no sign of Deirdre or anyone else having been there. Hopefully, that meant the constable had taken the girl away and they were rid of her. Maybe now he'd agree to let Caitlin have her wish.

Later that evening, Alex decided he could now approach Caitlin to continue their discussion of the clinic. Both of them had skirted around it long enough. The minute he came into the lodge and found her mixing her potions, he began.

"I think it's time we finished our talk about ye having a clinic in the village. I still have my reasons for not wanting ye to go down there, and . . ."

Before he could go any farther, however, Caitlin jumped him with both feet.

"Alex MacKinnon, you'll not tell me what I can and can't do. I'm intelligent enough to make my own decisions and I've decided about this clinic. I'm going to have one!"

Caitlin's temper had once again raised its ugly head, but she'd kept it at bay for longer than usual, so she felt she was making progress. To her surprise, Alex responded in a manner she had not expected.

"Aye, lass, I know the clinic is important to ye. Just promise me ye'll always take Willie with ye. Da says he'll go as often as

287

possible, too. He knows everyone in the village and they'll likely let ye treat them if he's with ye. At first anyway."

Well, what brought that about? Maybe he's finally beginning to understand I need to follow my own path. And maybe he's learning I can make good decisions, too.

Caitlin had the presence of mind to realize this was a great concession on Alex's part. It might be good if she, too, thought to make a gesture of understanding. She walked over to him, placed her arms around his waist and looked up at him, admiring his cleft chin that marked him from all the others.

"Alex, I understand you are concerned about me. I promise that Willie will always be at my side, and Da can accompany me whenever he wishes. I couldn't have better protection than those two, unless it is you, *mo chridhe.*" Alex's smile at her use of his term of endearment sent a shiver down her spine. He was still exactly what she wanted.

As for Alex, he would always want to protect her, but was slowly realizing she would retain a certain degree of independence no matter what. He'd stay in the background as much as he could, but he'd have to work diligently to tame his propensity to make her decisions, just as she would have to work hard at keeping her temper at bay. Alex recalled that Mam had often said our strengths and weaknesses are but a flip side of each other.

~ * ~

Caitlin and Millie were putting the final touches on the crofters' hut, the larger one, getting it ready for Uncle Andrew and his lady friend. Kenny and Hamish had spent most of their workweek making sure the thatching was fresh. They'd whitewashed the walls and the interior had been scrubbed by Millie and Caitlin

288

until it was as clean as it had ever been . . . maybe even cleaner.

When the two women had discovered mam's keepsakes and found the oil paintings, there were numerous other items they were excited about — beautiful linens, sheets of music, pieces of handmade pottery, several woven rugs, and a very old diary. When they had found the diary, however, Caitlin and Millie had agreed they would not read it.

"These words were meant for someone special. They were not written for our eyes. Let them remain private," Caitlin said. Millie nodded in agreement and they carefully rewrapped the diary in its silk cover and returned it to the trunk where Alice had placed it years ago.

But the other items, the paintings, the linens, the colorful rugs and pottery were arranged in the hut. These small additions added a fine touch to what otherwise would have just been a deserted crofter's hut. The shed out back was also filled with unused bits of furniture, and a few pieces still had some life left in them. The two ladies created an inviting place. Any woman would recognize this as a gesture of welcome.

~ * ~

Alex and Jack left early, the dew still clinging to the ground, and headed to look at another flock of sheep at the Fraser place. Two of their sheep had died recently and Fraser had sent word by one of his workers that something had killed several of his also. The MacKinnon brothers knew what a disaster disease could mean to any sheep farm. If it was contagious, then a whole flock could be wiped out.

Winter had been difficult for everyone at the MacKinnon place. Now spring was almost upon them and that was a relief for all, and no one more so than Alex. More than a month had passed now and no one had seen Deirdre. Just to ease his mind, however, he made a trip to the village to see Constable Stewart two days ago.

"She's in Edinburgh, Alex. She has an aunt there, her mother's sister. I put her on a coach and gave her enough funds to tide her over till she could get to her aunt's home. I know ye have yer own feelings about her, Alex, but she deserves a chance."

"She'll not get another chance with me, Stewart. If she ever shows her face here again, I promise ye I'll kill her." The constable sincerely hoped the lass would stay away, as Alex MacKinnon always made good on his promises.

The Highlander walked out and slammed the door behind him.

Well, good riddance. Some of her kin have taken her in and she's gone from here.

~ * ~

Caitlin was busy with her new clinic, although it was dawning on her it might be better to have it at the lodge. With all the children there now, Millie had her hands full, and she was excellent with the children, especially Charlie.

Caitlin taught everyone to stand in front of him when they spoke to him. Slowly but surely, he was beginning to understand lip reading, a skill Uncle Wabi had talked to her about. It took a lot of patience and Charlie wasn't always easy to work with, but even he was liking that he didn't always have to have Bridget right next to him.

Caitlin was happier than Alex had seen her since she came to his home. Her skin glowed and her ever-present smile was back. The laughter he had so liked had returned as well. Millie had seen this new excitement in Caitlin, too, and was glad. These two women had already suffered more than most ever did.

Life was always full of surprises, certainly, but the days were so filled with activity that none stopped to think about what might happen next. The orphaned children had a place here, just as Da had said. This lodge would always find room for a child who needed a home.

Alex was relieved to hear the Frasers' sheep had been attacked by wolves, not stricken by a disease. He wasn't sure what had caused the death of his two, but for the moment he wouldn't worry about it.

His latest worry was, as usual, Caitlin and her clinic. The lass was so full of energy he could hardly keep up with her. In fact, he'd thought the work would slow her pace, but not so. She'd just gotten home, Da at her side, and had reported that his presence in the village helped with getting the old ones to let her treat them.

Hector had left this morning headed to the estate again. He, Millie and Jack had laid out careful plans for the next phase of their project and Hector's mind wouldn't let him have a moment's peace.

Now, where in the world am I going to find women to help with the children?

And not just anyone, he remembered, but ones that would meet Millie's approval.

~ * ~

It was a late spring evening with the days beginning to lengthen, and Caitlin was missing. Alex knew the circle of stones continued to call to her, and he was pleased she no longer tried to hide it from him. The longer they were together, the greater their bond. She was his woman and his life with her was just as he had hoped—complete.

This evening the lodge was brimming with children laughing,

dogs being chased, and Millie calling out to Jack to come get Midge. Willie had learned to keep his distance from the children as much as possible. But Tess had lived with a house full of lads and knew the children were harmless. Da and Alex watched the activity and grinned at each other.

"Alex have ye ever seen such? I suppose ye lads must have been this active, but for the life of me I can't remember it. Alice always seemed to keep things more ordered that this, but just look at Jack and Millie, and those bairns."

Alex looked about, finding the scene one he approved of. He nodded to Da and, knowing where to find Caitlin, walked out the front door. Standing on the porch, he could just see her outline. Only yesterday she had talked with him about the henge and how she was drawn to it.

"Alex, there's a problem I have to figure out. I must go inside the circle. Every day the pull gets greater. And even though the nightmares have decreased, I still dream about someone — but I don't know who it is. Please understand. I can no longer put it off. I must settle this."

Apparently, she had decided today was the day. He had wondered about the cave incident. What had really happened there? Had she used her powers then? He wasn't sure why she hadn't done away with Nezerra if she had known she was there. Was she afraid of her powers? Or was she just caught off guard and didn't have time to react?

I'll give her a few minutes alone. Then I'll go to her. Maybe if I try to help her get to the bottom of this we'll have peace.

He slowly made his way up the moor and saw her with that same look on her face—serenity, peace. As he got closer he saw her bend down and, to his amazement, he watched as she lifted the square stone in the center, the one with the smooth edges. She gently turned it over. It was a small stone and had been there as long as he could remember. It was just part of the circle. Of course, until the incident recently, he had never been inside the circle.

When he got closer, Caitlin called out to him.

"Alex, you must come inside. It's all right now. I promise you. If it weren't, I would know it. But you must see this."

Alex wasn't at all sure he wanted to do this, but she was insistent.

"Come, hurry. Look at this."

Alex walked through the opening and reached Caitlin's side, bending to see what she was pointing to. She held the stone in her hands and read the inscription. "A.A.M. February 22, 1719." And there was a small etching, a drawing of a sprig of heather, drawn at the bottom of the small stone. "Alex, I think it's a gravestone. For a child. I can't explain it, but I know this child is the one calling to me. It's looking for someone — maybe its mother."

Alex ran his fingers over the letters and numbers, as a blind person who reads braille would have done. When he looked at Caitlin, there was much confusion in his face. And for a moment she thought he registered a quick moment of pain.

"What? What is it? Do you know whose stone this is?"

"Nae, lass. But that date — February 22, 1719— that's the day I was born."

"What do you think this means?"

"I don't know, but we'll corner Da and ask him. He's always been one to keep a lot to himself, but we need to know more about this. Maybe he doesn't know any more than we do. After all, the stone's been here for as long as I can remember and no one's ever turned it over before."

"I had no choice, Alex. It called me. But I still don't know

293

the reason. And why me?"

"Come on. Let's get to the lodge. Let's get the bairns fed, bathed and settled for the night. Then we'll approach Da. But he may decide not to tell us anything he doesn't want us to know."

"He's entitled to keep some things to himself, Alex. We all are. We'll have to accept what he wants us to know and let the rest go." Caitlin had learned from Uncle Wabi as a child that certain memories belonged only to us and were not to be shared.

~ * ~

Millie brought in a pitcher of cider and made sure everyone had a cup. It was the quiet period of the evening when they all gathered round and discussed their day.

"Now that the wild ones are settled I would like to ask a question, if I may."

Caitlin had thought carefully about this and still wasn't sure she should bring it up. But until she knew the answer to her question it would continue to run around in her head, so she might as well get it out.

"Da, I've been inside the circle of stones several times since I've come here to this home. And when I enter, there's such a feeling of peace and contentment. From what Alex tells me, Alice thought the circle was a place of reverence. But the last few times I've been there, I sense more than just peace. I'm being called, summoned. I need to ask this question. Are there any children buried in the burial plot? I believe the one calling me is a child. I don't understand it, but it's very real to me."

Alex spoke then, and he watched Da's face. "Da, Caitlin picked up the small stone in the middle of the circle. It has the initials A.A.M. and the date February 22, 1719, etched on the back side. I'm familiar with that date. Is there anything ye can tell us about that stone and that date?"

Alex thought it best that he ask the question rather than Caitlin.

Daniel rested his head against the tall back of his chair, the one Alice had selected for him. It was taller than the others. He thought for a moment before he responded to Caitlin, this healer who had powers that even she didn't understand yet.

Well, yes, perhaps now is the time for me to tell a few more secrets. Alice would want them to know.

"I'll answer all yer questions the best I can. Most things can't be told until the time is right, so just bear that in mind. And ye lads, ye must understand that yer mam had her reasons for asking for certain things to be done, and it's not yer place to question those now. She thought the sun rose and set in every one of ye. Yeah, I know ye heard her say Ian was 'her special boy,' but what ye don't know is that she said that about each of ye when ye were the youngest lad. Yer mother was the finest woman I've ever known, and that's the first thing that needs to be understood. I've kept the promises I made her. Now perhaps I'll share a few of them with ye.

"February 22, 1719, was a special day here at this lodge. 'Course then it was only a hut and I'd just added a small room off the right side, a place to put a crib for the bairn we were expecting. And yer mam, well, she was so excited about a bairn coming she was beside herself. She took one of her dresses, took it apart and fashioned curtains—for the nursery, ye ken. Then, finally, the day came when she sent me off to fetch old Harriet. She's been gone for years now, but she was the midwife here, and a fine one she was. She came and spent practically the entire night with yer mam. Andrew and Florence were here, too, and we sat together talking about how we would have to learn about taking care of a bairn. They lived just next door in that old hut that's still standing. They never had any children, but they were as excited about a bairn as we were.

"We kept hearing Alice's cries, and just when I thought I couldn't stand it another minute there came a wail that had us all grinning. A hardy cry if I ever heard one. Old Harriet called me in and handed me this small bundle wrapped tightly in a blanket and told me to 'hold this squirming little thing.' I looked into your face, Alex, and those black eyes looked back at me as if studying my face to make sure I was someone ye recognized. Well, I took ye into the kitchen and was showing ye off to Andrew and Florence when, Holy Jesus, another cry filled the hut!

"Andrew went flying into the room and Harriet handed him another blanket with a baby! And the child was giving Andrew the once over jest as ye had done with me. But these eyes were so sparkling Andrew had to smile—blue eyes, ye ken, and a tuft of hair as bright as a fox's tail.

'What do ye think of that Andrew? Two bairns in one night?' I called out. Then I went to Alice's side and she was still crying, but these were happy tears.

'Daniel, I felt a lot of activity going on the last few days, but I never expected two. Whatever are we going to do with two bairns?'

'Well, I expect we'll find room for both of them, don't you *mo chridhe?*'

"Then old Harriet gathered the two bairns and continued to check them out head to toe. 'This lad's quite a fine one, he is. Look at his legs — long as a sapling and kicking up a storm. And a head full of dark hair, just like yers, Daniel MacKinnon.' She snuggled the lad next to Alice and started checking out the other.

'Well now, aren't ye just the picture of health too, me lass. That hair the same auburn color as yer Mam. A mite smaller than yer

296

brother, but ye've got a set of lungs fer sure.'

'Lass? Did ye say lass? Andrew we've got one of each. Looks like we'll be needing to add on another room shortly.'

'Aye, Daniel. I believe this calls for a wee dram, don't ye brother?'

"And Florence poured us a small amount into our cups and we drank to celebrate our blessings, two fine bairns. Yes, it was quite a night. But just a short while later, after we'd all slept for a few hours, I heard Alice crying, calling out to me.

'Daniel, Daniel, come. Help me!'

"I raced to her bed, still in awe of the sight — my Alice with a bairn on either side. And ye, Alex, ye were kicking and screaming for something to eat apparently. But on the other side, the wee lass was still, very still. Not a sound was coming from her. One look at Alice and I knew what she was telling me. Her heart was broken and I felt like the world had stopped spinning. We weren't expecting to have two bairns, but to lose one in just a few hours was devastating."

"I had a twin sister? No one ever told me that."

"Aye, lad. Yer Mam and I discussed it often. We both agreed there was no point in telling ye lads about the sister ye lost. She was gone and we'd dealt with our own grief. Alice didn't wish to bring any grief to her other bairns. Losing a child leaves a wounded place in yer heart, ye ken? No matter how many years pass, the pain still lingers. So we kept it to ourselves and Andrew and Florence were the only ones who knew about her. It's just as well I tell ye now, however, as Andrew has almost finished his written history of our family. And the birth of Amber Alicia MacKinnon will be listed on the same date as her brother, Alexander Daniel MacKinnon."

"A sister. A twin sister. And her name was Amber Alicia — after Mam, I see. Just as I was named Alexander Daniel, after you."

"We had already chosen those names before ye were born.

We'd decided on one for a lass and one for a lad."

"Is Amber a name from another relative long ago?"

"Nae, Alex. Yer Mam wanted to call a lass that. She was taken with the color, and had a beautiful piece of amber stone, a small one almost like a bird's egg, that she kept in her jewelry box. Probably still there today. It glowed from within she told me. So we agreed on that name for our first-born daughter."

"I'm sure there was no way to ever know why the lass died, Daniel. But I know now she must be the one calling me. I'll try to figure out more of this dilemma, but telling us about her is helpful. Now I know I haven't lost my mind. Somehow I just knew there was a child in the circle. Now I have to understand what she wants me to know."

"Then maybe I can help ye with that too, lass. Alice was so distraught over the death of our lass, Amber, and couldn't bear to think of the little bairn lying in that cold burial plot at the top of the moor all by herself. She always understood more about the circle of stones than any of us, including meself. She asked that we bury Amber in the circle where the "others" could watch over her. As I'm getting older, I am only now beginning to see Alice had her own special understanding of things I never did. But I never tried to have her abandon them. I just accepted her and her ways.

"So we laid the wee lass to rest in the circle and I created the small stone for her. Alice went within the circle often, and if you watched you'd see her rubbing her fingers around the edges of the stone. Over the years, the edges became smooth and thin. I suppose it was her way of connecting with the lass."

"Yes, the stone is so inviting, Daniel. It's light and when I touch it I feel a connection. And now I know it's Amber. But I'm not sure why she's connecting with me. Still, it's such a comforting feeling when I'm there."

"Nor do I, Caitlin. But to finish this story, there's one more piece of information I need to pass on to all of ye. When yer mam only had a few days left, she made a request that I promised I would follow through on."

"Request? What did she want, Da?" Jack was almost afraid to ask the question. He'd learned more about his family in the last six months than he had known in his whole life. And he wondered about much of it. "Is it something ye can do?"

"Well, yes, it's an easy enough task. But it wasn't anything I thought I had to hurry with just yet, ye ken? Yer mam asked me to move Amber's remains before I die and have them placed between her grave and the place where I'm to be buried. That way we would keep her close. Yes, I know, it's a request from a dying woman, but it's not much to ask for and easy to do. I always thought I would get around to it, but perhaps I should go ahead and take care of doing what Alice wanted. There's a place already waiting for me, so I'll just move Amber's remains and when my day comes I'll have already fulfilled my promise to Alice."

"We can do it for ye, if ye like." Alex nodded to him.

"Nae, lad. I would prefer to do it myself. But perhaps we could have a small prayer and gather round on the day. Yer mam would have liked that."

And the old man stood slowly and made his way up the stairs, to where his new family slept.

CHAPTER 29

Holy sheep shite!" Ian yelled. The time-weaving trip had been spectacular, but he was not expecting to see such an array of glittering stars when they finally landed in the field at Wabi's place on the Isle. There must be millions of them.

"Well, yes, but watch that tongue, Ian. I'm not yer mam, but I'm pretty sure she wouldn't approve of those words. As for the blinking stars, most of what you see is light sparkling from the water and being bounced back and forth from them. Of course, it's dark out here so the stars seem brighter than they are. One day we'll fly among them and you can get a closer view. You'll get use to it."

"Sorry, Uncle Wabi. Didn't think before I opened me mouth. It won't happen again."

"Of course it won't. Now, let's take a walk across the way and I'll introduce you to Mrs. Favre. She'll have taken care of Groucho while I've been gone. He's a bit too old to go time weaving anymore and she spoils him rotten. So you might expect he'll give us the cold shoulder at first. He's been with me for several lives now. I believe he showed up when I was about the same age you are now."

Owl immediately took his place in the rowan tree at the rear of the house. *I'll take a rest now, Master, if it's all the same to you.* Time weaving was for the birds as far as this bird was concerned.

"Ian, I see you have a companion already, too. Where did

301

you find your Henson?"

"To tell ye the truth, I don't know where he came from, Uncle Wabi. I was in the barn grooming Merlin a few months ago and this huge cat wandered into the stall. Merlin stomped and snorted, then leaned his head down. It looked like they were talking to each other and the next thing I knew the cat had jumped on Merlin's rump and was rubbing his face against my hand. He's the biggest cat I've ever seen. And those black tipped ears and tail. He's unusual for sure. Looks more like a puma than a cat. And his coat is the color of old lady Henson's hair — some light areas and then some dark ones, like his tail and ears. Old lady Henson always had sweets, though, and I'd visit her cottage just to get some."

More like a puma, huh? Then, perhaps he found you, my boy.

"I've seen such a cat once before, in another lifetime. In the Orient. I feel sure that's where his origins are. But from what I've observed, he's attached himself to you already. Perhaps there will be a great friendship between the two of you."

"Yeah. He sleeps at my feet at night. I kinda like having him there."

"Just so. Groucho claimed that spot too. And Ian, be patient with your new friend. He may surprise you in ways you aren't expecting. Always remain open to new understandings. When we start closing our minds to new ideas and understandings, then we cease to grow. And the Creator chose you for a specific purpose. Your understanding of his purposes will come. Slowly."

They rapped on the door and it opened quickly.

"Wabi, I was hoping you'd get here soon. I picked the currants yesterday and have already baked goodies. I assume I could bribe you with a cup of tea and a slice of current pie?"

With a quick embrace and a peck on the cheek, Wabi took

her arm and turned to Ian. "Ian, this lovely lady is Aned Favré. She's an even better cook than I, and I don't say that lightly. She's a dear friend and I want you to get to know her."

Ian reached out his hand as Mam and Da had taught him. "It's my pleasure I'm sure, mam." He made a quick bow as well. This woman was much older than his mother had been when she passed away, but this young lad from the Highlands was taken by her beauty and the warmth that emanated from her. Her silver hair and eyes that twinkled were not lost on him and he was intrigued by her. He'd always thought everyone old would be ugly as well. Not so. This woman was most attractive still.

"Wabi told me there was a special young man in the Highlands, and I assume he meant you, Ian. Please come and have tea and a taste of pie. Wabi has been a friend for years and I am sure you will be also."

Groucho finally made an appearance, and just as Wabi had predicted, he lifted his nose, looked around for a second, and appeared to ignore them. Then finally he climbed into Wabi's lap and waited for his head rubbing. He and Wabi communicated in their own way and the old feline was always glad to see his Master.

"So tell me, how is Caitlin? Is she adjusting to life in the Highlands? It's so much different than here on the coast I am sure." She had addressed Ian, rather than Wabi.

"Uh, yes mam. I think she's all right. She's got a clinic going and now with the new children about the place she's really busy."

"New children? Wabi? I don't know anything about any children. Other than the child of the other woman, Millie, I believe you told me."

Aned had a memory that never ceased to amaze Wabi. She was not called, but certainly could have been. As it was, she followed the stories of his travels and Caitlin had been a constant visitor when she lived with Wabi.

"That girl always was one to keep you on your toes." She laughed.

"Yes, mam. Alex would agree with ye. He said the same thing just recently. He's getting used to her, though. We all have had to figure out a few things with Caitlin and Millie around. We'd just forgotten a few of our manners, I guess."

"Well, we all must make adjustments. And now I want to know all about you. What is your favorite book? Wabi has told me that you read a lot. I just finished, for the third time, *Alexander's Travels*, one of the few books I have left which is written in French. I speak English so-so, but reading is much easier for me if it's in French."

~ * ~

First thing next morning, Wabi took Ian to the village to show him around and have him meet his friends. This was the first time Ian had ever left the Highlands, and he was taking in all the sights.

"Uncle Wabi, this place looks a lot different from the Highlands. I didn't know there were ruins here. Can't wait to walk around them. And did you see that mist hovering over the water this morning?"

"Yes, my lad. *Eilean`a Chèo* (Isle of Skye) literally means 'island of mists' and some days the mist lingers most of the day and surrounds us in a warm blanket. And there's something comforting about it, I think. But today the sun is bright so we'll go to the Wild Boar. There'll be a number of folk there getting their scones and coffee this time of the morning. Maybe we'll see some of my friends."

Walking through the door of the Wild Boar, Wabi was never

so surprised. The place was filled to over-flowing and there was laughter and chattering folk everywhere. And to boot, Thomas was hurrying over to greet them.

"Ah, Mr. Wabi. So good to see you again. You've been away I see. And who is this fine young lad?" He reached out to shake Ian's hand. "Come over here, I've got a nice table just for you two. And try the scones, just made this morning."

Wabi started laughing and Ian was confused. "What's funny Uncle Wabi?"

"Oh, Ian. You have no idea what a despicable man Thomas was. He even tried to harm Caitlin once. It's an amusing story. Let's just say that I "convinced" him he'd be better off to treat folk with respect and refrain from thoughts of harming others."

"Looks like you must have convinced him well. He's ever so happy today."

"Yes. Power in the right hands, at the right time, can be quite helpful."

After a quick stroll around the perimeter of the village, the two started back to Wabi's place. There was always work to be done there, and Wabi was ready to begin his mentoring of Ian. The lad was just remarkable. Wabi decided he'd take the time to create a plan that would have him mentoring the lad in a way that would be efficient and satisfying for both. Too much too soon wouldn't work. The boy had always read, but his formal schooling was limited. But Wabi knew the lad would make great strides in a short amount of time.

On the way to Wabi's cottage, they walked passed Laird Gordon's estate with its tall, ornately scrolled gates. Wabi was suddenly attacked from the rear and found himself stumbling, then finally landed on his stomach and felt a very wet tongue licking his face.

"Maximo, you little beast. What are you doing outside the estate gates?"

The little beagle's tail flicked back and forth so rapidly that he could have flown if he had wanted to.

"Your master will not like it when he sees you've gotten outside. We'd better take you home, fella."

He picked the small dog up and headed for the iron gates that marked the opening at Laird Gordon's estate. He saw they were ajar, so he entered and walked to the front of the large, grand house. He rapped the brass knocker and waited for a short minute before the door was opened by the butler, dressed in the finest livery.

"Oh, good morning. I'm Wabi and I've come to return Maximo to Laird Gordon. I believe he's gotten out the gate and I'm sure his master would want him to be returned."

"Wait here, sir." The butler glanced down at the small dog, let out a loud sigh, then held his head high and walked down the hallway taking slow, measured steps.

Laird Gordon appeared shortly, outfitted in his hunting gear apparently headed out to shoot. "Ah, Wabi. Good to see you again. And I see you've found my long-lost hunting dog. He's been gone for a couple of days — this time. After his first few escapes, I searched and searched for him before finding him out at your place. Now when he's gone, I know where to look."

"Oh, he's been out to my place? I've been gone for a bit now, so I wouldn't't' know about that."

"Well, I tell you what, Wabi. If you think you could manage it, I'd appreciate it if you'd just take the dog with you. He's a great hunting dog and can run a rabbit farther than I can, that's for sure. But he's your dog, Wabi. That's obvious to me now. He'll never be happy with me. Do you think you could take him with you?"

Wabi bent down and held the dog's face in his hand, looking deep into his eyes.

Yes, you do belong to me. Then so be it.

He straightened, his back erect. "Of course I'll take him. What's one more animal? I've got an old tomcat, a cantankerous owl, and several hawks that live in my barn, and Ian has brought a young feline with him. I believe Maximo will fit right in."

They left the estate and headed to Wabi's place. This was quite a crew, the old man and the young lad, and one happy beagle prancing beside them, his tail curled over his back and his nose twitching in the air.

Ian was anxious to go exploring around Wabi's place. It was located right on the water's edge and he had spotted those ruins this morning. There were bound to be places where he would find interesting items. He supposed when Wabi was ready they would begin their work, but until then he'd spend his time doing what he loved more than anything . . . learning something new.

CHAPTER 30

Caitlin, I can't do this by myself! I know your clinic is important to you, but handling these children is a fulltime job. And I'd like to work on my ideas for the school. But as it is, you've left me here to take care of everything. Jack and Alex are out with the sheep, you and Daniel leave for the clinic and someone has to feed these children and know where they are every second. Mrs. Murray helps on the days she's here, but that's not every day. It's like trying to herd kittens! I have to do the wash each day, and then I have to prepare food for this large group. I tell you I've had it!"

Tears ran down her face and she made a quick exit down the hallway, her long, dark hair streaming behind her.

Caitlin stood watching her friend as she fled to her room.

Caitlin, my girl, looks like you still have that selfish streak inside. You've never had to think of others much. Uncle Wabi catered to your every whim and you never had to consider anyone else's needs. Looks like you better start thinking of others instead of yourself. Holy Rusephus, how could I be so blind.

She gathered her herbs and placed them on the shelf alongside her medicines that she placed in the highest cupboard, well out of the reach of the children. She'd been chastised, certainly, and knew she deserved it.

~ * ~

Alex and Jack had taken on a new farm hand, Boder, as Hector was spending all his time at the estate. And even though Jamie had been old, he had contributed to the daily work and his presence was missed in more ways than one. He had never let his age become an excuse for not doing his share of the work. The brothers had had a tiring day, too. Lambing season was upon them and their days started early and lasted well into the evening. When they finally arrived at the lodge, a bath and supper was about all they were good for.

"Is that rabbit stew I smell? We haven't had that in quite a while. That's a treat."

Jack had thought to find Millie at her usual spot preparing their evening vittles, but she wasn't there. Just now Caitlin was stirring a large pot, and even though she certainly knew her way around the kitchen they all knew that was Millie's domain.

Alex came up behind her and leaned over her shoulder, sniffing at her hair. "Where's Millie?"

"She's taking a short rest. I've got the children bathed already and we'll feed them shortly. Maybe Daniel will tuck them in with a story and we can all have a few quiet minutes. Today has been just a trifle busy around here."

"What are ye saying lass?" Jack picked at the loaf of bread that was laying on the counter, just begging for him to taste it. "Is Millie all right, then?"

"Yes, yes. But Dugald climbed the ladder in the stable and fell out the hay door opening. He's fine, but bruised his arm and has a knot on his head. Then Bridget ate all the apples Millie had sliced for her pie. That meant quite a stomachache for the lass. Finally, Charlie cried through Millie's entire reading lesson and refused to cooperate with her on anything she tried. It's been quite a trying day for her, Jack. You might want to take care of Midge for the rest of the evening. Let's let Millie have a few moments to herself."

"And how was yer day at the clinic? Da says the old ones think ye hung the moon, lass."

"My day was busy and Daniel is a Godsend. He knows everyone by first name, and thanks to him I know most of them now. But we need to consider moving the clinic up here, to the lodge. I hadn't thought about how much work we were putting on Millie's shoulders. When we first talked about her school plans and mine for a clinic, we didn't have the children we have now. Of course we want them here, but we all need to give Millie a hand. She's pretty fragile at the moment. I've just realized how selfish I'm been. Uncle Wabi told me there were two things I would always need to work on — my selfish nature and my quick temper. It looks like he was right, as usual."

"Ah, lass. Don't be so hard on yerself. But maybe ye've got a good idea there. Moving the clinic to the lodge. Da could talk the villagers into coming up here. Where do ye think Hector got his negotiating skills? Let's talk it over with him after supper. Not to worry so, lass. We'll work it out."

Alex was overjoyed with Caitlin's decision to move the clinic to the lodge. Of course, that meant another one of the huts needed to be cleaned and readied for her use. Kenny and Hamish knew just what to do now, having just finished the larger one for Uncle Andrew and his friend. Those two hadn't shown their faces yet, but it was ready when they did get here.

That evening, Caitlin cornered Da about her thoughts. "Daniel, it'll be a lot easier if I move my clinic here to the lodge. Millie needs help with the children, and it looks like there will be a dozen or more students from our area. Probably even more once word gets around about 'the Lady' and her school."

Both of them laughed and Daniel agreed with her about the clinic. The villagers were thrilled to finally have a healer, and they would make time to come to her, even if it did mean coming up the mountain a ways.

~ * ~

Caitlin's clinic was sporadic at first. It might take a while before the villagers came, but they eventually would. The move was certainly a help to Millie. Now that their daily routine was not quite so hectic, the women sat together to make plans for officially opening the school.

Millie began teaching the three children at the lodge, that way she could see what she might need to change before the school formally began. As might have been expected, Charlie was the child who demanded everyone's attention, and their patience as well. There were days Millie was at wit's end.

Today Caitlin walked in, placing several items on the table. "I told Uncle Wabi about Charlie and his hearing difficulty. He made a couple of suggestions that we might try when we're working with the lad. Here, sit and try this. Close your eyes now, and tell me what I've laid on the table."

Millie closed her eyes then, using her fingers, worked her way up and down the item Caitlin had placed in front of her.

"What is it? Can you tell?"

"Of course. It's a hairbrush. I use one every morning."

"Right. Now, close your eyes again. What's this?"

Millie felt the new item carefully, then turned it over. And she nodded. "It's one of my cookbooks. It's the one that has a picture of birds on the front. I can feel them. There are raised letters that read Blackbirds in a Pie."

Caitlin nodded to her friend. "So it was easy to identify both pieces, wouldn't you say?"

"Yes, of course."

"But you couldn't see them, could you?"

"Well, no, but I could tell what they were just by feeling them."

"Right. That's one of the suggestions Uncle Wabi made. He says people who are blind see with their hands. He also says people who are deaf hear with their eyes. We must teach Charlie to use his eyes to hear. Does that make any sense to you?"

"No. Not at all. If the child can't hear, then how does seeing help him with that?"

"Wabi says we should have him in the same class with the other children you are teaching to read. We should write the words on the board, and maybe draw a picture of the item, the word you're teaching him. Like the word 'book.' Write the word and draw a picture of a book next to it. That's a visual picture of the word.

Then, when you pronounce the words, slowly, look directly at Charlie, as I've seen you doing with the other children, and he can 'hear' in his own way. Uncle Wabi says we should have him take a finger and draw the letters of the word, then take his fingers and feel around the picture of the book. Apparently touching the letters and picture makes a connection that helps him remember the word. Like closing your eyes and feeling the trunk of a tree. You don't need anyone to tell you it's a tree. Your fingers 'see' it's a tree and a picture comes to your mind immediately. He may never be able to speak, but he can certainly learn to hear in his own way."

"Well, it's worth a try. But Caitlin, you have to help me with this. It's bound to be a challenge for him."

"And a challenge for us, too. But of course I'll help. Should

313

have been more thoughtful all along. I've been told more than once that I have a selfish streak, Millie. But it's a trait I'm working on. Trust me, I'll not leave everything to you again."

"Ah, Caitlin. It was just a bad day, I suppose. But it occurs to me once we really get this school going and your clinic is at full speed, we could use more help. Hector will find a buyer for my jewels, so perhaps we could use those proceeds to hire a helper, or two? And Dorothea will be here soon. She'll be a big help."

"Hmm. That's not a bad idea. But we'll need to get Jack and Alex behind us. I've already learned they have a real need to be consulted on our plans. Yeah, let's ask their opinion first."

They laughed together, as they always did.

~ * ~

"Alex, would ye look at that. I never would have believed it," Jack said.

He and Alex watched from the window as a coach pulled up in front of the lodge, creaking loudly as it came to a halt. Uncle Andrew opened the door, stepped down from the carriage and held out his hand.

"We're here finally, lass. Come now, it's only family here. The whole clan has been waiting to meet ye."

For the longest minute he stood there, waiting. Finally, with another bit of coaxing, his companion stepped out as well.

Jack looked at Alex and they called to the girls. "Millie, Caitlin, Come look!"

"Jack MacKinnon, stop your gawking and walk out to meet them. Mam taught you better manners than that."

"But Millie, she's not at all what we were expecting."

Alex nodded his agreement with that statement.

314

"Nevertheless, you two get yourselves out there and invite her in. Andrew's kin, but a gesture of welcome would be in order. Go now."

Alex led the way and, after a hug for Uncle Andrew, he bowed from the waist and introduced himself. "Good evening, mam. I'm Alex and this is Jack. We're glad you finally made it to our home. Please come in and meet everyone."

Jack just nodded when he was introduced.

Uncle Andrew addressed the two. "Alex, Jack. 'Tis good to see ye, lads. Coming by coach takes a wee bit longer than I expected it would, but it seemed like the most comfortable way to bring Camille to her new home."

The woman had yet to say a word. She stood close by Andrew's side and held on to his hand. She was rather tall. Not as tall as Millie, but much taller than Caitlin. And she was thin. Her hair was a rich, deep brown with silver threads running through it and she had tied it back with a yellow ribbon, with curls managing to escape their confines in several places. Her large brown eyes were her best feature, and her smile began in them before it got to her lips. She was a most attractive woman, and somewhat younger than Andrew.

"Camille, these two young lads, excuse me, young men, are my nephews. They'll grow on ye lass — just give 'em a little time." He laughed and pulled Camille's arm, moving her forward.

Entering the great room, Daniel met them at the door. He greeted Andrew, shook hands with Camille and took her coat, hanging it on a peg with the others.

Caitlin and Millie came in and Daniel introduced them to Uncle Andrew's lady friend.

Millie spoke first. "Camille, it's such a pleasure to meet you. We've been so excited since Uncle Andrew informed us of your plans. Another woman at this place will be most welcome I assure you."

"And I'm Caitlin. Millie couldn't have put it any better. We're outnumbered here and a woman from the city will be such a treat for us. It's not everyday we meet one who can tell us what's happening in the rest of the country. We're delighted to have you here."

It was obvious Camille was painfully shy, but she straightened her shoulders and smiled to the two ladies, and spoke quietly. "You are so very kind. Andrew has told me stories of you, his family. I'm very hopeful that not all of them are true."

That brought laughter from the group.

"And I thank you for your hospitality." She nodded her head slightly, and then took Andrew's hand in hers once again.

Daniel was passing around cups of cider when a shrill scream rang out from the top of the stairs. "Alex, help me!" The voice was high-pitched and filled with giggles.

Alex smiled as he watched Bridget come flying down the stairs into his waiting arms.

"Whoa, now. What's going on here?"

"Dugald found a spider and tried to put it down the back of my dress. I hate spiders!"

"Well, then. We'll have to talk to Dugald, I suppose." He grinned at the girl and let her slide to the floor. She was off before he could say another word.

"Alex? I know time flies quickly, especially at my age, but I've only been gone a short while and ye've got a daughter it appears." Andrew lifted his eyebrows and looked to Daniel to see if he had any information to parcel out. But nothing was coming from that quarter.

"Actually, Uncle Andrew, I've a daughter and two sons. But

316

I'm not really sure if they're mine, ye ken? They could be Jack's too, I suppose. Or maybe Hector's — even Da's."

Andrew laughed a hardy laugh and shook his head. "So ye see, lass, it's just as I told ye. These lads are always coming up with surprises and I never know what to expect when I return."

Daniel took a seat next to the couple and gave them a rundown on the children. "Andrew, it's a lot like it was when the lads were wee ones. Lots of laughter, lots of screaming, and lots of food being prepared. So ye may have to add another page to yer history. I suppose there's a way to indicate orphans in the recording?"

"Well, what I don't know, Camille does. She's been working in the Department of Ancestry at the library in Edinburgh for a number of years now. No doubt we'll make a way to record it properly."

Following Millie's fine dinner of roasted woodcock and clootie dumplings for dessert, Daniel took Andrew and Camille over to their recently renovated hut.

"The ladies had the lads, Kenny and Hamish, do a cleaning job on the hut. Had them do it twice, as I recollect. And they found a few items they thought would make the place a bit more hospitable."

He walked in and lighted several candles that Caitlin and Millie had placed throughout the hut. The lads had built a small peat fire in the fireplace and it glowed and gave off a softness that made the place so inviting.

"Oh, Andrew, will you look at that. A brass bed and a duvet. Oh, and look here — this rug is hand woven. And look at the beautiful colors. It will feel so good on a cold morning."

She walked quietly about the room, touching the small items Caitlin and Millie had arranged — the heather in a bowl, Mam's potpourri they found in the closet, and a small pitcher of cider and two glasses sat on the old oak table next to the bed. She stopped then, as if embarrassed she had spoken so freely.

Andrew grinned and winked at Daniel. "Tell the lasses it's verra fine. Verra fine indeed."

Daniel excused himself and left the couple to themselves.

Inside the lodge, Jack and Alex were still wondering how in the world this couple had gotten together.

"Alex, I bet ye a crown she's a good ten years younger than Andrew."

"I'm not a betting man, Jack. That dark hair is streaked with silver strands, and those crinkles around her eyes tell me she's no spring chicken. But she's a beautiful woman, no doubt. And thin, too. Sorta like Mam, huh?"

"Yeah, and to think Uncle Andrew has talked her into coming here and she's agreed to live with him. No ceremony as I understand it."

More change. More change, Jack thought to himself.

"It's called hand fasting, Jack. It was common in earlier years. She probably has her reasons for not wanting a ceremony. Let's just accept that it's what the two of them want," Millie suggested.

Millie could think of many reasons to not marry. She'd already had one marriage she hadn't wanted. Though now, with Jack, she saw how wonderful it could be. But the fact she'd made her own decisions about it was what was important.

CHAPTER 31

"Whoa now. Whoa. Stopping here young lass. Stopping here." Responding to Deirdre's tap, tap, tap on the roof, the coachman pulled hard on the reins and shortly the lumbering vehicle came to a jostling halt. Each turn of its creaking wheels created unbearable nausea for the lass inside and the driver had to stop numerous times for her to expel her stomach contents. Some three hours into the journey he realized this was going to be a very long trip. Thankfully, the only other rider, an elderly man who slept most of the way, didn't seem too irritated by all the stops. His own hangover from last evening's affair was obvious to the coachman.

Constable Stewart had never been so glad to get anyone off his hands. The lass cried the entire time she was in his station and he wasn't sure whether to believe her or not when she spoke of a relative in Edinburgh. Finally deciding he could no longer stand her incessant noise, he put her on the first coach he could find going that way. He paid her passage and included a few coins to ensure she didn't lack for food.

As she held her head in her hands trying to fight back another wave of nausea, Deirdre wondered how she was going to explain her situation to Aunt Margaret, her mother's sister. The truth was that she had only met her once when she was a young child. Her mother never spoke much of her, and when she did it was always in reference to "my sister, the Lady Margaret." The sisters never had agreed on much of anything, and keeping in touch was not something that either spent much time pursing.

Deirdre knew full well she was suffering the abrupt cessation of the potion she had been using for some time. Nezerra was gone now, and as Deirdre's mind began to surface from the fog that had surrounded it she desperately needed to find someone to replace Nezerra. Well, actually, she only needed the potion, and at this moment she would have given her right arm for just a small taste. Her memory of that evening in the cave was hazy at best, but she hadn't forgotten that Alex MacKinnon had been the one to take her to the constable. She also recalled how he refused to even look at her. That he loathed her very presence came through loud and clear.

I'm ill at the moment and unable to follow ye, Alex MacKinnon, but our business is not finished. Ye'll find I don't give up so easily.

Even as the thought of finding him again ran through her head, she knew he'd never want her as she had hoped. That red-haired lass had captured his heart as surely as Deirdre had captured her. As she thought back on the evening when she had kidnapped Caitlin following the wedding ceremonies, she realized her plan could have been better laid out.

Yes, just a bit more planning and it would have worked. Still, who knows what tomorrow may bring? Perhaps the lass will still meet an untimely death. He may not want me, but I can keep him from having her. That would be his reward for his treatment of me.

Arriving in Edinburgh, she made her way to the address on the last letter her mother had received from her sister. Deirdre hoped the woman would remember her, as she had no idea where she would go if she didn't. Thankfully, the nausea had subsided greatly and she had straightened her hair and tied it back. When she got to the address, she was surprised at the size of the dwelling. She stared at the tall black door, complete with a brass knocker — a lion's head — for a long minute before rapping. In a few moments, an elderly woman, rather short and stout and very bent over, answered.

"Good morning, Aunt Margaret. It's me, Deirdre — Ellen's daughter from the northern Highlands. Remember me?"

The old woman pushed her glasses up, peered closely at the girl and looked a bit confused. "You be looking for your aunt you say?"

Deirdre realized quickly that she had made a mistake. This woman was not her aunt. "Oh, perhaps I have the wrong address. Excuse me, please." As she began to turn away, the old woman called out to her.

"Mrs. Margaret lives here, lass. Come in and I'll get her for you."

Deirdre followed as the woman slowly went back in.

"Wait here and I'll bring her to you."

Deirdre stood staring at the place, the many paintings on the walls, the luxurious drapes at the tall windows, and the black and white tiled floor that shone as if just polished.

So this is what my mother meant by the Lady Margaret.

She could hear voices coming from farther inside, but couldn't distinguish what was being discussed. Shortly, the old woman returned with another woman, this one almost as old as the one answering the door. The only real difference was that this one was dressed in a very fine frock and was rather tall and thin. Her hair was pulled up in a bun and the lace at her throat and sleeves was exquisite.

"Hello. I'm Margaret Finlayson. May I help you?"

"Yes . . . I mean, I hope so. I'm Deirdre, Ellen's daughter. Your sister, Ellen?"

"Ellen's daughter. What a pleasant surprise. Come in child, come in." She smiled at the girl and led her to a large room at the rear of the house. The room had floor-to-ceiling windows and fresh flowers in a crystal vase that sent out splinters of color as the light bounced off it.

"Here, my girl, sit next to me. My hearing is not quite what is used to be, so I must listen closely."

Deirdre sat next to her aunt and had difficulty concentrating on the conversation as she was so distracted by the sheer opulence surrounding her. She had never seen such fine furniture and art.

"Ellen didn't write me back after my annual Christmas letter to her. I suppose we'll never see eye-to-eye, but one would think a letter once a year wouldn't be too much for either of us. Tell me, is she well?"

"Oh, nae. She's passed on just recently, ye see. The arthritis has kept her in bed for the last year or so and she come down with a cough that finally got the best of her. She was laid to rest next to me da, and now I've no one. Lately I've been sick meself, and I've come here hoping I might have a place to rest, just for a short white, ye ken?"

The woman folded her hands under her chin. "Oh, heavens. Ellen's gone? I do wish I had known she was sick. Perhaps Henry could have sent a doctor to help her. But then, knowing Ellen, she wouldn't have agreed to anything I might have suggested. Still, it grieves me to know she's gone. I must tell Henry about this situation. Now, what did you say your name was again?"

~ * ~

During the first few days, her aunt's resemblance to her own mother stirred nostalgic memories that had Deirdre longing for her family as they were in her younger years. She and her mother would often take baked goods to neighbors who could no longer get about. She remembered mother's voice even now. "Caring for your neighbor is not a chore, Deirdre. It is a chance to return the gifts that have been given us."

It was one of these neighborly errands to the MacKinnon home that had facilitated the girl's fascination with Alex. When her mother heard Mrs. MacKinnon was under the weather, they made sure to take some home-baked goods to her. Everyone knew that with a house full of men another plate of food would be welcome. The lass had known the MacKinnon lads all her life, but she was only now seeing how handsome the oldest one, Alex, had become and her mind was made up on that day that he would be hers. But that was not what had happened as she well recalled.

Aunt Margaret was thrilled to have a young niece in residence, even though she usually couldn't recall her name nor remember why she had come. It only took Deirdre a few days to see that her aunt was able to get around fairly well with the help of a cane, but was having great difficulty with her memory and often went about her home talking to her late husband, Henry. The old servant, Tilly, kept the place up, but had no idea what to do when her employer walked about talking to someone that wasn't there. She kept the knowledge to herself, as she totally depended on her wages for her existence. Apparently Aunt Margaret's husband had been a man of means and had left the widow well-heeled.

Edinburgh was turning out to be quite an exciting adventure for Deirdre. She took several weeks to regain her strength, then began to make her way about the city, learning everything about the place. She had never been there before, and the sheer size of the city was thrilling to her. Her favorite place was the High Street with its castle and where there were many merchants selling their wares.

She'd never seen so many tempting items.

Quickly realizing that her aunt was not mentally sharp, Deirdre took over the management of her household and, most conveniently for her, the funds. Among the merchants on the High Street, there was one that Deirdre became close friends with. This merchant was more than glad to supply her with another potion, much like Nezerra's. Now, with her aunt's money, keeping a supply on hand was much easier, and she put Alex MacKinnon out of her mind — for the moment.

CHAPTER 32

Caitlin discovered that having her clinic at the lodge was much more convenient than in the village. The village folk were beginning to come almost daily now, and she and Millie worked together in the school. Word about the Lady's school had gotten around and presently there were a dozen children coming each morning for instruction. Millie had one group working on arithmetic and another on reading. She wanted to teach them French and maybe a bit of science, but there were only the two of them and Caitlin was often busy tending her patients.

"Caitlin, I know we've talked about it already, but we're going to have to hire help. We've got to convince Jack and Alex that we're making a contribution to this place."

"Aye. By the end of the day I've barely got enough energy to get the children bathed, fed and to bed."

"Then we'll have to get on this right away. I know if we look around, surely we can find a person who's able to teach. Certainly to help with the reading. That's the key to all the rest. If they can't read, then nothing else matters."

~ * ~

Daniel had made the decision to move the gravesite of the child, Alex's twin, Amber. He thought Easter Sunday would be a most appropriate day.

"That seems like a perfect day to do something this important. Alice made me promise, and I don't want to go back on my word."

"Da, let Alex and me dig for ye." Jack thought it would be too much for Da to take on that chore.

"If you must, then, all right. It's just the tiniest little coffin, lads. She was only one day old, so it'll not be difficult. But I'm ready to put her next to her mother. My soul would never rest if I should pass on before I get that task done."

So here it was, Easter morning. Spring in the Highlands was a most welcome sight. And on this day, even the wind on top of the moor was not as brisk and chilly as it was most days. The clan all gathered around and Uncle Andrew had thought it appropriate to have a short scripture reading followed by a prayer. The small little coffin was laid to rest in its new place, right next to Mam's grave. Millie had remembered to bring a wreath, and the daffodils that had just bloomed seemed perfect for a child's grave.

It was a short ceremony, and even though the lads had never known their sister, this Amber, they felt a connection. Da's face was peaceful and he smiled at the group.

"My thanks to ye all. She'll be more at peace here, I believe. I know Alice is pleased, as I am."

Uncle Andrew and Camille strolled about the cemetery, Andrew pointing out gravestones of the various family members. Millie and Jack followed behind as the children ran down the hill. Alex and Caitlin stayed a few moments and walked about the burial plot. They placed a wreath on Mam's grave also. They had recently noticed that the fresh flowers that were always on her grave were not there now.

326

"Yes, of course—Ian. The lad always thought she was special . . . think it went both ways." Alex nodded.

"I want to go inside the circle while we're here. It'll only take a moment." Caitlin looked at him closely to see his reaction.

Alex stood tall, then walked over to the circle with her.

"Wait here."

He looked on as she went to the center, bowed her head and then lifted her face to the sky. Immediately the golden light made an appearance and Caitlin's face registered her feelings. A few minutes passed in which Alex watched Caitlin, wondering what she experienced in the circle. "Oh, Alex, it's gone. The crying's gone. The child is quiet now. She doesn't call to me anymore."

She smiled and the relief was so great she hardly knew how to react. Just then she experienced a novel happening, and it was pleasing to her. "Come inside, Alex. Come, hurry."

Alex had lost his fear of the circle, but still thought he should be reverent when he entered in. He knew Caitlin's presence would protect him, but he still wasn't too keen on going inside. He walked to her and she smiled up at him and took both his hands.

"Alex, the child is at peace now. It was Amber calling to me. She's where she wants to be now. With her mother."

"But why would she single you out? Because you're one of the called?"

"I'm not sure, but maybe that could be part of it. But at this moment, I know another reason why she called to me. Alex, I've just experienced the quickening."

"Quickening? What does that mean?"

"It's the small fluttering in my stomach that tells me I'm about to be a mother also. I believe Amber sensed that. I've been so busy I didn't pay attention to the signals, but she did. I was drawn to the circle from the first day I came, before I was pregnant, but lately even more so."

"Caitlin? Are ye sure, *mo chridhe?*"

Caitlin's smile grew even wider. "Yes. I'm sure. All the signs were there. They just didn't register with me. The irrational moods I've been having, the blazing energy, and then the lack of it. Yes. I'm sure."

"Jesus. Whatever are we going to do with another child?" He was thrilled, but at the same time he just couldn't see how they would manage.

"Oh, I think we'll probably make room somewhere, don't you?"

Alex held her close and sent a prayer of thanksgiving to whomever was listening.

"Aye. I'm quite sure we will."

The two of them walked together quietly, each with their own thoughts. Alex was grinning so big his face hurt. Finally, he let out a "WooHoo!" that echoed from one end of the moor to the other. The others, almost home already, heard him. Probably not what he should have done following this ceremony, but he couldn't hold back another second.

"Wonder what's got into Alex. He never shows that much emotion over anything." Jack looked at Millie, who just shrugged.

They waited up a bit to let Alex and Caitlin catch them.

"So are ye gonna tell us, or are we gonna have to pull it out of ye? What's got ye so excited, brother?"

"Well, Jack, it appears we're going to have to add another room onto the lodge."

"What? It's pretty big already Alex. Not sure why we would need to do that."

"Why did Da always add another room, Jack?" Millie asked.

She grinned and gave her friend a hug.

"Oh, that's so exciting, Caitlin. There's nothing like your own bairn, I can tell you that much."

"What? Yer gonna have a bairn? Well, why didn't ye just say so?" Jack hadn't given a lot of thought to more children. He loved little Midge and the new children seemed to fit right in. But it looked like he may have to start thinking more about that, children that is. "Then I believe we'd better start making plans, huh?"

"Yes, I suppose we'd better. I'll continue with the clinic and the school until I waddle too much to do so," Caitlin laughed. "But I don't think there's any question but that we'll need help. What do you think, Alex? Jack? Maybe we can find someone to help us out a little? The village needs this school and the clinic is getting busier every day."

"Aye, lass, we'll put our heads together. We'll figure it out when we get back. Jack and I'll be gone a couple of days next week, and we'll need Boder, the new hand, to go with us. We're taking a few sheep to MacDonald. He lost a few this past winter and wants to increase his flock. Our lambing season was good, so we can easily get rid of a handful. With Hector at the estate, that means you and Millie will be here by yerselves. Think ye'll manage?"

"Daniel and Andrew are here. Willie, too. And Da's as good with those children as either of us. We'll be fine."

She had no qualms about the men leaving them now. Deirdre was banished from the village, the school was going well, and her clinic was beginning to serve many folk. The fact that the circle of stones was no longer calling to her also put Caitlin's mind at ease. She'd finally figured out the nightmares and crying of the child.

She stopped for a moment as a particular thought flashed into her head. What had Uncle Wabi said? "The answer to your nightmares lies in the circle of stones."

That's what he meant. She was lying in the circle of stones all this time.

She started to walk again, but then another quick flash of memory registered. "In your condition, putting up a protective barrier was exactly the right thing to do. And when you are thinking of this, ask yourself who is the most protective creature on the earth?"

Of course. A mother is the most protective creature ever. He knew. He knew all along.

But in his usual way, he'd let her figure it out on her own. She missed him still and was glad Ian was with him. That arrangement would be good for both of them.

~ * ~

"Daniel, do you think we could go to the village and look for another woman to help us here? Millie and I are stretched already and Mrs. Murray's getting on in years. She does the scrubbing of the floors and helps with the laundry, and we need her of course, but with more than a dozen children in our school we could use another hand."

"Aye, lass. Surely we can find a body who's needing work. A small bit of coin will help folk for sure. But it'll be better if I come with ye. Together we'll make a better decision about who to choose. Tomorrow we'll head down and try to get this chore done."

Next morning Millie and Caitlin were dishing out breakfast bowls of porridge and toast. Jack and Alex had left early headed to the MacDonald farm, and Daniel was making himself useful, refilling porridge bowls and wiping sticky fingers.

"Guess Alice might could have used a little help in her day, too, but I was so busy trying to make a living with the sheep. So she did it all by herself. Course, she wouldn't have wanted it any other way, she was like that."

The back door opened and Uncle Andrew stuck his head in. "Could a neighbor get a cup of coffee, ye think?"

"I believe there's a fresh pot brewing on the stove. Come in and we'll find a cup for ye. Ah, Camille, come in lass. There's plenty for everyone."

The couple had pretty much kept to themselves these first weeks and the others gave them their privacy. They usually ate the supper meal with the clan, but the rest of the day they were either at the hut or they'd walk about the moor, her staying close to him.

"Good morning, Camille. We're having porridge and toast. Would you care for a taste?"

"No, thanks, Millie. I had toast and current jelly earlier — a jar that I brought with me. But coffee would be just right."

The children were hustled off to the great room where they were to sit by the fire until such time as Millie indicated the school day was to start. Then she'd gather them and take them out to the smaller hut where the classroom was organized. Until then, however, Tess and Willie would put up with their pulling and riding. Willie had taken to staying close to Charlie, but often he could still be seen sitting wherever Caitlin was. He was hers, and that would never change. But at the moment, he sensed Charlie was needy and he allowed the lad a bit of his attention.

Andrew sipped his coffee, and cleared his throat. "Ahem. We've been wondering, the two of us, about a situation and would like to ask your opinion. All of ye."

"What's that, Andrew?" Da asked.

Daniel was pleased Andrew had found Camille. He, himself, had no interest in any other woman in his life. Alice was his only love, and that was that. But this Camille was special to Andrew and he to her.

"From what we've observed for a few weeks now, it looks like ye two ladies have a lot on yer plate. As ye know, Camille has been employed at the Department of Ancestry in Edinburgh. She's recorded and researched clan histories for years now and was the person who got me going on my own work. There's not much the lass doesn't know about tracing a family line to the earliest days. What you don't know is that she was educated at the University in Edinburgh. She's studied history, the sciences, mathematics, and she speaks French as well as Gaelic and English. Oh, and she plays the harpsichord, too. We were wondering if ye'd consider letting her help with the teaching."

Millie looked at Camille. She was never so surprised. This woman was so shy and quiet that this would have never occurred to her.

"Camille? You'd like to help us?"

"Yes. I might could help with teaching the sciences, I believe. It was my best subject at university and it still interests me. And I have had training in music — harpsichord and violin."

"My word, we had no idea we had such a learned person here at the lodge. Why, we would be ever so glad to have you."

Caitlin had great respect for those who had received an education at university. She'd read articles about the medical treatments being developed in Edinburgh, and she had heard Alex speak of a Dr. Lind, who was quite a learned man in the medical field. Perhaps one day she might take a trip to Edinburgh.

"Oh, Camille, that would be grand. Maybe later today we can sit together and make a schedule that will work for the three of us."

Daniel and Andrew exchanged a look they both understood.

Keep the women occupied and they'll make our lives easier.

CHAPTER 33

Hector hadn't been as fortunate as Millie and Caitlin in finding someone to help him — specifically, someone to manage the daily operations of the Cameron Sanctuary when he was finished with his role in setting it up. Clint and Ethel had spread the word around the village that they were looking for a woman to manage the Sanctuary, but none had appeared so far.

Sitting in his office, actually just a small area in a corner of the great room, he wanted to do one more final calculation before he could be assured his figures were correct and he was comfortable about submitting them to Millie. All the bedrooms had been outfitted with several small beds that could accommodate children and would also be large enough for the women, and the dining room now held three long trestle-type tables that would seat at least ten. The former gardeners had been re-employed and several gardens had been planted and were being cared for daily. Ethel had located the young girls that had worked at the castle before and, with a bit of coaxing, they had returned to their posts. There was still fear in the village, as the assailant of the Cameron ladies was still at large. Now that Clint and Winston had funds to work with, the sheep were being sheared and the proceeds already coming in from that. So the only hitch was their inability to find a manager.

As Hector was closing his ledgers, he heard someone

approaching. Clint made his presence known by clearing his throat. "Uh, excuse me, Hector, but there's a young woman here asking about getting work in the Sanctuary. Ye can find her outside in the flower garden. She was taken with that so I told her to wait there."

"Did she say what kind of work? Kitchen work or gardening?"

"Nae. I didn't ask her, ye ken? Didn't seem to be any of me business, and I knew ye'd do better talking to her than me."

Hector nodded, put his ledgers away and walked out to the flower garden. The gardeners not only worked wonders with vegetables and fruits, but the flower garden was bursting out with blossoms all over. Spring in the Lowlands came much sooner than it did in the Highlands, and it was obvious the gardeners were more than glad to have employment again.

For a few seconds he saw no one, thinking perhaps the woman had left. Then, just a few yards to his left, there was movement and he looked in that direction. A young woman was bent over examining a large bloom on a rosebush. She raised up and turned in his direction, then stood there staring at him. He stared back and neither of them said a word for the longest moment.

Hector was quite sure he had never seen a more beautiful woman. Her luxurious, long hair was a soft, light brown, a color he had seen on many young fawns, and it was held back with a blue ribbon. She was average height, rather thin, and was wearing a plain, very prim, blue dress with white collar and cuffs. However, there was nothing average or plain about her face. She appeared to look him over from head to toe and when she finally let her gaze meet his eyes, he took a deep breath and let it go slowly. The only word that would describe her eye color was violet — the color of the amethyst broach he'd seen Mam wear over the years. But that was impossible

— no one had violet eyes — but obviously this woman did.

Hector finally found his tongue and re-engaged his brain. He nodded his head and bowed slightly to the woman. "Hello, madam. I'm Hector MacKinnon. Clint tells me yer seeking work here at the Sanctuary. What kind of work are ye looking for, may I ask?"

She made a half-curtsy and introduced herself. "Hello, sir. I'm Regina Carmichael. I understand there is a position available here at Cameron Castle for someone to manage the new Sanctuary project."

"Yes, that's right. The Sanctuary is ready, but we're still seeking someone to manage it. We need someone with some experience, however. Do you have any experience running a business or a large house?"

"Yes, actually, I do. I've been Lodge Manager for the hunting lodge at the Wellington Estate for the past two years. My husband was the Games Keeper and I was in charge of organizing lodging and accommodations for the guests of the Wellingtons whenever they entertained hunting parties. They had shooting events and occasionally clan gatherings, which required me to plan meals for a large number of folk, keep the books, and organize the staff that was needed for the events."

"I see. That sounds like quite a lot of experience, but I must ask, why are ye looking for employment? Do ye no longer work there?"

"Nae, I am no longer needed there. My husband was killed in a shooting accident about six months ago. Master Wellington very graciously kept me on as a matter of courtesy, but I know they would prefer a new husband and wife team to take over. Without my husband there, I find it very lonely so I've decided to seek a new place and start my life again. I am in hopes that this position might be one that would provide me this new start."

Hector found himself staring at the woman again and struggled to find the words he needed. This woman could be the answer to his problem. She certainly spoke like an educated woman and her experience seemed adequate.

"Then perhaps we should talk further. This project is a new one and we'll all have to work together to make it a success. My brother's wife, Millie, is the granddaughter of Mrs. Cameron and the estate now belongs to her. It was her idea to have this Sanctuary. I agreed to help her get it going, but eventually I'll return to the Highlands. The manager will have a lot of responsibilities for sure."

The young woman had listened carefully, but as yet had said nothing more. Hector really didn't want to see her walk away so quickly, so he made a suggestion that might keep her for a while longer.

"Seeing as it's getting late, why don't we meet at the Mermaid Inn for supper and we'll talk more detail. Would that be agreeable to you?"

The woman nodded her agreement and thanked Hector for his time.

That evening, following a long meal during which Hector filled her in on as many details as he could think of, both of them agreed that this arrangement might work.

"It appears to me that you are just what we need for this position, so it's yours if ye want it. But ye must understand, if Millie disagrees with my choice, then that is that. Her decisions are the ones that really matter. She'll be down next week to see the changes we've made and I'll arrange for the two of ye to have some time together. But if yer willing, I'd like ye to start as soon as possible. We already have several women with children huddling in a lean-to at the back of the estate, desperate for help. Once yer here, we can begin to bring

336

those and others in."

"Tomorrow suits me and I'll be here early and see what needs to be done. Thank you, Mr. MacKinnon. I look forward to working with you and meeting my employer."

He stood up quickly and pulled out her chair. "Hector — call me Hector," he said as he helped her with her coat.

"And I'm Reggie," she said as she smiled at him and disappeared out the door of the Inn.

CHAPTER 34

In a short time, Caitlin's condition was obvious. Even she was surprised at how quickly her middle had grown. She had guessed the bairn would be born in June, but she wasn't sure. Alex was excited, but was anxious about this new situation. What if she died during childbirth? It was not uncommon and now, after learning about having a twin sister who died, that thought was running around in his head. And she looked really big to him already.

"Oh, Alex, don't be such a worrywart. Just look at Millie and Midge. That child was born out in the forest in the middle of a snowstorm, and they made it through just fine. And so will I."

~ * ~

Millie had her hands full. She'd spent hours making "word cards" for the class, but she had Charlie in mind when she was creating them. Writing the words on them was easy enough, but drawing the pictures was not so easy. But she needed a lot of cards in order to help Charlie, so she'd keep working on them. Now that they had Camille to help them, there was no need for Daniel and Caitlin to go to the village looking for help.

"Daniel, she's just too perfect. We could have scoured the entire Highlands and never come across one with her education, training and experience. Uncle Andrew has helped us in more ways than one."

"Then maybe he and I can get back to the discussions we always used to have. We've solved most of the world's problems, lass. Did ye know that? Then, with ye ladies well into yer routine today, perhaps the two of us might make a trip to the village ourselves. I'd like his opinion on a young pony I'm looking at. Murdock showed him to me last week, but I'm not sure he's what we need."

"Whatever do we need another pony for?" asked Caitlin.

"Well, lass, young Dugald will be needing a pony to learn to ride, ye ken? He's small, but now's the time to start him out, teaching him about taking care of the animal first, of course. Then, once he's got that down I'll be teaching him to ride."

"But why can't he ride Ian's horse, Merlin?"

"Oh, no. Merlin's not the easiest mount to ride. And besides that, something tells me Ian will be here to retrieve him shortly. They've been together a while now."

"I guess I hadn't thought about that. So, Da, does that mean you think Ian will never come back to the lodge? To live here with us?"

"That's not for me to say. It's clear to me he's where he needs to be, with Wabi. That one will take care of him well enough. But he's a MacKinnon, and that means he'll make his own decisions. A family trait I'm afraid."

"Yes, I'm familiar with that family trait." She smiled at him. "Then we'll see you two later this evening?"

"We wouldn't miss one of Millie's meals. We're old, but not without our good senses. Well, not yet anyway. And Alex and Jack should be here today, too, if they get their business with MacDonald finished. So we'll see ye at supper."

340

So the two old ones rode out, glad to have a few hours of man-to-man companionship.

Caitlin headed to the stable as Alex had told her she might find a few cages there. Camille had already made a list of items she would need for organizing her science class. The first items on the list were small animal cages, and a bird's nest. Caitlin decided not to ask what Camille was going to do with these items. Just the fact she was willing to help them was enough for Caitlin. Rounding up cages might be easy enough, but a bird's nest?

Willie walked beside her, attentive as always. Charlie had been marched into the classroom with the others so the wolf was free for a while. As soon as they arrived in the barn, however, Willie jumped in front of Caitlin and snarled. His hackles stood on end and he bared his teeth, showing the fangs that had been used more than once to protect his master.

"Easy, Willie. What is it?"

Caitlin had learned to always listen to messages from Willie. He stood even closer to her, prohibiting her to move another step. Every muscle in his body was taut and ready to spring at her command.

"Who's there? Where are you?" Caitlin called out. Her scalp was stinging and the hair on her arms was standing at attention.

There was a front door to the barn and also a small side door they used for loading hay from the loft. Both were open, but even with that much light there were shadowed corners in the building where anyone could be hiding.

For several moments there was not a sound in the stable save the wind whistling through the open door. Willie's growl filled the hollow emptiness, and the air quivered with his rumble. Caitlin immediately held her hands over her large abdomen — a protective gesture as natural as breathing.

341

Then she heard a small cry. "Oh!"

The cry was cut short, and then she heard a gasp, as if one were trying to get a breath of air. She turned in the direction of the noise, directly to her left. Apparently the intruder had come through the side door.

Turning all her senses on alert, Caitlin's nose was the first to send her information — a floral scent — then a voice confirmed the message from her nostrils.

"So, looks like ye did keep my Highlander warm through the winter, then. What he ever saw in a tiny lass like ye is beyond me."

Caitlin's eyes took in the scene in front of her — it was too awful to contemplate and her brain was having great difficulty organizing her thoughts.

Be still Caitlin. Think. Don't do anything that will anger her further.

Caitlin's reactions needed to be measured now, and she needed to give all her concentration to the task at hand. Most of all, she knew she had to keep her emotions corralled so as not to unleash her powers. What effect they could have on her unborn child was unknown. Uncle Wabi had reminded her that "you did what you needed to do to protect," so she needed to figure a way out of this situation without bringing down the wrath of power that was at her fingertips, the wrath she had brought on Lord Warwick and Commander Campbell.

But harnessing that power might prove to be a difficult task. She could already feel it simmering and boiling up inside her and, like Willie when he saw Deirdre, it just wanted to attack.

Deirdre was standing a few feet in front of her, holding young Charlie around his chest with her left arm, lifting him off his feet. Her right hand held a long-bladed knife at his throat, and a small trail of blood trickled down his thin neck. The little child's face was so white Caitlin feared he would faint. But he never uttered a sound. With the knife digging into his neck, he trembled from head to toe.

Deirdre stared at Caitlin, taking note of the fear in the pregnant woman's face.

"What? Ye thought I'd stay in Edinburgh with my daffy old aunt while yer here with Alex living the life that should have been mine? Not likely. And who does this bairn belong to? Huh? He came just at the right moment. And I see yer protector is still with ye. But if he comes any closer, I'll slice this lad's throat before ye can blink an eye. I will. Ye know that though, don't ye?"

"Deirdre, let that child go. He's done nothing to harm you. He's only a small lad."

"Oh, for sure. But he came into the barn and he was just what I needed — a prize to bargain with. So, Caitlin, I'll thank ye to put that wolf in his cage now. He never has cared much for me. If ye don't, then the boy will die. He means nothing to me, ye ken?"

Caitlin held onto Willie's fur, talking to him under her breath. It was all she could do to hold him back. He was ready to pounce and was pulling at her arms to let him go. But she'd put him away, as she didn't doubt that Deirdre would carry out her threat.

"Come, Willie. Let's put you away for a short while. Come, boy."

Willie stayed in place, clearly not liking this situation— his Master and a child that he'd been looking out for were both in danger.

"Now, Willie. It's all right. Come." Caitlin led him to the last stall, Merlin's stall, where he always stayed when she needed to put him away for safekeeping. He followed, but the growling never ceased and he looked to Caitlin, begging for permission to attack.

"Stay Willie. I'll take care of her. Stay." She pushed him through the opening of the stall and pulled the gate to behind her.

Her mind racing and her heart beating rapidly, Caitlin decided to try and talk Deirdre out of her insane actions.

"Deirdre, you need to let the lad go now and come inside with me. We'll sit together and see if we can't figure out how to help you. Your condition is all Nezerra's work. But if you'll let me, I can help you recover from her treatments."

Wild laugher filled the air. "Ha. Ye'd like that wouldn't ye? The chance to poison me just like she did. Well, that won't work again. Yer a witch just like she was. And Alex deserves better than that. So now I think it's time for ye to have a taste of *my* medicine. And it's verra tasty." She held the knife in her left hand now, then with her right, she pulled out a small bottle from her pocket and tossed it to Caitlin. The little lad never even tried to escape her clutches. He was petrified.

"Let's see ye drain that bottle — now. Else this little lad may have a verra short life I'm thinkin'."

Caitlin hesitated a moment, then just as she raised the bottle to her lips, a screaming screech came from the top of the barn and a large, feathered creature slammed into the back of Deirdre's head at full speed. Owl had come zipping through the loft window and his talons struck her head with a tremendous amount of force—a move he had perfected.

Deirdre's head snapped forward with her chin striking her chest. "Whaaaa?" She stumbled several steps, dropping Charlie in the process. Before she could gather her wits, however, another sound of indignation shattered the quiet. Willie's primordial call fractured the air — a call to his ancestors that signaled his wild nature was surfacing with a vengeance.

"HOOOOOWWW!" The great wolf came flying over the stall gate and was at Deirdre's throat in a heartbeat.

Caitlin felt rooted to the floor. Her feet wouldn't follow the instructions her brain was sending to them. Charlie had slumped to the floor, but still had not made a sound. He was beyond crying apparently. He was totally soundless. But he pleaded with his eyes and Caitlin understood the message.

"Noooooooo! Get off! Nooooooo!" Deirdre was lying on the ground, struggling to get Willie off her neck. She still held the blade and struck wildly at the beast — and the blade was ever so sharp. She lashed out again at Willie and he yelped only once. She lifted her hand to strike him again, but was having great difficulty breathing. Willie's fangs were buried deep in her throat and he had no intention of letting go. Her breath was all but gone when she heard a noise and glanced at the side door.

Alex. Yes. He'll help me.

Caitlin felt the power as it flooded her body. She lost all control when she saw Deirdre slashing at Willie, and in the next instant a blazing stream of fire streaked across the barn, finding its target — Deirdre's hands. In less than a second they burst into flame and were seared to a smoldering crisp, smoke rising from them in wisps. The blade was nothing but ashes as well.

Deirdre looked at them as if they belonged to someone else. Then unspeakable pain registered in her demented brain.

"Alex, help me!" She called to him, hoping against hope that he would put aside his anger and help her.

Then, with hands that were nothing but charred lumps of flesh, Deirdre turned her head once again toward the door as another sound tore through the stable. The pistol shot rang so loudly that Caitlin grabbed her ears in an effort to protect them from such an explosive noise.

Deirdre's body lay still on the ground. Her last thought was that Alex had chosen that tiny lass over her —again.

Caitlin's voice split the sudden silence. "Alex, help me. Charlie. Charlie's hurt. Help me!"

Caitlin was always one to keep her head in a frightful situation, but Alex could hear the fear in her voice. This was her first experience with a child of her own. Well, maybe Charlie was not exactly her own, but her heart told her it was the same.

Before he checked on Charlie, however, Alex held Caitlin close and gave thanks for her safety.

"Lass, are ye sure yer all right?" He could feel her trembling as he held her.

"I'm fine, but I just couldn't control the power. There was no way I could stop it. I've worked so hard to keep my temper in bounds, and I've tried to consider others as I never have before. Now I've killed a woman, a person who had a place in this world. And not only that, but I may have harmed our unborn bairn! Oh, Alex, will I never be able to control myself and these powers?"

"That power was given to ye for a reason, and I doubt the Creator would allow ye to use it if it would harm ye. And I believe I dealt her the lethal blow, Caitlin."

Alex quickly picked the lad up and carried him to a large bale of hay and laid him down. Caitlin spoke to the child soothingly while checking out his neck wound carefully. "There now, Charlie. It's all right lad. It's all right now." She saw the wound was only a slight one, but the poor lad was still trembling. She held him close and nodded to Alex. "He's all right now, Alex. Go see about Willie and Deirdre."

It took only a second to determine the extent of Deirdre's wounds. They were fatal. Between having most of her neck missing, hands that were nothing but withered, black, appendages, and a large hole in her chest, she was most definitely dead.

And that's what I should have done long ago. Not for one second would he wonder if he should have let her live.

As for Willie, Alex knelt and wrapped his arms around the great beast. "Now, Willie, let's see how ye be, huh?" He ran his hands down Willie's sides and along his neck. His sticky fingers told him the beast had been wounded. "Looks like she got ye pretty good just under yer belly there, fella. But ye've had worse and ye'll survive this, no doubt."

Caitlin got on her knees and hugged her great protector. "Ah, Willie, you've never failed me. And I seem to need you more than I ever knew I would." Tears were falling now, but as with everything else in the last few minutes, she didn't seem to have any control over them.

Alex lifted Charlie, holding the lad close to his body. "Easy lad. Caitlin will have ye fixed up in a second. She's quite a great healer, in case ye didn't know. She made our Ian well, and she'll get ye back on yer feet in a jiffy. It's all right, lad."

Caitlin quickly ran to the lodge and returned with a drink laced with just a tad of herbal medicine that would help him relax. He still hadn't uttered a sound, which had Caitlin concerned. He never spoke, but always made enough grunts and sounds to get attention when he needed it.

"Alex, he's been so frightened he can't even utter his usual sounds. We need to keep close by him. He's had quite an experience today."

"And so have ye, Caitlin. Are ye sure yer all right lass? I've never been so scared in my life as when I saw Deirdre holding the lad and ye standing there. There wasn't any time for thought, just action. And I have to tell ye, I'm not sorry I took her life. She was evil Caitlin, and that evil needed to stop with her."

"I know that was difficult for you. But I truly believe she would have hurt Charlie or me if you hadn't come. Your timing was perfect."

"Well, I may have had a little help with that, ye ken? Jack and I were coming up the lane and Owl flew so close to my head I had to duck. It didn't take much to know he wanted me to follow him, so I came as fast as Zeus would bring me. That owl knew something that I didn't. But I'm learning to not question, to just go with my intuition. Another lesson from Mam. Ye know, lass, I can't remember how often she must have said that. It didn't mean to be foolish, it just meant to trust yer feelings."

Jack had been just a minute or two behind Alex and had entered the stable just as the streak of fire struck Deidre's hands. He had witnessed Caitlin's powers once again, and he knew they had come at the right time. He was relieved even more so when Alex fired his pistol, completing the job. He'd decided to take a backseat and watch from the sidelines.

"Jack, give me a hand here. He's heavy."

Alex and Jack struggled to get Willie up on a large table that Caitlin used for drying herbs. She cleared the area and made room, but the great beast was almost more than they could handle. Finally the two of them managed to get the animal up where she could check him over.

"Willie, let's see what I can do for you. We've got to stop this, you know —this stitching you up every few months. You never cease to amaze me. Without you I'd have been done in several times. Uncle Wabi told me he was sure you and I have a connection that can never be broken, and I believe he's right. You and Alex always seem to show up just when I need you."

She stroked the great animal's head then went about stitching his underside. Following that, she bandaged him, which he really didn't like. Last time he pulled the bandage off before she would have done so, but maybe he'd known the healing was completed even if she didn't.

Just then a thought occurred to her.

"Alex, if Owl was there leading you home, then Uncle Wabi can't be too far behind. That owl stays with him unless he's been sent on an errand. Perhaps Wabi sensed something was going on. His powers are much greater than mine. He knows about events much sooner than I. Perhaps he and Ian will come soon. I hope so. I'm concerned about what releasing my powers may have done. But he'll know. I hope."

The three of them, Caitlin, Alex and Jack, got the lad and the wolf to the lodge and had a tale to tell to the others.

~ * ~

Sure enough, only a few hours later two men could be seen at the top of the moor. From a distance Ian looked just as much a man as Wabi. He was almost as tall, but at close range he still looked like the young lad he was. His legs were beginning to fill out, as was his chest. Apparently he was going to be another big MacKinnon lad.

"Holy sheep shiiii… uh, dung, Uncle Wabi. Do our landings always have to be so hard? My backside has just recovered from our last trip."

Wabi laughed at the young man, whom he was growing to appreciate more every day. He had only to look at the lad and see all the MacKinnon traits: dark hair and eyes, long limbs, and the makings of some very broad shoulders.

Just give him a few more years and he'll stand just as tall and broad as the other brothers.

"I'll leave that to you to figure out. I've been doing it so long I no longer think about it. But time weaving is the quickest way, no doubt. I'm sure you will have figured out it can be most tiring, however."

"Well, I've only done it a few times. But so far it seems to be all right. Sure beats walking."

The two looked about, taking in the circle of stones and burial plot. Ian was the first to notice the recently dug grave. "Look, Wabi. There's a new grave over there, right close to Mam's grave. With a new wreath on it. And Mam's grave has a new one too. Uncle Wabi, do ye think me da has passed? Or one of me brothers?"

"No, lad. As perceptive as you are, you would have felt it. No. It's someone else. But look. It's a very small grave, Ian."

Ian stooped and looked at the small square stone that had been laid on the grave. "A.A.M. February 22, 1719. I don't know who that is, Uncle Wabi."

"Well, you could go into the circle and probably learn who it is. Or you can go to the lodge and ask your brothers."

"Aye. Let's go to the lodge. It seems like forever since I've seen all of them. And they'll have stories for me. But I'll have tales for them, too." He laughed as they started down the hill.

Ian opened the back door and the two entered, certainly without knocking.

"Well, look at you, Ian, you've grown another foot. Wabi, what have you been feeding him?" Millie smiled broadly and embraced the two.

Calling out loudly, "Jack, Alex, we've got company," she wiped her hands on her apron and watched happily as the two older brothers came through the door.

"About time I say. We've been wanting to see yer face, brother." Jack hugged the young boy, and Wabi as well. The old wizard was as much a part of this clan as Caitlin now.

Alex came up and put an arm around Ian's shoulder. "Well,

just another couple of inches now, my lad. Jack, can ye believe it? Our little brother is about to catch up with us. Think we should knock him down to size?"

Ian smiled at the joking and his insides warmed just being here in the lodge. His life with Wabi was such an adventure and he never wanted it to stop, but his people were here and his heart was in this place.

Finally, another voice called out. "Hey, what's all the ruckus?" Da walked in, book in hand — a trait he and Ian had in common. "Now that's a sight for sore eyes. Three fine-looking MacKinnon lads. 'Course the really handsome one is at the estate."

That brought laughter all round and Da felt his throat tighten. He'd welcomed Wabi's tutoring of Ian, but the lad's absence left quite an empty place around the lodge. He hugged the young man and nodded to Wabi. Those two old ones didn't need words to communicate.

Dinner was a noisy affair with everyone talking at once, food being passed around, and children spilling milk and dropping biscuits on the floor. In other words, a typical meal at the MacKinnon lodge these days.

"And Jack, ye wouldn't believe this place called the Orient. That's where Henson came from originally, according to Uncle Wabi. And the lasses over there . . . they're even more beautiful than the Highland ones."

"What? Yer looking at the ladies already? Wabi, yer gonna have to watch him looks like."

Caitlin had placed Charlie on a pallet next to the fireplace and covered him with a blanket. Willie had taken up residence right next to the lad and the boy reached out to stroke his back.

The other two children thought Ian was just another child to play with, so they rolled about the floor with him, showing him how Tess would let the smaller one, Bridget, ride on her back.

"But now, you know you aren't the first ones to ride Tess, don't ye?"

"Who? Who rode her before us?"

"Well, I did as a matter of fact. She's been with us for years — she's even older than I am, so be easy with her, ye ken?"

The house was so different than when he had left. But it only took a moment for him to see this place was just right for all of them. The children had needed a home and it seemed to him Da had stepped right in and considered them part of his family.

Mam would really like this. The thought made him smile.

It was Alex's night to put the children to bed. He carried Charlie and the two others followed behind him. The three bairns were still sleeping in old Jamie's big bed and Caitlin had spoken with Alex tonight, just before he took them upstairs.

"Let's put Charlie in his usual bed, with the others. He lost a father, then a mother, both in a short period of time. And these two, his brother and sister, are the only constant things he's had in his entire life. Let him be with them. We'll watch him closely and I'll talk to Wabi about him."

Alex nodded and agreed with her suggestion.

Caitlin and Wabi sat at the old pine table, still shining from Millie's daily waxing. This had become the place where all decisions were made. There was something comforting about the old table that had been here even before the lads. It was scarred as were most of the lives of those who had sat at it over the years. But it still served its original purpose — a gathering place for a family. Caitlin poured a small amount of cider for herself and for Uncle Wabi.

"Wabi, it's been quite a day for all of us. I'm concerned about Charlie and not real sure if there's anything I can do."

"Charlie's a very young lad, Caitlin. He may surprise you. It's difficult to not rebound when you're surrounded by so many folk who care about you. He feels that inside and time will help him put this event behind him. All you can do is continue to care for him, as I am sure you will."

Da came strolling in and had a seat at the table, followed by Jack.

"Lass, ye did a verra brave thing today. Taking care of Deirdre as you did. I saw how ye stopped her from hurting our Charlie." Jack was not one to heap on praise, but today it was warranted. He was the one who had feared Caitlin's powers when they first appeared and had not particularly wanted her here at their home, but it was appropriate that he acknowledge that her actions had saved another of their loved ones — once more.

"We're in yer debt once again, lass. Looks like we may have to keep ye," he smiled at her.

"I don't think I was being brave. I was trying to keep my powers inside, but at the last moment I lost control and then it was too late. It's a good thing Alex came along. I don't know how it would have ended otherwise. Wabi, that's my real concern now. What did that moment, when I released that streak of fire, do to my bairn? Has it been harmed?"

She took a deep breath and refused to let her emotions get away from her again.

"Those powers were given to you by the Creator, for purposes known only to him. I rather doubt he would allow them to harm you when they come forth. Trust in yourself and the Creator, lass. All is as it should be. And I'm pleased to see you didn't need me to step in. You handled it on your own, my girl."

"Aye, well, Alex and Willie came to my rescue — as always. Now I have another question. This one is for you, Daniel. If you could spare just another moment, I want your opinion."

"Well, as I always tell ye, lass, I know a lot about sheep. But not much about anything else."

Wabi smiled at the old man. He knew Daniel was one of the most "educated" men he'd ever known. And he was very wise.

"Then, Alex and I were wondering, you see. Just a thought mind you."

"Lass, would ye come on out with it? It can't be all that bad."

"Well, as you know, Charlie is deaf — partially, if not completely. And Willie has been sort of staying close to him. I think he senses the lad can't hear and tries to look out for him. Now today, Willie wasn't with Charlie when the lad went to the stable. He was with me. Charlie couldn't hear Deirdre in the stable and she was able to come upon him before he even saw her. If Willie had been with him, that woman would never have gotten to Charlie. As Wabi has told me, Willie belongs to me. And that's the way it is. But Alex and I were wondering if maybe we should think about getting a protector for Charlie—like I have in Willie. You know, his own companion."

"A protector, ye say. Hmm. What do ye think Wabi? Would that be a good idea?"

"I think it's a grand idea, Daniel. That would give the lad confidence he doesn't have now. And he's going to be afraid for some time, I'm sure of that."

"As it is he almost always has to have Bridget with him. And she feels she can't leave him either. Perhaps it would help both of them," Caitlin continued.

"Then, there's nothing to be lost by trying, I say," Da nodded.

"As I happened to have trained quite a few dogs, I can find one for the lad. Let me look around a bit and I'll locate one and bring him to you," Wabi chimed in.

"Uncle Wabi . . . uh . . . ye don't mean another wolf do ye?" This question was coming from Jack.

Wabi laughed. "No, Jack. It's not the size of the animal that matters. Mostly we have to be sure the two of them bond. And that'll be easy enough to see in just a few days with each other. Caitlin, that's a good idea, lass. Healing takes many forms and Charlie's wounds require a different kind of medicine. Looks like you understood his needs. Always a healer."

With the bairns all tucked in, Alex came down and took his place next to Caitlin. It was quiet time and the fire was burning low, casting a warm glow throughout the great room. Candles were plentiful and they provided their own soft light. Then, as usual, a small voice called from the top of the stairs.

"Grand-Da, you promised!"

They all laughed as Da stood. Every evening he looked forward to story time with the bairns. It brought back memories for the old man and created new ones for the orphaned children. A special time for all of them.

Just as he rose to go upstairs, there was a loud rap on the front door.

"I'll get it. Up already. Hope nothing's wrong. A few sheep have probably gotten into somebody's garden, though it's a little late for neighbors to come calling."

He walked across the room and opened the door — and felt the blood drain from his face.

No. This can't be. No. He's here in this room. And he's not a lad any longer. He's a man. No.

His brain was telling him, no, it couldn't be. But his heart recognized the truth. The same thick shock of dark hair and even darker eyes that bore into your soul, long, gangly legs that had outgrown the rest of his body, and a cleft in his chin that couldn't be denied.

Oh, Alice, mo chridhe. Ye should see him.

Daniel finally found his voice and connected it to his floundering brain.

"Good evening, lad. Can I help ye?"

The young lad pulled off his tam and crumpled it, nervously shifting it back and forth from one hand to the other.

"Yes, sir. I'm looking for my da. I was told he lives here."

The riveting, intelligent eyes never left Daniel's face.

The old man nodded.

"Yes. I believe he does. Come in then, lad."

The boy entered and Daniel leaned against the door, just for a brief moment, regaining his equilibrium. Then he called out loudly.

"Alex! There's someone here who needs ye!"

"One more thing"...

Hallelujah! You made it and I'm very grateful that you took the time to read my work. However, your feedback is essential to improving my craft as an author. Therefore, if I could ask for "one more thing," please go to amazon.com/dp/B01FKI3QS4 and scroll down the page to favor me with your review.

If you would like to know more about Caitlin, Wabi, the MacKinnon brothers, and all the animals, please go to amazon.com/dp/B016CF714C for Highland Healer, the first novel in this series.

TO GET A QUICK GLIMPSE OF HIGHLAND
BLOODLINE, NOVEL #3 IN THIS SERIES, TAKE
A PEEK BELOW...

1

The MacKinnon lodge was a most inviting place this evening. Oil lamps and candles burned softly, while a small fire kept the damp chill at bay. The hills and moor were coming to life again after a long winter, and even though it was after eight in the evening it was still light outside.

All the bairns were abed and the MacKinnon men were enjoying a wee dram after a trying day. To an outsider peeking in, the scene was one of perfect calm and peace. Were that outsider to enter, however, he would be steeped in the anxiety and tension that sizzled in the room.

The topic of conversation was the same as it had been for several nights now, rumors the British military were rounding up Jacobite supporters who had survived the Battle of Culloden and either putting them in prison, executing them on the spot, or sending them to the islands to be sold as slaves.

These rumors were not new, and many supporters had already been captured. It had been some time since the battle and the MacKinnons had avoided being captured. Their lodge was a difficult place to find, it being well hidden high up in the Highlands.

Alex came in the back door, having needed a word with Boder, the new hand they had hired for the lambing season.

"What did Boder want this time?" Jack asked.

"Another complaint about his living quarters. He's not too keen on sharing the cottage with Hamish and Kenny. Says they talk too much and keep him awake at night. Mostly he's miffed because

I told him to put that cheroot out before he goes in the cottage at night as it wouldn't take much for that thatched roof to go up in flames. Don't think he much liked that. Thinks he should have a cottage to himself. He's a good hand, but I'm not of a mind to have the lads clean another cottage and make it ready just for his convenience. Let's see how he works out before we make any other arrangements for him."

From the kitchen, Caitlin was only half listening to the conversation. Her mind was occupied with the events of a few days ago. It wasn't every day she was called upon to use her extraordinary powers to save a loved one, and certainly it was not every day she caused the death of another human being. She was a healer after all, not a killer.

As she entered the room, her long skirt sweeping along the floor, Alex stood and turned his attention from Da and Jack to her, reaching for her hand as she came closer. He thought she was the picture of perfection. Her long, curly, flame-colored hair and sparkling aqua eyes seemed even more brilliant these days. Willie, her wolf companion and protector, trailed along beside her. He seemed to be aware of her condition and kept glued to her every moment. His role as her protector was one he never neglected.

"Lass, here, sit now, rest awhile. I know yer still worried about Charlie, but the ordeal's over and the little lad's safe. He's wounded to be sure, but he's young and he'll recover. Hear me on this now, *mo chridhe*."

Caitlin's large girth made sitting a bit of a chore these days. She and Alex were expecting their first bairn, and one look at the healer's body indicated the birth would be soon.

"I hope you're right. He's such a special lad, but he's had enough problems already. His deafness is quite a challenge for him, and since the incident with Drosera, he hasn't even made his usual sounds. Millie and Camille and I have worked diligently with him, and this is a major setback."

"Aye. But he's got this entire family to help him, lass, ye ken?"

Caitlin nodded and, finding the chair uncomfortable, stood again and walked to the window. As she looked out across the moor, Alex came up behind her and put an arm around her shoulders.

"*Mo chridhe*, ye don't need to worry so. Drosera was an evil woman if ever there was one, and if ye hadn't taken care of her she'd have killed our wee Charlie for sure. Don't forget, ye aren't totally responsible for her death. Yer bolt of lightning definitely started the process, but the shot from my pistol finished the job. So, I'm responsible also.

We both know it had to be done. If we hadn't taken action, she'd have found us again someday. Nae, ye needn't let her death weigh on yer mind. I know that's difficult for a healer, but let it go lass, let it go."

Alex thought he had gotten his message through to her, but Caitlin turned to face him, grabbed his shirt and jerked him closer.

"Alex, I killed a woman! A healer saves people, she doesn't kill them. I had no intention of destroying a life, I simply needed to save Charlie. I acted on an overwhelming instinct and in a matter of seconds I had taken Drosera's life. I don't want these powers. I'll never be able to control them!"

She burst into sobs and held her face in her hands. For a woman who remained calm in most trying situations, the emotional exhibition was out of character.

"Lass, ye saved the lad's life and that's all that matters. If ye hadn't stopped Drosera, Charlie would be dead now instead of that vile woman. Come now. Let's get ye settled here in the chair. We'll put yer feet up and I'll fetch ye a mug of Millie's hot cocoa."

He helped her into a larger chair and she sat quietly, sipping her cocoa and catching a few words of the discussion the men were having. Trying her best to turn her mind from her recent deplorable deed, she listened more closely to the men. She still found it amusing the true Highlanders spoke so differently than folks from other areas of the country. Their brogue was unique, certainly.

She had heard different accents in almost every village she came through on her way to the upper Highlands, where she now

361

lived. She was originally from Skye, the largest island of the Inner Hebrides. And even though Skye was considered part of the Highlands, the accent was still different from the accent she heard up here. She loved the way these brothers said "ye" instead of you and "yer" instead of your. She'd grown used to it now, but still enjoyed hearing the men and their brogue. It was like a language from another era and she found it refreshing.

Da and Jack expressed their thoughts openly, but she knew Alex would keep his thoughts to himself and only express them when he had worked out the details. But this latest issue, the Brits rounding up the Jacobites, this was a real problem and she could see the worry on Alex's face.

Her own thoughts, her worries, were about what would happen if the Brits managed to capture them, Alex and Jack. What would happen to the others? Da was still able-bodied but getting older now, as was Uncle Andrew. And Hector and Ian? Did the Brits know that all the brothers had been at Culloden? Would she and Millie have to fend for themselves and the bairns?

My life has changed so since coming to the Highlands. I was a carefree healer caring for the villagers in Skye and life was so easy. What was I thinking when I married this Highlander? It seems that we've gone from one calamity to another since we met. Of course, I was running from two men who were determined to kill me back then and Alex saved me from certain death. Oh, what a mess. I do love him so, but I wish life weren't so complicated.

These powers are very disturbing. I've used them twice now, and in neither case was I in control of them. Uncle Wabi says they were bestowed on me for a purpose, but I don't want them. I can just hear him now though . . . 'patience, dear girl, patience.' It seems to me if one is given powers, shouldn't they be able to control them?

Looking around the room, she saw all those she cared for gathered. If the Brits did manage to find them, Alex and Jack wouldn't be taken easily, but she also knew the Brits had plenty of soldiers and was aware there were informers, other Scots, who were aiding the soldiers in their quest. Brother had fought against brother in this battle, and in the end there was great heartache for all. There were too many unanswered questions. She had no doubt this problem was not going away, and time was not on their side.

~ ~ ~

For Alex, the leader of this band of brothers, his shoulders felt a heavy load of responsibility, as if they were carrying a heavy ewe, as they often had over the years. Da was still around, but he'd turned the reins over to Alex, the eldest son. Though they made decisions as a family, it was obvious the others looked to Alex to handle difficult situations, which certainly arose in such a large family. His intelligence was a great asset, but some situations were difficult to come to grips with.

Jack, the second oldest brother, and a very large Highlander, paced back and forth, his face flushed with excitement.

"But, Alex. We can't just sit here waiting on the Redcoats to come round us up. We've got to do something I tell ye!"

"I'm just as concerned as ye, Jack, but we have to think this through. We need a plan of action, not just a knee-jerk response that could get all of us killed. It's not just us menfolk now. We've got women and bairns to think about. Let's be rational about this and then take action." Alex had learned long ago to let Jack vent and then try to reason with him.

"Yeah, but if they show up tomorrow we might just be caught without a plan. What do we do if that happens?"

Then, as usual at the end of the day, a small voice called from the top of the stairs.

"Grandda, you promised!" That stopped the serious conversation, which was a good thing. No amount of talking had brought any answers so far anyway. They all laughed as Da stood.

Every evening he looked forward to story time with the wee ones. Reading to them brought back old memories for him and created new ones for them. The irony of the situation was that these were not even his own grandchildren. They were three orphans Hector had found hiding in Cameron Castle, an estate Millie inherited upon her grandmother's recent death. The orphans had been in the lodge for several months now and were an integral part of the MacKinnon family.

Just as Da rose to climb the stairs, there was a sharp rap on the front door. Alex was out of his chair in an instant. "Jack, pistols!"

Fearing it might be the Brits, Alex hurried to the kitchen to retrieve the pistol he kept hidden in the pantry. Jack flew down the hall to retrieve his own firearm, moving quickly for such a large man.

Before the brothers could get back, however, Da had gone to the door.

"I'll get it. I'm up already." He opened the door and felt the blood drain from his face. *No. This can't be. He's here. And he's not a lad any longer, he's a man. No.*

His brain kept telling him it couldn't be, but his heart recognized the truth. There was the same shock of dark hair, and even darker eyes that looked into your soul, and long, gangly legs that had outgrown the rest of his body. And the final touch, the cleft in his chin that couldn't be denied.

Oh, Alice, mo chridhe. Ye should see him.

Da finally found his voice and connected it to his brain. "Good evening, lad. Can I help ye?" He held his breath almost dreading to hear the answer to his question.

The young lad quickly pulled off his tam and crumpled it, shuffling it back and forth from one hand to the other. "Yes ... sir. I'm looking for my father. I was told he lives here." The dark, intelligent eyes never left Da's face.

The old man nodded. "Yes. I believe he does. Come in then, lad."

The boy entered and Da leaned against the door for a moment, trying to regain his equilibrium and feeling his age as never before. Then he called out. "Alex, there's someone here who needs ye!"

Alex heard Da calling and quickly walked that way, his kilt swinging as his long, muscular legs covered the distance quickly.

"What? Who is it?" He held his pistol tightly as

he reached the door, coming face-to-face with the young lad standing there.   *Certainly not the Brits. But who?*

Alex, too, seemed to have the same problem Da experienced—lack of connection between his tongue and his brain. His mind reeled as he stared at the lad and he had no doubt he was seeing the very image of himself at that age—the thick, dark hair, rather scruffy at the neck, in need of a trim as Alex's always was, and long legs that were out of proportion with the rest of his body. The lad already stood close to six feet tall. But most telling of all were his eyes, so dark and deep Alex could feel them searing into his face. Likewise, his own dark eyes were taking in every inch of the young lad's features, as if to etch them into his mind. Then the cleft chin said it all.

Holy Jesus. What have I done?

What was he to say? How do you address a stranger who is so like you there's no denying it? But it was impossible. He had no children, except, obviously that was not true. But when, where, who?

As Alex furiously ran a litany of questions through his mind, the lad looked away from him, then, turning back to face him, held his head at an angle that caused an avalanche of memories to come cascading through Alex's brain.

Yes, of course, Fiona. My English rose at university. Ye always cocked yer head in that manner when ye were about to question me about something I probably wasn't going to agree with. Why didn't ye let me know I had a son?

His held his pistol in his left hand, still pointed directly at the chest of the young lad, who stared at it as if he had never seen one. As his mind slowed down and reason returned, Alex finally spoke and let his pistol hang down by his side.

"Lad, I'm Alex MacKinnon. Please come in, join us." He held out his hand and offered it to the young lad. Much beyond that Alex wasn't sure how to proceed.

To his great relief, Caitlin had her emotions back under control and walked over to join him. The healer had only to take a quick look to understand the situation. The lad was the spiting image of Alex. And he was even more uncomfortable than Alex himself.

That was apparent to her as she, too, offered her hand to the stranger.

"Hello, I'm Caitlin MacKinnon. And what is your name?"

"I'm Robbie. Actually, Robert Alexander MacKinnon."

"Please come in, Robbie. Come warm by the fire and I'll make you a cup of cocoa. That'll get your insides warmed up. It's still a mite cold out."

Alex was grateful someone had stepped in and taken the lead. It was apparent to him that both he and Robbie were having difficulty speaking—maybe a familial trait or genetic problem.

Da excused himself. Alex had no doubt that he, too, was relieved his daughter-in-law had sorted the situation quickly and was trying to assist in making things a bit more comfortable for everyone. In her usual fashion, the healer started issuing instructions.

"Alex, introduce Robbie to everyone and then you two come to the kitchen. We should have a few moments together and see if Robbie is hungry as well."

"Yes, of course, come in lad. Come in." Alex stepped back and the lad came through.

Robbie was surprised to find so many people in the lodge. His mother had told him only a few facts about his father. He knew Alex came from a large family with several brothers and that they lived in the Highlands. Other than that, he really didn't know much. He stood in the middle of the room wishing he could drop through a hole in the floor.

What was I thinking? That he'd welcome me with open arms? He didn't even know I existed before today.

Alex, usually very adept at handling social situations, found himself struggling to find the right words. Finally he managed to utter something that at least got the conversation going.

"Uh, Robbie, the beautiful woman making the cocoa is Caitlin, my wife. This other lovely lady is Millie, and she's married to my brother, Jack."

The lad continued to shift his tam back and forth in his hands as he nodded to the ladies and briefly made a quick handshake with

Jack, who still held his pistol also. Young Ian stood up from his lying position on the floor. He, too, saw the unbelievable resemblance to Alex. The boy could be another MacKinnon brother from the looks of him.

"Hello, I'm Ian, Alex's youngest brother."

Robbie looked at Ian and felt a warmth he hadn't felt coming from the others. Perhaps it was that they were close in age. Whatever, it was a welcomed feeling.

Alex cleared his throat. "Um, everyone, this is Robert Alexander MacKinnon. Apparently he belongs in this family, so we'll get to know him. Now, Robbie, let's go to the kitchen and see if Caitlin has that cocoa ready."

Alex wasn't sure which was worse, standing with the lad, a son he didn't know he had, or seeing the expressions on the faces of his family. They were astounded.

The lad followed Alex and they took a seat at the old pine kitchen table, the one where all family matters got settled. Robbie liked the looks of the table, as there was something of permanence about it. There were many scars on the surface and someone's initials had been carved on one corner. Around the edges there were what looked like scratches made by an animal. But thanks to Millie's efforts, it was shining and smelled like lemons. In fact, the whole place smelled like a home should smell, not one that reeked like an infirmary with sick folk, like his own home had for the longest time now.

"So, Robbie, would you like a taste of Millie's apple cobbler? She's the main cook around here, and I assure you it's delicious."

"Uh, yes mum. I've not eaten all day, so that would be appreciated."

As for Caitlin, she had an ear that didn't miss the very proper pronunciation of his words. Apparently the lad had been reared with proper British English, and most probably proper manners as well. She observed that he waited for Alex to sit before he did, and he carefully lay his tam on the chair next to him.

367

She couldn't tell who was the most anxious, Alex or Robbie, and her heart was breaking for these two, a father and a son who had never met. She debated whether to retreat from the room and leave them alone to figure out how to communicate, or whether she should help them for a few minutes then take her leave. The healer in her desperately wished to bring some relief to the situation.

"Here, try this cocoa and have some cobbler. Your stomach will thank you, I'm sure. Alex, here's another cup of cider for you. I'll leave you two to yourselves now. You need to get acquainted, I believe." She left, holding her hands over her abdomen as she walked back toward the great room.

~ ~ ~

Da finished his story time with the bairns and stood at the window of the upstairs hallway, looking out over the moor. Thinking. Remembering. Alice, Mam, had a saying she used at times such as these: "Life is meant to be embraced, Daniel. If we run away from everything unpleasant or uncomfortable that is thrown at us, we'll cease to grow as people and never gain any new understanding. Rejoice in all experiences that ye encounter, even if ye don't completely understand them, and let them become part of yer soul."

Mo chridhe, this may be a great opportunity to embrace that which we don't quite understand.

He knew he must go down and lend Alex a hand, but thought he'd give him a few minutes alone with the lad then step in, as Alice would have done. Yes, she would have taken it all in stride. Eventually, he made his way slowly back down the stairs.

Jack, the largest of the MacKinnon brothers, and also the most hotheaded one who despised changes, accosted Da the minute he got to the bottom of the stairs.

"Da? Do ye think he's Alex's son? I mean, he looks just like him! What are we supposed to do? Alex has a son? Who would have ever thought that? And what are we to do with him? That's just more changes, Da, more changes."

368

"Oh, well, I feel sure we'll find room for him, don't ye? He's obviously a MacKinnon, so I don't believe we'll be throwing him out the door."

"No, but what will Caitlin think? She's about to have a bairn any day now and here, this evening, she learns Alex already has one."

"And she thinks it a very fine thing, too, Jack," a voice spoke behind him.

Caitlin joined them at the bottom of the stairs.

"The lad apparently is in need or he wouldn't be here. So, we all should make him welcome and try to see what we can do for him. He's fearful and anxious, certainly. I can see that on his face." The healer not only saw the pain in the boy's face, but she felt it at an even deeper level. Uncle Wabi had told her she would learn to shield herself from sensing others' pain, eventually, but as yet she still hadn't mastered that skill.

She was getting close to the end of her pregnancy and her emotions were riding a wave that crested high one day then crashed the next. The bairn wasn't due for several more weeks, and she knew these emotions were common in the last days, but she wished the child would get here, and soon.

"I think the best thing we can do this evening will be to find the lad a place to sleep and let him know we're glad he's with us."

Ian, the youngest of the brothers, stood again, which still took a bit of doing with his prosthetic foot. But he had no complaints, and didn't let his prosthesis stop him from doing most anything he wanted. Caitlin had been responsible for keeping him alive following a wound at the Battle of Culloden in which he lost his foot. The prosthesis was a gift from Da, Uncle Wabi and Uncle Andrew. The three had worked together to create it and now Ian was almost good as new.

"Let him come up to the attic with me. There's a small cot he can sleep on and I'll find some blankets for him. He'll like being up there. It's the best place in the lodge, trust me."

Ian would be returning to the Isle of Skye in a few days anyway, and his room would be vacant. The new lad could have full use of the room then. Being part of a large family had its good points, but Ian always liked that he could climb up to the highest part of the lodge and have his own space where he could light a candle, read to his heart's content, and watch out the window for the old stag that wandered the moor at night. He knew Robbie would like that too.

Millie and Jack made their way to the east wing where Millie's little daughter, Midge, was already asleep and they, too, retired for the evening. Jack and Millie had wed the same day Alex and Caitlin had. Millie, the former Lady Sinclair, had gone from being a lady in a castle in England, and wife to a despicable lord, to being wife to Jack, a Highlander whom she thought hung the moon. He had his strong points, and his weak ones as well. Most of all he disliked changes, but this past year had proved to him he didn't need to fear them. Sometimes they actually made things better.

"But, Millie. Another child, a lad, in the lodge? How many can we take in?"

"As Da said, we won't be throwing him out. I know how the lad feels, Jack. I, too, had no place to go and now I'm here with this family. It'll be alright."

With Caitlin and Millie having come into the family, the lives of everyone in the lodge had changed. Caitlin and Millie had become friends first, then Caitlin saved Ian's life after Culloden and the MacKinnons had come to her rescue in her time of need. Alex had been captivated by her from day one and had let nothing keep him from marrying her, not even family concerns about her.

The fact Caitlin possessed special powers had been a problem for Jack originally, but she had saved him, Alex, and Millie, as well as herself, on two occasions. That had gone a long way toward Jack accepting her and her abilities.

Caitlin slowly climbed the stairs, headed to the rooms she and Alex claimed in the west wing of the lodge. She particularly liked that wing as she had two large windows from which she could view the moor, and if she looked closely she could see the circle of stones at the top. She intuitively knew the circle was a special place and she longed to walk among the spirits that she was sure dwelled there.

This evening she found herself wondering what might happen next. Her handsome Highlander was her life, and his touch still sent chills along her spine. Watching him as he strode across the floor, his kilted body tall and muscular, was as appealing as ever, and the sound of his deep, resonating voice was soothing to her.

Her life was fulfilling and she never regretted leaving the Isle of Skye and Uncle Wabi, although she missed him greatly. He visited often and she could always "call" him if she really needed him. But this night she wished she could talk to another woman, perhaps Mam. That woman had raised this house full of lads who were a credit to her and Da. And now, as Caitlin was about to deliver the next bairn in this clan, a new MacKinnon lad had shown up.

She undressed and began to brush her hair. Tying a ribbon around the mass of curls, she pulled on a high-necked nightgown and crawled into bed. She was tired beyond belief, but her mind wouldn't stop its churning.

Holy Rusephus! Alex has a son. But why did he not know about him? Why would any woman keep such a secret from a father? This will be a tale worth hearing. I sounded so sure of myself downstairs, but I don't know how to handle this situation any better than Alex. A son? Just one more calamity.

Alex would be up eventually, but she knew he would remain quiet about his feelings regarding Robbie until he'd sorted them out in his own mind. Only then would he discuss them with her.

She felt like an elephant as she tried to get comfortable in bed, and fell asleep wishing the bairn would be born this very minute—several more weeks was unthinkable.

~ ~ ~

"So then, Robbie. I think we might better try to get acquainted, ye ken?" Alex shifted uncomfortably in his chair, not sure how to get this conversation going.

"Yes ... sir. I suppose that would be the logical thing to do."

Alex noted the lad all but refused to make eye contact, and an element of anger and resentment inside the boy was palpable.

"Well now, it's fairly obvious the two of us are a lot alike, physically, that is. So we can agree ye must be my son. Is that how ye see it?"

The lad looked to the floor and, in a most sullen voice, replied. "I guess so. Mother told me I was to find you when she was no longer here with me. That's why I came here this evening. She died a fortnight ago and I've been trying to determine what would be the best course of action for me to take."

Alex could feel anger and resentment coming off the lad in waves. Unconsciously crossing his arms across his chest in a defensive manner, he took a deep breath and leaned back, fearing what the next words from the lad might be. The boy sounded like a much older person, and other than observing that the lad was nervous, what with him picking his tam up again and constantly fiddling with it, Alex would have assumed he was an adult.

Suddenly realizing his posture might be sending out a message that wasn't exactly welcoming, Alex released his arms and leaned forward to rest them on the table and gave the lad his undivided attention. Seeing his own dark eyes staring back at him gave him pause, but he began.

"Oh, lad, whatever caused her to die? She was such a lovely young woman when I knew her. It grieves me to hear she has passed away."

Still addressing the floor, Robbie began his tale. "She'd been ill for quite some time ... sir. When she wasn't teaching, she volunteered at the Old Tolbooth, the prison in Edinburgh, where she contracted typhus a while back. The doctors at the Royal Infirmary of Edinburgh treated her, but finally there was nothing else to be done so she asked to leave hospital and come home for her final days. Mattie, our housekeeper, arranged to bring her back home and nursed her through the last weeks. She died on April 14th, which is ironic, as that happens to be my birthday.

"Lad, that's a heartache for ye, to be sure."

"Yes ... sir, but actually, it's a meaningful day already so it seems appropriate somehow."

372

Alex sipped at his cider, trying to decide how to further the conversation along. But then, what did he want to know? Surely he would offer to help the lad, but how were they to get any kind of relationship going?

"To be frank with ye, lad, I don't know any other way of figuring things out except to ask ye questions, ye ken?"

"Alright. I guess that's OK. I'll answer them if I can. But you must know, I don't especially want to be here even though Mother said I should find you. I'm a British citizen, not a Scot."

"Aye. Aye. I see. Then, do ye understand I never knew I had a son?"

"Yes ... sir. And you should know I never knew my father was alive until a couple of months ago. Mother had a birth certificate that has my name as Robert Alexander Edwards ... and another one that says Robert Alexander MacKinnon. She told me my father had been a soldier in service of the Crown and that he was brave and died in a battle with a battalion of French soldiers. There was never a lot of discussion about him, other than she always insisted he was a most intelligent man, very handsome, and a fine soldier. She even showed me a few charcoal drawings she said were of him. Of course, I now realize she invented this man in order for me to believe I had been a wanted child, and that is exactly what she accomplished. I did always feel wanted and cared for. Only now, since she's passed away, I'm aware of new feelings, of being without roots, drifting, not sure what to do next."

"Aye. Of course, lad. Ye naturally would feel that. Then, ye can be sure this family, the MacKinnon family—yer family, I suppose—will welcome ye. And I should also tell ye we're probably quite different from folk down in the Lowlands or Edinburgh and London. Speaking of that, where did ye come from?"

"I've lived in London and Edinburgh. In my early life we lived in London for some years then, for some reason, Mother insisted we move to Edinburgh. She'd been a tutor at university there early on, then went back to London and was headmistress at Her Majesty's Preparatory Academy, a school for young ladies. She taught

373

there for some time, but about five years ago she wanted to return to Edinburgh and the university. She had fond memories of her time there and missed the stimulation of the young students. So, we moved there and that's where I still live."

"So yer early years were pretty much spent in London then. I suppose that's why ye sound more English than Scot. But of course ye would. Fiona was English through and through."

"Yes ... sir."

Alex didn't miss the hesitancy of the lad to call him sir.

"But she always spoke highly of the Scots and their devotion to family and their strong work ethic. She was impressed with those characteristics. But not everyone I know feels that way about Scots."

"Then I thank her for that. She was a fine lady herself, and I never held it against her that she were English."

He smiled at the lad and the smile was returned briefly. But there was certainly a question written on the lad's face.

Ah, he seemed to take no offense and took that remark as it was intended. So, maybe we can get through this.

Robbie took a deep breath, then made his pronouncement. "I've always thought I was thoroughly British. But now, I guess I have to realize and admit I'm half Scot."

Alex thought for a moment before addressing this proclamation from the lad. The flat, non-emotional way in which he made the statement told Alex the lad would rather be a toad than a Scot.

Looks like I have a new problem to deal with. He was proud to be British, of course. Now he knows Scots blood flows in his veins as well, Highland blood at that.

"Well, then I suppose yer right. In my opinion a man, or lad, should be proud of his heritage, his country, and most of all his family. But I can understand ye might have some trouble agreeing with me on this. Ye've thought ye were British for some years now, and actually ye are half British, as it were. But there's goodness to be found in both peoples, I suppose, and areas where there will always be disagreements. Mam would have said 'that's life.'"

"Who's Mam?"

"Mam was my mother, yer grandmother. She's gone on now, but she always had sayings that seemed to fit most occasions."

And I know she could help me now if she were here.

"Robbie, we have a lot of catching up to do. It's late now so I think we'll call it a night and tomorrow we'll make more headway. Tonight ye need to rest and, again, ye are welcome here in our home. I'm not real sure how a father should act, but I'll do my best. I hope ye can find a way to understand that if I had known about ye, I'd have come looking for ye. This family cares for its own. Ye are my son. That makes ye important to all of us."

"Yes ... sir. Mother and I discussed you at length before she passed on. She held you in the highest regard and indicated I was to do the same ... even if you are a Scot."

"I'm glad to hear that, lad. Then let's see where we're to bed ye down. Come, I'll see what Caitlin has in mind."

As they stood, Da entered and stood for a moment, staring at his son and grandson. Alex was certainly a handsome man, and wore his kilt with pride. The lad was clad in long, dark trousers and a dark matching coat. Obviously their clothing was different, but if they were any more alike Da would eat his tam. The lad was several inches shorter than Alex and certainly not as filled out, but then he still had a few growing years ahead of him.

Stroking his bearded face, Da ran his finger down through the cleft in his chin.

Huh. Well now, guess that's at least one trait the three of us have in common. Wonder what others we may have.

He walked over and put his hand out and the boy took it for a short moment.

"Lad, I'm yer grandfather, Daniel. Ye found yer way here, and now that ye have, we're glad to make yer acquaintance. We MacKinnons take care of each other, and ye'll be treated like one of us, as ye certainly are from what I see."

"Thank you ... sir." The boy hadn't known what to expect, but this was not an anticipated response.

They don't even know me, but are going out of their way to make me feel welcome. But they're Scots, known to be scoundrels and uneducated heathens. I know I can't trust them.

"If it suits ye, Ian would like ye to share his space. It's up in the farthest part of the lodge, the attic actually. He's about yer age, maybe a tad older, I think. So, take the stairs all the way to the top and he'll find ye a bed. We'll talk tomorrow. Night to ye now."

Robbie nodded quickly to Da. "Yes ... sir. That sounds fine to me."

The young lad looked about, not sure where he was to go. He made a quick trip back to the porch and returned carrying a soft, leather valise in which he had brought a few items of clothing, some of his mother's personal documents, and his ever-present writing pad. This pad was much more important to him than any of the other articles, however.

Da made his way to his room at the end of the hall, a book tucked under his arm as always, and Alex waited at the foot of the stairs for the lad.

"Up there, lad—Robbie. All the way to the top. Ian's got a place for ye to rest yer head. He'll be going to the Isle of Skye in a couple of days and then ye'll have the place to yerself. So if you can manage to share a room a couple of nights, it will be helpful."

"Of course ... sir."

Alex hardly knew how to react to such a formal, polished young man. On the one hand, the lad obviously disliked learning he was half Scot and had made that very clear. But on the other, he had the manners of a young gentleman. Alex tried to remember himself at that awkward age. He was quite sure he was not polished, but Mam would have insisted on good manners. And if he was rebellious, then Da would have given him some extra chores to work off his angry feelings. No doubt, though, this lad was as much a MacKinnon as any of them.

Robbie lifted his valise and began the climb up the stairs. And it was a climb, too. Once he got to the top, he saw the faintest light coming from beneath one of the doors. He knocked and waited a second. Just as he was about to knock again, the door opened and Ian nodded to him.

"Aye, this is the right room. Mine. And I think ye'll like it, too. Come in."

Robbie slowly walked through the doorway and felt as if he had entered a room that had been designed with him in mind. There was an old wooden desk in front of one of the tall, many-paned windows. A candle had been lighted and there were several maps and drawings lying on the desk. He came closer and took a quick glance at them. The maps were very old and Robbie thought they were from a much earlier period, perhaps from early Roman times, and there was a scent in the room that was most pleasant—an herb, something green and fresh. Maybe rosemary.

"Put yer bag in the corner. I've put some blankets on the cot and that should keep ye warm enough. Ye'll find it's actually warmer up here than any other place. Da says it's something about the heat rising. But still, it can get cold up here in the Highlands, even in the spring. Probably different from where ye came from. Where was that exactly?"

"I came from Edinburgh, where I lived with my mother. She died recently and I'm not sure what I'm to do now."

Ian found himself searching for the right words, but wasn't sure there were any. "Oh, then, don't worry too much. Alex is a very intelligent man. He'll figure out the best thing for ye to do. I know how it is to lose yer mam, though. Ours passed on a couple of years ago and we all felt like our world had turned upside down. Maybe that's how everybody feels when their mam dies. But I'm learning that because she died doesn't mean she's lost to ye. She's just in a different place now. Ah, listen to me, going on so. Come over here and take a look out there."

Robbie walked closer to the tall window, the two young lads standing side by side. Ian snuffed the candle out and it was pitch-black in the room. Suddenly, the moor was easily seen beneath the light of a glowing moon. The snow that had covered the ground for so long had melted now as the days were warmer, even though the evenings were still chilly. The highest peaks of the mountains were still covered and pockets of snow could be found in the crags, but the green, spring sprouts were beginning to show and the heather on the moor was blossoming quickly.

"Now look just at the edge of that stand of pine trees on the left side, look closely."

"I don't see anything. There's nothing there but trees. No, wait. Oh! Is that a stag?" Robbie stared at Ian, his face registering his excitement.

"Yeah. He's been here as long as I can remember. He shows himself sometimes on an evening such as this. I sometimes wonder if he can see me too."

Robbie continued to look at Ian. The two could have been brothers. But there was something about this young lad Robbie didn't quite understand. He acted as if Robbie was not a stranger but had always been here, in this lodge, as if he had always been a member of this family. There was also an element of mischief, or adventure that emanated from him. But then, there was an element of warmth, also. Robbie had lived in London and Edinburgh, but he had never come across a young person who was as interesting as Ian.

"Do you think he can see us now?"

"I'm learning that the animals know a lot, and we've a lot to learn from them if we only will. Just some of the things Uncle Wabi is teaching me."

"Uncle Wabi? Who's that?"

"He's actually Caitlin's uncle, but he feels like mine too so I call him Uncle Wabi. He's a very unusual man and I'm studying with him. I'll tell ye about him tomorrow. Right now I think we'd better get to bed. If I know Alex, he'll be expecting both of us to be down in the kitchen early, ready to listen to his instructions for the day." He smiled when he made this remark and Robbie smiled in return.

To continue, your copy is available at

https://www.amazon.com/dp/B06WWNJTQV.

Made in the USA
Middletown, DE
16 March 2018